The Best
AMERICAN
ESSAYS
2011

GUEST EDITORS OF
THE BEST AMERICAN ESSAYS

1986 ELIZABETH HARDWICK

1987 GAY TALESE

1988 ANNIE DILLARD

1989 GEOFFREY WOLFF

1990 JUSTIN KAPLAN

1991 JOYCE CAROL OATES

1992 SUSAN SONTAG

1993 JOSEPH EPSTEIN

1994 TRACY KIDDER

1995 JAMAICA KINCAID

1996 GEOFFREY C. WARD

1997 IAN FRAZIER

1998 CYNTHIA OZICK

1999 EDWARD HOAGLAND

2000 ALAN LIGHTMAN

2001 KATHLEEN NORRIS

2002 STEPHEN JAY GOULD

2003 ANNE FADIMAN

2004 LOUIS MENAND

2005 SUSAN ORLEAN

2006 LAUREN SLATER

2007 DAVID FOSTER WALLACE

2008 ADAM GOPNIK

2009 MARY OLIVER

2010 CHRISTOPHER HITCHENS

2011 EDWIDGE DANTICAT

The Best
AMERICAN
ESSAYS®
2011

Edited and with an Introduction
By EDWIDGE DANTICAT

Robert Atwan, Series Editor

A MARINER ORIGINAL
HOUGHTON MIFFLIN HARCOURT
BOSTON · NEW YORK

www.hmhbooks.com

ISSN 0888-3742
ISBN 978-0-547-47977-4

Printed in the United States of America

DOC 10 9 8 7

Contents

Contents

Foreword: Confessions of an Anthologist

WHILE SPEAKING AT A PANEL devoted to the essay a few years ago, I was surprised to be introduced as one of America's noted anthologists. No one had ever called me that before, nor had I ever thought of myself that way, but afterward I began to reflect on the unusual compliment, which I assume it was.

I had never considered anthologizing as a special talent, but, I admit, I have compiled quite a few. Not just this annual—which is now in its twenty-sixth edition—but numerous collections of short stories, poems, political and cultural commentary, memoirs of movie stars, even historical advertisements. Had my early submissions of poems and stories met with more receptivity or had my first publication, a 1973 college anthology called *Popular Writing in America* (the title is still in print), which I coedited with a very good friend, Don McQuade, not been a success, I may not have risen to the esteemed rank of a "noted anthologist." But in publishing (as in so many industries) a success in one endeavor is often followed by an invitation to do something similar, and so one anthology followed another, but not always successfully.

I'm certain that no one ever set out to be an anthologist. It is hardly a conventional career path. "What would you like to be when you grow up, kid?" "That's easy, sir—a noted anthologist." But I did possess the one important characteristic that qualified me for the job. As far back as first grade, I enjoyed reading anything and everything. I even loved to read the required Baltimore catechism with its endlessly fascinating questions—"Why did God make us?—and all the textbooks the good sisters passed out to us on the first day of every school year. On the opening day of third grade I brought our reader home and finished it that night. Given the typeface and all the illustrations, it was hardly a challenge; I would realize in time that as the books got harder, the print got smaller.

I was not just a voracious and indiscriminating reader, I was an obsessive one. This sometimes worried my father, who never read anything other than the New York tabloids and daily racing sheets, which of course I devoured as well once he was done. He was concerned that a kid who always had "his nose in a book" would grow up unfit for the rough-and-tumble conditions of our sketchy environment. So I reduced his worries by playing baseball, though there were many times while standing alone out in center field inning after inning waiting for a fly ball that I wished I had hidden a Zane Grey paperback inside my perfectly oiled Rawlings.

I'm not usually sold on epiphanies, especially of the life-transforming type. I'm more interested in the opposite experience: not those rare moments of startling insight or realization, but— what I suspect are more common—those sudden flashes of anxious confusion and bewilderment. I distinctly recall experiencing one of these reverse epiphanies (is there a word for these?) shortly after I began high school. Before then I had been a regular visitor to our cozy, storefront branch library, where I borrowed book after book, usually biographies of Hall of Fame baseball stars, all through the summer months. But during the first week at St. Joseph's High School, one of the nuns suggested we obtain a card from the main branch of the Paterson Free Public Library. I had never set foot inside this imposing building with its stately columns that looked a little like the Lincoln Memorial (and no wonder—the same architect, I would later learn, had designed both). I entered the expansive lobby with some trepidation, not yet feeling a sense of belonging; libraries had not yet become the convivial community centers they are today. Libraries then were all about books, and librarians were the stern guardians of those books. An intimidating decorum of absolute silence prevailed as I timidly glanced about, astonished to find more books in one place than I had ever pictured, awed by the gleaming mahogany card catalogues that looked longer than the Erie Railway boxcars that click-clacked by our house hour after hour. As I walked out past the columns and cautiously down the steps, now a card-carrying member of this humbling institution (and, by some sort of worrisome magical extension, an adult), I rejoiced that with so much available to read, I would never be bored in my entire life. And yet with a dizzying sense of unease, I simultaneously felt a terrifying rush of unknown possibilities.

The word *anthology* derives from the Greek *antholegein,* which literally means to gather (*legein*) flowers (*anthos*). The anthologist in a sense gathers a literary bouquet. Or as the founding father of all anthologies, Meleager of Gadara (now the city of Umm Qais), and apparently my ancient countryman, called his first-century B.C. compilation of short verse, a garland. Despite its unusual etymology, one that very few readers probably know, the anthology has remained a popular publishing product for over two millennia. So we anthologists possess a long literary tradition, though I know of no history that charts our endeavors or the progress of Meleager's *Garland* into the *Norton Anthology of Poetry.*

The first anthology I remember owning was Oscar Williams's *Pocket Book of Modern Verse.* I acquired this while a high school senior and read it for years until it finally fell to pieces. Williams became one of the nation's most influential promoters of poetry, and his inexpensive paperback collections could be found in the 1950s and '60s in every bookshop, on drugstore racks, and in countless college classrooms. They are still being sold on Amazon.com, to the accompaniment of many warm and nostalgic reviews, a few of which informed me that my copy was not the only one read to pieces. Any history of the modern anthology would need to include Oscar Williams, a Ukrainian Jewish immigrant, born Oscar Kaplan. Williams was also a poet about whom Robert Lowell wrote, "Mr. Williams is probably the best anthologist in America today."

Although *The Pocket Book of Modern Verse* was well thumbed and well loved by thousands of readers, it did not approximate the literary impact of Harriet Monroe's famous 1917 collection, *The New Poetry: An Anthology.* That authoritative book proved to the public that something indeed had happened to poetry around the start of the century's second decade. Monroe's collection was the literary equivalent of the groundbreaking 1913 Armory Show, a visual "anthology" that mapped the enormous changes occurring in the world of art. By gathering a large sampling of the emerging poets of her time, Monroe (who included a dozen of her own poems) was able to demonstrate—as no single collection by an individual poet could—that a distinct movement was afoot and that modern readers had better start to swim with Ezra Pound rather than sink with Alfred, Lord Tennyson.

I've mentioned two influential poetry anthologies and I could mention others. Poetry movements have often been accompanied by anthologies that serve as manifestoes. But what about essays? Although there have been a number of excellent essay collections, mostly with a historical sweep—the best of which is Phillip Lopate's comprehensive and indispensable *The Art of the Personal Essay* (1994)—I can think of no dedicated, single-volume twentieth-century essay anthology that did for the modern essay what Harriet Monroe's book did for modern poetry. That might be because the essay was so slow in coming to terms with modernism: as I've written before, the essay, with very few exceptions, was the vehicle for understanding modernist literature, not a key part of that literature. Perhaps the most important anthology to showcase essays with a new voice and edge was Alain Locke's 1925 landmark collection, *The New Negro: An Interpretation,* which served as the major statement of the Harlem Renaissance. Though multigenre, the collection featured a preponderance of essays that clearly disassociated the form from the popular genteel essay and positioned it solidly in the new century. Another collection that would give voice to a new movement, not essayistic yet closely related, was Tom Wolfe's and E. W. Johnson's *The New Journalism,* the 1973 manifesto/anthology which celebrated a new style of nonfiction prose that had grown out of the ashes of the finally deceased novel.

But unlike *The New Poetry* or *The New Journalism,* there was no twentieth-century anthology entitled *The New Essay,* no gathering of key selections from a single period that demonstrated a vital literary movement gaining momentum. But as the twenty-first century opened, one young essayist, John D'Agata, noticed a new, hard-to-label form of essayistic prose that didn't resemble the traditional personal essay or nonfiction narrative or literary journalism. He collected these in a 2003 anthology that he called *The Next American Essay.* To be sure, some of these essays went back a few decades (such as John McPhee's brilliant 1975 *New Yorker* piece

"The Search for Marvin Gardens"), but all the selections had something in common: a determination by their authors to push the genre into new territory, to feature prose that—to put it quickly —depends more on poetic fragmentation than rhetorical coherence and discontinuous narrative than straightforward self-presentation. The trick, of course, is to employ innovative forms without sacrificing ideas, substance, or urgency.

This annual anthology represents no movement or literary agenda and is wholly receptive to the "next" American essay, as can be seen by the fact that nearly half of the authors collected in D'Agata's fine anthology have appeared in this series. In the 2011 volume readers will find essays of lyric power as well as those that are more dependent upon reflection and reporting and that do their literary work within more conventional parameters. We will wait and see whether the second decade of the twenty-first century will resemble that of the previous century and introduce seismic changes in the arts, though it is difficult to imagine the disappearance of time-honored essays that narrate compelling personal stories or engage head-on with controversial issues or ruminate about ideas both large and small.

The Best American Essays features a selection of the year's outstanding essays, essays of literary achievement that show an awareness of craft and forcefulness of thought. Hundreds of essays are gathered annually from a wide assortment of national and regional publications. These essays are then screened, and approximately one hundred are turned over to a distinguished guest editor, who may add a few personal discoveries and who makes the final selections. The list of notable essays appearing in the back of the book is drawn from a final comprehensive list that includes not only all of the essays submitted to the guest editor but also many that were not submitted.

To qualify for the volume, the essay must be a work of respectable literary quality, intended as a fully developed, independent essay on a subject of general interest (not specialized scholarship), originally written in English (or translated by the author) for publication in an American periodical during the calendar year. Today's essay is a highly flexible and shifting form, however, so these criteria are not carved in stone.

Magazine editors who want to be sure their contributors will be considered each year should submit issues or subscriptions to: Robert Atwan, Series Editor, The Best American Essays, P.O. Box 220, Readville, MA 02137. Writers and editors are welcome to submit published essays from any American periodical for consideration; unpublished work does not qualify for the series and cannot be reviewed or evaluated. Please note: all submissions must be directly from the publication and not in manuscript or printout format. Editors of online magazines and literary bloggers should not assume that appropriate work will be seen; they are invited to submit printed copies of the essays (with full citations) to the address above.

I'd like to thank my assistant, Kyle J. Giacomozzi, once again for all his help throughout every phase of this book, and I wish him well-deserved success as he now departs to pursue an MFA in nonfiction. As always, the Houghton Mifflin Harcourt staff did everything to bring so many moving parts together in so short a time, and I once again appreciate the efforts of Deanne Urmy, Nicole Angeloro, Liz Duvall, and Megan Wilson. Working on this volume with Edwidge Danticat was a delightful experience, and I believe the 2011 book represents one of the most diverse in the series, both in its range of writers and in its exciting array of themes and topics. Given the remarkable reach of her own fiction and nonfiction, this should come as no surprise.

R. A.

Introduction

THROUGH RECENT EXPERIENCES with both birth and death, I have discovered that we enter and leave life as, among other things, words. Though we might later become daughters and sons, many of us start out as whispers or rumors before ending up with our names scrawled next to our parents' on birth certificates. We also struggle to find, both throughout our lives and at the end, words to pin down how we see and talk about ourselves.

When my brothers and I first learned, in the fall of 2004, that our father was dying, one of my brothers bravely asked him a question which led to my father narrating his life to us.

"Pop, have you enjoyed your life?" my brother wanted to know.

Stripped bare of any pretense and fully vulnerable, my father gifted us with his life experiences to do with as we pleased. We could use them, as such statements are often said to do, to inform, instruct, or inspire ourselves, or we could simply revel in them, or in the fact that he was even sharing them with us, then move on.

Seven years later, we have still not moved on. I can't say that I remember every single word my father uttered on his deathbed, but every story somehow feels like it's still within reach.

Such is the power of the stories we dare tell others about ourselves. They do inform, instruct, and inspire. They might even entertain, but they can also strip us totally bare, reducing (or expanding) the essence of everything we are to words.

Having written both fiction and nonfiction, I sometimes have my choice of the shield that fiction offers, and perhaps bypassing it, when I do, leaves me feeling even more exposed. As most people who take on this task know, along with self-revelation often comes self-questioning of a kind that is perhaps more obvious in some essays than others. When we insert our "I" (our eye) to search deeper into someone, something, or ourselves, we are always risking a yawn or a slap, indifference or disdain. How do we even know that what interests or delights us, alarms or terrifies us, will invoke a raised eyebrow in someone else? Perhaps the craft, the art, in whatever form it takes, is our bridge. We are narrating, after all (as my father was), slivers of moments, fragments of lives, declaring our love and hatred, concerns, and ambivalence, outing our hidden selves, and hoping that what we say will make sense to others.

The beauty of this series is that it reminds a handful of the many persistent and gifted practitioners of the various forms of this craft that they are being heard. Essayists, it seems, occasional or regular, are a bit more vulnerable these days, and as if the backlit screens of computers or smart phones were a metaphor for this, essays are now read under an even more glaring spotlight. This also forces us to push beyond certain boundaries, to be less formulaic and stereotypical, however that might manifest itself. But essentially we are guided in part by what Ralph Ellison in his groundbreaking essay "Little Man at Chehaw Station: The American Artist and His Audience" calls "art hunger," and what he defines as our urgent desire to put faith in our ability to communicate with others both directly and symbolically.

The *Best American Essays 2010* guest editor, Christopher Hitchens, who is a contributor to this year's edition, recently wrote a moving essay about what it means for a writer to have a "voice" when he has lost his ability to speak. "The most satisfying compliment a reader can pay is to tell me that he or she feels personally addressed," he wrote in the June 2011 issue of the magazine *Vanity Fair.* I hope you feel, as I did, personally addressed by each of these essays.

In the beginning, it is biblically said (not a flawless transition from Mr. Hitchens), was the word. And no matter where we are along the span of our existence, we are perhaps all searching for that word, the one that is sometimes conciliatory and sometimes contrarian, enlightening or disturbing, the one word that will launch us stumbling into a sea of other words, most of which we will discard and some of which we will keep, as we write ourselves anew.

On January 12, 2010, I was home in Miami—as I am most days —trying to get a bit of writing done while looking after my two young daughters. If thirty-five tumultuous seconds had not rattled Haiti, the country of my birth, at 4:53 P.M., that day would probably have blended into all the others, except that my girls and I had been scheduled to take a photograph that afternoon.

I did not want to take the photograph. I had grown photo-averse because of some baby weight that I just couldn't seem to shake. My girls, however, were very excited. A friend had given them identical embroidered white dresses and they wanted to wear them. (At least the older one did; the one-year-old did not get a vote.) So off we went that afternoon to a photographer neighbor's studio to get our picture taken.

Of all the pictures we took, my favorite is one of my five-year-old leaning her head ever so gently on my shoulder as her younger sister tries to choke me by yanking the heavy necklace around my neck. When I look at that picture now, it further deepens for me the sadness of that day. Looking at our serene, half-smiling faces reminds me how much we instinctively trust the banality and predictability of daily life. Until something larger shatters our world.

After the photo session, I drove to a supermarket in Miami's Little Haiti neighborhood and picked up a few things for dinner. As soon as I cleared the checkout aisle, my cell phone began to ring, and from that moment on the lives of 10 million Haitians and others, and to a much lesser extent my own life, have never been the same. Losing two family members and countless friends who had no time for last words was the least of it. Watching hundreds of thousands of others continue to struggle to survive adds daily to the weight of those losses.

"We tell ourselves stories in order to live," the novelist and essayist Joan Didion famously wrote. We also tell ourselves stories in order not to die. And at any moment these stories can change.

In "Port-au-Prince: The Moment," Mischa Berlinski recalls surviving the January 2010 earthquake. However, his essay, which poignantly and powerfully describes the height of disaster, echoes an instinct we might also display even as we attempt to capture the quietest, most predictable moments: our yearning to preserve our words. Berlinski was working on his novel when the earthquake struck. When his chair began to roll, his first thought was to press Control+S on his laptop keyboard and save his novel. He started

leaving with his laptop, then went back and put it on the table, rea-
soning that the book would be safer inside than outside. Though
we might disagree on some things—that, for example, "without
the presence—and the guns—of the United Nations, the [Hai-
tian] government would have been nothing but a band of refugees
and exiles"—reading, like writing, is never a dispassionate act. Essays, in the end, are not monologues. Whether we are nodding our
heads or shouting back or writing protest letters in response, the
most compelling essays often demand a reaction, either instantly
or much later, when the words have settled inside us, under our
skin, within us.

In "A Personal Essay by a Personal Essay," Christy Vannoy writes,
"I am a Personal Essay and I was born with a port wine stain and
beaten by my mother." Thankfully, essays like the twenty-four included in this collection are brilliant examples that the essay, port-
wine-stained or otherwise, continues not only to survive but to
thrive.

Edwidge Danticat

The Best
AMERICAN
ESSAYS
2011

Buddy Ebsen

FROM *The Believer*

IT'S THE QUEERS who made me. Who sat with me in the automobile in the dead of night and measured the content of my character without even looking at my face. Who—in the same car—asked me to apply a little strawberry lip balm to my lips before the anxious kiss that was fraught because would it be for an eternity, benday dots making up the hearts and flowers? Who sat on the toilet seat, panties around her ankles, talking and talking, girl talk burrowing through the partially closed bathroom door, and, boy, was it something. Who listened to opera. Who imitated Jessye Norman's locutions on and off the stage. Who made love in a Queens apartment and who wanted me to watch them making love while at least one of those so joined watched me, dressed, per that person's instructions, in my now-dead aunt's little-girl nightie. Who wore shoes with no socks in the dead of winter, intrepid, and then, before you knew it, was incapable of wiping his own ass—"gay cancer." Who died in a fire in an apartment in Paris. Who gave me a Raymond Radiguet novel when I was barely older than Radiguet was when he died, at twenty, of typhoid. Who sat with me in his automobile and talked to me about faith—he sat in the front seat, I in the back—and I was looking at the folds in his scalp when cops surrounded the car with flashlights and guns: they said we looked suspicious; we were aware that we looked and felt like no one else.

It's the queers who made me. Who didn't get married and who said to one woman, "I don't hang with that many other women," even though or perhaps because she herself was a woman. Who walked with me along the West Side piers in 1980s Manhattan, one summer afternoon, and said, apropos of the black kids vogueing, talking, getting dressed up around us, "I got it; it's a whole style." Who bought me a pair of saddle shoes and polished them while sitting at my desk, not looking up as I watched his hands work the leather. Who knew that the actor who played the Ghost of Christmas Past in the George C. Scott version of *A Christmas Carol* was an erotic draw for me as a child—or maybe it was the character's big beneficence. Who watched me watching Buddy Ebsen dancing with little Shirley Temple in a thirties movie called *Captain January* while singing "The Codfish Ball," Buddy Ebsen in a black jumper, moving his hands like a Negro dancer, arabesques informed by thought, his ass in the air, all on a wharf—and I have loved wharfs and docks, without ever wearing black jumpers, ever since.

It's the queers who made me. Who talked to me about Joe Brainard's *I Remember,* even though I kept forgetting to read it. Who keep after me to read *I Remember,* though perhaps my reluctance has to do with Brainard's association with Frank O'Hara, who was one queer who didn't make me, so interested was he in being a status-quo pet, the kind of desire that leads a fag to project his own self-loathing onto any other queer who gets into the room—How dare you. What are you doing here? But the late great poet-editor Barbara Epstein—who loved many queers and who could always love more—was friendly with Brainard and O'Hara, and perhaps the Barbara who still lives in my mind will eventually change my mind about all that, because she always could.

It's the queers who made me. Who introduced me to Edwin Denby's writings, and George Balanchine's "Serenade," and got me writing for *Ballet Review.* Who wore red suspenders and a Trotsky button; I had never met anyone who dressed so stylishly who wasn't black or Jewish. Who, even though I was "alone," watched me as I danced to Cindy Wilson singing "Give Me Back My Man" in the basement of a house that my mother shared with her sister in Atlanta. Who took me to Paris. Who let me share his bed in Paris. Who told my mother that I would be okay, and I hope she believed him. Who was delighted to include one of my sisters in a night out —she wore a pink prom dress and did the Electric Slide, surrounded by gay boys, and fuck knows if she cared or saw the difference between herself and them—and he stood by my side as I watched my sister dance in her pink prom dress, and then he asked what I was thinking about, and I said, "I'm just remembering why I'm gay."

It's the queers who made me. Who laughed with me in the pool in Lipari. Who kicked me under the table when I had allotted too much care for someone who would never experience love as suchness. Who sat with me in the cinema at Barnard College as *Black Orpheus* played, his bespectacled eyes glued to the screen as I weighed his whiteness against the characters' blackness and then my own. Who squatted down in the bathtub and scrubbed my legs and then my back and then the rest of my body the evening of the day we would start to know each other for the rest of our lives. Who lay with me in the bed in Los Angeles, white sheets over our young legs sprinkled with barely there hair. Who coaxed me back to life at the farmers' market later the same day, and I have the pictures to prove it. Who laughed when I said "What's J. Lo doing in the hospital?" as he stood near his bed dying of AIDS, his beautiful Panamanian hair—a mixture of African, Spanish, and Indian textures—no longer held back by the white bandanna I loved. Who gave me Michael Warner's *The Trouble with Normal*, and let me find much in it that was familiar and emotionally accurate, including the author's use of the word *moralism*, to describe the people who divide the world into "us" and "them," and who brutalize the queer in themselves and others to gain a foothold on a moralish perch.

It's the queers who made me. Who introduced me to a number of straight girls who, at first, thought that being queer was synonymous with being bitchy, and who, after meeting me and becoming friends, kept waiting and waiting for me to be a bitchy queen, largely because they wanted me to put down their female friends, and to hate other women as they themselves hated other women, not to mention themselves, despite their feminist agitprop; after all, I was a queen, and that's what queens did, right, along with getting sodomized, just like them, right—queens were the handmaidens to all that female self-hatred, right? And who then realized that I didn't hate women and so began to join forces with other women to level criticism at me.

It's the queers who made me. Who said: Women and queers get in the way of your feminism and gay rights. Who listened as I sat, hurt and confused, describing the postfeminist or postqueer monologue that had been addressed to me by some of the above

women and queers, who not only attacked my queer body directly
—you're too fat, you're too black, the horror, the horror!—but
delighted in hearing about queers flinging the same kind of pimp
slime on one another, not to mention joining forces with their girl-
friends of both sexes to establish within their marginalized groups
the kind of hierarchy straight white men presumably judge them
by, but not always, not really. Who asked, "Why do you spend so
much time thinking about women and queers?" And who didn't
hear me when I said, "But aren't we born of her? Didn't we queer
her body being born?"

It's the queers who made me. Who introduced me to the performer Justin Bond, whose various characters, sometimes cracked
by insecurity, eaglets in a society of buzzards, are defined by their
indomitability in an invulnerable world. Who told me about the
twelve-year-old girl who had been raised with love and acceptance
of queerness in adults, in a landscape where she could play without imprisoning herself in self-contempt, and who could talk to
her mother about what female bodies meant to her (everything),
which was a way of further loving her mother, the greatest romance
she had ever known, and who gave me, indirectly, my full queer
self, the desire to say "I" once again.

It's my queerness that made me. And in it there is a memory of
Jackie Curtis. She's walking up Bank Street, away from the river, a
low orange sun behind her like the ultimate stage set. It's my queer
self that goes up to Jackie Curtis—whom I have seen only in pictures and films; I am in my twenties—and it is he who says, "Oh,
Miss Curtis, you're amazing," and she says, in front of the setting
sun, completely stoned but attentive, a performer to her queer
bones, snapping to in the light of attention and love, "Oh, you
must come to my show!" as she digs into her big hippie bag to dig
out a flier, excited by the possibility of people seeing her for who
she is, even in makeup.

MISCHA BERLINSKI

Port-au-Prince: The Moment

FROM *The New York Review of Books*

MY CHAIR WAS ON CASTERS and began to roll. A large earthquake starts as a small earthquake. I saved my novel: Control+S. The horizon swayed at an angle. I had time to think many things —that's how long the quake lasted. I thought that I should stand under the lintel of the doorway. I took my laptop and started to leave. Then, unsteady on my feet, I wondered whether the laptop wouldn't be safer where it was. I put it back on the table. I went outside.

The office was a bungalow in a residential complex owned by a man who had made his fortune in powdered sugar. His wife had planted an elaborate garden of hanging and potted vases; they were falling or had fallen. The quake was a series of rolling waves, each sharper than the one before. I expected them to stop but they didn't. The visual effect was precisely that of the grainy videos that would later be shown on television, as of somebody shaking a camera sharply. It was tremendously loud—like huge stones grinding; I am not sure now if the sound was produced by the movement of the earth or by the simultaneous collapse of so many buildings.

I was alone on the sugar magnate's flowery terrace. I dropped to one knee, not shaken to the ground, but unbalanced, as if I had spun around in circles too many times. It did not occur to me for a second that I might die. I was panting heavily. A fissure in the earth opened up in the concrete beside me, perhaps a foot wide, a foot deep, and at least thirty feet long. The earthquake seemed to last an immensely long time, seemed to gain in power always, and when it was over the movement of the earth did not subside or taper down: it simply stopped. For five seconds or perhaps longer, the world was perfectly still and immensely quiet. Then the screaming began.

I knew that Cristina, Leo, and Bruno—my wife, my ten-month-old son, and my father-in-law, on vacation from Italy—were at home, and that I had to get to them as quickly as possible. But I wasn't worried. I knew that something could have happened to them but I knew that nothing had happened to them; a kind of reptilian optimism. I began to run. I had always imagined that the adrenaline response augmented one's energies. But the opposite was true: the run to the house was all downhill, yet I was gulping for air, almost vomiting. Cristina, Leo, and Bruno were waiting for me at the bottom of the driveway. Cristina was in tears. The baby was collected and calm.

Port-au-Prince is a city of high walls, all of which came down. At first glance, the city seemed prettier in the fading light of day as all over Port-au-Prince secret gardens and hidden terraces covered in flowers and lawn furniture emerged from behind the collapsed walls. Inside these clandestine gardens, security guards fingered their guns and householders sat on curbsides. A wall had fallen on a neighbor's pickup truck. A barrel of gasoline had overturned, leaving the road slick. Crowds began to arrive almost immediately at the Primature, the residence of the prime minister. There was a mood of fragile gaiety in the air, like the first minutes of a very lively party, ripples of giggles and laughter. A few women were in complete hysterical collapse—wailing, pounding the pavement, dragged along by men to the relative safety of the Primature.

A cluster of women began singing hymns; soon other women would join them; they would not relent for days. There were women dancing. A very large woman wearing a yellow bra cradled an un-moving bloodied child in her arms. (For some reason, my memories of the event are chiefly of women: women wailing, singing, dancing, crying, cradling the wounded, or wounded themselves; then later as corpses.) Beside my office, a large apartment complex had been in construction, two buildings, each four stories. It was a landmark on the horizon. Now one building was gone, and the other listed at a sharp angle.

All evening long there were aftershocks. We pulled a couch and chairs out of the house and sat in the driveway. Our house had suf-

fered almost no damage; we were in no immediate danger. We had
food and water for at least a week. We arranged Leo in his portable
crib and covered him well with a mosquito net. He fell asleep at his
habitual hour and did not wake up until the morning. We heard
singing and drumming all night long — and high throbbing prayer
like chanting, which as the aftershocks came redoubled in intensity to shouting. *"Tanpri Jezi. Tanpri,"* they chanted. We beg you, Jesus. We beg you. Every now and again through the night there was
a thud or an explosion. Our cellular telephones did not work. Our
neighbor claimed to have been able to call on his network, but his
phone, which functioned like all Haitian phones on a prepaid basis, was out of credit. I went out to look for cell-phone credit.

A large knot of people had gathered on the cul-de-sac leading to
my office: a woman there had Internet access via satellite. She allowed me to write to our families that we were fine. Cristina's radio
with the Mission des Nations Unies pour la Stabilisation en Haïti
(MINUSTAH) did not function. "Sierra Base, Sierra Base, this is
Papa Golf 224," she said. There was no response, only static. We
listened to the car radio. Across a normally busy dial, there were
only three operating stations. One was playing lively konpa music.
Another was Radio France Internationale. On the hour they had
news briefings announcing first a quake in Haiti, then an hour
later a massive quake in Haiti, then two hours later a catastrophic
quake in Haiti; this was between news of an African coup and in-
terviews with French artists, writers, and intellectuals. Then there
was a Creole news station. The director of a private morgue was
on the air, asking for the emergency donation or loan of a 10- to
15-kilowatt generator. Later there was a preacher on the same station, announcing the *"fin des temps."*

It was a remarkably clear and beautiful night. The electricity was
out all over Port-au-Prince, and when the moon set in the absence
of light pollution and as the dust settled, a night sky of remarkable
clarity emerged — the Big and Little Dipper, clouds of constella-
tions. The night had a chill to it. Cristina was worried that Leo was
cold and covered him with blanket after blanket. Even between aftershocks the earth did not feel stable but rather seemed to sway
slightly as on the deck of a ship. The cat finally came home, tentatively meowing her presence, only to have the neighbor's dog chase
her off. She fled to the roof of the house.

The very strange thing was this: there were no sirens, no helicopters. We spent the better part of the night making lists of people we knew: our nanny, our friends, Cristina's colleagues. Smith the real estate agent—he had a newborn daughter; so did Pierre the taxi driver. Boss Reginald the mechanic. We were alone in the driveway of our house as if the earthquake had sheared off the rest of the world, but for the sound of the praying, which finally abated not long before dawn.

In retrospect, the chief emotion I suffered in the days immediately following the quake was a powerful curiosity; an overwhelming desire to see for myself just what had happened. This was one of the most powerful emotions I have ever experienced. The next morning, I went on foot to the Hotel Montana. I had heard a rumor in the night that it had collapsed but did not believe it—the Hotel Montana was like a fortress! I was in San Francisco for the Loma Prieta quake of 1989. We had heard rumors that the Golden Gate Bridge had fallen into the Pacific, that the UC Berkeley library had burned to the ground. I imagined that now, too, the rumors far outstripped the truth. In this case, however, nobody knew what had really happened to Port-au-Prince.

Those who had come to the neighboring Caribbean islands or the Dominican Republic on vacation must have been delighted with the weather that morning, warm with a deep blue sky. Now the great lawn of the Primature was almost full. There was no organized aid or assistance, no Red Cross station, no sirens, no sign of the Police Nationale d'Haïti. The only official presence was a single security guard cradling a shotgun and dozing in a chair. People were stringing tarpaulins from trees to shelter themselves from the strong midmorning sun. One shady patch of the Primature served as cemetery, the bodies wrapped in blankets and discarded there, a few powdered limbs escaping. The predominant smell of the earthquake in my experience was not decomposing bodies, as has been often reported in the press, but piss and shit.

The road to the Montana hugs a deep ravine, on both flanks of which and in the valley below a vast *bidonville* had been constructed, a cinder-block city densely reticulated in its narrow passageways like an Arab souk. This was not the housing of the very poorest, but of the Port-au-Prince middle class: people who could afford to rent or buy shelter. In our own house, one bottle had broken while its neighbor remained upright. In the *bidonville,* some houses had collapsed and the collapse of one house brought down the next; but in other places a patch of ten or twenty houses clung stolidly to the side of the hill. The collapsed houses were a smear of cement. Within the *bidonville* there were large open spaces—a soccer field, for example—and in these open spaces clusters of people had settled. Afterward, people who were not in the quake always asked about the bodies. But at the time, the bodies were far less shocking than the collapsed houses. The dead were discreet. The massive untidy solidity of a collapsed building was awful.

The side of the mountain had collapsed on the road, partially burying a pickup truck. A woman had been caught in the flatbed. Her eyes were open; the impact had split open her guts; she was covered in a film of gray dust. I thought to myself that she would haunt my nightmares but in fact writing this now is the first time I have recalled her since the event. On the side of the road there were souvenir vendors with brightly painted metal lizards and other handicrafts.

The mountain reeked of cologne: a small *parfumerie* had collapsed. On a large green lawn, wounded from the hotel lay in the deck chairs in which they had been evacuated. One man was still in a swimsuit. An Argentine helicopter landed, one or two of the wounded were loaded up, and the helicopter took off again, disappearing out of view into the vastness of the city. The twenty-foot steel wall surrounding the Montana was still standing and its gate was closed, hiding the damaged hotel from view. Under ordinary circumstances, the hotel loomed far above the walls. Now it had simply disappeared.

My wife and I came to Haiti in the spring of 2007 when she found a job with MINUSTAH. We had spent almost two years in the provincial town of Jérémie, then after Leo's birth moved to Port-au-Prince. I was writing a novel about MINUSTAH. The protagonist of the novel was a former deputy sheriff from Florida, who joined the mission as an UNPOL—a police officer working with the UN to monitor, mentor, and support the Police Nationale d'Haïti. I wrote:

In the restaurant, they had a DVD of Aristide on the television. Jean-Bertrand Aristide was Haiti's crazy ex-President. In his time in power, he dismantled the military and the police force, fearing, not without rea-

son, a *coup d'etat* from one or the other. Then he distributed arms to his
class allies, the gang lords who ran the slums. This created social stabil-
ity to about the extent you can imagine. By the time Aristide fled Haiti
in 2004 and the United Nations arrived, the country had fallen apart.
Some blame Aristide, some blame his enemies. Drunken rebels ran riot
on the streets of Port-au-Prince. Coke-mad teenage gangs controlled the
cities. The new government of Haiti, such as it was, had no military and
no police force. That's why there was a United Nations Stabilization Mission in Haiti: soldiers were brought in to maintain order; I was there to
train the new police force, the one that was going to keep order in the
absence of the old police force.

My wife, unlike my protagonist, was a civilian employee of MIN-
USTAH. A lawyer herself, she worked with lawyers from a dozen
other countries in an attempt to reform and stabilize the Haitian
legal system—an effort that had so far borne only limited results.
There were still several thousand Haitians in prison awaiting trial;
some had been waiting for years. (The main prison collapsed in
the earthquake and the surviving prisoners all escaped, effectively
resolving this particular problem.) But there was only so much the
United Nations could do: the UN in Haiti—unlike in Kosovo—
did not possess executive authority. In my wife's case, MINUSTAH
could do little but gently coax local judicial authorities. At best, the
UN and the government of Haiti had a delicate coexistence: the
United Nations was in Haiti only with the permission of the government; but without the presence—and the guns—of the United
Nations, the government would have been nothing but a band of
refugees and exiles, some in Miami, some in Brooklyn, still others
in Montreal.

That afternoon, leaving the baby with my wife, I went along the
same road that led to the Hotel Montana but in the opposite direction, toward my wife's offices in the Hotel Christopher. The impasse leading to the Christopher was blocked by barbed wire and
protected by a few Filipino soldiers. A small crowd of Haitians
stood at the wire; a man was pleading to be admitted, on the
grounds that his car was parked inside. A Filipino said, "If I let you
in, I have to let everybody in." This debate continued in reasonable voices on both sides. I presented my wife's badge and was allowed in.

It was eerily quiet in the cul-de-sac. The place had once bustled
with purposeful movement. The Hotel Christopher and its adja-

cent buildings had been like a small college campus: the faces one encountered there were enthusiastic and alert, about half white and half black, either Africans or local Haitian staff. Signs had pointed the way to "Justice" or "Elections" or "Human Rights." On the walls of the Christopher there were giant photographs illustrating inspiring moments in MINUSTAH history: Sri Lankan soldiers in uniforms and blue helmets pushing a stalled pickup truck, a Jordanian soldier with a bushy mustache holding hands with a little girl. A peacock and a peahen had patrolled the grounds. Now the Brazilian army had transformed the narrow impasse into a staging ground for heavy equipment in which the bulldozers and cranes were parked. There couldn't have been more than a couple of dozen soldiers in all. A few Jordanians stood around taking pictures of the rubble.

My wife worked in a building one hundred meters from the Hotel Christopher—her building had collapsed. Cristina had been home only because her father was visiting. The UNDP had collapsed. Human Rights had collapsed. UNAIDS had collapsed. Villa Privé, the headquarter of the UNPOL program, had collapsed. We later learned that many UN staff members had died. I walked into the courtyard of the Hotel Christopher, where the vehicles of VIPs were under ordinary circumstances parked. This tall building too was gone, eight stories reduced to one—but the collapse was neat. It might simply have been a one-story building. Then I was alone in the courtyard, directly in front of the empty parking place of the special representative of the secretary general.

By the next day or the day after that, the faces of those except the most profoundly bereft had returned to normal—normal in the sense that they were commensurate with the experience that we had undergone. Faces in the days to come would reveal weariness, despair, misery, grief, and very often joy. But everywhere I went on that first day after the quake, I saw a facial expression I had never before seen; I suppose I must have worn it as well. Our faces suggested only the most profound surprise.

KATY BUTLER

What Broke My Father's Heart

FROM *The New York Times Magazine*

ONE OCTOBER AFTERNOON three years ago, while I was visiting my parents, my mother made a request I dreaded and longed to fulfill. She had just poured me a cup of Earl Grey from her Japanese iron teapot, shaped like a little pumpkin; outside, two cardinals splashed in the birdbath in the weak Connecticut sunlight. Her white hair was gathered at the nape of her neck, and her voice was low. "Please help me get Jeff's pacemaker turned off," she said, using my father's first name. I nodded, and my heart knocked.

Upstairs, my eighty-five-year-old father, Jeffrey, a retired Wesleyan University professor who suffered from dementia, lay napping in what was once their shared bedroom. Sewn into a hump of skin and muscle below his right clavicle was the pacemaker that helped his heart outlive his brain. The size of a pocket watch, it had kept his heart beating rhythmically for nearly five years. Its battery was expected to last five more.

After tea, I knew, my mother would help him from his narrow bed with its mattress encased in waterproof plastic. She would take him to the toilet, change his diaper, and lead him tottering to the couch, where he would sit mutely for hours, pretending to read Joyce Carol Oates, the book falling in his lap as he stared out the window.

I don't like describing what dementia did to my father — and indirectly to my mother — without telling you first that my parents loved each other, and I loved them. That my mother could stain a deck and sew an evening dress from a photo in *Vogue* and thought of my father as her best friend. That my father had never given up easily on anything.

Born in South Africa, he lost his left arm in World War II, but later earned a PhD from Oxford; built floor-to-ceiling bookcases for our living room; coached rugby; and with my two brothers as crew, sailed his beloved Rhodes 19 on Long Island Sound. When I was a child, he woke me, chortling, with his version of a verse from *The Rubaiyat of Omar Khayyam:* "Awake, my little one! Before life's liquor in its cup be dry!" At bedtime he tucked me in, quoting Hamlet: "May flights of angels sing thee to thy rest!"

Now I would look at him and think of Anton Chekhov, who died of tuberculosis in 1904. "Whenever there is someone in a family who has long been ill, and hopelessly ill," he wrote, "there come painful moments when all timidly, secretly, at the bottom of their hearts long for his death." A century later, my mother and I had come to long for the machine in my father's chest to fail.

Until 2001, my two brothers and I—all living in California—assumed that our parents would enjoy long, robust old ages capped by some brief, undefined final illness. Thanks to their own healthful habits and a panoply of medical advances—vaccines, antibiotics, airport defibrillators, 911 networks, and the like—they weren't likely to die prematurely of the pneumonias, influenzas, and heart attacks that decimated previous generations. They walked every day. My mother practiced yoga. My father was writing a history of his birthplace, a small South African town.

In short, they were seemingly among the lucky ones for whom the American medical system, despite its fragmentation, inequity, and waste, works quite well. Medicare and supplemental insurance paid for their specialists and their trusted Middletown internist, the lean, bespectacled Robert Fales, who, like them, was skeptical of medical overdoing. "I bonded with your parents, and you don't bond with everybody," he once told me. "It's easier to understand someone if they just tell it like it is from their heart and their soul."

They were also stoics and religious agnostics. They signed living wills and durable power-of-attorney documents for health care. My mother, who watched friends die slowly of cancer, had an underlined copy of the Hemlock Society's *Final Exit* in her bookcase. Even so, I watched them lose control of their lives to a set of perverse financial incentives—for cardiologists, hospitals, and especially the manufacturers of advanced medical devices—skewed to promote maximum treatment. At a point hard to precisely define, they stopped being beneficiaries of the war on sudden death and became its victims.

Things took their first unexpected turn on November 13, 2001, when my father—then seventy-nine, pacemakerless, and seemingly healthy—collapsed on my parents' kitchen floor in Middletown, making burbling sounds. He had suffered a stroke.

He came home six weeks later permanently incapable of completing a sentence. But as I've said, he didn't give up easily, and he doggedly learned again how to fasten his belt; to peck out sentences on his computer; to walk alone, one foot dragging, to the university pool for water aerobics. He never again put on a shirt without help or looked at the book he had been writing. One day he haltingly told my mother, "I don't know who I am anymore."

His stroke devastated two lives. The day before, my mother was an upper-middle-class housewife who practiced calligraphy in her spare time. Afterward, she was one of 37 million people in America, most of whom are women, who help care for an older family member.

Their numbers grow each day. Thanks to advanced medical technologies, elderly people now survive repeated health crises that once killed them, and so the "oldest old" have become the nation's most rapidly growing age group. Nearly a third of Americans over eighty-five have dementia (a condition whose prevalence rises in direct relationship to longevity). Half need help with at least one practical, life-sustaining activity, like getting dressed or making breakfast. Even though a capable woman was hired to give my dad showers, my seventy-seven-year-old mother found herself on duty more than eighty hours a week. Her blood pressure rose and her weight fell. On a routine visit to Dr. Fales, she burst into tears. She was put on sleeping pills and antidepressants.

My father said he came to believe that she would have been better off if he had died. "She'd have weeped the weep of a widow," he told me in his garbled, poststroke speech, on a walk we took together in the fall of 2002. "And then she would have been all right." It was hard to tell which of them was suffering more.

As we shuffled through the fallen leaves that day, I thought of my father's father, Ernest Butler. He was seventy-nine when he died, in 1965, before pacemakers, implanted cardiac defibrillators, stents, and replacement heart valves routinely staved off death among the very old. After completing some long-unfinished chairs, he cleaned his woodshop, had a heart attack, and died two days later in a plain hospital bed. As I held my dad's soft, mottled hand, I vainly wished him a similar merciful death.

A few days before Christmas that year, after a vigorous session of water exercises, my father developed a painful inguinal (intestinal) hernia. My mother took him to Fales, who sent them to a local surgeon, who sent them to a cardiologist for a preoperative clearance. After an electrocardiogram recorded my father's slow heartbeat— a longstanding and symptomless condition not uncommon in the very old—the cardiologist, John Rogan, refused to clear my dad for surgery unless he received a pacemaker.

Without the device, Dr. Rogan told me later, my father could have died from cardiac arrest during surgery or perhaps within a few months. It was the second time Rogan had seen my father. The first time, about a year before, he recommended the device for the same slow heartbeat. That time, my then-competent and prestroke father expressed extreme reluctance, on the advice of Fales, who considered it overtreatment.

My father's medical conservatism, I have since learned, is not unusual. According to studies publicized by the Dartmouth Atlas public-health research group, patients are far more likely than their doctors to reject aggressive treatments when fully informed of pros, cons, and alternatives—information, one study suggests, that nearly half of patients say they don't get. And although many doctors assume that people want to extend their lives, many do not. In a 1997 study in the *Journal of the American Geriatrics Society,* 30 percent of seriously ill people surveyed in a hospital said they would "rather die" than live permanently in a nursing home. In a 2008 study in the *Journal of the American College of Cardiology,* 28 percent of patients with advanced heart failure said they would trade one day of excellent health for another two years in their current state.

When Rogan suggested the pacemaker for the second time, my father was too stroke-damaged to discuss, and perhaps even to weigh, his tradeoffs. The decision fell to my mother—anxious to relieve my father's pain, exhausted with caregiving, deferential to doctors, and no expert on high-tech medicine. She said yes. One

of the most important medical decisions of my father's life was over
in minutes. Dr. Fales was notified by fax.

Fales loved my parents, knew their suffering close at hand, continued to oppose a pacemaker, and wasn't alarmed by death. If he
had had the chance to sit down with my parents, he could have explained that the pacemaker's battery would last ten years and asked
whether my father wanted to live to be eighty-nine in his nearly
mute and dependent state. He could have discussed the option of
using a temporary external pacemaker that, I later learned, could
have seen my dad safely through surgery. But my mother never
consulted Fales. And the system would have effectively penalized
him if she had. Medicare would have paid him a standard office-
visit rate of $54 for what would undoubtedly have been a long
meeting—and nothing for phone calls to work out a plan with Rogan and the surgeon.

Medicare administrators are aware of this problem, and in the
House version of the health-care reform bill debated last summer,
better payments to primary-care doctors for such conversations
were included, but after the provision was distorted as reimbursement for "death panels," it was dropped. In my father's case, there
was only a brief informed-consent process, covering the boilerplate
risks of minor surgery, handled by the general surgeon.

I believe that my father's doctors did their best within a com-
partmentalized and time-pressured medical system. But in the absence of any other guiding hand, there is no doubt that economics
helped shape the context in which doctors made decisions. Had
we been at the Mayo Clinic—where doctors are salaried, medical
records are electronically organized, and care is coordinated by a
single doctor—things might have turned out differently. But Middletown is part of the fee-for-service medical economy. Doctors
peddle their wares on a piecework basis; communication among
them is haphazard; thinking is often short-term; nobody makes
money when medical interventions are declined; and nobody is in
charge except the marketplace.

And so on January 2, 2003, at Middlesex Hospital, the surgeon
implanted my father's pacemaker using local anesthetic. Medicare
paid him $461 and the hospital a flat fee of about $12,000, of
which an estimated $7,500 went to St. Jude Medical, the maker of
the device. The hernia was fixed a few days later.

It was a case study in what primary-care doctors have long bemoaned: that Medicare rewards doctors far better for doing procedures than for assessing whether they should be done at all. The incentives for overtreatment continue, said Dr. Ted Epperly, the board chairman of the American Academy of Family Physicians, because those who profit from them—specialists, hospitals, drug companies, and the medical device manufacturers—spend money lobbying Congress and the public to keep it that way.

Last year, doctors, hospitals, drug companies and medical equipment manufacturers, and other medical professionals spent $545 million on lobbying, according to the Center for Responsive Politics. This may help explain why researchers estimate that 20 to 30 percent of Medicare's $510 billion budget goes for unnecessary tests and treatment. Why cost containment received short shrift in health-care reform. Why physicians like Fales net an average of $173,000 a year, while noninvasive cardiologists like Rogan net about $419,000.

The system rewarded nobody for saying "no" or even "wait"— not even my frugal, intelligent, *Consumer Reports*–reading mother. Medicare and supplemental insurance covered almost every penny of my father's pacemaker. My mother was given more government-mandated consumer information when she bought a new Camry a year later.

And so my father's electronically managed heart—now requiring frequent monitoring, paid by Medicare—became part of the $24 billion worldwide cardiac device industry and an indirect subsidizer of the fiscal health of American hospitals. The profit margins that manufacturers earn on cardiac devices is close to 30 percent. Cardiac procedures and diagnostics generate about 20 percent of hospital revenues and 30 percent of profits.

Shortly after New Year's 2003, my mother belatedly called and told me about the operations, which went off without a hitch. She didn't call earlier, she said, because she didn't want to worry me. My heart sank, but I said nothing. It is one thing to silently thank the heavens that your beloved father's heart might fail. It is another to actively abet his death.

The pacemaker bought my parents two years of limbo, two of purgatory, and two of hell. At first they soldiered on, with my father no better and no worse. My mother reread Jon Kabat-Zinn's

Full Catastrophe Living, bought a self-help book on patience, and rose each morning to meditate.

In 2005, the age-related degeneration that had slowed my father's heart attacked his eyes, lungs, bladder, and bowels. Clots as narrow as a single human hair lodged in tiny blood vessels in his brain, killing clusters of neurons by depriving them of oxygen. Long partly deaf, he began losing his sight to "wet" macular degeneration, requiring ocular injections that cost nearly $2,000 each. A few months later, he forgot his way home from the university pool. He grew incontinent. He was collapsing physically, like an ancient, shored-up house.

In the summer of 2006, he fell in the driveway and suffered a brain hemorrhage. Not long afterward, he spent a full weekend compulsively brushing and rebrushing his teeth. "The Jeff I loved is gone," my mother wrote in the journal a social worker had suggested she keep. "My life is in ruins. This is horrible, and I lasted for five years." His pacemaker kept on ticking.

When bioethicists debate life-extending technologies, the effects on people like my mother rarely enter the calculus. But a 2008 Ohio State University study of the DNA of family caregivers of people with Alzheimer's disease showed that the ends of their chromosomes, called telomeres, had degraded enough to reflect a four- to eight-year shortening of lifespan. By that reckoning, every year that the pacemaker gave my irreparably damaged father took from my then-vigorous mother an equal year.

When my mother was upset, she meditated or cleaned house. When I was upset, I Googled. In 2006, I discovered that pacemakers could be deactivated without surgery. Nurses, doctors, and even device salesmen had done so, usually at deathbeds. A white ceramic device, like a TV remote and shaped like the wands that children use to blow bubbles, could be placed around the hump on my father's chest. Press a few buttons and the electrical pulses that ran down the leads to his heart would slow until they were no longer effective. My father's heart, I learned, would probably not stop. It would just return to its old, slow rhythm. If he was lucky, he might suffer cardiac arrest and die within weeks, perhaps in his sleep. If he was unlucky, he might linger painfully for months while his lagging heart failed to suffuse his vital organs with sufficient oxygenated blood.

If we did nothing, his pacemaker would not stop for years. Like the tireless charmed brooms in Disney's *Fantasia,* it would prompt my father's heart to beat after he became too demented to speak, sit up, or eat. It would keep his heart pulsing after he drew his last breath. If he was buried, it would send signals to his dead heart in the coffin. If he was cremated, it would have to be cut from his chest first, to prevent it from exploding and damaging the incinerator's walls or hurting an attendant.

On the Internet, I discovered that the pacemaker—somewhat like the ventilator, defibrillator, and feeding tube—was first an exotic, stopgap device, used to carry a handful of patients through a brief medical crisis. Then it morphed into a battery-powered, implantable, and routine treatment. When Medicare approved the pacemaker for reimbursement in 1966, the market exploded. Today pacemakers are implanted annually in more than 400,000 Americans, about 80 percent of whom are over sixty-five. According to calculations by the Dartmouth Atlas research group using Medicare data, nearly a fifth of new recipients who receive pacemakers annually—76,000—are over eighty. The typical patient with a cardiac device today is an elderly person suffering from at least one other severe chronic illness.

Over the years, as technology has improved, the battery life of these devices has lengthened. The list of heart conditions for which they are recommended has grown. In 1984, the treatment guidelines from the American College of Cardiology declared that pacemakers were strongly recommended as "indicated" or mildly approved as "reasonable" for fifty-six heart conditions and "not indicated" for thirty-one more. By 2008, the list for which they were strongly or mildly recommended expanded to eighty-eight, with most of the increase in the lukewarm "reasonable" category. Ethical cautions regarding their use in the aged and chronically ill were given little more than a glance.

The research backing the expansion of diagnoses was weak. Overall, only 5 percent of the positive recommendations were supported by research from multiple double-blind randomized studies, the gold standard of evidence-based medicine. And 58 percent were based on no studies at all, only a "consensus of expert opinion." Of the seventeen cardiologists who wrote the 2008 guidelines, eleven received financing from cardiac device makers or worked at institutions receiving it.

This pattern—a paucity of scientific support and a plethora of industry connections—holds across almost all cardiac treatment, according to the cardiologist Pierluigi Tricoci of Duke University's Clinical Research Institute. Last year in the *Journal of the American Medical Association,* Tricoci and his coauthors wrote that only 11 percent of 2,700 widely used cardiac treatment guidelines were based on that gold standard. Most were based only on expert opinion.

"Experts are as vulnerable to conflicts of interest as researchers are," the authors warned, because "expert clinicians are also those who are likely to receive honoraria, speakers bureau [fees], consulting fees, or research support from industry." They called the current cardiac research agenda "strongly influenced by industry's natural desire to introduce new products."

Perhaps it's no surprise that I also discovered others puzzling over cardiologists who recommended pacemakers for relatives with advanced dementia. "78-year-old mother-in-law has dementia; severe short-term memory issues," read an Internet post by "soninlaw" on Elderhope.com, a caregivers' site, in 2007. "On a routine trip to her cardiologist, doctor decides she needs a pacemaker . . . Anyone have a similar encounter?"

By the summer of 2007, my dad had forgotten the purpose of a dinner napkin and had to be coached to remove his slippers before he tried to put on his shoes. After a lifetime of promoting my father's health, my mother reversed course. On a routine visit, she asked Rogan to deactivate the pacemaker. "It was hard," she later told me. "I was doing for Jeff what I would have wanted Jeff to do for me." Rogan soon made it clear he was morally opposed. "It would have been like putting a pillow over your father's head," he later told me.

Not long afterward, my mother declined additional medical tests and refused to put my father on a new anti-dementia drug and a blood thinner with troublesome side effects. "I take responsibility for whatever," she wrote in her journal that summer. "Enough of all this overkill! It's killing me! Talk about quality of life—what about mine?"

*

Then came the autumn day when she asked for my help, and I said yes. I told myself that we were simply trying to undo a terrible medical mistake. I reminded myself that my dad had rejected a pacemaker when his faculties were intact. I imagined, as a bioethicist had suggested, what a fifteen-minute conversation with my independent, pre-dementia father would have been like and knew he would shake his head in horror over any further extension of what was not a "life" but a prolonged and attenuated dying. None of it helped. I knew that once he died, I would dream of him and miss his mute, loving smiles. I wanted to melt into the arms of the father I once had and ask him to handle this. Instead, I felt as if I were signing on as his executioner and that I had no choice.

Over the next five months, my mother and I learned many things. We were told, by the Hemlock Society's successor, Compassion and Choices, that as my father's medical proxy, my mother had the legal right to ask for the withdrawal of any treatment and that the pacemaker was, in theory at least, a form of medical treatment. We learned that although my father's living will requested no life support if he were comatose or dying, it said nothing about dementia and did not define a pacemaker as life support. We learned that if we called 911, emergency medical technicians would not honor my father's do-not-resuscitate order unless he wore a state-issued orange hospital bracelet. We also learned that no cardiology association had given its members clear guidance on when, or whether, deactivating pacemakers was ethical.

(Last month that changed. The Heart Rhythm Society and the American Heart Association issued guidelines declaring that patients or their legal surrogates have the moral and legal right to request the withdrawal of any medical treatment, including an implanted cardiac device. It said that deactivating a pacemaker was neither euthanasia nor assisted suicide, and that a doctor could not be compelled to do so in violation of his moral values. In such cases, it continued, doctors "cannot abandon the patient but should involve a colleague who is willing to carry out the procedure." This came, of course, too late for us.)

In the spring of 2008, things got even worse. My father took to roaring like a lion at his caregivers. At home in California, I searched the Internet for a sympathetic cardiologist and a caregiver to put my dad to bed at night. My frayed mother began to shout at him, and their nighttime scenes were heartbreaking and frightening. An Alzheimer's Association support group leader suggested that my brothers and I fly out together and institutionalize my father. This leader did not know of my mother's formidable will and had never heard my mother speak about her wedding vows or her love.

Meanwhile my father drifted into what nurses call "the dwindles": not sick enough to qualify for hospice care, but sick enough to never get better. He fell repeatedly at night and my mother could not pick him up. Finally, he was weak enough to qualify for palliative care, and a team of nurses and social workers visited the house. His chest grew wheezy. My mother did not request antibiotics. In mid-April 2008, he was taken by ambulance to Middlesex Hospital's hospice wing, suffering from pneumonia.

Pneumonia was once called "the old man's friend" for its promise of an easy death. That's not what I saw when I flew in. On morphine, his eyes shut and unreachable, my beloved father was breathing as hard and regularly as a machine.

My mother sat holding his hand, weeping and begging for forgiveness for her impatience. She sat by him in agony. She beseeched his doctors and nurses to increase his morphine dose and to turn off the pacemaker. It was a weekend, and the doctor on call at Rogan's cardiology practice refused authorization, saying that my father "might die immediately." And so came five days of hard labor. My mother and I stayed by him in shifts, while his breathing became increasingly ragged and his feet slowly started to turn blue. I began drafting an appeal to the hospital ethics committee. My brothers flew in.

On a Tuesday afternoon, with my mother at his side, my father stopped breathing. A hospice nurse hung a blue memorial light on the outside of his hospital door. Inside his chest, his pacemaker was still quietly pulsing.

After his memorial service in the Wesleyan University chapel, I carried a box from the crematory into the woods of an old convent where he and I often walked. It was late April, overcast and cold. By the side of a stream, I opened the box, scooped out a handful of ashes, and threw them into the swirling water. There were some curious spiraled metal wires, perhaps the leads of his pacemaker, mixed with the white dust and pieces of bone.

*

A year later, I took my mother to meet a heart surgeon in a windowless treatment room at Brigham and Women's Hospital in Boston. She was eighty-four, with two leaking heart valves. Her cardiologist had recommended open-heart surgery, and I was hoping to find a less invasive approach. When the surgeon asked us why we were there, my mother said, "To ask questions." She was no longer a trusting and deferential patient. Like me, she no longer saw doctors — perhaps with the exception of Fales — as healers or her fiduciaries. They were now skilled technicians with their own agendas. But I couldn't help feeling that something precious — our old faith in a doctor's calling, perhaps, or in a healing that is more than a financial transaction or a reflexive fixing of broken parts — had been lost.

The surgeon was forthright: without open-heart surgery, there was a fifty-fifty chance my mother would die within two years. If she survived the operation, she would probably live to be ninety. And the risks? He shrugged. Months of recovery. A 5 percent chance of stroke. Some possibility, he acknowledged at my prompting, of postoperative cognitive decline. (More than half of heart-bypass patients suffer at least a 20 percent reduction in mental function.) My mother lifted her trouser leg to reveal an anklet of orange plastic: her do-not-resuscitate bracelet. The doctor recoiled. No, he would not operate with that bracelet in place. It would not be fair to his team. She would be revived if she collapsed. "If I have a stroke," my mother said, nearly in tears, "I want you to let me go." What about a minor stroke, he said — a little weakness on one side?

I kept my mouth shut. I was there to get her the information she needed and to support whatever decision she made. If she emerged from surgery intellectually damaged, I would bring her to a nursing home in California and try to care for her the way she had cared for my father at such cost to her own health. The thought terrified me.

The doctor sent her up a floor for an echocardiogram. A half-hour later, my mother came back to the waiting room and put on her black coat. "No," she said brightly, with the clarity of purpose she had shown when she asked me to have the pacemaker deactivated. "I will not do it."

She spent the spring and summer arranging house repairs, thinning out my father's bookcases, and throwing out the files he collected so lovingly for the book he never finished writing. She told someone that she didn't want to leave a mess for her kids. Her chest pain worsened, and her breathlessness grew severe. "I'm aching to garden," she wrote in her journal. "But so it goes. ACCEPT ACCEPT ACCEPT."

Last August, she had a heart attack and returned home under the care of hospice. One evening a month later, another heart attack. One of my brothers followed her ambulance to the hospice wing where we had sat for days by my father's bed. The next morning, she took off her silver earrings and told the nurses she wanted to stop eating and drinking, that she wanted to die and never go home. Death came to her an hour later, while my brother was on the phone to me in California—almost as mercifully as it had come to my paternal grandfather. She was continent and lucid to her end.

A week later, at the same crematory near Long Island Sound, my brothers and I watched through a plate-glass window as a cardboard box containing her body, dressed in a scarlet silk *ao dai* she had sewn herself, slid into the flames. The next day, the undertaker delivered a plastic box to the house where, for forty-five of their sixty-one years together, my parents had loved and looked after each other, humanly and imperfectly. There were no bits of metal mixed with the fine white powder and the small pieces of her bones.

STEVEN CHURCH

Auscultation

FROM *The Pedestrian*

Chamber 1

IN AUGUST 2007 we all waited to hear news of six miners trapped
1,500 feet underground by a massive cave-in at the Crandall Canyon coal mine in Utah, a catastrophic collapse so intense that it
registered as a 3.9 magnitude earthquake on seismographs. As rescuers began the arduous three-day process of digging the men out,
they also erected seismic listening devices on the surface and set
off three dynamite charges, a signal to any surviving miners to
make noise. Lots of noise. The electronic ears listened for the
sound of hammers pounding on the rock and on roof bolts, the
telltale rap-and-thump of human life. We listened and listened but
never heard a thing.

Six miners missing. Six boreholes drilled into different areas
of the mine. They sent oxygen sensors, cameras, and microphones
down through PVC pipe, fishing in each hole, searching every possible area for the men. Oxygen levels were misread, confused, and
ultimately determined to be dangerously low. Three rescue workers trying to dig the trapped miners out were also killed when a
wall of the mine "exploded," crushing them. We never saw or heard
any sign of the miners, and all six men were considered missing
and presumed dead. All rescue efforts were eventually abandoned.
I don't know if there is a signal for this, another series of blasts to
say goodbye, or some other ceremonial end to the search. Maybe
they just switch off the drills and unplug their ears.

The owner of the mine, Bob Murray, held a press conference and said, "Had I known that this evil mountain, this alive mountain, would do what it did, I would never have sent the miners in here. I'll never go near that mountain again."

Finally a seventh hole was bored into the mountain, and through this hole they pumped thousands of gallons of mud and debris, filling all remaining cavities and sealing the tomb off permanently with the missing miners still inside.

Researchers today at Utah State University are working to create more effective listening and noisemaking devices to help trapped miners—some of them seemingly crude and simplistic, yet still effective. One plan calls for four-by-four-inch iron plates to be placed at regular intervals in the tunnels, with sledgehammers kept nearby—the idea being that a trapped miner can find his way to a station and slam the hammer into the iron plate over and over again. Think of the noise below. Think of your ears. Geophones on the surface—the kind of sensors they use to anticipate earthquakes—would register the sound waves created by the hammer pings and create a listening grid, a kind of sound map of the mine, which they would then use to pinpoint the exact location of any miners still kicking below the rugged skin.

Chamber 2

Recall the ice-cold press of the metal disk against your cavity, the sting and soft burn as it warms on your clavicle, your breastbone, fingers moving metal across your naked chest, around behind, fingertips stepping down your spine, one hand on your hip, maybe your shoulder, the other sliding around your rib cage, always, always with the whispered command *Breathe . . . breathe . . . good,* and the eyes staring not at you but at the cold diaphragm, the metallic spot on your body, listening as if your body possesses a voice of its own and speaks in a language only others understand. The diaphragm will only broadcast its secret to the touch. It knows you. And when it touches you, it sings sounds of your body, noises you can barely imagine—the hypnotic pump of organs, the soft ebb and flow of blood in your veins, and the breathy whisper of lungs at work—noises that can name you *normal, healthy,* or *not.* The intimate instrument—the stethoscope—knows your body in a way your own hands and ears never can.

Chamber 3

Some heart doctors train their ears on classical music—Mozart and Bach and Chopin—learning to discern the individual instruments: to hear baritone from trombone, trumpet from sax, and the *tum-tum* of kettle over bongo or bass. They learn to listen for the flaws and failings of the heart, to recognize the music of machinelike muscle efficiency, and to understand when a noise is a bad noise. They depend on the stethoscope for more than diagnoses. They need it to be whole. Nothing promises *doctor* like a stethoscope draped around an exposed neck or curled over a pressed, collared shirt, perhaps tucked neatly into the pocket of a white lab coat, or clutched firmly in hand, authoritatively like a craftsman's hammer, a plumber's seat wrench, or a surgeon's scalpel—the only tool for a specific job. You are familiar with the flexible latex tubing, the chrome-plated ear tubes, the hard metal diaphragm—cold, round, smooth as pearl, reflective as a mirror. The stethoscope immediately identifies a doctor—an icon of care and pain management, a reliquary of body knowledge, someone you trust with your life. Think of the things you've allowed another person to do and say to you, mainly because he wore the uniform of doctor and carried a stethoscope. We don't check resumés or credentials, don't ask for service reviews or certificates. We expect and accept the object. Even if it's never used (but it's always used), its appearance conjures a sense memory of that repeated sweet burn when pressed to your flesh. Regardless of physical context or attire (say at a crowded beach, in a subway, or on a mountain trail), the stethoscope speaks. It says, "I am a doctor," and in so doing it grants rights and responsibilities, obligations and expectations. It tells us you will do no harm. It tells us you know what you are talking about. Every child's doctor play-set comes with a plastic stethoscope, because you can't dress up as a doctor without one.

As object, it functions as both necessary and sufficient condition of "doctorness." But this identity and image—of the doctor as listener, as diviner of significant sounds through a stethoscope, the magician of auscultation—is a relatively new one, just over 150 years old. The French doctor René Laennec is credited by many for inventing the first stethoscope, or at least for introducing the diagnostic practice of auscultation. In a paper published in 1819, he says:

> I was consulted by a young woman with symptoms of a diseased heart . . . percussion was of little avail on account . . . of fatness. The application of the ear . . . inadmissible by the age and sex of the patient. I recollected a fact in acoustics . . . the augmented sound conveyed through solid bodies . . . I rolled a quire of paper into a cylinder and applied one end to the heart and one end to the ear . . . and thereby perceived the action of the heart . . . more clear and distinct. I have been enabled to discover new signs of the diseases of the lungs, heart and pleura.

It wasn't until the 1851 invention by Arthur Leared, and the refinement in 1852 by George Cammann, of the binaural stethoscope—a simple but incredibly significant instrument—that the practice of refined auscultation began to develop and doctors could listen in stereo to the sounds of the body. Before that it was a crude monaural amplifying horn, Laennec's ear trumpet, which offered little more than a distant thump against the rib cage. Without binaural stethoscope technology, auscultation was more like listening for trees falling in a distant forest or miners tapping faintly in a deep pit. But doctors still pressed ears to chest cavities and listened for the pings, trying to read the heart's noises and tremors. L. A. Conner (1866–1950), the founder of the American Heart Association, is said to have carried a silk handkerchief to place on the wall of the chest for ear auscultation.

For one hundred years cardiologists relied on Cammann's binaural scope to detect the slightest abnormality, arrhythmia, skip, hop, hammer, block, or stutter. Nineteen fifty-two and 1964 saw further refinements of the traditional binaural stethoscope, with many cardiologists believing that the now all-but-obsolete Rapport-Sprague was the finest auscultation device ever made or used, allowing them unprecedented clarity and consistency.

Current research is focused on developing a reliable electronic amplified stethoscope, which is not actually a listening device but a noise translator that generates a reproduction of the heartbeat, bullying the human ear out of its place as the direct register of the heart.

I first heard the *whoosh-whoosh* of my daughter's heart as reproduction, as an electronic transmission through a fetal heart monitor strapped to my wife's belly—an electronic stethoscope. The sound is less a *thump* than a *slosh.* More valve and flap than muscled push. But it is still a treasured sound. For most of our prenatal visits, medical intervention extended only as far as placement of the fetal heart monitor. The first thing we did—doctor and parents— was listen. All together. We awaited the news of life. And anyone who's been in this place understands the simple comfort of that sound, the reassurance of that noise—or, more directly, the doctor's recognition that this is *normal* noise.

A baby's heartbeat is the first sensory experience a father has with his child, often the first moment that a father begins to think of the fetus as a child. A baby: body and brain and lungs and drumming heart. An identity: the first hint of possibility filtered through an electronic translator, reproduced from a tiny speaker. Nothing promises *person* like these first heart sounds. Nothing says *It begins* like the *wish-wish-wish* noise of the stubborn pump—and I say this with both knowledge and ignorance of the ethical implications for some.

Perhaps because of facts, stats, opinions, and ideas—or perhaps because I had no other way to feel my wife's pregnancy—fatherhood was mostly an abstraction. I never really began to *feel* like a baby's father until I heard the thumping inside, that telltale tapping. Or perhaps my son was not a son, my daughter not a daughter, at least in part, until their first heart noises registered in my ear —a formation of identity that wasn't even possible when my grandfather was born, in 1906, or my father, in 1945, and was still only a rough science when I was born, in 1971. But I know that in many ways I did not identify myself as a father until I heard my child's heart, and that I couldn't have heard this without the aid of a stethoscope. Most of us identify a doctor by the stethoscope, that intimate disk. But it also identifies parent and child. All three fledgling identities intertwine in that examination room, hopelessly dependent on the curl and twisting turns of simple listening technology, the only tool for the vital job of reading and feeling the rhythmic thumps of the heart, that *tap-tap-tap* signal of life we cannot see and I can in no other way sense.

Chamber 4

The year is 2002, and nine coal miners are trapped in the Quecreek Mine in Pennsylvania by rising water released after a drilling machine punches through a wall into an underground spring. The nine men—a father and son among the crew—retreat to the highest spot in the mine and rope themselves together. They listen for the signal from the surface—three small explosions—but don't hear anything. They start pounding on the roof bolts with their hammers, hoping to make some noise the surface can recognize. They pound and pound, but background noise on the surface interferes, and the seismic listening devices can't hear them. The men write notes to family members, seal them in a metal lunch box, and wait to die. As rescuers work frantically to pull water from the mine with massive diesel-powered pumps, they also drill down from the surface to pump oxygen into the cave where the rescuers hope the men have retreated. If the miners are alive, they can only be in one place, all of them protected by a small womb of air against the rising flood. The miners continue pounding on the roof bolts, but they get no response. The miners' families gather on the surface, huddled in a tent around the drill operator—because perhaps he is more than an operator and more than muscle: he's more like the human side of the machine, the listening side, the man with the touch, who watches the spin of metal, waiting. When the drill finally reaches the lightless room, 240 feet down, and punches like an amnio needle into the pocket, the drill operator shuts off the machine, quiets the crowd, and listens. I wonder what it was that he listened for. How faint? How rhythmic? He listens, his hands on the machine, until he finally hears or feels the rhythmic noise of the trapped men hammering at the steel—the sole musical evidence of survival. Above them, on the outside, the expectant wives and mothers rejoice. They hug the man at the drill and slap each other on the back and think of how they can't wait to see and touch and smell their babies again.

PAUL CRENSHAW

After the Ice

FROM *Southern Humanities Review*

WHEN I WAS SEVENTEEN an ice storm moved through my hometown in Arkansas and coated the roads and trees with a thin layer of ice. I remember the ice only because later that morning I would receive a phone call that my nephew Keith was in the hospital. There were few details, just that he was hurt in some way and it looked serious, and driving there, the day was so bright it hurt the muscles behind my eyes. Ice covered the fields where cows searched for grass, their breath fanning the air before them. On top of telephone poles hawks sat waiting, sharp eyes scanning the fields for movement. The few drivers on the road drove slowly, fearing the ice, though by that time it was melting, and small streams ran across the road, the water turned brown and dirty from the salt and cinders the county road crews had dumped the night before.

At the hospital, my family gathered in the hall outside the emergency room. Every few minutes the door opened and a nurse came out, and when the door opened we could see my nephew laid out on the operating table, tubes down his throat, his pajamas open and his small chest, thin and frail as a bird's, failing to rise and fall. He was eighteen months old. In a few hours he would be pronounced dead, and not long after that one of the nurses on duty would call the police to report that this was not an accident. There were bruises on his neck and shoulders, and before night fell again Keith's stepfather was under investigation for murder.

I have scans of the old newspaper articles saved on my computer now. My mother, at my request, found old microfilm reels at the library and e-mailed them to me. I read them sometimes, late at night, when my daughters are asleep, though when they first arrived in my in box, it took me months to open them.

The first one is dated February 8, and is titled "Boy's Death Investigated." According to the article, the unnamed boy died of "severe head injuries," and after his death his body was sent to the state medical examiner in Little Rock. The Logan County sheriff stated that police were waiting on an autopsy, but they suspected the boy's death was related to child abuse.

The next article is six months later. After three days of trial, and a jury deliberation of less than two hours, the stepfather was convicted of first-degree murder. In his testimony, he said that his stepson had wandered outside while he was on the phone. In the courtroom he was clean-shaven, his hair cut short, and he wore a long-sleeved blue shirt with a dark blue tie. His hands moved as he talked, and his eyes roamed about the courtroom, not landing on anyone. When he hung up the phone, the stepfather said, he saw the boy outside, by the woodpile. He lay on his back, not moving.

At the hospital, the nurses first noticed, and later the medical examiner confirmed, four small bruises on Keith's forehead. There were large pictures set up on exhibit stands in the courtroom, and the medical examiner pointed to each one with a pointer. He made a circling motion around the four bruises, spaced apart like knuckles. There were also deep bruises on Keith's neck. In the courtroom the picture sat next to another picture of my nephew in overalls, holding a stuffed tiger. He was smiling then, laughing at whatever silly toy the cameraman was holding up. In the picture he had only a few teeth, and his blond hair was combed so fine you could hardly see it, like the way a baby's hair will disappear in the bathtub. As he was shaken, his brain crashed around inside his skull. The blood vessels feeding his brain were torn. Blood pooled within his skull, creating pressure. His brain swelled. At some point he lost consciousness. He was not breathing when he arrived at the hospital. In the hours he lay on the emergency room table, he did not breathe on his own. In the parking lot my brother lit one cigarette from the butt of another. In the hallway outside the room, we all waited, impotent and raging. In the big corner mirrors the nurses came and went.

I reconstruct the physical injuries from newspaper reports and courtroom testimony to cement the crime in my head. Years later I sometimes feel forgiveness creeping in, so I list in my head the bruises and choke marks. I think about time, how long this must have gone on, and some strange feeling builds up in me, though it is not sadness, or anger. Perhaps it is despair. But in the years since, most of the sadness has fled, and what remains exists only on an intellectual level. I have no visceral reaction, and I am surprised to find no emotion, only a place where that emotion used to be. I'd like to say sadness has replaced it, but in the time that has passed what is left is a feeling deeper than sadness. But it is less painful. It is like trees in November, or birdsong before first light; something intangible, full of memory and heartache: a child's clean smell, a faint memory of your mother, a daughter's first steps.

If my nephew had lived he might have had physical and learning disabilities, seizures, behavioral disorders, cerebral palsy, and speech and hearing impairment. He might not have walked again, or spoken. He might not have ever learned his name, or his mother's birthday. He might not have remembered what happened to him, and for some reason I cannot explain, though I am ashamed to say it, this seems unbearable to me—that he might have smiled when his stepfather came into the room, or reached up his arms for his stepfather to pick him up, or laid his head on his stepfather's chest late at night on the couch, the TV the only light in the room, changing from light to dark.

The last article is the shortest of all. It recounts the sentencing hearing, in which the stepfather was sentenced to life in prison. When the sentence was given, his attorney put a hand on his shoulder. He was not wearing a tie this time. He was in jailhouse orange sweats, with black numbers stenciled on them, and his hands were handcuffed in front of him. It is an image I will remember for a very long time, held up against the one of my nephew with tubes down his throat, but the two of them do not cancel one another out, just as rereading the newspaper articles does not cancel out the story inside my head.

The funeral was in a church I had never been to before. The service exists now in a cloistral space—nothing before it or after it. It is an isolated incident, faint at the edges of memory. There was an easel set up with a picture of Keith on it, the same picture of overalls and a stuffed tiger that would sit in the courtroom when the trial started. The casket was closed. I suspect it would have been too hard any other way. I sat in a balcony of the church with my grandmother. I suspect it was a strategic positioning, that from the distance of the balcony her failing eyes could not make out the picture, the flowers, the casket.

Two police officers sat near the stepfather, their uniforms crisply ironed. He sat near the front of the church and stared straight ahead. From the balcony I studied his profile — red hair that reached to the nape of his neck, a mustache not trimmed well. His face was red, with a pale blotch that crept higher up his neck and side of his face, and his jaw worked as the service went on.

During the service my eyes wandered from the tiger to the step-father to the state troopers, then made the loop again and again. My grandmother moaned beside me, a noise she did not know she was making, just as she didn't know what had happened, or why, and I realized in a strange moment of clarity, one that announced my emergence into adulthood, that we would never understand, that for the rest of our lives when any of this was mentioned, we would shake our heads sadly and stare at the floor until the moment passed.

After the funeral, while my family gathered in the living room of my grandmother's house and some of the men stood on the front porch and talked of violence, I walked through the woods on my grandmother's land. It was stifling inside the house, and loud with the sounds that accompany death, but outside it was cold and still. The air hovered right at freezing, and the light mist that fell could not decide whether it wanted to be snow or rain. Late in the afternoon, the dark came early, and by the time I turned around to walk back only the porch light was visible. The rain had finally made a decision, and the only sound around me was ice on frozen leaves.

I have never been in the house where it happened. The house is turned sideways to the road. The front yard is thick with trees and shrubs, blocking a clear view, but what you can see is a small rock house huddled on a quiet street in what might be any town. The front yard needs mowing, and the gutters are filled with leaves.

The inside of the house I must imagine, though in the years

since the murder I have done the imagining enough times that the memories feel real. I start from the street, seeing the carport as it would have been that day—the stepfather's brown Chevy truck idling in the drive, smoke leaking from the exhaust. Just off the carport is the woodpile, and past the carport is a chainlink fence separating the house from the one next door, only a few feet away.

From the carport a door opens into the kitchen. The kitchen is narrow, with a green linoleum floor. Above the sink a window looks out on the backyard. Past the kitchen, moving farther into the house, is a small dining table, and past the dining table is the living room. A short hall opens off the living room, and two bedrooms are tucked into the back. The phone hangs on the wall beside the sliding glass door, in the transitional space between the kitchen/dining room and living room.

Because I have so few memories of my nephew, I sometimes create false ones. I replace Keith with images stolen from my own life, put him in the place of my youngest daughter rubbing spaghetti into her hair or riding her tricycle in the driveway. I picture his walker rattling across the hardwood floor of my grandmother's house as we sat at the table or watched TV, the same noise my oldest daughter made rattling across the linoleum of our kitchen. I see myself walking outside holding him sometime in the late fall, geese veering south overhead and the wind cold around us, Keith pointing at the geese much as my youngest daughter pointed years later, eyes wide with wonder. I see my sister holding him, rocking back and forth to coax him to sleep, the same as I did with my daughters night after night for years. And I see Keith falling and bumping his head on the coffee table once. It was a minor accident, the kind my daughters had many times, but when my sister picked him up, she cried longer than he did, though I had no idea why she was crying until many years later.

If I can do it, if I can remember my nephew smiling or laughing or holding out his arms to be picked up, I can forget the cold morning, the truck idling outside, and something happening that caused the stepfather to open and close his hands as he moved toward Keith. Instead I can imagine my nephew standing at the sliding glass door in diapers, watching the dogs play in the backyard, or huddling scared from fireworks on the Fourth; I can imagine him with his mother in a plastic wading pool she bought at Walmart, one with ducks on it, her son splashing her as she sits on the edge of the pool laughing; as a young boy running through the sprinkler in the backyard.

The last time I drove past, the house was empty. As far as I can remember it had always been rented, changing hands from one family to the next with the same regularity as the seasons. This was only a few years ago, and though I know the house hadn't been empty long and would not remain that way, in my mind it stands empty now. There is no dining table, no phone hanging from the wall. There is no sprinkler in the backyard, and no one to run through it.

My first daughter was born in the hospital where my nephew died. We lived in a small house at the time, on a small side street in a small town. When we brought my daughter home, my wife held her for days. At night we lay in bed together, the three of us, my daughter between us, her chest rising and falling rapidly, her lungs small and frail, and neither of us could sleep for fear of rolling over on her. Late at night I carried her to her crib, and my wife and I stood staring down at her. Later, when the house was quiet and everyone was asleep, I went out and stood in the backyard. It had snowed a few days earlier, and at some point I realized it was the anniversary of Keith's death, but I don't remember what I did there, or what I thought about, only that the stars were bright and the night was cold.

I have never told my wife this story. Lying in bed late at night I open my mouth to speak, then close it again. On the second floor above us, our daughters sleep. I wonder what they dream, if, when they get older, they will know the kind of fear that sometimes creeps into my heart.

When my first daughter was eighteen months old my wife came home from a routine doctor's visit crying. Our daughter's head was forming incorrectly, the doctors told her, the sutures misaligned. Her brain could be squeezed together, trapped between the bones of her skull. A few days later we took her for a CAT scan. My wife dug her fingernails into my arm as nurses slid our daughter, unconscious, into the machine. She was asleep for hours afterward. We sat in a little alcove, separated from the main room by a curtain. We could see the feet of nurses passing outside, and every few minutes one would stick her head through the curtain and check on us.

I don't remember the details of that little room, or what my daughter was wearing. I remember her waking, and smiling, and the nurse coming to tell us that the CAT scan showed nothing abnormal. Afterward, we drove home, though I have forgotten what time of year it was, or how bright the snow might have been or if the sun was shining or if it was night, and sometimes I wonder how, if there had been something wrong, it would feel twenty years later. Would I have to dredge up the memories or would they come to me at times unbidden, moving from one to the next: her riding her tricycle in the driveway; shying away from the neighbor's dogs that barked at her; running through the sprinkler in the backyard?

There was no picture of the stepfather in the paper, just as there was no picture of Keith. What I have, I have had to recreate from memory. I hold hard to my recreation of the little house because it is easier than understanding or forgiveness: the truck idling in the driveway, the stepfather's hands opening and closing, the ice on the roads as I drove to the hospital.

But sometimes a different memory creeps in, no matter what I do to keep it out. It is Thanksgiving, four months before Keith's death. We have gathered at my grandmother's house. We have eaten until we are sick with food and now we lie back and watch football on TV, or else walk slowly in the yard to work off the food we have eaten. It is damp, and cool. It has rained the night before.

I am standing in the kitchen, looking out onto the backyard through the sliding glass door. The stepfather is playing with Keith. The stepfather holds his hands up and growls like a monster. Keith laughs and tries to get away but he totters and falls. He is fourteen months old and has just learned to walk and the world beneath him is still shaky and suspicious. But when he falls the stepfather scoops him up and holds Keith above his head and Keith squeals with delight as the stepfather laughs. The boy's eyes are bright. When he laughs, I can see his front two teeth, just coming in.

I wish I were more forgiving. I wish the world made more sense sometimes. I wish some memories did not drive wedges through others, that a moment could be defined in sharper terms—black or white, love or hate, good or bad. I watch the game of chase, laughing with them, until the stepfather turns and sees me. He offers a little wave, and I wave back.

My father has not spoken his grandson's name in twenty years. But sometimes, in the years after it happened, before I moved away and went to college and then started a family of my own, I'd come home late at night and find him smoking in the dark of the living room. He never spoke to me on these nights, just nodded his head as I passed, the smell of his cigarette following me to my bedroom, where I would try to sleep. In bed, I'd think of him in there, smoke curling above him, headlights from the road occasionally sweeping the wall. I knew he was thinking of something. Some nights I'd climb out of bed and join him. We'd sit until very late, until morning was coming outside, both of us staring into whatever thoughts occupied us, whatever dreams we could not handle while asleep. We'd both be very quiet, listening to the silence gathering around us.

My family does not mention Keith's name. I wonder who visits his grave. I do not even know where it is. There was no graveside service, not until weeks later, when the state medical examiner had outlined the history of violence on his body. I could find out, could make the long drive back to Arkansas and stand some November with the wind in the trees and the clouds racing above me and look down at his name. But I wonder if I would only be doing it for me —if whatever comfort provided by the act would be for me alone —and it saddens me to suspect this about myself.

Six months after we moved to North Carolina I rose past midnight and dressed. It had been snowing all day, and earlier my wife and I had taken our daughters out to make snow angels and snowmen and chase each other with snowballs. Late that night it was still snowing, the roads blanked out, everything bright in the reflected light. I walked to the university where I took graduate classes. My youngest daughter was about the age Keith had been when he died. My oldest daughter was years older than he had ever been. On a small hill overlooking the soccer field, I knelt and watched the snow fall. There were no cars on the roads, no sounds passing in the night. The lights in the dorms and buildings were out, and it was easy to think I was alone in all the world. In the classes I teach, I have heard myself saying that winter often represents death, the world shriveling and dying, until spring comes and life bursts forth once again. When I get home I will lean over each of my daughters, my youngest still in her crib, and when my wife wakes and finds me there, I will not be able to explain any of it to her.

The stepfather was sent to prison in December. I do not how it was arranged, if he was forced to turn himself in, if family members stood and watched him go, watched the handcuffs put on, watched him loaded into the back of the waiting car. He might have been forced to surrender himself the night before and to spend his last night in jail, but I know none of this. My imagining of how this occurred comes from prison movies, where white vans wired with steel mesh roll through gates topped with concertina wire, and the veteran prisoners whistle at the newcomers, who look around wild-eyed and frightened, while a burly guard with a shaved head slaps a nightstick into his palm.

Nor can I imagine the inside of the prison without a movie or TV show creeping in: a stacked tier where burning paper rains down on the normally stoic guards, or a yard where every space belongs to one gang or another, and even standing in the wrong place can lead to a violent attack, and though I was raised by forgiving people there are times when I feel he deserves a violent place, that there should be no forgiveness.

But at other times I can begin to find sympathy for him, if not exactly forgiveness. I see him sitting on the edge of the bed, elbows propped on his knees, staring at the wall. Or shuffling through the prison yard alone on a cold day in early February, or waking up in the middle of the night to a muffled sob, what might be a strange sound in a world of violent men, and wondering if he had made it.

I was the first to hold my oldest daughter, before the doctor, before my wife. We were on the fifth or sixth floor of the hospital, and I could see the city stretched out below, dingy in winter but ringed with blue hills all around. Her eyes were not open and she was crying as only a newborn can, but I held her near the window as if to show her the world she had come into.

The first year of her life is chronicled in pictures, and in each one I am holding her, or my wife is, or my mother or father or brother, each of us with a hand cupped gently under her head. She grows larger in each one, until she is standing, holding on to the edge of a chair or the coffee table, then walking unsteadily from parent to parent. There are pictures of her fine blond curls, of her riding a tricycle in the driveway, of her standing by a Japanese maple I planted in our front yard.

While she is growing, my mother comes to our house every day to see her. My father makes strange faces at her and babbles like an idiot, something I have never seen him do. When I make fun of him for it, he tells me to shut up, then hugs me with enough strength to compress my ribs and kisses me on the forehead, as if I am two years old. When we move to North Carolina, my parents fly in three or four times a year. By this time my wife and I have a second daughter, and our oldest starts kindergarten. We stand outside one hot August morning and watch her get on the bus. As the bus pulls away, my wife cries for several minutes, holding our youngest and kissing her repeatedly.

When they are gone sometimes, when the morning is quiet, when my parents have not flown in unexpectedly, when I am turning some old memory over and over, trying to make sense of it, I dig through an old shoebox of photos. I go through the pictures one by one, seeing the linear and vertical progression of my daughters' lives, or myself, looking slightly older in each one, yet somehow less wise as the years go past.

In the pictures in my mind I see a house, a carport, a man coming home from work. His stepson is crying. The man is tired. He wants a drink and to sit in front of the TV, but the child is crying. The rattle doesn't work. The cartoons the child watches don't work either. The teething ring, the blue one with fishes on it, also does not work, so he reaches for the child, and what were cries before become something else entirely. Outside, the crunch of ice under tires.

Once before my nephew's death his stepfather brought him into the grocery store where I worked, near closing time one night. Keith was crying, throwing his head back and screaming, and the stepfather had little idea what to do.

I was a teenage boy then, and many years later, I would grow up to be a writer who spent a lot of time trying to make sense of the past. The stepfather looked frustrated or angry or even lost, so I held out my arms and Keith came to me and stopped crying. There were few people in the store, so I wandered around talking to him while his stepfather bought cigarettes. He smelled fresh and clean and I thought we had something in common, though at the time I couldn't put a name to it, couldn't see that what we had in common was the life that lay ahead of us, both of them just beginning. In a few years I would be a young father holding a daughter for the first time, worried and scared for all the things in the world that could happen to her, but of course I knew none of that then. Winter had just set in and the dark came early and no one knew Keith had only a few months to live, and when I handed him back to his stepfather he started crying again, though it would have been impossible, I am sure, to have known the reason why.

TOI DERRICOTTE

Beds

FROM *Creative Nonfiction*

Trauma is not what happens to us, but what we hold inside us in the absence of an empathetic witness.

— *Peter Levine,* The Unspoken Voice

I.

THE FIRST WAS A BASSINET. I don't remember what it was made of; I think it was one of those big white wicker baskets with wheels. When I couldn't sleep at night, my father would drag it into the kitchen. It was winter. He'd light the gas oven. I remember the room's stuffiness, the acrid bite of cold and fumes.

My father didn't like crying. He said I was doing it to get attention. He didn't like my mother teaching me that I could cry and get attention. Nothing was wrong with me, and even if I was hungry, it wasn't time to eat. Sometimes I screamed for hours, and my father—I do remember this—would push his chair up to the lip of the bassinet and smoke, as if he were keeping me company.

After a few nights, he had broken me. I stopped crying. But when he put the bottle to my lips, I didn't want it. I was too exhausted to drink.

II.

My second was a crib in the corner of my parents' room. We moved to the attic when I was eighteen months old, so it must have been before that. I still didn't sleep at night. I'd see a huge gray monster outside the window, swaying toward me and side to side. I was afraid that any moment it would swoop in and get me. But I couldn't wake my parents. What if it wasn't real but only the huge blue spruce outside the window? If I woke them for nothing my father would be angry. I was more afraid of my father than I was of the monster. If I just kept watching, it couldn't get me.

III.

My aunt brought home a present for me every day when she came from work. I'd wait by the kitchen door as soon as I could walk. Sometimes she'd fish down in her pocketbook, and the only thing she could find was a Tums, which she called candy. But mostly she'd bring colored paper and pencils from the printing press where she worked.

When I was two or three, I began to draw things and to write my name. I wrote it backward for a long time: *I-O-T.* I drew houses, cars, money, and animals. I actually believed everything I drew was real; the house was a real house, as real as the one we lived in. I held it in my hand. It belonged to me, like a chair or an apple. From then on, I did not understand my mother's sadness or my father's rage. If we could have whatever we wanted just by drawing it, there was nothing to miss or to long for. I tried to show them what I meant, but they shrugged it off, not seeing or believing.

(This sideways escape—the battle between my father's worst thought of me and this proof, this stream of something, questioned and found lacking, which must remain nearly invisible—pressed into what leaks out as involuntarily as urine, a message which must be passed over the coals, raked, purified into a thin strand of unambiguous essence of the deep core.)

IV.

When I was seven, we moved to the Forest Lodge. We lived in D12 on the fourth floor. My mother and father slept in the living room on a bed that came down out of the wall. I slept on a rollaway cot kept in the same closet and pulled out at night. I helped my mother roll it into a corner of the kitchen, push the kitchen table back, and open the cot, its sheets and blankets still tight. (Whatever I had, I kept nice. I had to. My bed was my bed, but it was in my mother's space. If she needed the space, my bed would go.)

Someone had given me an easel-shaped blackboard with a sheet of clear plastic that you could pull down and paint on. In the morning, my mother would set it up in a small area between the dining room and the kitchen. She didn't mind if the colors spilled, if a few drops fell on the newsprint she had put down. After she scrubbed every Saturday, she liked to put newspaper over the linoleum to keep it clean of our footprints. Wednesday, halfway through the week, she'd take the torn, dirty papers up, and underneath, the floor was like new.

V.

Most times I liked my food. I didn't mind eating until my daddy started making me clean my plate and either struck me off my chair if I didn't or lifted me up by my hair and held me midair if I was slow. He wanted me to eat faster; he didn't have all day.

He'd hold me off the floor until I pleaded. I'd sputter in fear and humiliation—I don't remember pain—but I had to button up before he put me down to do exactly what he had told me to do, fast.

Slowness was a sign of insubordination. If I missed a pea or a crumb, I was trying to outwit him. I must have thought he was stupid. And if I pleaded that I hadn't seen the pea, he'd know I was lying. "Your story is so touching till it sounds like a lie."

I swallowed it down; I wiped that look off my face. But still he would notice my bottom lip beginning to quiver. This was a personal insult, as if I had taken a knife and put it to his face. If my brow wrinkled in a question— "Do you love me, Daddy? How could you hurt me like this?"—this implied I was pursuing my own version of the truth, as if I were his victim.

It was a war of wills, as he so clearly saw, and these were my attempts to subvert him, to make my will reign, to plant my flag.

He was the ruler of my body. I had to learn that. He had to be deep in me, deeper than instinct, like the commander of a submarine during times of war.

VI.

Thinking was the thing about me that most offended or hurt him, the thing he most wanted to kill. Just in case my mind might be heading in that direction, here was a stop sign, a warning: "Who do you think you are?" But the words weren't enough. They'd bubble out of him like some brew exploding from an escape hatch, a vortex that pulled in his whole body, his huge hands, which grabbed me up by my hair.

Where could I go? I was trapped in what my father thought I was thinking. I couldn't think. My thinking disappeared in casc I had the wrong thought.

It was not the world that I needed to take in, but my father's voice. I had to see exactly what my father saw in me—and stay out of its way.

VII.

In the morning, I'd fold up my bed and put it away. On those days and nights when my father didn't come home, we didn't need the space in the kitchen for breakfast or dinner, so we didn't put my bed away. I'd make it without a wrinkle, the pillow placed carefully on top, and it would stay in the little space under the window.

Maybe the black phone had rung saying he'd be late. Or maybe she had put him out.

I didn't know how they slept in the same bed because they never touched. Once, I saw them kiss. Maybe it was her birthday or Mother's Day. They blushed when they saw I saw them.

VIII.

> Those caught in such a vicious abuse-reactive cycle will not only continue to expose the animals they love to suffering merely to prove that they themselves can no longer be hurt, but they are also given to testing the boundaries of their own desensitization through various acts of self-mutilation. In short, such children can only achieve a sense of safety and empowerment by inflicting pain and suffering on themselves and others.
> —Charles Siebert, *"The Animal-Cruelty Syndrome,"* New York Times Magazine, *June 11, 2010*

I am trying to get as close as possible to the place in me where the change occurred: I had to take that voice in, become my father, the judge referred to before any dangerous self-assertion, any thought or feeling. I happened in reverse: My body took in the pummeling actions, which went down into my core. I ask myself first, before any love or joy or passion, anything that might grow from me: "Who do you think you are?" I suppress the possibilities.

IX.

My mother used the small inheritance she received from her mother to put my father through embalming school. He moved to Chicago for the few months of training at Worsham, the college for black undertakers. She hoped to raise us up—her mother had been a cook—to become an undertaker's wife, one of the highest positions of black society. But when he came back from the school, my father wouldn't take the mean five dollars a week his stepfather offered him to apprentice. He wouldn't swallow his pride. He also wouldn't take jobs offered by his stepfather's competitors. That too was a matter of pride, not to sell out the family name.

My father never did practice undertaking for a living. Though sometimes, when I was young, friends would ask him to embalm someone they loved and my father would acquiesce. He would enter the embalming room at Webster's Funeral Home, put on the robe, take up the tools, and his stepfather would step back. His reputation grew in this way. People who saw the bodies he had worked on—especially the body of the beautiful and wealthy Elsie Roxborough, who died by her own hand and was buried in a head-to-foot glass casket like Sleeping Beauty—marveled at his art and agreed he had the best touch of anyone.

People praised him for conducting the most elegant service; for knowing exactly what to say to comfort the bereaved, for holding their arms and escorting them to the first funeral car, for convincing those who needed to cry that it was all right, yet knowing too how to quiet them so there were no embarrassing "shows."

My father knew the workings of the heart; that's why so many people—my grandmother; his stepfather; and even his best friend Rad, whose heart he had crushed—loved him even after he let them down completely and many times, even after he abandoned them or did the meanest things. My father was with each of them, holding their hands, when they died. My handsome, charming father, the ultimate lover, the ultimate knower of the heart.

X.

My father knew all about the body. He had learned in embalming school. For a while after his mother died, he stopped smoking and drinking and came home at night. He'd get out the huge leather-bound dictionary (*Webster's*—the same as our last name!) that my grandmother had given him when he graduated. He would open it to a picture of the bones in the middle of the book, which had three see-through overlays: on the first, the blue muscles; on the second, the red blood vessels; and finally, on the third, the white nerves.

He loved the body, loved knowing how things worked. He taught me the longest name of a muscle, the sternocleidomastoid, a cradle or hammock that was strung between the sternum and mastoid. He'd amaze me with long, multisyllabic words; then he'd test me on the spelling.

My father always explained. He always showed me the little smear on the plate that I had set to drain before he'd make me do all the dishes over again. He'd explain how he had studied hard so he knew where to hit me and not leave a single mark. He'd brag about it. He wanted me to appreciate the quality of his work. Like any good teacher, he wanted to pass it down.

XI.

During the summer when my mother and aunt were cleaning and wanted me out of the house, I would go out to the side of the house with a fly swatter and command the flies not to land on my wall. There were hundreds of flies, and though I told them not to, they continued to land. I don't think I said it out loud. I think I said it —screamed it, really—in my mind. Sometimes I believed that the things in the world heard your thoughts, the way God heard your prayers. When I was very young, not even out of my crib, I'd ask the shades to blow a certain way to prove they had heard me.

The flies were disobeying me. Whenever one landed, I would go after it with the fly swatter. I was furious that they would do what I had commanded them not to. I knew they understood, or would understand finally. I killed tens, hundreds—didn't they see?—but they wouldn't stop.

I knew I was murderous, and yet, was it murder to kill flies? My aunt and mother never stopped me.

XII.

Before my grandmother died, when I was ten, she had three dogs. Each had a short life. Patsy was the "good" dog, who died of a chicken bone in her stomach, and Smokey was the "bad" dog who growled at people and would jump over the second-story banister on the porch and walk around on the outside of the rail. When my grandmother and grandfather were downstairs in the undertaking parlor, they would leave me alone with Smokey. I was about seven, and I had learned the voice the nuns used to say cruel things to the children who were slow. Sometimes the nuns hit those children over the knuckles with a ruler, but mostly they just humiliated them, made them sit in the back and never called on them to do errands. I tried to teach Smokey to stay behind the gate to the pantry. I would open the gate and tell him to stay, and when he went out in the kitchen, I'd hit him with his leash. I believe I hit him hard, maybe as hard as my father hit me. I wanted to feel that power.

I did this two, three, or four times, and though it seems impossible that my grandparents didn't know, no one stopped me. One time I came over, and my grandmother said Smokey had escaped, jumped over the second-story banister to the street, and didn't die but ran away. He was never seen again. Was he that desperate to get away? I felt sad and responsible. I felt glad.

XIII.

I was nine when we moved to a bigger apartment on the first floor. Now my father had only one flight to carry me up by my hair. He didn't mind going public — the stairs were right in the lobby — but he refused to allow me to scream in terror when he grabbed me. Not because he was afraid people would see. My screaming made him furious because I knew he was only going to carry me up the stairs and scream at me, only beat me on the thighs and calves (where it wouldn't show), and only until I made every look of pain, confusion, and fury disappear from my face. He knew I knew that. So what was all that broadcasting, as if something really bad was going to happen, as if he was going to kill me?

XIV.

Life is something you have to get used to: what is normal in a house, the bottom line, what is taken for granted. I always had good food. Our house was clean. My mother was tired and sad most of the time. My mother spent most of her day cleaning.

We had a kitchen with a little dining space, a living room, a bedroom, a bathroom, and two halls, one that led to the bathroom and the bedroom and one that led to the front door. There was a linen closet in the hall between the bedroom and the bathroom. My books and toys all went into a drawer that I had to straighten every Saturday. There was a closet in the bedroom for my mother's clothes, a closet in the front hall for my father's, and a closet off the living room that held my mother's bed.

It was a huge metal apparatus that somehow swept out on a hinge. I can't imagine how my mother and I, as small as we were, brought it out and put it back every night and every morning, for my father was hardly ever there. We just grabbed on, exerted a little force, and pulled it straight toward us. It seemed to glide by itself, swinging outward around the corner; then it would stand up, rocking, balancing, until we pulled it down.

XV.

My father and I shared the small bedroom, and my mother slept on the pullout in the living room so that she wouldn't wake us when she got dressed in the morning to go to her new job. We slept in twin beds she had bought us, pushed up close together.

I had special things given to me, special things she paid for: the expensive toys I got for Christmas that took a whole year to pay for and the clothes I wore from Himelhoch's while my mother wore an old plaid coat for eleven years. Now I was a big girl moving from a little cot in the kitchen to my own bed in a bedroom. My father and I always got the best.

XVI.

My mother shopped after work every Thursday, so my father would come home and fix dinner for me. He'd stop at Fadell's Market and get a big steak with a bone in it. He'd bring it home and unwrap the brown paper, slowly, savoring one corner at a time, like someone doing a striptease or opening a trove of stolen diamonds. He'd brag about how much money he had spent. He'd broil it right up next to the flame, spattering grease, fire, and smoke, only a couple of minutes on each side, cooked still bloody, nearly raw, the way we liked it, he said—different from my mother. He'd say he liked it just knocked over the head with a hammer and dragged over a hot skillet. His eyebrows would go wild, and he'd rub his hands together like a fly.

XVII.

Once my father took me to the movies. We walked downtown to the Fox Theater on one unusually warm Thursday evening during my Christmas vacation to see Bing Crosby in *The Bells of St. Mary's.* My father frequently promised things he didn't deliver, like the time he promised to come home and pray the family rosary every night for a week when I carried the huge statue of the Virgin home in a box as big as a violin case. He never came home once. When I turned the Virgin back in at school, I had to lie to the nun. After that, I rarely asked for anything. But going to the movies was his idea.

I was never happier than when I was with my father and he was in a good mood. He liked to tease me and make me laugh. He was so handsome that I felt proud when people noticed us. I thought they were thinking that my father really enjoyed me, that I was a very special girl. I acted like a special girl, happy and pretty, until I almost believed it. I had dressed up, and we stopped for a Coney Island and caramel corn, which were his favorites.

XVIII.

By this time, my father didn't come home most nights. Sometimes he and my mother wouldn't speak to each other for months. Sometimes they wouldn't even speak to me when we were in the house together, as if we had to be quiet, like in a church, and respect their hatred for each other.

My father thought I hated him like my mother did or else he didn't think I was worth talking to, for he'd often go months without speaking even when we were in the house alone.

I tried to make him change. I'd make up special names like "D-dats." "Hi, D-dats," I'd meet him at the door when he came home at night. I knew he liked to feel young and hip. I'd make my voice happy. I actually was happy when I was with him—I had to be! He could see inside me. He could tell my moods. My unhappiness blamed him.

Maybe all that silence and beating was because he thought nobody loved him, not my mother and not his mother. He told me how his mother had knocked him down when he was a grown man. He told me how my mother always picked up his ashtrays to wash them as soon as he put his cigarette out. I tried to make him feel loved. Sometimes we played "Step on a crack you break your mother's back" when we were coming home from his mother's house, the two of us in cahoots.

XIX.

Once, when I was ten or eleven, he came home for lunch, and I asked him if I could dance for him. I had seen Rita Hayworth dance the Dance of the Seven Veils. I had stayed home sick and practiced. I liked to dance on the bed so I could see myself in my mother's dressing table mirror.

I wore old see-through curtains and my mother's jewelry on my head like a crown. I must have had something underneath for I knew some things mustn't show. I thought maybe if he saw I was almost a woman and could do what beautiful women do, he might find a reason to love me.

At the end, I spun around and around until most of the drapes, towels, and my mother's nightgown fell to the floor. I don't remember what remained to cover me.

XX.

Sometimes, on the nights he came home, I'd sneak up on him while he was reading the newspaper and pull off his slipper.

He'd put the paper down very deliberately, put on his "mean" play-face, and say, "Oh, you want to play, huh?" And he'd grab me up like an ogre. He'd hold me down and jab his fingers into my ribs.

"No," I'd scream, "I'm sorry," and I'd plead that I would pee if he didn't let me up.

Finally he'd relent. "You're not going to do it again?" And he'd tickle me more.

"Never, never," I'd scream.

"Are you sure?"

As soon as he picked up the paper again and seemed to turn his attention away, I'd go back.

My father could make me laugh. He knew just where to hit the funny bone. Always, my father was the only one who could make me swallow pills or sit still while he administered burning iodine. When I fell or took the wrong step over a picket fence, I'd come to him, crying. "I'm going to have a big scar and nobody will love me." And he'd tease, "Oh, my poor little baby, all the boys are going to call her 'old scar leg,' and she's going to be alone for the rest of her life"; but he'd do what had to be done, hold the leg in place, put the iodine on the raw spot, right where it was needed, direct and quick, without flinching, never afraid to cause the necessary pain.

XXI.

On Saturday mornings, my mother and I would have toast and coffee in her bed. She let me lie there while she planned our day. She'd get up barefoot and put the coffee on and make me sugar toast. I loved those Saturday mornings near her: her big bed, her cold cream smell.

I had always thought my mother was frightened of my father. She never seemed to fight straight. She got him by going the back route, like the look on her face when she got in the orange and yellow truck that he bought when he started the egg business. She sat on the orange crate—he called it the passenger seat—and never laughed, never joined in on the fun as he took us around Belle Isle. He had been so happy when he jingled the keys, but you could tell she thought that old truck was nothing to be proud of, as if even a joke about such a poor thing was in bad taste.

Then one Saturday morning, I spotted a big roach, a water bug, on the living room floor. I jumped up on the bed and started screaming; she came from the kitchen, grabbed her house shoe, and got down on all fours. The thing charged her from under the chair like a warrior. I was screaming like crazy. I realized she was my last protection. And she started punching at the thing, punching the floor, anywhere she could punch. She didn't stop until it was flattened.

I had never seen my mother brave. I had never seen that she would fight to the death. It was a part of her she never showed. I had thought she didn't stop my father from beating me because she was afraid. I was confused by her braveness.

XXII.

My mother was sad. She didn't feel appreciated. I didn't do enough to help. She hurt inside. Her body suffered. Her feet swelled black with poison. She had a dead baby. She had womb problems. They had to take the knotted thing out. The doctor rubbed her stomach for hours until she went to the bathroom. She got TB. She got a goiter. She shouldn't clean so hard; she should rest, at least late in the afternoon. But she wouldn't. She had to keep doing what hurt her.

My mother and father were at war; whoever loved the other first would lose.

XXIII.

Nobody thought the little marks were worth looking at. I cried and showed how they went up my arm all the way to my elbow, ran all over my ankles and the tops of my feet, even up my thighs. I could see them, but when anyone else looked, the marks disappeared.

Maybe they didn't itch. Maybe they weren't serious. Maybe I was causing trouble. (I had an active imagination, my mother and father said.) I couldn't sleep because something was happening in my bed—a misery—and everybody acted as if it wasn't. It didn't hurt after a while. I could take my mind off it and put it somewhere else.

I think the only reason my mother finally believed me was because I kept showing her that Monday mornings, after I had spent the weekend with my aunt, I didn't have the marks, but Tuesdays, after I had slept in my own bed, I had the marks again.

In an instant of recognition, she raced into the bedroom, flipped my covers off the bed, and saw the little bits of blood. She turned over the mattress, and there, in the corners, were the nests of a thousand bedbugs, lethargic or crawling. She looked close. They had gotten so far inside that the room had to be sealed with tape, a bomb put in.

He had been sleeping with another woman. He had brought her dirt into his own home (though he said the bugs came in egg crates).

Bedbugs were what poor women had, women who couldn't do better, women who didn't matter. Some other woman's bedbugs were making my mother the same as that woman.

He had brought in everything she hated, everything she couldn't control: the helplessness of slavery, bad births, poverty, illness, and death. Everything she had risked her life to clean out of our apartment.

My mother had reason for outrage.

I only had reason to itch.

XXIV.

The living room was off-limits. There was too much that might get messed up or broken. I guess he chose rooms to beat me in honor of the sacrifices my mother had made to make our home beautiful.

In the bedroom, where could I go when I fell? I wouldn't fall on the wooden footboards. There was an aisle between my mother's closet and my father's bed. That was too narrow. On the left side of the doorway was my mother's dressing table, where I'd sit and put on necklaces, earrings, and nail polish and look in the mirror. There wasn't room for me to flail around, so my father had to be very specific about the direction in which his blows would aim me.

If my cousin was visiting, he would inform her, his voice sincere but matter-of-fact—"I'm going to have to take Toi to the bathroom." He preferred the bathroom when she was visiting, except when my mother was in on it, and then we needed a bigger space. If, for example, my mother had told him I talked back, he'd say, "We're going to have to speak to Toi in the kitchen." He'd pull me by my arm and close the kitchen door, which had glass panes so that my cousin could see.

But she said she averted her eyes, knowing it would humiliate me. She remembers him sliding off his belt; she remembers me pleading each time the belt hit; she remembers him telling me, as he was beating me, in rhythm, why he was doing it and what I shouldn't do the next time. I would come out, trying not to show how I had been afraid for my life, how I had pleaded without pride. I thought these things would have made her hate me.

I remember the hitting, but not the feeling of the hits; I remember falling and trying to cover my legs with my hands.

I remember the time I came home with a migraine and begged him not to beat me. "Please, please, Daddy, it hurts so bad." I could hardly speak. I had to walk level, my head a huge cup of water that might spill on the floor.

Why couldn't he see my pain? My head seemed to be splitting open, my eyes bleeding. I didn't know what might happen if I tipped my head even slightly. He saw me walking like that, as if someone had placed delicate glass statues on my arms and shoulders. I begged him, "Not now." I knew I had it coming. I had gone out with the Childs, and he had left a note telling me not to go out.

The Childs lived on the fourth floor. Sometimes they brought down the best rice with butter and just the right amount of salt and pepper. They had no children. They had a little bubble-shaped car. We all seemed glad to roll the windows down and go out to their niece's house. She turned her bike over to me. It was so much fun pumping it up and down the hill, letting my hair fly. I forgot my father, as I had forgotten the bug bites, as I forgot what it felt like to be beaten. I just thought, *I'm pumping harder so I will go faster and let the air hit my face and arms, and then I'll stop pumping at the top and fall down and down, my feet up off the pedals.* And I didn't feel fat: my body lost weight—it just went with everything going in that direction, and the wind flew against me in the other direction. Though it blew in my face and began to sting, I couldn't stop pumping, couldn't stop trying, one more time, to bring myself to that moment of pleasure and accomplishment right before I'd let go.

I had never felt such power, earning it by my own work and skill.

I could ride it. I was the girl in charge; I had the power to bring myself there.

XXV.

Shortly after I was married, we had a dog that kept shitting on the floor. Once I took a coat hanger and was going to hit her with it, but she drew back her lips and snarled at me in self-defense and fury. I had no idea that she would defend herself. I was shocked. I thought she was going to attack me, and I put the hanger down. I respected her in a different way after that.

She lived for sixteen years and was a great mothering presence in our household. Every dog and cat that came in the house had to lie beside her, with some part of its body—a paw, the hind—touching hers. Once I heard a strange noise during the night and went to investigate. A kitten my son had found on the railroad tracks was nursing from her, and she was sleeping, as if she expected to be a mother. When I would come home, after I had been away for a while, she'd jump up on the bed and curl her butt into my belly, and I'd put my arms around her and hold her like a lover. When she died, I missed her so much I realized that she had been my mother too. She taught me it was beautiful to defend yourself—and that you could be unafraid of touch.

I remember how, occasionally, my father's dogs would pull back and snarl at him when he was viciously beating them. His anger would increase immeasurably. They had truly given him a reason to kill them. "You think you can get away with that in my house?" he'd ask, the same as he'd ask me.

Once, to get away from him, one of his dogs leapt through the glass storm door in the kitchen and ran down Fourteenth Street bleeding to death.

XXVI.

You would think that the one treated so cruelly would "kill" the abuser, throw him out of the brain forever. What a horrific irony that the abuser is the one most taken in, most remembered; the imprint of those who were loving and kind is secondary, like a passing cloud. Sometimes I thought that's why my father beat me. Because he was afraid he would be forgotten. And he achieved what he wanted.

In the deepest place of judgment, not critical thinking, not on that high plain, but judgment of first waking, judgment of the sort that decides what inner face to turn toward the morning—in that first choosing moment of what to say to myself, the place from which first language blossoms—I choose, must choose, my father's words.

The twisted snarl of his unbelief turned everything good into something undeserved, so that nothing convinces enough—no man or woman or child, no play or work or art. There is no inner loyalty, no way of belonging. I cannot trust what I feel and connect to; I cannot love or hold anything in my hand, any fragile thing—a living blue egg, my own baby—in the same way that I never convinced my father I was his. And I must rest on it, as on bedrock.

XXVII.

The time I had the migraine, after my father had beaten me, he made me bathe. He drew the bath, felt the water with his fingers, and made sure it wouldn't burn. He told me to go in there and take off my clothes.

The water, when I put my toe in, was like walking in fire. I stood there, holding myself.

And then—instead of letting my father kill me or bashing my own head against the tile to end all knowing—I crouched down, letting the lukewarm water touch me.

Oh, water, how can you hurt me this bad? What did I do to you? I was whimpering. I don't know if I still had hope he would hear me, or if I just couldn't stop the sound from leaking out of my body.

But my father came and lifted me out of the water in his arms, took me naked, laid me on my bed, and covered me lightly with a sheet. Then he went away and left me in the dark as if to cool down, and he brought cut lemon slices for my eyes and a cool towel or pads of alcohol to put on my forehead. He bathed me in tenderness, as if he really knew I was suffering and he wanted me to feel better.

I wondered if he finally believed. If he realized from within himself that I had been telling the truth, that I wasn't evil. Maybe he had some idea of how much he had hurt me. I knew that sometimes men beat their women and then make up. I didn't know which daddy was real.

Afterword:

I hear in myself a slight opposition, a wounded presence saying, "I am me, I know who I am." But I am left with only a narrow hole, a thin tube of rubber that the words must squeak through. Where words might have gushed out as from a struck well, now, instead, I watch it—watch every thought. It wasn't my father's thought that I took in; it was his language. It is the language in me that must change.

MEENAKSHI GIGI DURHAM

Grieving

FROM *Harvard Review*

THERE ARE PEOPLE who love their jobs. I am not one of them, and so I am both awed and envious when I meet people who tell me about their passion for their work. My friend Heather, who performs daedal and dicey heart transplants on children, is one of them; my colleague's wife, Maria, who brews hausfrau-friendly concoctions in a test kitchen, is another; and the librarian at my kids' school, shuffling through stacks of Magic Schoolbus and Maisie books, seems to be that way too. I have learned, over the years, that it is not the work itself that inspires passion, but something much more elusive, some kind of cosmic alignment between a personality and an occupation. Those who find it emanate a potent, mystical energy; to me, they seem enlightened and serene, while I hover in a state of constant self-doubt and questing, like a lovelorn adolescent, wondering what I should do with my life and how to find lasting fulfillment.

My husband, Dallas, on the other hand, has been in an ardent relationship with his job from the moment he set foot in graduate school, and in truth, this has always been a source of tension between us. That is why it came as such a blow when he lost it. When he showed me the letter that said he had been denied tenure at the university where we both teach, and where I had been tenured six years earlier, we were both silent. I could see how white his lips were, how his hands were shaking; it was as though he had been hit by a car, or a blunt object. The cosmos had come undone.

They—the experts, the gurus—talk about job loss in terms of trauma, separation, death. On the Internet, I learned that there are stages of grief after a job loss, just like after any other bereavement: denial, anger, frustration, acceptance. "Losing your job can trigger a range of emotions—some of which may be uncomfortable or upsetting," pontificated one website. Looking at the deep bruises under Dallas's eyes and hearing the pain in his voice in the days after he got the letter, I found those feeble words—*uncomfortable, upsetting*—to be vapid, even delusory. In the aftermath of that letter, we lay awake at night, silent and rigid in our bed, thinking the fevered thoughts that brew up at 4 A.M. At first, of course, came questions of money and the well-being of our two young daughters; but as the days passed, those issues seemed trivial. We could always get other jobs, or move to a smaller house and live on my salary, or something. The real crisis was the blunt negation of Dallas's identity, an identity that had been slowly, delicately building since he had been a star doctoral student in a star graduate program—building in pulsating fragments, like a coral reef. This identity had evolved into a complex organism, an intricate structure composed of symbiotic elements—the natural and gifted teacher who garnered glowing evaluations, the brilliant scholar, the articulate and tactful faculty member whom everyone knew would be a dean or provost one day. The academic.

"If Professor D— were single and I were a woman, I would marry him," wrote a student on one of Dallas's evaluation forms. "I love his lectures, I love his ideas," wrote another. "I even love his exams." Dallas has told me often that he is happiest in the undergraduate classroom, that he relaxes when he is sharing ideas with students, even though they most often comment on his vitality and enthusiasm. I cannot relate to this: teaching is a challenge for me, an anxiety-producing event, even after more than a decade of doing it. I still quiver with nerves before classes, collapse limply with relief afterward. Dallas has never quite understood my teaching jitters, nor my need to prep for hours before each class. He can walk into a room without notes or preparation and earn a standing ovation. I have heard that strangers attend his lectures, people who are not enrolled in his classes or even at the university, just to experience his teaching. I am prepared to be skeptical about this rumor, but it has been repeated to me by several students, so I suppose it is true. I have never heard this about any other teacher, ever.

He enrolled in a PhD program deliberately; I, by accident. (How does one "accidentally" do a doctorate? There's another story there.) More to the point, Dallas knew what he was doing. I have had graduate students who came to doctoral programs to hide from "the real world," or to recover after a divorce, or because they had borderline personality disorders that rendered them unsuitable for everyday life. But Dallas applied to graduate school because he wanted to be a college professor and a scholar. He researched the best programs in our field and applied to them; on the day I turned in my completed dissertation, feeling depleted and numb, he was admitted to an elite doctoral program—several cuts above the one I had stumbled into. I was ready to flee academe, to return to the penurious but provocative world of journalism I had reluctantly abandoned for higher learning. He was ready to leap joyously into it, looking ahead to the hooding ceremony and a job at a research university and beyond—to the PhD's holy grail. Tenure.

The U.S. Department of Education reports that only 45 percent of faculty members nationwide have tenure. Of these, more than two-thirds are men. The numbers at our university are comparable. There is concern, nationally and here, about the low numbers of women and minorities who are tenured, and about the retention of women and minority faculty.

Dallas is a white male. Statistically, he should have succeeded.

In fact, race and gender aside, he should have succeeded. Every indicator, until the letter arrived, had been positive. We learned, as we set about (as academics will) analyzing and dissecting the denial, that the carefully laid-out steps on the path to tenure meant precisely nothing. There are markers on the tenure track that are treated with the reverence of religious rituals and given the symbolic weight of law. In fact, they have neither, as we came to find out. These markers include annual reviews, especially the third-year review that anticipates the contract renewal; the report of the departmental faculty when the tenure dossier is ready for submission (which was laudatory and contained a unanimous vote in favor of Dallas's tenure and promotion); and the letters from external reviewers (which in Dallas's case were from schools as reputable as Stanford and Cornell, and all of which were positive). These portents had lulled us into a false sense of security.

"It means I failed," Dallas said as we reviewed the facts, like forensic detectives on *CSI*. "It means I can't do this. I'm not good enough to do this." That was what mattered: not the job per se, but the opportunity to keep doing the work he loved. An end to the cosmic alignment that had put him in such perfect harmony with the universe. He had done everything right, it seemed, but . . . But. Robert Burns wrote about that, about the best-laid plans "gang aft agley," leaving "nought but grief and pain."

When you appeal a tenure denial, it is called a grievance, and the process is formally known as grieving.

The proper period of time in which to grieve a death was, in Victorian England, as much as four years; anything less indicated a lack of respect for the decedent. In India, at least for women, grieving has no time limit: a widow is traditionally in mourning for the rest of her life. I was not sure how long Dallas would grieve his loss, the loss of Associate Professor D—. "All my classmates are deans now," he said once. "What happened?"

There were times when he wondered aloud what he had done to tempt fate, whether he was marked in some way with the number of the beast, or whether this was a matter of bad karma. "I wake up wanting it to be a dream," he told me on many bleak mornings. "And then I realize it is happening, and I keep wanting to scream and come out of it and I can't."

In chilling contrast to the piles of effusive plaudits that preceded it, the denial was contained in two terse lines: "Insufficient record of publication. Lack of participation in the graduate program." We were stunned by these formulae. They were not even sentences, they were sentence fragments. And there was a deadly poetry in them, the fragments that rendered us fragmented; ashes to ashes; *quia pulvis es et in pulverem reverteris*. For dust you are and to dust you will return, as the liturgy has it. We read and reread the fragments, as though they were runes whose meaning we could unlock with sufficient slavish study.

"What do they mean?" Dallas would ask, bewildered, running his hands through his hair, readjusting his spectacles. I did not know. He had published in the requisite prestigious peer-reviewed journals; he had signed off on—we counted—fourteen dissertations. Those facts seemed to negate the reasons for the denial.

So there had to be some deeper, more mystical significance to the fragments. We meditated on them, hoping they would reveal their inner meaning. Were there seven Demotic signs contained in them? Were they based on a system of code that we needed to crack? Perhaps it would come to us in a blinding flash. Legend has it that Champollion fainted dead away after translating the Rosetta Stone in 1824. I could see that; could imagine the rush of blood to the head, the buckling of the knees, the dizzying relief that comprehension would bring.

The denial became the constant topic of our conversation; we could not speak of anything else. We worried at it in the car, on the phone with our families and friends, in our workplace, at the hairdresser's, at the local farmers' market, and with our yard man, Roberto. But we had decided, virtuously, not to say anything to our young daughters, who were nine and six. No need to scare them. As good parents, we had an obligation to keep them secure, not to destabilize their happy little worlds with job issues they didn't need to know about. The weeks went by, and we were on the phone with lawyers and the AAUP and our financial adviser, and I realized eventually that the girls had been hearing every word, and that Dallas and I were both stupid and derelict to avoid talking to them about it. So in the kitchen one evening I asked my older daughter if she knew what was going on. She looked directly at me.

"Daddy didn't get tenure," she said, and burst into tears. She clung to me, sobbing, for a long time. "It doesn't mean anything yet," I murmured into her soft, sweet-smelling hair. "It doesn't mean we have to move, or leave, or anything, yet. Don't be scared."

In his often-assigned and overanalyzed essay "Experience," Emerson reflects on grief as an illusion, a passion of the moment, in its way as meaningless as every other sentiment or perception, all the while acknowledging its power to rack us with pain. "I grieve," he writes, "that grief can teach me nothing."

*

"The Investigating Officer is empowered to request and to receive the cooperation of . . . the grieving faculty member . . ." Section III 29.6d of the university's faculty dispute procedures.

The grievance procedure involves memos, lots of memos. The memos, crafted by Dallas and vetted by both our lawyer and me, generated responses from institutional authorities that seemed completely irrational, even insane, to us. Everything had to be done in writing. "Can't I *talk* to anyone?" Dallas asked, plaintively. "Why won't anyone meet with me and hear me out?" We pointed out, hotly, to each other that even common criminals get to face their accusers and defend themselves in person. *Not that Dallas had done anything wrong.* That Dallas himself was only known to his superiors (his inquisitors, we told each other) through a growing pile of byzantine paperwork and procedural documents seemed bizarre, and it represented a new kind of effacement, another loss of self. "I take this evanescence and lubricity of all objects, which lets them slip through our fingers then when we clutch hardest, to be the most unhandsome part of our condition," notes Emerson. And, "I distrust the facts and the inferences."

My husband, who is constitutionally thin and pale, grew thinner and paler. He slept badly, as did I, even though I knew there was no point in worrying. This was not a cancer diagnosis, I reminded him, in my jolliest tones. It's not like anything terrible has happened to the kids or anything. It's just a job. You can apply for other jobs in the fall, or you could do something else. Maybe you could go to law school. Maybe you could work in PR.

These were not the right things to say. For me, these ideas represented options, opportunities, a chance for a new direction. For Dallas, they were like sucker punches. I could see his body recoil slightly with each word, and when I looked at him, I understood a little more about grieving.

I am a stranger to grief. I have lost no one close to me: neither parents nor friends nor children. I empathize with such losses, of course; I can imagine how it might feel to suffer such an event. I had not imagined, before it happened, the profound and searing sorrow that would attend Dallas's job loss. I was frightened by the depth of his anguish and by its incessant presence; it ravaged him like a consumptive disease.

He went to see a counselor through the university's faculty assistance program. He said her face changed when he told her he was grieving. A grieving faculty member, one who was initiating a formal inquiry process against the university, could not be counseled in her office. "Let me wear my human resources hat now," she told him brightly, making a switching-hats gesture with her hands. "There are legal issues here I can't get into. You need to realize that the university makes good decisions, and that there are systems of checks and balances in place that mean what happened to you was properly done. You need to figure out how to get on with your life."

"It's the politburo," he said to me later, head in hands. "She thinks I need deprogramming." Grief counseling, we learned, is not grievance counseling.

Many people interceded on Dallas's behalf. And finally Dallas found a way to face them, the inquisitors of his heretical depravity, the ones who had ordered his excommunication. They granted him an audience, after repeated appeals from champions who had appealed to them from across the university, from Europe, from Asia, from all parts of the continental United States. They were bombarded with letters and e-mails. Did these missives cause them to cave? I don't know. But anyway, they granted him face time. He was given a half-hour appointment with the provost.

He went in to the august administrator's office without hope, but filled with righteous anger. He said (and I know this only from his reports, which grew more thrilling with each telling), *I hope you are happy. I hope you believe you did the right thing. I want you to know I was willing to give this institution my very best. I ask you to reconsider; please review my file.* He held his head up; he looked them in the eyes. *You can burn me at the stake. You can torment me on the rack. But I am of noble heart.* He did not say that last part, but it should be part of this adventure. In your mind's eye, Dallas should wear a hair shirt and a halo. His green eyes blaze with light. Angel song swells around him.

In fact, we won. On a Thursday afternoon in May, as tornado sirens wailed and we huddled in our dining room watching silvery cords of rain strike the windows of our prairie house, the phone rang. The provost had reversed the tenure denial.

Pandemonium. We are jumping around and yelling with joy, all four of us; we are louder than the storm; the kids look dazed and delirious. Our six-year-old gets out her markers and writes "I ♥ tenure! I ♥ Daddy!" in uneven, sprawling, rainbow-colored letters. We put her sign up on our front door. The next day, we buy balloons and champagne and get Thai take-out, the kids' favorite.

Letters and phone calls come in from all over the world in the next few weeks. At the farmers' market, people walk up and hug Dallas. Our mail carrier congratulates him, and so does Roberto. This is a small town, and word gets around.

Dallas writes to thank the provost, and I am moved by his reply. "Glad to help, Dallas. It was the right thing to do. So very sorry you had to go through hell in the meantime."

We do not know, with any clarity, how it happened, how the core of Dallas's being was excised, then restored, almost daemonically. It all smacks of witchcraft, or thaumaturgy, or something. Once, long ago, I worked with a woman who was diagnosed with inoperable brain cancer. She had six months to live, people said. I did not know her well, but I watched her at work: young, vivacious, doomed. In her eyes lurked a new knowledge, a searing awareness that was almost tangible in its intensity. And then, suddenly, the tumor disappeared without a trace. Her death sentence had been erroneous.

Perhaps she thinks about that diagnosis still; perhaps she is haunted by memories of the days and nights when she thought she was dying. I can imagine that the light looked different during that time, that her senses were sharpened and quickened by the knowledge of death. I can imagine how every moment might cause panic; I can feel the bitterness of her sorrow. The careless indifference to life you enjoy when you are not haunted by death's specter —you can probably never feel that again once you have contemplated death.

Or perhaps you can just leave it behind, gleefully, once the threat is gone: *not dead yet*. It seems to me that the latter response would be preferable—easier, lighter. I wouldn't know, though. I have not had to confront these issues.

But Dallas has. His grieving has abated, yet grieving has deepened his passion for the work that was his lifeblood. Glimpsing how profoundly this episode affected him has humbled and silenced me. How can I reject, or mock, or decry, the very source of his psyche, his *atman*? There must be something there that makes this work that we do, this process of teaching and connecting and writing and coming-to-consciousness, more than just work. I have to come to grips with that: to see beyond the mundane to the numinous.

I had not known, before, that a job could rend and then restore a person's soul. "Grief too," writes Emerson, "will make us idealists."

BERNADETTE ESPOSITO

A-LOC

FROM *The North American Review*

I AWOKE IN A FIELD, on my back. My left eye was sealed shut. Out of the corner of my right eye I spotted a girl. She sat with her legs crossed. Her torn clothes hung off her shoulders. At the elbow she cradled her arm and shook her head. Down my right cheek I felt something wet. When I caught myself trying to wipe it away, I readjusted my head. The girl looked over at me and held up her arm. From wrist to elbow it shone black and slick, with a single suppurated crease folding in on itself. "My skin will never be the same," she lamented.

Tactically scattered at the end of the runway were suitcases, a car seat, and a teddy bear. Some of the suitcases were closed, but had sticking out from their zippers and pockets a sock or a shirtsleeve. To an outsider this gave the impression of a hastily done packing job. One of the suitcases hit the ground near the girl. When it did something popped and sirens came alive. I couldn't see the flames, but when the girl looked up, her irises blazed and I heard a *whoosh*. In the distance the air traffic control tower loomed over a bright green field and some taxiing regional jets. A warm southwesterly breeze blew the smoke our direction. With the back of my hand I covered my mouth.

"Couldn't have picked a better day for—" started a fireman. His sentence was blotted out by the screams of a nearby woman. "I've got burns over eighty percent of my body and I've been waiting fifteen minutes for an ambulance!"

"Ma'am—" began the fireman.

"I guess I'm just not burned enough," shouted the woman.

Someone laughed and someone else said, "Relax. The man seated next to me had a heart attack and it took them forty-five minutes to get to him."

"He should have been dead," murmured the girl.

Something exploded.

The girl began to rock herself.

Seconds later a woman was seen running. "My baby! My baby!" she yelled. "Help me find my baby!"

The morning breeze blew loose hair across my cheek and settled it into one of the cuts. A woman wearing a blue uniform walked over and knelt down beside me. "What's your name?" she asked, taking two fingers to my wrist.

"Bernadette," I told her.

"How old are you?"

"Thirty-three."

"You've got significant trauma to the bridge of your nose, Bernadette. I'm concerned that if these bones are fractured they may cause the brain to connect with the outside environment. Where does it hurt?"

"I can't see out of my eyes," I told her.

"What's the last thing you remember?"

"Flamingos. Six of them, in the marsh along the runway."

"Flamingos?" She slid a green tag onto my wrist.

"Yes. Pink ones."

She wrote something down, stood up, and gestured toward the fire. "We've got a confused head injury, right over here."

As we ascended over the Mediterranean on a routine flight to Paris, the engine over which I was seated *exploded*. It was a systematic and orderly blow. It did not build as in a Berlioz cantata or culminate from a collection of small, meaningless gestures—a whistle, a hiss, a persistent rattle—in a cacophony of tearing metal, snapping cables, and shattering glass. It was a noise so full and palpable, so concise and final, that whatever followed I hoped would follow swiftly.

The source of the explosion was not immediately discernible to all passengers—it seemed to come from the back of the airplane, yet it had an all-encompassing quality leaving those seated forward or aft craning their necks like hungry birds. Not far from where I rested my head against the window of an over-wing seat, a smoke-choked engine burned. The flames, refracting through the window, illuminated my reflection. We were in a sharp right bank and I looked down, astonished to see the deep green of the Mediterranean against the fire and smoke.

My first reaction was not one of tragic realization—I did not bury my face in my hands or scream or yell or weep. In other circumstances I might have found comic the heady response with which the universe had answered my persistent and recurring dreams, but this felt like a cruel cosmic joke, like Hamlet laughing along with the gravediggers. *Holy Mother Fuck!* I said aloud. *You've got to be kidding me.* The lights went out. The plane shuddered and yawed. The woman across the aisle began to cry.

A disquieting silence I interpreted as a French response to crisis followed. No announcements were made, no instructions given. I slid the shade down over the window and stared ahead. The tray table in front of me, the seatback cover, and the armrests all took on the dreadful significance objects acquire in bad dreams. I began to pray aloud. *Hail Mary, full of grace, the Lord is with thee.* It was not so much a prayer as an uninflected mantra modulated by my strained breathing. *Blessed art thou among women.*

"Are you all right?" the man seated next to me asked in a French accent. He patted my clenched hand. "We've just *lost* an engine," he assured.

But *lost* was too passive, too quiet a word. People lost dogs or lost family to cancer, when in actuality cars ran over dogs and cancer metastasized. What I felt and what I witnessed prior to this *loss* of engine power was an *explosion:* an earsplitting bang, accompanied by a forceful jerk of the airplane and the sudden and lurid and unrelenting spewing of fire and sparks and smoke.

"I am a pilot," the Frenchman said. "The airplane can fly on one engine. But not for very long."

My memories of crashing planes date as far back as I can remember. As a five-year-old I saw on the news a photograph of an American Airlines DC-10 taken by an amateur photographer seconds after it took off and seconds before it rolled over. The plane hung perpendicular to the ground, a thin white stream of leaked hydraulic fuel trailing from the place where the engine had severed. The news described the photographer as "stunned" and "shaking." The photographer described the plane as "slow-moving" and "horrify-ing." At seven, I watched coverage of an Air Florida DC-9 after it crashed into the 14th Street Bridge during a blizzard. Passengers, bobbing around the Potomac River, clung to chunks of ice as a he-licopter tried and failed to toss them life preservers. At fifteen, live coverage of the United DC-10 crash in Sioux City, Iowa, aired on TV. Midflight, on its way to Chicago from Denver, the plane experi-enced catastrophic hydraulic failure rendering it unable to steady itself, make left turns, or slow down. The wingtip hit first, leaving a three-foot gouge in the runway. It cartwheeled. Broke into four pieces. Survivors who, from their hospital beds, saw the crash on the news asked, "What crash was that?" and "Were there any survi-vors?"

When my sister called to tell me she heard something on the ra-dio "about that crash in Iowa you always talk about," I took down the information. They were interviewing Jerry Schemmel, "the voice of the Denver Nuggets," who went back into the burning plane to save a baby whose cries he heard from the cornfield. I or-dered a used copy of his book *Chosen to Live*. Aside from the title's unsettling suggestion that those who perished had been so chosen, I stopped reading after Schemmel prosaically describes the feeling of the crash as "exactly how you'd expect it to feel if you'd dropped thousands of feet out of the sky and hit the ground."

Schemmel's account of the moments between the failure of the number-two engine on the tail of the plane and the crash landing in an Iowa cornfield is vivid as far as it goes. What's more interest-ing is the exchange he has with a crying woman and her seven-year-old son seated in front of him in row 22. Compelled to soothe the two after he overhears the child ask his mother if they are go-ing to die, he lies and tells them that he is a pilot, and assures them that they are not going to die: planes are made to fly normally when an engine fails.

My fear of flying was not so much informed by memories of crash-ing planes as it was characterized by a priori knowledge of a crash. Loosely translated, I feared receiving a sign, a peremptory warn-ing that an airplane might at any moment send me a crazy vibe before hurling itself from the sky. The fear was accompanied by a lesser, secondary fear, that upon receipt of the sign, I might take the wrong course of action. Earlier in my life, I had become so

anxious after booking a flight to Chicago that I swallowed a roommate's prescription sleeping pills on the way to the airport. The
pills induced a paranoid delusion involving New Age prophet Edgar Cayce and an elevator. Edgar Cayce could read auras, a gift
I discovered we had in common when I began working at a psy-
chic fair in my late teens. For five dollars customers could stand in
front of a white backdrop while I outlined in Crayola marker the
colors emanating from their crown chakras. A green aura meant
healing; a yellow, intelligence; pink, love. There were vibrant auras, indicating health and vitality, and lackluster auras, indicating
the soul's withdrawal from the body. One day while shopping for
sweaters Edgar Cayce stepped into a department store elevator. It
was brightly lit and full of shoppers, yet it felt "dark," a feeling he
ascribed to catastrophe and impending doom. When he could not
see the auras of the other occupants, he quickly stepped out. The
doors closed, the cables snapped, the elevator fell to the basement,
killing everyone aboard.

If I could not see the auras of the other passengers, I would get
off the airplane. But the effects of the sleeping pills had grown
more intense, heightening my paranoia. The closer I got to the
gate, the more I feared misreading luggage for auras and vice versa.
As I walked down the jetway, I decided that unless either of my recently deceased grandparents appeared on the flight, I would stay
on the airplane. From then on, I avoided certain flight numbers,
flying on certain dates, during inauspicious astrological aspects
such as squares and oppositions, as well as on the days leading up
to the peaks of these aspects, which, as it turned out, were also terrible for bill-paying and dental treatments.

The Rockwell Collins hangar looks like the set of a zombie movie.
Inside, children dressed in torn T-shirts and old pajama bottoms,
their faces and arms smeared with shades of red, gray, and purple
paint, chase one another. "We're dead! We're dead!" yells a boy
covered in gray paint. He points behind me. "See that plastic bag?"
I turn to where I think he is pointing and shake my head. "Right
there. Can't you see it? It's filled with DEAD people!" He laughs
maniacally.

I ask his friend, who is less cheerful and also painted gray, if he
too is dead. He nods solemnly, lifting his arm to reveal the tag on
his wrist: DOA. "My grandma gets to ride in an ambulance to the

hospital and watch TV all day and I have to lay there," he says. "*So* unfair."

The grandma walks up, covered in fake blood. A blue poker chip juts from her forehead. "*What* happened to you?" she asks me.

I hold up my wrist: *lacerations.*

Since my teenage years my sleep has been disrupted by crashing planes. So vivid and specific are the dreams in terms of make and model of the airplane that for a while I believed them an augury of a crash to come. "Those are anxiety dreams," my mom pointed out when I told her about a disturbingly vivid crash in which a Russian airliner carried some uniformed schoolchildren. "You're worried about teaching," she said. Over the years I have followed the trajectory of the dreams in a journal and notice that they fall into three categories. In the first kind of dream, I watch from a verdant field as the distressed plane struggles to stay aloft; in the second, I stand in line with other passengers preparing to jump from the falling airplane and devising my strategy for hitting the ground; and in the third, I sit patiently in my seat waiting for the plane to crash, telling myself it will all end soon enough. There are nuances, of course. Often, as I stand in the field, watching the distressed airplane, the engines or the wings fall off. Often the plane takes off too steeply, makes it about fifty feet into the air, stalls, and falls back to earth. Sometimes, when I am on the airplane, I take off my shoes before jumping.

In my waking life, I understand the impossibility (not to mention the ensuing complications were it possible) of opening a bulkhead door and leaping from a cruising 747. But the dreams do not obey the laws of physics. One feature remains immutable in all of them, and yet it contains the single most frightful aspect of a crashing plane: the unmitigated spinning with which it drops from the sky. Never do they fall the way Alaska Airlines fell from 31,500 feet to 23,000 feet in eighty seconds and then fell again in an inverted nosedive at 18,000 feet for eighty-one seconds off the coast of Ventura, where a passenger seat and tray table had washed up on the beach and I learned to surf.

The idea of a one-and-three-quarter-inch-thick piece of fiberglass separating me from cold water beneath which thrived a vast and unforgiving ecosystem did not inveigle me. Still, something about the surfers bobbing on the sea, sleek and elegant, shiny and black, had me wondering what sort of Elysian secret propelled them into all that deep water again and again. My board was seven feet one inch long, a cumbersome thing, with the maker's name, Total Commitment, written across it. I liked taking my Total Commitment out late in the morning or early in the afternoon when the sun was bright and the white water came in full and frothy. Waves are best in the early morning and evening, but at midday the white water was beautiful: it gathered around my knees like big tufts of tulle from a ballerina's skirt. Once I got my board beyond the break it took a great deal of effort—my duck dives were not efficient. I could not push the nose of my board far enough beneath the wave without it dislodging me several yards closer to shore. I stretched out belly down, exhausted, hung my hand over the top, and let the water lap over it in neat little swirls.

More often I found myself floating around at dusk, staring at the line on the horizon where the water meets the sky. I was content to float and had even begun to enjoy the firmament reflected in the water around me. The saltwater had the same effect as that of cold, clear air passing across a glacier on Mount Rainier and the hot, sagey smell of the Mojave Desert and the rustling of corn on a Midwest highway. But floating was not typical surfing behavior. It caused other surfers to paddle over, suggesting I slide my body a little further up or reach my arms like this or kick my feet *while* reaching my arms like this. These are helpful suggestions when you are trying to paddle beyond the surf. But if you are trying to get back to shore, as I was when I finished floating, you must negotiate the crashing waves around you. And so, quite unintentionally, I caught my first wave. A tug and a pull nudged me from behind and in one smooth motion I was dropped into and carried down the face. It happened so fast that by the time I thought to pop up onto my feet, the g-force was too strong. I sped along, my stomach soldered to the board, the shore out of the corner of my eye approaching at an angle.

Anyone who has caught a wave knows that once you catch your first and ride it to shore, you will—as long as you are near water and there are waves—seek another and another after that. But knowing which waves to paddle for and which to let pass is not instinctual; my timing was off. I was too far in front of the wave: the

nose of my board pitched forward and up. When the wave began
to break, the nose pitched down. As frequently as this happened, I
was never prepared for the plunge followed by the violence with
which the wave would thrash me and toss me and press me into the
ocean floor. But I knew the drill: take in as much air as you can
hold, grab the back of your neck with your hands, brace.

The hangar opens to a road designated for emergency vehicle
transport only. Members of the county medical community, the
Transportation Safety Association, search and rescue, firefighters,
and police officers eat doughnuts with reporters whose cameras sit
on tripods and chat with members of local news stations who are
testing mikes. The children linger on the precipice, making faces
at the cameras and daring one another to step outside of the hangar. The morning is beautiful and dew-filled, with clear skies and a
warm breeze. In the distance an air traffic control tower looms over
a bright green field and some taxiing regional jets. "Couldn't have
picked a better day for a crash," says a fireman. Soon all the partic-
ipants, nearly one hundred volunteers—all victims—have gathered at the opening—crossed arms, shifting—while those whose
various suppurations are punctured by poker chips and oozing
Vaseline and fake blood stand still and supine. The man next to me
acknowledges those around him by bending his torso and nodding
adroitly like the Tin Man. A fake plastic bone protrudes from his
forearm, a red poker chip from his leg. The morning May breeze
blows loose hair across my cheek and settles it into one of the cuts.
I smile and try not itch where the fake blood has sealed my eyelashes to the upper eyelid, forcing my eye open. We grow quiet.
Some of the dead are restless, asking to go home already. The airport transit buses arrive and cheers erupt. We are herded back to
the cafeteria tables in the center of the hangar for a debriefing. Attention is called. Sincere thanks are given. Special thanks are given.
Time taken from our busy schedules is given appreciation. And
then the tone of voice changes and instructions are given: It's *very*
important that you take your individual role seriously. You are actors and we expect, when the time comes, you act your designated
part. That means no laughing. If you start laughing the person
next you starts laughing and pretty soon everyone is laughing. If
you have a *real* emergency and you need attention, you need to say

I have a real emergency; otherwise the medical teams will assume you are playing your designated role. Finally, when the drill is over, please return any shrapnel you have on your person, including the poker chips, the Plexiglas, and the plastic intestines. Thank you.

I booked my flight from Paris to Los Angeles for the ten-year anniversary of the death of Jerry Garcia. I had notions of arriving in Southern California to various commemorations involving drum circles and calico dresses, and to ensure my August ninth arrival, I booked in haste a flight from the South of France to Paris for the evening of August eighth. The flight had been delayed. I sat in the airport eating black licorice and reading the letters of Abelard and Héloise. When I finally took seat 22F on an over-wing window, I was bored with the patriarchal prerogatives of twelfth-century France and wanted to go home. I closed the book and propped my head against the window. The long starboard wing of the Airbus spread out before me, the engine hummed, and the slats retracted. As we began to ascend I noticed the flamingos.

A decade earlier, in my daydreams, I played the protagonist in a small southern French village redolent of lavender. Between smoking cigarettes and writing doleful descriptions of old windows and doors in an outside café, I spent my days flirtatiously stirring the foam of a café crème while charming locals named Etienne or Solange chuckled at my broken French and asked in broken English my thoughts on American policymaking. When the sun dropped below the lavender fields, I carried my baguette and fruit in a bicycle basket along with fresh flowers and a bottle of Bordeaux. I imagined myself at night sipping wine and rereading what I had written, smugly telling myself that these descriptions suffused with significance would one day enlighten the curious reader.

My old journals are full of entreaties earnestly titled "THE LIST OF WHAT I WANT AND HOW I CAN GET IT," offset by roman numerals that included such headings as Graduate College, Run Boston Marathon, Write in the South of France, under which were suggestions for doing so: Pell Grant, fix foot, cross-train, yoga, money, time, other people. My friend MuRasha told me that you cannot desire that which is not possible to manifest somewhere in the universe. MuRasha channeled Pleiadians, beings of Love and Light, from the constellation Taurus. Pleiadians do not come in darkness, she said. They come in Light, where all things are revealed. MuRasha's tiny studio apartment in Olympia was lined with old milk jugs. Every couple of months she took the jugs to Mount Shasta, where she filled them with Saint Germain water. Ascended Master of the Seventh Ray, Saint Germain, who has come to earth embodied as a high priest of Atlantis, Plato, Saint Joseph, Hesiod, Christopher Columbus, and Francis Bacon, fed the poor, worked for peace, and wrote the plays of William Shakespeare. One day in 1930, he was met on Mount Shasta by another hiker. Together the two took astral trips through time and space, to other worlds and lost civilizations. One of these, an interplanetary, interdimensional portal whose citizens travel on electromagnetic subways and use amino-acid-based computer systems, is the mythological underground city of Telos. Telos lies beneath the town of Shasta. Its people are descendents of Lemurians, highly evolved beings, who were given permission to build their city after a tussle with the Atlantians over whether less evolved civilizations ought to be left to evolve at their own pace. The Pleiadians instructed MuRasha to collect and drink the water from Mount Shasta. She says she doesn't ask why, she just does what they tell her to do. When I visit MuRasha she puts beautiful translucent stones in a glass and pours the Saint Germain water over the stones. After I drink it, she instructs me to lie down with my eyes closed. She takes the stones out of the glass and places them on my heart chakra and solar plexus. Her voice pitches several octaves higher in a kind of operatic yodel she describes as a dolphin call.

"You *can* see them," she coaxes. "Pleiadians work through consciousness." In my mind's eye I feverishly erase the chalkboard, open my consciousness to the vibrational frequencies, the octaves of the fifth dimension, as she calls them. A few short minutes pass.

"Are they blue?" I ask.

"Yes! Yes! What shade?"

"Cobalt?"

"Yes! Yes! What are they doing?"

"Sitting in the window of my childhood bedroom?"

The first time I saw a silver cigar-shaped object float quietly and unobtrusively in the evening sky I began to scream. My sister turned around. When she saw what I saw she began to scream. My mom came running out of the house, her arms in the air, her eyes wild. We pointed up. She shielded her eyes and put her hand flat on her chest. "It's a blimp," she yelled. "The Goodyear Blimp." To my sister she said, "Don't ever scream like that unless you crack your head open," and to me she said, "Don't ever scream like that, unless your sister cracks her head open." She went back inside. Full of relief and disappointment, we flopped down in the front yard and watched the blimp make its silent way over the tree line until it disappeared behind the towers of Wheaton Center. I imagined lots of people huddled cozily inside the blimp, its curved surfaces cradling them like beanbag chairs. But I did not get to steep for very long in my blimp fantasy. "That's not the way a blimp works," my mom told me. People don't sit *in* the blimp. They sit in a tiny gondola beneath it, *in* seats *with* seat belts, just like driving in a car or flying in an airplane. This came as a disappointment. I wanted badly for there to exist a flying object whose occupants, inside of which, lolled around in Mickey Mouse sleeping bags watching *The Wizard of Oz* in color and eating sugary cereals. Blimps are really just big balloons, my mom said. They float because they are filled with an invisible, lighter-than-air substance called helium.

In my world things that float in the air float because they *are* balloons or because they *are* clouds or bubbles. I was four and I could not accept that a blimp was nothing more than a colossal silver balloon, whose contents I was now being told were lighter than air *and* invisible. I accepted other systems: inside my chest was a heart, inside my head a brain. Between the spaces of my four fingers an orange hue I knew to be blood glowed as I pressed them together in the light. But the blimp with its big open space of invisible substance meant there were objects unobstructed, unobscured in my line of sight whose contents I could and would not, under any circumstances, ever see.

Inside the falling airplanes of my dreams a sober scene belies the vertiginous horror passengers must have felt when, in full view of the Pittsburgh airport, US Air flight 427 rolled out of the sky. In my dreams no spidery fissures race up the walls, no overhead bins pop open, no chunks rip loose the plane's belly. The g-force does not drain the blood away from my brain or pull down my rib cage. The force of the acceleration does not cause bruising or a rash of broken blood vessel called *geezles*. While federal crash standards require that a passenger in a *typical* accident not experience g-loading for longer than thirty-six milliseconds, a *typical* person can function under heavy g-loads within the first five seconds. After five seconds a loss of peripheral vision and color perception called a *grayout* occurs, followed by the complete loss of eyesight called a *blackout*. Unfortunately, graying and blacking out does not ensure a loss of consciousness, which passengers of Pan Am flight 103, who were not injured from the explosion or the decompression or the disintegration of the aircraft, are believed to have regained at some point during their 35,000-foot fall. A mother was found holding her baby, seatmates were found hand-in-hand, passengers were found clutching crucifixes. During a grayout or a blackout, an altered state of awareness called A-LOC (Almost Loss of Consciousness), characterized by the disconnection between cognition and the ability to act on it, overcomes you—you will still hear and think and feel—before G-LOC (loss of consciousness) occurs. When it does, you will lose bladder and bowel control. You will experience sudden muscle contractions called myoclonic convulsions or *jumps,* similar to those we feel just as we are dropping off to sleep. During the jumps, you will have vivid and memorable dreams.

I was a reverent and devout Catholic child, named for a young missionary and messenger of the Immaculate Conception. When my mom was nineteen she watched *The Song of Bernadette*. In it a young peasant girl named Bernadette is taking off her shoes to cross a canal when she feels a gust of wind. A bright light catches her eye in the cliff face running along the canal. Something white in the shape of a lady motions for her to come closer. Bernadette is fearful. She begins to say the rosary. Over several visits the apparition, dressed in white and holding her own rosary, tells Bernadette to return for fifteen days. News spreads and crowds gather. Though they do not hear what she hears, they see Bernadette's lips move. And though they do not see what she sees, they watch her dig in the muddy ground below the grotto. As the water pools before her, she scoops it into her hand to drink. She is crazy, they whisper.

Later, Bernadette tells the priest, "She indicated that I drink from the spring and wash in it."

"Why did she ask you to do that?" wonders the priest.

"I am drawn there by an irresistible force," Bernadette tells him.
"When I see her I feel I am no longer in this world. When she disappears I am amazed to find myself still here."

I believed in the Holy Spirit, who proceeds from the Father and
the Son. I prayed to Saint Anthony for my lost crayon barettes, a
missing two-dollar bill, the mouthpiece from my alto sax. Each
time my faith in the procession of the saints was matched by my
faith in the power of prayer, both of which were reaffirmed when
the lost object was discovered under my pillow, in the desk of Andy
Besh, or inside the neck of my alto sax by a confused music store
employee. I was too young to ask for clarity or strength or fore-
sight, but old enough to feel the weight of my conscience. I confessed to thinking a classmate ugly or my sister stupid, and for those
I was asked to say three Hail Marys and a Glory Be. But the weight
was no more than a jab. I feared the real urge to clear my conscience came less from a penitent heart than from a belief in the
conditional: If I confess, then I can receive the Body of Christ. For
a child, the silent contemplation of Catholic mass — the forty-five
minutes of sitting, standing, and kneeling — is finally broken when
at last we file out of the pew and down the long line to receive the
Eucharist. The break is enhanced by the belief that something real
and holy happens as the host dissolves on the tongue. Despite
learning all the secrets of wafer-making from my altar-boy friends
and despite a detailed account from my neighbor, who said she was
given loaves of white bread and taught to press the slices into tiny
half-dollars after she and her friend were caught in the sacristy eating the wafers, I *felt* the Holy Spirit move through me. Many years
later I discovered that the perceived physiological effects — the
rush of energy, the pounding in my chest, the flush on my cheeks
— I had long ascribed to the profound sacrifices made for me by
Jesus were really just the effects of oxygen coursing through my
body after forty-five minutes of stillness and silence.

When, decades later, I arrived at a writing workshop in the South
of France and a self-proclaimed recovering alcoholic Buddhist
poet told me to *Go to the dark place,* I had well embraced the notion
that thoughts dictate reality. I believed in the laws of attraction.
And while I understood that they did not exactly promise fulfillment, I had only partially begun to accept that if you put attention
and thought into something you wanted, you got it. But if you put

attention and thought into something you didn't want, you got that too.

The moments that elapsed between the engine explosion and the subsequent emergency landing on one instead of two engines were, physically, some of the most uneventful of my life. As a young person I loved being flung and spun and tossed into the air. I rode roller coasters that twisted and dropped so fast they left strings of saliva across my face. I jumped out second-story windows and balconies, off rooftops and into piles of snow, out of trees and into raked leaves, and when I was sure I could not get any higher, I jumped from the apex of the longest swing in the playground, savoring that airborne second before landing with a thud and a roll. Once during a school assembly I volunteered to sit on the shoulders of a blindfolded man riding a unicycle. I trusted the laws of motion: action-at-a-distance and the tendency of objects to resist change, that all would end with the intact simplicity of a falling apple. Airplanes followed that course. I not only believed in them, I wanted to be a part of a cast that kept the belief alive.

I was six when I was given a flight manual. That year my first-grade class stood outside to watch the flicker that was the Space Shuttle *Columbia* launching out of Cape Canaveral. When I was ten I wrote to Sally Ride. By then I had cemented my career choice. By then I had also become suspicious after reading that Amelia Earhart had fallen victim to the Bermuda Triangle. Uncle Tom took me up in his Cessna, attached a pair of headphones around my ears, talked me through the preflight check, telling me where to push and pull: that pedal to turn the plane, this steering wheel to lift the nose up and down. The plane wants to fly itself. During climb out you want your flaps at zero degrees. This dial right here. You want the nose of the plane to touch the place where the horizon and the sky meet. Keep an eye on the wingtips. When we're in the air, your job is to keep the nose of the plane one fist below the horizon at all times. Calm your hands. Calm your hands. If you pull your steering wheel up too high and the nose of the plane lifts too far too fast, you'll stall. You feel it? This is what happens when you stall.

The plane shuddered and yawed and banked momentarily before steadying itself. The cabin lights came on, the woman across the aisle stopped crying, and I resumed my praying, silently. Anyone could *hear* that the engine was no longer powering the airplane, but the illusion of normalcy alarmed me.

In kindergarten, Eddie told me that in his backyard beneath the big blue slide lived the Devil. Uncle Tom told me that the Spanish moss which hung limp on the cypress trees during the day came alive when the sun set. A certain white house on the main thoroughfare gave me "the heavies." As I grew up, books filled with dead bodies floating in quarries were read in front of curtainless picture windows after dark. Scenes were snuck from *The Exorcist* and *Halloween:* foot-long needles sliding through eyeballs, flesh melting in loose, serrated chunks. When the Ted Bundy made-for-TV movie aired the year I turned twelve, my siblings and I taped it. *The Deliberate Stranger,* a two-part series, follows Ted Bundy from Washington to Utah to Colorado to Florida as he lures women into his tan VW. We loved *The Deliberate Stranger.* We argued over his victims as if we were arguing over the backyard shenanigans of friends and neighbors. "They did not find Carrie-Anne's skull at Lake Sammamish," insisted my nine-year-old sister. "That was Dawn's, you idiot." We clutched one another each time Ted flashed a fake badge or emerged from a wooded state park, when hair and dental records were collected and scrutinized by baffled pathologists.

Why are we still ascending? I asked the pilot. They have to disengage autopilot, he answered.

"They did a real number on you," says the grandma, aiming her camera.

I point to the poker chip in her forehead. "Looks painful," I joke. "Bad gambling accident?"

"Shrapnel," she says, pointing her camera at two teenage girls who walk past us calmly and importantly. They hold their heads as though they're balancing books so as not to disturb the oozing cuts across their necks.

"I am actually *dying* from this," says the taller girl. She points to her friend. "You're already *dead.*"

"I'm not *actually* dead," says her friend.

There's an evident hierarchy. The survivors, who consequently look in much worse shape than the deceased, are getting all the press, while the dead, played mostly by younger children who will not be required to do anything but lie in the grass, vie for attention —and fake blood.

The boy grabs his neck and rolls his eyes into his head. The girls keep walking. "Grandma?" he asks. "Don't you want more fake blood?"

"No, I don't want more fake blood."

The friend brightens. "You know you can eat it," he says, stretching his tongue across his cheek to where the blood has splattered.

"Don't eat it," says Grandma.

I am told the fake blood is a mixture of corn syrup, flour, and red food coloring and most of the children participating are scouts or members of school drama clubs and church groups.

"We do this *all* the time," says the boy.

"Every *few* years," says Grandma. "FAA requirement."

If the other dreams were about approaching a crash, the strangest dream, which did not fit into any of the other categories, was about reaching it. In it I watched the ground through a window on the floor of the airplane as it ricocheted violently from one side to the other. We knew we were in trouble, but were kept calm by a woman who talked us through the final moments. She spoke in the soothing way a yoga teacher might talk you through a difficult posture.

"The closer we get to impact," she said, "the slower time will move."

As she spoke my limbs grew heavy, my movements full of effort.

"We will see the crash happen before our eyes," she said, "but we will not feel anything or remember anything at the moment of impact.

"We are all going to die," she added, "Except for Steve."

I felt disappointed that I had not been "chosen" and annoyed by what seemed to be a presumption of the outcome. Yes, I could see the ground moving toward us through the window on the floor of the airplane, but who was she to tell me death was imminent? The farther we fell and the slower we approached the end, the less I believed her.

The scene changed. We were being ushered into a large conference room, with big picture windows along the walls. When we were told that we had died in the plane crash and this was the beginning of our afterlife, some people began to cry. "Where are we going?" "What are we doing?" "It's not true!" they yelled.

I looked around and noticed that we were all dressed in the same green shirt. We were ushered up to a long conference table on which were stacks of brochures and bowls full of tiny gold charm medals. The medals, intended to hang from gold chains, were the size of silver dollars. On them were inscriptions and illustrations appropriate for the occasion: a seagull flying over water, hands folded in prayer. We were told to choose one we felt represented who we were in life. The inscription on mine read, "I was a nice person."

The dead and dying have already been chosen, says the woman at the registration table. She looks apologetic and, in a cheerful voice, suggests I play a survivor. After I sign a release form stating my understanding of the terms and conditions (damage of personal effects and stains to clothing are not the responsibility of the county), I walk to a long cafeteria table on the other side of the hangar. "Dead, dying, or surviving?" asks a woman with a clipboard. I hand her my release form and she instructs me to take a seat.

"We're gonna make you look really gross." She grins, nodding to a man who is opening a jar of Vaseline. "Should we cut off her arm?"

He shakes his head. "Lacerations!"

"This is Don's first time," she says, winking at Don.

Don pushes my hair away from my face. "Don't worry," he says. "I'm trained."

In three minutes he maneuvers the Vaseline and the putty and the fake blood, starting at my forehead, along the bridge of my nose, under my left eye, and down my cheek. He holds up a mirror. I not only look more infected than newly lacerated, I look like I hit the ground face first. Cameras click. Video cameras roll. A man from the county shouts, "That's one hell of a facial!" Another says, "I'd be writing a letter."

"What happened to me?" I ask.

Don grins. "I think it'll be pretty obvious."

Topic of Cancer

FROM *Vanity Fair*

I HAVE MORE THAN ONCE in my time woken up feeling like death. But nothing prepared me for the early morning last June when I came to consciousness feeling as if I were actually shackled to my own corpse. The whole cave of my chest and thorax seemed to have been hollowed out and then refilled with slow-drying cement. I could faintly hear myself breathe but could not manage to inflate my lungs. My heart was beating either much too much or much too little. Any movement, however slight, required forethought and planning. It took strenuous effort for me to cross the room of my New York hotel and summon the emergency services. They arrived with great dispatch and behaved with immense courtesy and professionalism. I had the time to wonder why they needed so many boots and helmets and so much heavy backup equipment, but now that I view the scene in retrospect I see it as a very gentle and firm deportation, taking me from the country of the well across the stark frontier that marks off the land of malady. Within a few hours, having had to do quite a lot of emergency work on my heart and my lungs, the physicians at this sad border post had shown me a few other postcards from the interior and told me that my immediate next stop would have to be with an oncologist. Some kind of shadow was throwing itself across the negatives.

The previous evening, I had been launching my latest book at a successful event in New Haven. The night of the terrible morning, I was supposed to go on *The Daily Show* with Jon Stewart and then appear at a sold-out event at the 92nd Street Y, on the Upper East Side, in conversation with Salman Rushdie. My very short-lived campaign of denial took this form: I would not cancel these appearances or let down my friends or miss the chance of selling a stack of books. I managed to pull off both gigs without anyone noticing anything amiss, though I did vomit two times, with an extraordinary combination of accuracy, neatness, violence, and profusion, just before each show. This is what citizens of the sick country do while they are still hopelessly clinging to their old domicile.

The new land is quite welcoming in its way. Everybody smiles encouragingly and there appears to be absolutely no racism. A generally egalitarian spirit prevails, and those who run the place have obviously got where they are on merit and hard work. As against that, the humor is a touch feeble and repetitive, there seems to be almost no talk of sex, and the cuisine is the worst of any destination I have ever visited. The country has a language of its own—a lingua franca that manages to be both dull and difficult and that contains names like ondansetron, for anti-nausea medication—as well as some unsettling gestures that require a bit of getting used to. For example, an official met for the first time may abruptly sink his fingers into your neck. That's how I discovered that my cancer had spread to my lymph nodes, and that one of these deformed beauties—located on my right clavicle, or collarbone—was big enough to be seen and felt. It's not at all good when your cancer is "palpable" from the outside. Especially when, as at this stage, they didn't even know where the primary source was. Carcinoma works cunningly from the inside out. Detection and treatment often work more slowly and gropingly, from the outside in. Many needles were sunk into my clavicle area—"Tissue is the issue" being a hot slogan in the local Tumorville tongue—and I was told the biopsy results might take a week.

Working back from the cancer-ridden squamous cells that these first results disclosed, it took rather longer than that to discover the disagreeable truth. The word *metastasized* was the one in the report that first caught my eye, and ear. The alien had colonized a bit of my lung as well as quite a bit of my lymph node. And its original base of operations was located—had been located for quite some time—in my esophagus. My father had died, and very swiftly too, of cancer of the esophagus. He was seventy-nine. I am sixty-one. In whatever kind of a "race" life may be, I have very abruptly become a finalist.

*

The notorious stage theory of Elisabeth Kübler-Ross, whereby one progresses from denial to rage through bargaining to depression and the eventual bliss of "acceptance," hasn't so far had much application in my case. In one way, I suppose, I have been "in denial" for some time, knowingly burning the candle at both ends and finding that it often gives a lovely light. But for precisely that reason, I can't see myself smiting my brow with shock or hear myself whining about how it's all so unfair: I have been taunting the Reaper into taking a free scythe in my direction and have now succumbed to something so predictable and banal that it bores even me. Rage would be beside the point for the same reason. Instead, I am badly oppressed by a gnawing sense of waste. I had real plans for my next decade and felt I'd worked hard enough to earn it. Will I really not live to see my children married? To watch the World Trade Center rise again? To read—if not indeed write—the obituaries of elderly villains like Henry Kissinger and Joseph Ratzinger? But I understand this sort of nonthinking for what it is: sentimentality and self-pity. Of course my book hit the bestseller list on the day that I received the grimmest of news bulletins, and for that matter the last flight I took as a healthy-feeling person (to a fine, big audience at the Chicago Book Fair) was the one that made me a million-miler on United Airlines, with a lifetime of free upgrades to look forward to. But irony is my business and I just can't see any ironies here: Would it be less poignant to get cancer on the day that my memoirs were remaindered as a box-office turkey, or that I was bounced from a coach-class flight and left on the tarmac? To the dumb question "Why me?" the cosmos barely bothers to return the reply: Why not?

The *bargaining* stage, though. Maybe there's a loophole here. The oncology bargain is that, in return for at least the chance of a few more useful years, you agree to submit to chemotherapy and then, if you are lucky with that, to radiation or even surgery. So here's the wager: you stick around for a bit, but in return we are going to need some things from you. These things may include your taste buds, your ability to concentrate, your ability to digest, and the hair on your head. This certainly appears to be a reasonable trade. Unfortunately, it also involves confronting one of the most appealing clichés in our language. You've heard it all right. People don't have cancer: they are reported to be battling cancer. No well-wisher omits the combative image: You can beat this. It's even in obituaries for cancer losers, as if one might reasonably say of someone that they died after a long and brave struggle with mortality. You don't hear it about long-term sufferers from heart disease or kidney failure.

Myself, I love the imagery of struggle. I sometimes wish I were suffering in a good cause, or risking my life for the good of others, instead of just being a gravely endangered patient. Allow me to inform you, though, that when you sit in a room with a set of other finalists, and kindly people bring a huge transparent bag of poison and plug it into your arm, and you either read or don't read a book while the venom sack gradually empties itself into your system, the image of the ardent soldier or revolutionary is the very last one that will occur to you. You feel swamped with passivity and impotence: dissolving in powerlessness like a sugar lump in water.

It's quite something, this chemo-poison. It has caused me to lose about fourteen pounds, though without making me feel any lighter. It has cleared up a vicious rash on my shins that no doctor could ever name, let alone cure. (Some venom, to get rid of those furious red dots without a struggle.) Let it please be this mean and ruthless with the alien and its spreading dead-zone colonies. But as against that, the death-dealing stuff and life-preserving stuff have also made me strangely neuter. I was fairly reconciled to the loss of my hair, which began to come out in the shower in the first two weeks of treatment, and which I saved in a plastic bag so that it could help fill a floating dam in the Gulf of Mexico. But I wasn't quite prepared for the way that my razor blade would suddenly go slipping pointlessly down my face, meeting no stubble. Or for the way that my newly smooth upper lip would begin to look as if it had undergone electrolysis, causing me to look a bit too much like somebody's maiden auntie. (The chest hair that was once the toast of two continents hasn't yet wilted, but so much of it was shaved off for various hospital incisions that it's a rather patchy affair.) I feel upsettingly denatured. If Penélope Cruz were one of my nurses, I wouldn't even notice. In the war against Thanatos, if we must term it a war, the immediate loss of Eros is a huge initial sacrifice.

These are my first raw reactions to being stricken. I am quietly resolved to resist bodily as best I can, even if only passively, and to seek the most advanced advice. My heart and blood pressure and many other registers are now strong again: indeed, it occurs to me that if I didn't have such a stout constitution I might have led a much healthier life thus far. Against me is the blind, emotionless alien, cheered on by some who have long wished me ill. But on the side of my continued life is a group of brilliant and selfless physicians plus an astonishing number of prayer groups. On both of these I hope to write next time if—as my father invariably said—I am spared.

PICO IYER

Chapels

FROM *Portland Magazine*

GIANT FIGURES ARE TALKING and strutting and singing on enormous screens above me, and someone is chattering away on the miniscreen in the cab from which I just stepped. Nine people at this street corner are shouting into thin air, wearing wires around their chins and jabbing at screens in their hands. One teenager in Sacramento, I read recently, sent 300,000 text messages in a month —or ten a minute for every minute of her waking day, assuming she was awake sixteen hours a day. There are more cell phones than people on the planet now, almost (ten mobiles for every one at the beginning of the century). Even by the end of the last century, the average human being in a country such as ours saw as many images in a day as a Victorian inhaled in a lifetime.

And then I walk off crowded Fifth Avenue and into the capacious silence of St. Patrick's. Candles are flickering here and there, intensifying my sense of all I cannot see. Figures are on their knees, heads bowed, drawing my attention to what cannot be said. Light is flooding through the great blue windows, and I have entered a realm where no I or realm exists. I notice everything around me: the worn stones, the little crosses, the hymnbooks, the upturned faces; then I sit down, close my eyes—and step out of time, into everything that stretches beyond it.

When I look back on my life, the parts that matter and sustain me, all I see is a series of chapels. They may be old or young, cracked brown or open space; they may be lectories or afterthoughts, hidden corners of a city or deserted spaces in the forest. They are as variable as people. But like people they have a stillness at the core of them which makes all discussion of high and low, East and West, you and me dissolve. Bells toll and toll and I lose all sense of whether they are chiming within me or without.

The first time I was asked to enter a New York office building—for a job interview twenty-eight years ago—I gathered myself, in all senses, in St. Patrick's, and knew that it would put everything I was about to face (a company, a new life, my twittering ambitions) into place. It was the frame that gave everything else definition. Ever since, I've made it my practice to step into that great thronged space whenever I return to the city, to remind myself of what is real, what is lasting, before giving myself to everything that isn't. A chapel is the biggest immensity we face in our daily lives, unless we live in a desert or in the vicinity of the Grand Canyon. A chapel is the deepest silence we can absorb, unless we stay in a cloister. A chapel is where we allow ourselves to be broken open as if we were children again, trembling at home before our parents.

Whenever I fly, I step into an airport chapel. The people there may be sleeping, reading, praying, but all of them are there because they want to be collected. When I go to San Francisco, I stay across from Grace Cathedral, and visit it several times a day, to put solid ground underneath my feet. Returning to the college I attended, I sit on a pew at the back, listening to the high-voiced choir, and think back on that shuffling kid who wandered the downy grounds and what relation he might have to the person who now sits here.

So much of our time is spent running from ourselves, or hiding from the world; a chapel brings us back to the source, in ourselves and in the larger sense of self—as if there were a difference. Look around you. Occasional figures are exploring their separate silences; the rich and the poor are hard to tell apart, heads bowed. Light is diffused and general; when you hear voices, they are joined in a chorus or reading from a holy book. The space at the heart of the Rothko Chapel is empty, and that emptiness is prayer and surrender.

In 1929 the British Broadcasting Corporation decided to start broadcasting "live silence" in memory of the dead instead of just halting transmission for two minutes every day; it was important, it was felt, to hear the rustle of papers, the singing of birds outside, an occasional cough. As a BBC spokesman put it, with rare wisdom, silence is "a solvent which destroys personality and gives us leave to be great and universal." Permits us, in short, to be who we are and could be if only we had the openness and trust. A chapel is where we hear something and nothing, ourselves and everyone else, a silence that is not the absence of noise but the presence of something much deeper: the depth beneath our thoughts.

This spring I came, for the first time, to the Chapel of Christ the Teacher at the University of Portland, to give a talk as the light was falling. Great shafts of sunshine stretched across the courtyard, catching and sharpening the faces of students returning to their rooms. Later in the evening, since this was Holy Week, an enormous cross was carried into the space, in darkness and reverence and silence. Now, however, people were walking in from all directions, leaving themselves at the door, putting away their business cards and gathering in a circle. They said nothing, and looked around them. The light through the windows began to fade. A scatter of seats became a congregation. And whatever was said, or not said, became less important than the silence.

Many years ago, when I was too young to know better, I worked in a twenty-fifth-floor office four blocks from Times Square, in New York City. Teletypes juddered the news furiously into our midst every second — this was the World Affairs department of *Time* magazine — and messengers breathlessly brought the latest reports from our correspondents to our offices. Editors barked, early computers sputtered, televisions in our senior editors' offices gave us the news as it was breaking. We spoke and conferred and checked facts and wrote, often, twenty or twenty-five pages in an evening.

I left all that for a monastery on the back streets of Kyoto. I wanted to learn about silence. I wanted to learn about who I was when I wasn't thinking about it. The Japanese are masters of not saying anything, both because their attention is always on listening, on saying little, even on speaking generically, and because when they do talk, they are very eager to say nothing offensive, outrageous, or confrontational. They're like talk-show hosts in a nation where self-display is almost forbidden. You learn more by listening than talking, they know; you create a wider circle not by thinking about yourself, but about the people around you, and how you can find common ground with them. The Japanese idea of a dream date—I've been with my Japanese sweetheart for twenty-three years and I've learned the hard way—is to go to a movie and come out saying nothing.

Perhaps I wouldn't need this kind of training in paying attention and keeping quiet were it not for the fact that I used to love babbling, and my colleges and friends in England and the U.S. trained and encouraged me to talk, to thrust myself forward, to assert my little self in all its puny glory. Perhaps we wouldn't need chapels if our lives were already clear and calm (a saint or a Jesus may never need to go into a church; he's always carrying one inside himself). Chapels are emergency rooms for the soul. They are the one place we can reliably go to find who we are and what we should be doing with our lives—usually by finding all we aren't, and what is much greater than us, to which we can only give ourselves up.

"I like the silent church," Emerson wrote, "before the service begins."

I grew up in chapels, at school in England. For all the years of my growing up, we had to go to chapel every morning and to say prayers in a smaller room every evening. Chapel became everything we longed to flee; it was where we made faces at one another, doodled in our hymnbooks, sniggered at each other every time we sang about "the bosom of the Lord" or the "breast" of a green hill. All we wanted was open space, mobility, freedom—the California of the soul. But as the years went on, I started to see that no movement made sense unless it had a changelessness beneath it; that all our explorations were only as rich as the still place we brought them back to.

I noticed, in my early thirties, that I had accumulated 1.5 million miles with United Airlines alone; I started going to a monastery. It wasn't in order to become religious or to attend services in the chapel, though I did go there, over and over, as Emerson might have done, when nobody was present. The real chapel was my little cell in the hermitage, looking out on the boundless blue of the Pacific Ocean below, the Steller's jay that just alighted on the splintered fence in my garden. Chapel was silence and spaciousness and whatever put the human round, my human, all too human thoughts, in some kind of vaster context.

My house had burned down eight months before, and kind friends might have been thinking that I was seeking out a home; but in the chapel of my cell, I was seeking only a reminder of the inner home we always carry with us. To be a journalist is to be beholden to the contents of just now, the news, the public need; to be a human—even if you're a journalist—is to be conscious of the old, what stands outside of time, our prime necessity. I could only write for *Time,* I thought, if I focused on Eternity.

I've stayed in those little cells in a Benedictine hermitage above the sea more than fifty times by now, over almost twenty years. I've stayed in the cloister with the monks; spent three weeks at a time in silence; stayed in a trailer in the dark, and in a house for the monastery's laborers, where I'd come upon monks doing press-ups against the rafters on the ground floor and planning their next raid upon the monastery computer.

Now the place lives inside me so powerfully that my home in Japan looks and feels like a Benedictine hermitage. I receive no newspapers or magazines there, and I watch no television. I've never had a cell phone, and I've ensured that we have almost no Internet connections at all. We own no car or bicycle, and the whole apartment (formerly, population four, my wife and two children and myself) consists of two rooms. I sleep on a couch in the living room at 8:30 every night, and think this is the most luxurious, expansive, liberating adventure I could imagine.

A chapel is where you can hear something beating below your heart.

We've always needed chapels, however confused or contradictory we may be in the way we define our religious affiliations; we've always had to have quietness and stillness to undertake our journeys into battle, or just the tumult of the world. How can we act in the world, if we haven't had the time and chance to find out who we are and what the world and action might be?

But now Times Square is with us everywhere. The whole world is clamoring at our door even on a mountaintop (my monastery has wireless Internet, its workers downloaded so much of the world recently that the system crashed, and the monastery has a digital address, www.contemplation.com). Even in my cell in Japan, I can feel more than 6 billion voices, plus the Library of Alexandria,

CNN, MSNBC, everything, in that inoffensive little white box with the apple on it. Take a bite, and you fall into the realm of Knowledge, and Ignorance, and Division.

The high-tech firm Intel experimented for seven months with enforcing "Quiet Time" for all of its workers for at least four consecutive hours a week (no e-mails were allowed, no phone calls accepted). It tried banning all e-mail checks on Fridays and assuring its workers that they had twenty-four hours, not twenty-four minutes, in which to respond to any internal e-mail. If people are always running to catch up, they will never have the time and space to create a world worth catching up with. Some colleges have now instituted a vespers hour, though often without a church; even in the most secular framework, what people require is the quietness to sink beneath the rush of the brain. Journalist friends of mine switch off their modems from Friday evening to Monday morning, every week, and I bow before them silently; I know that when I hop around the Web, watch YouTube videos, surf the TV set, I turn away and feel agitated. I go for a walk, enjoy a real conversation with a friend, turn off the lights and listen to Bach or Leonard Cohen, and I feel palpably richer, deeper, fuller, happier.

Happiness is absorption, being entirely yourself and entirely in one place. That is the chapel that we crave.

Long after my home had burned down, and I had begun going four times a year to my monastery up the coast, long after I'd constructed a more or less unplugged life in Japan—figuring that a journalist could write about the news best by not following its every convulsion, and writing from the chapel and not the madness of Times Square—I found a Christian retreat house in my own hometown. Sometimes, when I had an hour free in the day, or was running from errand to errand, I drove up into the silent hills and parked there, and just sat for a few minutes in its garden. Encircled by flowers. In a slice of light next to a statue of the Virgin.

Instantly, everything was okay. I had more reassurance than I would ever need. I was thinking of something more than an "I" I could never entirely respect.

Later, I opened the heavy doors and walked into the chapel, again when no one was there. It sat next to a sunlit courtyard overlooking the dry hills and far-off blue ocean of what could have

been a space in Andalusia. A heavy bell spoke of the church's private sense of time. A row of blond-wood chairs was gathered in a
circle. I knelt and closed my eyes and thought of the candle flickering in one corner of the chapel I loved in the monastery up the
coast.

When I had to go to Sri Lanka, in the midst of its civil war, I went
to the chapel to be still; to gather my resources and protection, as
it were. I went there when I was forcibly evacuated from the house
that my family had rebuilt after our earlier structure had burned
down, and our new home was surrounded by wild flames driven by
seventy-mile-per-hour winds. In the very same week, my monastery
in Big Sur was also encircled by fire.

I went there even when I was halfway across the world, because I
had reconstituted the chapel in my head, my heart; it was where I
went to be held by something profound. Then another wildfire
struck up, and a newspaper editor called me in Japan: the retreat
house near my home was gone.

Where does one go when one's chapel is reduced to ash? Perhaps it is the first and main question before us all. There are still
chapels everywhere. And I go to them. But like the best of teachers
or friends, they always have the gift of making themselves immate-
rial, invisible—even, perhaps, immortal. I sit in Nara, the capital
of Japan thirteen centuries ago, and I see a candle flickering. I feel
the light descending from a skylight in the rotunda roof. I hear a
fountain in the courtyard. I close my eyes and sit very still, by the
side of my bed, and sense the chapel take shape around me.

If your silence is deep enough, bells toll all the way through it.

VICTOR LaVALLE

Long Distance

FROM *Granta*

THE MOST LOVING RELATIONSHIP of my early twenties cost me ninety-nine cents per minute. Her name was Margie, and while I was charged to talk with her, she was not a pro. She was a fifty-year-old woman who lived in New Jersey. Two or three nights a week we called each other on a chatline. I'd dial 970-DATE and agree to have the charges billed to my telephone while Margie dialed the same number but never paid a fee. Much like at nightclubs and bars, it's a lot harder to get ladies into the room. So Margie, and the hundreds of women like her, would call the number and register as a woman, then punch through the recorded greetings from thousands of guys who were waiting to talk with them. One of those men was me.

Each guy's greeting was his name and a little something about himself. Our messages were either lewd or pornographic, nothing else. Using euphemisms about your penis counted as a true gentleman's move. I was no better than the rest. Twenty-one and horny and incapable of getting a real-world date. So instead I listened to the recorded greetings of anonymous women from all over the northeastern United States. The women's greetings tended to differ from the men's; they spoke about amusement parks and dining out and walks on the beach. Ridiculous shit. We all knew why we were here and it wasn't to line up any dates. We were there to talk dirty into our telephones and masturbate in our separate darkened rooms. At least that was true for me and Margie.

We liked each other's voices—each other's imaginations—enough to keep calling back. We'd make appointments for the

next "meeting" and then call the line. Scroll through the many recorded messages, listening for the voice we recognized. She was
Margie and I was Michael. We spent two years having phone sex
and, eventually, speaking to each other off the line, but we never
told each other our real names.

But why was I doing this? At twenty-one? I was in college and, in
theory, surrounded by eligible women. *Besieged* by more appropriate partners. My little crew of friends enjoyed no end of sex, but
my crew consisted of some sterling men. But even that's a cop-out,
because the schlumps and losers were actually doing all right too,
juggling a couple of women on campus. Not me, though.

I was 350 pounds and didn't stand nine feet tall, so the weight
didn't sit well on me. As big as a house? No. I was as big as a housing project. Lumpy and lazy; I *aspired* to lethargy. Second year of
university I missed half my classes just because I couldn't pull my
big butt out of bed.

But here's the thing: I was charming. Funnier than you and all
your friends. Well read and well spoken. Observant and even kind.
Not too easily suckered. Street-smart. In other words, I was kind of
a fucking catch. And I *knew* this was true. As long as you couldn't
see me. If you saw me you'd think I was the sea cow that had swallowed your catch.

Margie lived alone in the home she owned in northern New Jersey.
Her daughter had grown up and married and moved away to Boston. Margie had retired because she got sick, but she'd saved her
money all these years. Even leaving the workforce as young as fifty
didn't give her much concern. She had enough in the bank and
the mortgage had been paid off. She felt quite proud of herself,
and rightly so. She never mentioned a husband, the father of her
only child, and I didn't ask. During the day Margie ran errands
and spent time with her neighbors. At night Margie entertained
her gentleman callers.

One of them was me, Michael, a college student in upstate New
York. A kid from Queens who was paying for school with a part-
time job and loans. A former high school baseball player who
wanted to become a lawyer someday. I told her I looked like Derek
Jeter. She said she resembled Gina Lollobrigida. Did I know who
that was? The first time she told me I said, "Of course," and then
looked the actress up.

Both our exaggerations were probably true *enough*. I did have one black parent and one white parent and I had played baseball in high school. I might as well be Derek's twin brother! As for Margie, I felt sure she was at least a woman who had brown hair. But when we finally found each other on the chatline, all suspicions fell away. She was there and I was too. Our rooms so dark we could imagine each other—and ourselves—exactly as we wanted.

"Hello, Michael."

"Hello, Margie."

"I missed you," she said.

"I'm there with you now."

"Right here in bed?"

"No. I'm outside. Looking in through your window."

She blew out a breath. "My neighbors will see you."

"Then I'd better break in."

"Aren't you afraid I'll hear you?"

I said, "I'll hide until you're sleeping."

"I don't keep much money in the house."

"I don't want your money."

"I don't have jewelry."

"I don't want your jewels," I said.

"Why me?" she asked.

"I saw you at the supermarket. You were wearing those tight shorts."

"You followed me home?" she asked.

"And now I'm standing by your bed."

Margie sighed. "It gets so dark in here at night. I can't see anything."

"But you can feel me getting on the bed."

Quiet.

"Yes," she said.

"I'm going to have to stop you from getting away, though."

She whispered, "You could climb on my chest. Pin my arms down with your knees."

"That would hurt you."

"Yes," she said.

Quiet, a little longer.

"Now open your mouth," I said.

"I won't."

"Don't make me smack you," I told her.

"I'm sorry," she said.

Even quieter now. The longest silence yet.

I said, "If you say no to me again, I'm going to get rough."

Margie blew into the phone softly.

"No," she said.

Margie and I were "together" for about two years. After the first year she gave me her home number and I would call at our appointed times. Neither of us expected the other to stay off the chatlines. If I happened to hear her recorded message there, on one of our off days, calling out the name of a different man, I didn't mind. I was usually listening for a different woman. We'd defeated the madness of monogamy! It only required that we never actually see or touch each other. Sometimes we talked about me taking a bus up to her town, or her meeting me for coffee in New York City, on one of my visits home. But we never did that. And never would. Both of us knew it. She was a fifty-year-old woman with some undefined illness that forced her to retire fifteen years early. Maybe it took some toll on her physically. Maybe she was in a wheelchair, or had purple spots on her ass, I don't know. But I sure as hell never would let her see me either. If she did, how could we ever fantasize about me crouching over her chest again? In real life I'd suffocate the poor woman between my meaty thighs if we ever tried.

And yet, somehow, I convinced myself that Margie was helping to keep me tethered to the "normal" world of relationships. I knew what we had wasn't complete, but at least we were two human beings sharing some kind of real affection. I still felt like this was infinitely better than the alternative: have you ever known men or women who don't get *any* kind of loving for years? They get *weird.* The women become either monstrously drab or they costume themselves in ways that make them seem unreal; they externalize their inner fantasies and come to believe — on some level — they really are elves or princesses or, most disturbing of all, children again. And the men? They're even worse. Men who are denied affection too long devolve into some kind of rage-filled hominoid. Their anger becomes palpable. You can almost feel the wrath emanating from their pores. Lonely women destroy themselves; lonely men threaten the world.

So with that fate in mind, I felt truly grateful for Margie. While I enjoyed phone sex with other women, Margie and I would also have real conversations after the sex was done. She'd want to know what I'd been reading in class and I'd ask about the home-improvement work she'd been doing. I enjoyed her company, her voice. And she sounded sincere when she told me she'd missed me.

So it came as a real shock when she said we'd have to stop talking.

Her daughter's husband had lost his job and their home had gone into foreclosure. The two of them, and their three-year-old child, would be moving in with Margie. There was no other way to go. Margie had plenty of space in her home. Plus she'd been so good with her money that she could afford to carry the three of them until the husband found work. And Margie wanted to do this; she loved the idea of having them close. Her only regret was that she'd have to say goodbye to me. (And to the other dudes she'd had relationships with, I gathered.) Someone would always be home and she couldn't risk the embarrassment if one of them overheard us.

So in 1995 my fifty-year-old girlfriend, the one I'd never met, broke up with me.

While she and I were "together" I'd thought of myself like an astronaut going on one of those spacewalks outside the space shuttle. Below me I could see Earth, the glorious terrain. The place where true couples dwelled. And while I wasn't there, I could still view it. I knew what it looked like. And in time I'd make my way back into the shuttle; I'd hit the thrusters on my spaceship and return to that good soil.

But when Margie and I stopped talking it was as if the craft had blown to bits. I had plenty of oxygen in my suit, but I was no longer tethered to anything.

And the shock waves of the blast didn't send me hurtling down to Earth.

Instead, they blew me backward.

Deeper into space.

It's funny to have to relate all this first. Because I really want to tell you about my life *after* I lost weight. What sex was like once I'd exercised and dieted myself down to 195 pounds. That's from the lifetime high of somewhere just north of 350. How did I manage the miracle? I bought a refurbished StairMaster and used it four days a week. And I joined Jenny Craig, the weight-loss system that used out-of-work celebrities in their ads. Ridiculous as it sounds, it worked.

To belabor the astronaut metaphor just a minute longer: I'd found my way back to Earth after having drifted through the lifeless void for two years. Victory parades were thrown in my honor. The president offered me heartfelt congratulations. (By which I mean my mother was incredibly proud of my change.) Here's our man, finally height and weight proportionate! Once again a member of the human race.

But in the time I'd been away—when I'd been inhuman, I guess —I'd journeyed well past phone sex of any kind. Leapfrogged over message boards and heated Internet exchanges. I'd found another phone line where each side really did want to meet and make things happen.

I had sex—lots of it—with women who were, essentially, just like me. By which I mean more than 350 pounds *and* crippled by self-loathing. We made our introductions on the phone line, essentially negotiating the details of our affections in advance. *I want this and you want that; I won't do any of those things, but I will try these.* As a result I'd show up at some woman's apartment for the first time and we'd be naked in about ten minutes. Engaging in the kind of sexual fantasies that usually require six months of dating before anyone will even broach the subject. And then they probably still wait another six months before they trust each other enough actually to try it. We covered all that ground in a single night.

And I'll tell you what I learned during those two years: fat people are perverts.

By which I mean to say, loneliness perverts you.

I'm not talking about the sex. Or not exclusively, anyway. My first date as a trimmer man scared me more than my very first fistfight. Part of the reason was that I didn't even realize we were on a date.

We met each other at a party in a bar. We shook hands and exchanged a few words and then mingled among other friends. Once or twice we sat in the same frame for some of those group photos people take as a party wears on. When she sat next to me at a table and smiled before I'd said anything, I had the notion that she might be flirting with me, but the phenomenon had been so rare these last few years that I didn't trust my lying eyes. I figured my intuition had probably shriveled up and died long ago. She wasn't flirting, she was just being friendly.

But then, a few hours into the party, she came up and asked if I liked her blouse. Her friend stood nearby, at the bar, a glass of beer in front of her mouth to try and hide the way she giggled at her friend's boldness. I was seated and she stood over me. She asked again if I liked her blouse, and this time she flipped the bottom of it up and showed me her stomach.

Now *that* was flirting. Impossible to ignore. Plus, I didn't want to ignore it. This woman was beautiful by any measure. When she flipped her shirt up I saw her skin and I realized how long it had been since I'd seen a belly without stretch marks. Five years? Ten? I'm including my own in that count.

Before I left I asked if she'd go to dinner with me, and when she said yes she actually went up on her tiptoes, like a kid.

I took her to a sushi restaurant and sat across from her, but after a few minutes it was clear her face showed none of the same enthusiasm as at the bar. I asked her questions about her job as a magazine editor, but she hardly answered in full sentences. I made jokes, each one worse than the last. Maybe it was just that she'd been drunk at the party. I couldn't think of an explanation for why she was acting so damn uninterested now.

Then, during another moment of silence, I looked away from her and out of the window. There were no couples between us and the store's large front windows. I saw her reflection. She was as lovely as the other night, maybe more so. She wore a sheer sweater and a skirt that flattered her long legs.

And me?

I was still wearing my coat.

Not a jacket. My *winter* coat. We'd been inside for half an hour and I hadn't taken it off. No wonder she seemed distant, even dismayed; it looked like I couldn't wait to get away.

And it wasn't just the coat. I had so many layers on. A sweater *and* a button-down shirt. And a T-shirt under them. It wouldn't have surprised me if I had thermal underwear layered down there as well. In other words, I was dressed like a fat person. We make the mistake of thinking those layers of clothing are serving to hide us.

A kind of protection. Instead they only serve to make us look even bigger. Or, in this case, to make me seem like an asshole.

I wanted to explain everything to her. *I'm going through a big transition*. But I couldn't bring myself to tell her. No matter how I phrased it in my head, it always sounded like a bad pun, a sad joke. Finally, I slid my coat off, but the gesture must've seemed like pity. I popped mine off and she pulled on hers. We ate the rest of our meal quickly. I took her home on the F train, but when we reached her station she said I didn't have to walk her home.

All this changed after I dated the woman with the violent boyfriend. We became friends first. We worked in the same space and at lunchtime we sometimes ate together and talked. We were attracted to each other, but did nothing about it for months. She continued to date the aforementioned bruiser and I was busy trying to live like a normal-sized man, meaning I stayed off the phone lines, I ate sensible meals, I exercised regularly, and I told no one that I'd ever been fat. The last seemed particularly important. If enough other people believed it, I hoped that I'd come to believe it too. If they treated me like a guy who'd never knocked out a dozen Krispy Kreme original glazed doughnuts in one sitting, then I'd forget I ever had. I needed the outside world to convince me because I still couldn't quite believe the transformation had been real.

So all of the fall of 1998, I'm flirting with this woman but keeping a respectful distance. Getting closer and then pulling away. And she was doing the same. This slow build felt exciting and frustrating. But each time I saw her again my feelings seemed even stronger. And that was a shock too. *Feelings*. Not to be too self-pitying (or self-aggrandizing), but I hadn't really cared about a woman outside my family since Margie and I hung up our phones in 1995.

Christmas 1998. A little bit of partying. A lot of alcohol. I remember the first time she put her arms around me, outside a bar. I held my breath as she clasped her hands around my waist; then she rested her head against my chest.

And finally the two of us are stumbling back to her building. We climb the stairs to her apartment. Open the front door, listen for her roommate, and when it seems we're alone we fall across her living room couch. I'm on my back and she's on top of me. She undoes my jeans and slides them down and lifts her skirt. She climbs back on top of me.

And as much as I'm enjoying myself, as I anticipate the next step with three years' worth of pent-up glee, I'm also not really there. As soon as my pants slide down to my knees and my shirt rides up above my belly I feel myself wince, as if preparing for an explosion. And I realize I've been thinking of my clothes as if they were the casing around a live bomb.

Have you ever had out-of-body sex? It's not the same as that tantric business. As soon as my skin touched open air my mind drifted away. I watched myself and this woman having some wonderfully energetic sex. I even felt proud of the guy down there because he seemed so free. *He* was laughing and gripping her hips, but *I* was floating up by the ceiling. That body and the person inside it weren't connected to each other. While the body worked up a sweat, I remained cool on the outside, keeping watch; I felt sure that if this woman saw me at the wrong angle, or in the wrong light, her lust would suddenly fold up and be packed away.

Then she reached down and touched my stomach; I'd lost a lot of weight but the skin there was a little loose, and there were faint stretch marks along the bottom that looked like dried-out riverbeds. She put her hand on my stomach and I sucked my belly in. Understand, I didn't even have that belly anymore, but that didn't make the belly any less real to me.

Her hand stayed there on my stomach and I waited to hear her say, "Stop." Or, "Get off me." Or a groan of disgust.

But instead she did the most perfect thing. For which I remain grateful.

She lifted her hand and then brought it back down hard. She smacked me.

But not out of revulsion; not to punish me.

She looked down at me and gritted her teeth.

"Harder," is the only thing she said.

Later that night the violent boyfriend showed up. We were in her bedroom by now, zonked out from sex and bourbon, when the sound of the building's buzzer woke us up. In my tired mind it was the sound of a wasp, a swarm of wasps, and I woke up swatting at the air. Finally I realized someone was downstairs, in the lobby, trying to get in.

"It's him," she said quietly.

"How do you know it's not your roommate?"

"My roommate doesn't ring the bell. My roommate has the keys."

Now we both sat up and listened as the buzzing continued. I'd met the boyfriend before, when he'd visited her at work. Not intimidating. The guy reminded me of Jean-Paul Sartre, actually, owlish like that. After he'd left she'd told me about how violent he could get and I thought she was making a confession about her own abuse. But it wasn't like that. He'd never swung on her. Or even used a cross word. But she swore she'd watched him chop down guys the size of redwood trees. You can't always guess that kind of thing, just from looking.

I slid out of bed and said, "I'll go talk to him."

But she frowned. "You really don't want to do that."

I thought of her stories about him. I was *much* smaller than a redwood now.

I slid back next to her and we lay there as he continued zapping the buzzer. We wondered if her roommate would show up and let him in. Caught sleeping in bed with another man's woman: that's a sure-fire way to get your ass snuffed. She fell asleep long before I did. I spent hours lying there, alert.

By dawn I still hadn't gone to sleep, but I had stopped worrying over the violent boyfriend long ago. I lifted my hand until it was bathed in the morning light coming through the thin curtains. I still couldn't believe what I saw. My new hand, slim enough to show the wrist bones; the knuckles no longer lost in flesh. But this hand hadn't replaced the old one; instead it was like this hand had grown *around* the fatter one somehow. Both were there, but only one could be seen.

CHARLIE LeDUFF

What Killed Aiyana
Stanley-Jones?

FROM *Mother Jones*

IT WAS JUST AFTER MIDNIGHT on the morning of May 16 and
the neighbors say the streetlights were out on Lillibridge Street. It
is like that all over Detroit, where whole blocks regularly go dark
with no warning or any apparent pattern. Inside the lower unit of a
duplex halfway down the gloomy street, Charles Jones, twenty-five,
was pacing, unable to sleep.

His seven-year-old daughter, Aiyana Mo'nay Stanley-Jones, slept
on the couch as her grandmother watched television. Outside,
Television was watching them. A half-dozen masked officers of the
Special Response Team—Detroit's version of SWAT—were at the
door, guns drawn. In tow was an A&E crew filming an episode of
The First 48, its true-crime program. The conceit of the show is that
homicide detectives have forty-eight hours to crack a murder case
before the trail goes cold. Thirty-four hours earlier, Je'Rean Blake
Nobles, seventeen, had been shot outside a liquor store on nearby
Mack Avenue; an informant had ID'ed a man named Chauncey
Owens as the shooter and provided this address.

The SWAT team tried the steel door to the building. It was unlocked. They threw a flash-bang grenade through the window of
the lower unit and kicked open its wooden door, which was also
unlocked. The grenade landed so close to Aiyana that it burned
her blanket. Officer Joseph Weekley, the lead commando—who'd
been featured before on another A&E show, *Detroit SWAT*—burst
into the house. His weapon fired a single shot, the bullet striking

Aiyana in the head and exiting her neck. It all happened in a matter of seconds.

"They had time," a Detroit police detective told me. "You don't go into a home around midnight. People are drinking. People are awake. Me? I would have waited until the morning when the guy went to the liquor store to buy a quart of milk. That's how it's supposed to be done."

But the SWAT team didn't wait. Maybe because the cameras were rolling, maybe because a Detroit police officer had been murdered two weeks earlier while trying to apprehend a suspect. This was the first raid on a house since his death.

Police first floated the story that Aiyana's grandmother had grabbed Weekley's gun. Then, realizing that sounded implausible, they said she'd brushed the gun as she ran past the door. But the grandmother says she was lying on the far side of the couch, away from the door.

Compounding the tragedy is the fact that the police threw the grenade into the wrong apartment. The suspect fingered for Blake's murder, Chauncey Owens, lived in the *upstairs* flat, with Charles Jones's sister.

Plus, grenades are rarely used when rounding up suspects, even murder suspects. But it was dark. And TV may have needed some pyrotechnics.

"I'm worried they went Hollywood," said a high-ranking Detroit police official, who spoke on the condition of anonymity due to the sensitivity of the investigation and simmering resentment in the streets. "It is not protocol. And I've got to say in all my years in the department, I've never used a flash-bang in a case like this."

The official went on to say that the SWAT team was not briefed about the presence of children in the house, although the neighborhood informant who led homicide detectives to the Lillibridge address told them that children lived there. There were even toys on the lawn.

"It was a total fuck-up," the official said. "A total, unfortunate fuck-up."

Owens, a habitual criminal, was arrested upstairs minutes after Aiyana's shooting and charged for the slaying of Je'Rean. His motive, authorities say, was that the teen failed to pay him the proper respect. Jones too later became a person of interest in Je'Rean's murder—he allegedly went along for the ride—but Jones denies it, and he's lawyered up and moved to the suburbs.

As Officer Weekley wept on the sidewalk, Aiyana was rushed to the trauma table, where she was pronounced dead. Her body was transferred to the Wayne County morgue.

Dr. Carl Schmidt is the chief medical examiner there. There are at least fifty corpses on hold in his morgue cooler, some unidentified, others whose next of kin are too poor to bury them. So Dr. Schmidt keeps them on layaway, zipped up in body bags as family members wait for a ship to come in that never seems to arrive.

The day I visited, a Hollywood starlet was tailing the doctor, studying for her role as the medical examiner in ABC's new Detroit-based murder drama *Detroit 1-8-7*. The title is derived from the California penal code for murder: 187. In Michigan, the designation for homicide is actually 750.316, but that's just a mouthful of detail.

"You might say that the homicide of Aiyana is the natural conclusion to the disease from which she suffered," Schmidt told me.

"What disease was that?" I asked.

"The psychopathology of growing up in Detroit," he said. "Some people are doomed from birth because their environment is so toxic."

Was it so simple? Was it inevitable, as the doctor said, that abject poverty would lead to Aiyana's death and so many others? Was it death by TV? By police incompetence? By parental neglect? By civic malfeasance? About 350 people are murdered each year in Detroit. There are some 10,000 unsolved homicides dating back to 1960. Many are as fucked up and sad as Aiyana's. But I felt unraveling this one death could help diagnose what has gone wrong in this city, so I decided to retrace the events leading up to that pitiable moment on the porch on Lillibridge Street.

People my mother's age like to tell me about Detroit's good old days of soda fountains and shopping markets and lazy Saturday night drives. But the fact is Detroit and its suburbs were dying forty years ago. The whole country knew it, and the whole country laughed. *A bunch of lazy, uneducated blue-collar incompetents. The Rust Belt. Forget about it.*

When I was a teenager, my mother owned a struggling little

flower shop on the East Side, not far from where Aiyana was killed. On a hot afternoon around one Mother's Day, I was working in the back greenhouse. It was a sweatbox, and I went across the street to the liquor store for a soda pop. A small crowd of agitated black people was gathered on the sidewalk. The store bell jingled its little requiem as I pulled the door open.

Inside, splayed on the floor underneath the rack of snack cakes near the register, was a black man in a pool of blood. The blood was congealing into a pancake on the dirty linoleum. His eyes and mouth were open and held that milky expression of a drunk who has fallen asleep with his eyes open. The red halo around his skull gave the scene a feeling of serenity.

An Arab family owned the store, and one of the men—the one with the pocked face and loud voice—was talking on the telephone, but I remember no sounds. His brother stood over the dead man, a pistol in his hand, keeping an eye on the door in case someone walked in wanting to settle things.

"You should go," he said to me, shattering the silence with a wave of his hand. "Forget what you saw, little man. Go." He wore a gold bracelet as thick as a gymnasium rope. I lingered a moment, backing out while taking it in: the bracelet, the liquor, the blood, the gun, the Ho Hos, the cheapness of it all.

The flower shop is just a pile of bricks now, but despite what the Arab told me, I did not forget what I saw. Whenever I see a person who died of violence or misadventure, I think about the dead man with the open eyes on the dirty floor of the liquor store. I've seen him in the faces of soldiers when I was covering the Iraq war. I saw him in the face of my sister, who died a violent death in a filthy section of Detroit a decade ago. I saw him in the face of my sister's daughter, who died from a heroin overdose in a suburban basement near the interstate, weeks after I moved back to Michigan with my wife to raise our daughter and take a job with the *Detroit News*.

No one cared much about Detroit or its industrial suburbs until the Dow collapsed, the chief executives of the Big Three went to Washington to grovel, and General Motors declared bankruptcy— one hundred years after its founding. Suddenly Detroit was historic, symbolic—hip, even. I began to get calls from reporters around the world wondering what Detroit was like, what was happening here. They were wondering if the Rust Belt cancer had metastasized and was creeping to Los Angeles and London and Barcelona. Was Detroit an outlier or an epicenter?

Je'rean Blake Nobles was one of the rare black males in Detroit who made it through high school. A good kid with average grades, Je'Rean went to Southeastern High, which is situated in an industrial belt of moldering Chrysler assembly plants. Completed in 1917, the school, attended by white students at the time, was considered so far out in the wilds that its athletic teams took the nickname Jungaleers.

With large swaths of the city rewilding—empty lots are returning to prairie and woodland as the city depopulates—Southeastern was slated to absorb students from nearby Kettering High this year as part of a massive school-consolidation effort. That is, until someone realized that the schools are controlled by rival gangs. So bad is the rivalry that when the schools face off to play football or basketball, spectators from the visiting team are banned.

Southeastern's motto is *Age Quod Agis:* "Attend to Your Business." And Je'Rean did. By wit and will, he managed to make it through. A member of JROTC, he was on his way to the military recruitment office after senior prom and commencement. But Je'Rean never went to prom, much less the Afghanistan theater, because he couldn't clear the killing fields of Detroit. He became a horrifying statistic—one of 103 kids and teens murdered between January 2009 and July 2010.

Je'Rean's crime? He looked at Chauncey Owens the wrong way, detectives say.

It was 2:40 in the afternoon on May 14 when Je'Rean went to the Motor City liquor store and ice cream stand to get himself an orange juice to wash down his McDonald's. About forty kids were milling around in front of the soft-serve window. That's when Owens, thirty-four, pulled up on a moped.

Je'Rean might have thought it was funny to see a grown man driving a moped. He might have smirked. But according to a witness, he said nothing.

"Why you looking at me?" said Owens, getting off the moped. "Do you got a problem or something? What the fuck you looking at?"

A slender, pimply-faced kid, Je'Rean was not an intimidating figure. One witness had him pegged for thirteen years old.

Je'Rean balled up his tiny fist. "What?" he croaked.

"Oh, stay your ass right here," Owens growled. "I got something
for you."

Owens sped two blocks back to Lillibridge and gathered up a
posse, according to his statement to the police. The posse allegedly
included Aiyana's father, Charles "C.J." Jones.

"It's some lil niggas at the store talking shit—let's go whip they
ass," Detective Theopolis Williams later testified that Owens told
him during his interrogation.

Owens switched his moped for a Chevy Blazer. Jones and two
other men, known as Lil' James and Dirt, rode along for Je'Rean's
ass-whipping. Lil' James brought along a .357 Magnum—at the
behest of Jones, Detective Williams testified, because Jones was
afraid someone would try to steal his "diamond Cartier glasses."

Je'Rean knew badness was on its way and called his mother to
come pick him up. She arrived too late. Owens got there first and
shot Je'Rean clear through the chest with Lil' James's gun. Clutching his juice in one hand and two dollars in the other, Je'Rean stag-
gered across Mack Avenue and collapsed in the street. A minute
later, a friend took the two dollars as a keepsake. A few minutes after that, Je'Rean's mother, Lyvonne Cargill, arrived and got behind
the wheel of the car that friends had dragged him into.

Why would anyone move a gunshot victim, much less toss him in
a car? It is a matter of conditioning, Cargill later told me. In Detroit, the official response time of an ambulance to a 911 call is
twelve minutes. Paramedics say it is routinely much longer. Sometimes they come in a Crown Victoria with only a defibrillator and a
blanket, because there are no other units available. The hospital
was six miles away. Je'Rean's mother drove as he gurgled in the
backseat.

"My baby, my baby, my baby. God, don't take my baby."

They made it to the trauma ward, where Je'Rean was pronounced
dead. His body was transferred to Dr. Schmidt and the Wayne
County morgue.

The raid on the Lillibridge house that took little Aiyana's life came
two weeks and at least a dozen homicides after the last time police

stormed into a Detroit home. That house too is on the city's East Side, a nondescript brick duplex with a crumbling garage whose driveway funnels into busy Schoenherr Road.

Responding to a breaking-and-entering and shots-fired call at 3:30 A.M., Officer Brian Huff, a twelve-year veteran, walked into that dark house. Behind him stood two rookies. His partner took the rear entrance. Huff and his partner were not actually called to the scene; they'd taken it upon themselves to assist the younger cops, according to the police version of events. Another cruiser with two officers responded as well.

Huff entered with his gun still holstered. Behind the door was Jason Gibson, twenty-five, a violent man with a history of gun crimes, assaults on police, and repeated failures to honor probationary sentences.

Gibson is a tall, thick-necked man who, like the character Omar from *The Wire*, made his living robbing dope houses. Which is what he was doing at this house, authorities contend, when he put three bullets in Officer Huff's face.

What happened after that is a matter of conjecture, as Detroit officials have had problems getting their stories straight. Neighbor Paul Jameson, a former soldier whose wife had called in the break-in to 911, said the rookies ran toward the house and opened fire after Huff was shot.

Someone radioed in, and more police arrived—but the official story of what happened that night has changed repeatedly. First, it was six cops who responded to the 911 call. Then eight, then eleven. Officials said Gibson ran out the front of the house. Then they said he ran out the back of the house, even though there is no back door. Then they said he jumped out a back window. It was Jameson who finally dragged Huff out of the house and gave him CPR in the driveway, across the street from the Boys & Girls Club. In the end, Gibson was charged with Huff's murder and the attempted murders of four more officers. But police officials have refused to discuss how one got shot in the foot.

"We believe some of them were struck by friendly fire," the high-ranking cop told me. "But our ammo's so bad, we can't do ballistics testing. We've got nothing but bullet fragments."

A neighbor who tends the lawn in front of the dope house out of respect to Huff wonders why so many cops came in the first place, given that "the police hardly come around at all, much less that many cops that fast on a home break-in."

But the real mystery behind Officer Huff's murder is why Gibson was out on the street in the first place. In 2007, he attacked a cop and tried to take his gun. For that he was given simple probation. He failed to report. Police caught him again in November 2009 in possession of a handgun stolen from an Ohio cop. Gibson bonded out last January and actually showed up for his trial in circuit court on February 17.

The judge, Cynthia Gray Hathaway, set his bond at $20,000— only 10 percent of which was due up-front—and adjourned the trial without explanation, according to the docket. Known as Half-Day Hathaway, the judge was removed from the bench for six months by the Michigan Supreme Court a decade ago for, among other things, adjourning trials to sneak away on vacation.

Predictably, Gibson did not show for his new court date. The day after Huff was killed, and under fire from the police for her leniency toward Gibson, Judge Hathaway went into the case file and made changes, according to notations made in the court's computerized docket system. She refused to let me see the original paper file, despite the fact that it is a public record, and has said that she can't comment on the case because she might preside in the trial against Gibson.

More than four thousand people attended Officer Huff's funeral at the Greater Grace Temple on the city's Northwest Side. Police officers came from Canada and across Michigan. They were restless and agitated and pulled at the collars of dress blues that didn't seem to fit. Bagpipes played and the rain fell.

Mayor Dave Bing spoke. "The madness has to stop," he said.

But the madness was only beginning.

It might be a stretch to see anything more than Detroit's problems in Detroit's problems. Still, as the American middle class collapses, it's worth perhaps remembering that the East Side of Detroit—the place where Aiyana, Je'Rean, and Officer Huff all died—was once its industrial cradle.

Henry Ford built his first automobile assembly-line plant in Highland Park in 1908 on the east side of Woodward Avenue, the thoroughfare that divides the east of Detroit from the west. Over the next fifty years, Detroit's East Side would become the world's machine shop, its factory floor. The city grew to 1.3 million people from 300,000 after Ford opened his Model T factory. Other auto plants sprang up on the East Side: Packard, Studebaker, Chrysler's Dodge Main. Soon the Motor City's population surpassed that of Boston and Baltimore, old East Coast port cities founded on maritime shipping when the world moved by boat.

European intellectuals wondered at the whirl of building and spending in the new America. At the center of this economic dynamo was Detroit. "It is the home of mass-production, of very high wages and colossal profits, of lavish spending and reckless instalment-buying, of intense work and a large and shifting labour-surplus," British historian and MP Ramsay Muir wrote in 1927. "It regards itself as the temple of a new gospel of progress, to which I shall venture to give the name of 'Detroitism.'"

Skyscrapers sprang up virtually overnight. The city filled with people from all over the world: Arabs, Appalachians, Poles, African Americans, all in their separate neighborhoods surrounding the factories. Forbidden by restrictive real estate covenants and racist custom, the blacks were mostly restricted to Paradise Valley, which ran the length of Woodward Avenue. As the black population grew, so did black frustration over poor housing and rock-fisted police.

Soon the air was the color of a filthy dishrag. The water in the Detroit River was so bad, it was said you could bottle it and sell it as poison. The beavers disappeared from the river around 1930.

But pollution didn't kill Detroit. What did?

No one can answer that fully. You can blame it on the John Deere mechanical cotton-picker of 1950, which uprooted the sharecropper and sent him north looking for a living—where he found he was locked out of the factories by the unions. You might blame it on the urban renewal and interstate highway projects that rammed a freeway down the middle of Paradise Valley, displacing thousands of blacks and packing the Negro tenements tighter still. (Thomas Sugrue, in his seminal book *The Origins of the Urban Crisis,* writes that residents in Detroit's predominantly black lower East Side reported 206 rat bites in 1951 and 1952.)

You might blame postwar industrial policies that sent the factories to the suburbs, the rural South, and the western deserts. You might blame the 1967 race riot and the white flight that followed. You might blame Coleman Young—the city's first black mayor—and his culture of cronyism. You could blame it on the gas shocks of the '70s that opened the door to foreign car competition. You might point to the trade agreements of the Clinton years, which allowed American manufacturers to leave the country by the back door. You might blame the UAW, which demanded things like full pay for idle workers, or myopic Big Three management, who instead of saying no simply tacked the cost onto the price of a car.

Then there is the thought that Detroit is simply a boomtown that went bust the minute Henry Ford began to build it. The car made Detroit, and the car unmade Detroit. The auto industry allowed for sprawl. It also allowed a man to escape the smoldering city.

In any case, Detroit began its long precipitous decline during the 1950s, precisely when the city—and the United States—was at its peak. As Detroit led the nation in median income and home-ownership, automation and foreign competition were forcing companies like Packard to shutter their doors. That factory closed in 1956 and was left to rot, pulling down the East Side, which pulled down the city. Inexplicably, its carcass still stands and burns incessantly.

By 1958, 20 percent of the Detroit workforce was jobless. Not to worry: the city had its own welfare system, decades before Lyndon Johnson's Great Society. The city provided clothing, fuel, rent, and $10 every week to adults for food; children got $5. Word of the free milk and honey made its way down South, and the poor "Negros" and "hillbillies" flooded in.

But if it weren't for them, the city population would have sunk further than it did. Nor is corruption a black or liberal thing. Louis Miriani, the last Republican mayor of Detroit, who served from 1957 to 1962, was sent to federal prison for tax evasion when he couldn't explain how he made nearly a quarter of a million dollars on a reported salary of only $25,000.

Today—seventy-five years after the beavers disappeared from the Detroit River—"Detroitism" means something completely different. It means uncertainty and abandonment and psychopathology. The city reached a peak population of 1.9 million people in the 1950s, and it was 83 percent white. Now Detroit has fewer than 800,000 people, is 83 percent black, and is the only American city that has surpassed a million people and dipped back below that threshold.

"There are plenty of good people in Detroit," boosters like to say. And there are. Tens of thousands of them, hundreds of thousands. There are lawyers and doctors and auto executives with nice homes and good jobs, community elders trying to make things better, teachers who spend their own money on classroom supplies, people who mow lawns out of respect for the dead, parents who raise their children, ministers who help with funeral expenses.

For years it was the all-but-official policy of the newspapers to ignore the black city, since the majority of readers lived in the predominantly white suburbs. And now that the papers do cover Detroit, boosters complain about a lack of balance. To me, that's like writing about the surf conditions in the Gaza Strip. As for the struggles of a generation of living people, the murder of a hundred children, they ask me: "What's new in that?"

Detroit's East Side is now the poorest, most violent quarter of America's poorest, most violent big city. The illiteracy, child poverty, and unemployment rates hover around 50 percent.

Stand at the corner of Lillibridge Street and Mack Avenue and walk a mile in each direction from Alter Road to Gratiot Avenue (pronounced Gra-*shit*). You will count thirty-four churches, a dozen liquor stores, six beauty salons and barbershops, a funeral parlor, a sprawling Chrysler engine and assembly complex working at less than half capacity, and three dollar stores—but no grocery stores. In fact, there are no chain grocery stores in all of Detroit.

There are two elementary schools in the area, both in desperate need of a lawnmower and a can of paint. But there is no money; the struggling school system has a $363 million deficit. Robert Bobb was hired in 2009 as the emergency financial manager and given sweeping powers to balance the books. But even he couldn't stanch the tsunami of red ink; the deficit ballooned more than $140 million under his guidance.

Bobb did uncover graft and fraud and waste, however. He caught a lunch lady stealing the children's milk money. A former risk manager for the district was indicted for siphoning off $3 million for personal use. The president of the school board, Otis Mathis, recently admitted that he had only rudimentary writing skills shortly before being forced to resign for fondling himself during a meeting with the school superintendent.

The graduation rate for Detroit school kids hovers around 35 percent. Moreover, the Detroit public school system is the worst performer in the National Assessment of Educational Progress tests, with nearly 80 percent of eighth-graders unable to do basic math. So bad is it for Detroit's children that Education Secretary Arne Duncan said last year, "I lose sleep over that one."

Duncan may lie awake, but many civic leaders appear to walk around with their eyes sealed shut. As a reporter, I've worked from New York to St. Louis to Los Angeles, and Detroit is the only big city I know of that doesn't put out a crime blotter tracking the day's mayhem. While other American metropolises have gotten control of their murder rate, Detroit's remains where it was during the crack epidemic. Add in the fact that half the police precincts were closed in 2005 for budgetary reasons, and the crime lab was closed two years ago due to ineptitude, and it might explain why five of the nine members of the city council carry a firearm.

To avoid the embarrassment of being the nation's perpetual murder capital, the police department took to cooking the homicide statistics, reclassifying murders as other crimes or incidents. For instance, in 2008 a man was shot in the head. ME Schmidt ruled it a homicide; the police decided it was a suicide. That year, the police said there were 306 homicides—until I began digging. The number was actually 375. I also found that the police and judicial systems were so broken that in more than 70 percent of murders, the killer got away with it. In Los Angeles, by comparison, the unsolved-murder rate is 22 percent.

The fire department is little better. When I moved back to Detroit two years ago, I profiled a firehouse on the East Side. Much of the firefighters' equipment was substandard: their boots had holes; they were alerted to fires by fax from the central office. (They'd jury-rigged a contraption where the fax pushes a door hinge, which falls on a screw wired to an actual alarm.) I called the fire department to ask for its statistics. They'd not been tabulated for four years.

Detroit has been synonymous with arson since the '80s, when the city burst into flames in a pre-Halloween orgy of fire and destruction known as Devil's Night. At its peak popularity, 810 fires were set in a three-day span. Devil's Night is no longer the big deal it used to be, topping out last year at around 65 arsons. That's good news until you realize that in Detroit, some 500 fires are set every single month. That's five times as many as New York, in a city one-tenth the size.

As a reporter at the *Detroit News,* I get plenty of phone calls from people in the neighborhoods. A man called me once to say he had witnessed a murder but the police refused to take his statement. When I called the head of the homicide bureau and explained the situation, he told me, "Oh yeah? Have him call me," and then hung up the phone. One man, who wanted to turn himself in for a murder, gave up trying to call the Detroit police; he drove to Ohio and turned himself in there.

The police have been working under a federal consent decree since a 2003 investigation found that detectives were locking up murder witnesses for days on end, without access to a lawyer, until they coughed up a name. The department was also cited for excessive force after people died in lockup and at the hands of rogue cops.

Detroit has since made little progress on the federal consent decree. Newspapers made little of it—until the U.S. attorney revealed that the federal monitor of the decree was having an affair with the priapic mayor Kwame Kilpatrick, who was forced to resign, and now sits in prison convicted of perjury and obstruction of justice.

The Kilpatrick scandal, combined with the murder rate, spurred the newly elected mayor, Dave Bing—an NBA Hall of Famer—to fire Police Chief James Barrens last year and replace him with Warren Evans, the Wayne County sheriff. The day Barrens cleaned out his desk, a burglar cleaned out Barrens's house.

Evans brought a refreshing honesty to a department plagued by ineptitude and secrecy. He computerized daily crime statistics, created a mobile strike force commanded by young and educated go-getters, and dispatched cops to crime hot spots. He assigned the SWAT team the job of rounding up murder suspects, a task that had previously been done by detectives.

Evans told me then that major crimes were routinely underreported by 20 percent. He also told me that perhaps 50 percent of Detroit's drivers were operating without a license or insurance. "It's going to stop," he promised. "We're going to pull people over for traffic violations and we're going to take their cars if they're not legal. That's one less knucklehead driving around looking to do a drive-by."

His approach was successful, with murder dropping more than

20 percent in his first year. If that isn't a record for any major metropolis, it is certainly a record for Detroit. (And that statistic is true; I checked.)

So there should have been a parade with confetti and tanks of lemonade, but instead, the complaints about overaggressive cops began to roll in. Then Evans's own driver shot a man last October. The official version was that two men were walking in the middle of a street on the East Side when Evans and his driver told them to walk on the sidewalk. One ran off. Evans's driver—a cop—gave chase. The man stopped, turned, and pulled a gun. Evans's driver dropped him with a single shot. An investigation was promised. The story rated three paragraphs in the daily papers, and the media never followed up. Then Huff got killed. Then Je'Rean was murdered. Then came the homicide-by-cop of little Aiyana.

Chief Evans might have survived it all had he too not been drawn to the lights of Hollywood. As it turns out, he was filming a pilot for his own reality show, entitled *The Chief*.

The program's six-minute sizzle reel begins with Evans dressed in full battle gear in front of the shattered Michigan Central Rail Depot, cradling a semiautomatic rifle and declaring that he would "do whatever it takes" to take back the streets of Detroit. I saw the tape and wrote about its existence after the killing of Aiyana, but the story went nowhere until two months later, when someone in City Hall leaked a copy to the local ABC affiliate. Evans was fired.

But in Evans's defense, he seemed to understand one thing: after the collapse of the car industry and the implosion of the real estate bubble, there is little else Detroit has to export except its misery.

And America is buying. There are no fewer than two TV dramas, two documentaries, and three reality programs being filmed here. Even *Time* bought a house on the East Side last year for $99,000. The gimmick was to have its reporters live there and chronicle the decline of the Motor City for one year.

Somebody should have told company executives back in New York that they had wildly overpaid. In Detroit, a new car costs more than the average house.

Aiyana's family retained Geoffrey Fieger, the flamboyant, brass-knuckled lawyer who represented Dr. Jack Kevorkian—AKA Dr.

Death. With Chief Evans vacationing overseas with a subordinate, Fieger ran wild, holding a press conference where he claimed he had seen videotape of Officer Weekley firing into the house from the porch. Fieger alleged a police coverup. Detroit grew restless.

I went to see Fieger to ask him to show me the tape. Fieger's suburban office is a shrine to Geoffrey Fieger. The walls are covered with photographs of Geoffrey Fieger. On his desk is a bronze bust of Geoffrey Fieger. And during our conversation, he referred to himself in the third person—Geoffrey Fieger.

"What killed Aiyana is what killed the people in New Orleans and the rider on the transit in Oakland, and that's police bullets and police arrogance and police coverup," Geoffrey Fieger said. "People call it police brutality. But Geoffrey Fieger calls it police arrogance. Even in Detroit, a predominantly black city. They killed a child and then they lied about it."

I asked Fieger if Charles Jones should accept some culpability in his daughter's death, considering his alleged role in Je'Rean's murder, the stolen cars found in his backyard, and the fact that his daughter slept on the couch next to an unlocked door.

"So what?" Fieger barked. "I'm not representing the father; I'm speaking for the daughter." He also pointed out that while Jones remains a person of interest in Je'Rean's murder, he has not been arrested. "It's police disinformation."

As for the videotape of the killing, Geoffrey Fieger said he did not have it.

I was allowed to meet with Charles Jones the following morning at Fieger's office, but with the caveat that I could only ask him questions about the evening his daughter was killed.

Jones, twenty-five, a slight man with frizzy braids, wore a dingy T-shirt. An eleventh-grade dropout and convicted robber, he said he supported his seven children with "a little this, a little that—I got a few tricks and trades."

He has three boys with Aiyana's mother, Dominika Stanley, and three boys with another woman, whom he had left long ago.

Jones's new family had been on the drift for the past few years as he tried to pull it together. His mother's house on Lillibridge, he said, was just supposed to be a way station to better things.

They had even kept Aiyana in her old school, Trix Elementary, because it was something consistent in her life, a clean and safe school in a city with too few. They drove her there every morning, five miles.

"I can accept the shooting was a mistake," Jones said about his daughter's death as a bleary-eyed Stanley sat motionless next to him. "But I can't accept it because they lied about it. I can't heal properly because of it. It was all for the cameras. I don't want no apology from no police. It's too late."

I asked him if the way he was raising his daughter, the people he exposed her to, or the neighborhood where they lived—with its decaying houses and liquor stores—may have played a role.

Stanley suddenly emerged from her stupor. "What's that got to do with it?" she hissed.

"My daughter got love, honor, and respect. The environment didn't affect us none," Jones said. "The environment got nothing to do with kids."

Aiyana was laid to rest six days after her killing. The service was held at Second Ebenezer Church in Detroit, a drab cake-shaped megachurch near the Chrysler Freeway. A thousand people attended, as did the predictable plump of media.

The Reverend Al Sharpton delivered the eulogy, though his heart did not seem to be in it. It was a white cop who killed the girl, but Detroit is America's largest black city with a black mayor and a black chief of police. The sad and confusing circumstances of the murders of Je'Rean Blake Nobles and Officer Huff, both black, robbed Sharpton of some of his customary indignation.

"We're here today not to find blame, but to find out how we never have to come here again," said Sharpton, standing in the grand pulpit. "It's easy in our anger, our rage, to just vent and scream. But I would be doing Aiyana a disservice if we just vented instead of dealing with the real problems."

He went on: "This child is the breaking point."

Aiyana's pink-robed body was carried away by a horse-drawn carriage to the Trinity Cemetery, the same carriage that five years earlier had taken the body of Rosa Parks to Woodlawn Cemetery on the city's West Side. Once at Aiyana's graveside, Charles Jones released a dove.

Sharpton left and the Reverend Horace Sheffield, a local version of Sharpton, got stiffed for $4,000 in funeral costs, claiming Aiyana's father made off with the donations people gave to cover it.

"I'm trying to find him," Sheffield complained. "But he doesn't return my calls. It's always like that. People taking advantage of my benevolence. They went hog-wild. I mean, hiring the Rosa Parks carriage?"

"I don't owe Sheffield shit," says Jones. "He got paid exactly what he was supposed to be paid."

While a thousand people mourned the tragic death of Aiyana, the body of Je'Rean Blake Nobles sat in a refrigerator at a local funeral parlor; his mother was too poor to bury him herself and too respectful to bury him until after the little girl's funeral anyhow. The mortician charged $700 for the most basic viewing casket, even though the body was to be cremated.

Sharpton's people called Je'Rean's mother, Lyvonne Cargill, promising to come over to her house after Aiyana's funeral. She waited, but Sharpton never came.

"Sharpton's full of shit," said Cargill, a brassy thirty-nine-year-old who works as a stock clerk at Target. "He came here for publicity. He's from New York. What the hell you doing up here for? The kids are dropping like flies—especially young black males—and he's got nothing but useless words."

The Reverend Sheffield came to see Cargill. He gave her $800 for funeral costs.

As summer dragged on, the story of Aiyana faded from even the regional press. As for the tape that Geoffrey Fieger claimed would show the cops firing on Aiyana's house from outside, A&E turned it over to the police. The mayor's office is said to have a copy, as well as the Michigan State Police, who are now handling the investigation. Even on Lillibridge Street, the outrage has died down. But the people of Lillibridge Street still look like they've been picked up by their hair and dropped from the rooftop. The crumbling houses still crumble. The streetlights still go on and off. The landlord of the duplex, Edward Taylor, let me into the Jones apartment. A woman was in his car, the motor running.

"They still owe me rent," he said with a face about the Joneses. "Don't bother locking it. It's now just another abandoned house in Detroit."

And with that, he was off.

Inside, toys, Hannah Montana shoes, and a pyramid of KFC cartons were left to rot. The smell was beastly. Outside, three men were loading the boiler, tubs, and sinks into a trailer to take to the scrap yard.

"Would you take a job at that Chrysler plant if there were any jobs there?" I asked one of the men, who was sweating under the weight of the cast iron.

"What the fuck do you think?" he said. "Of course I would. Except there ain't no job. We're taking what's left."

I went to visit Cargill, who lived just around the way. She told me that Je'Rean's best friend, Chaise Sherrors, seventeen, had been murdered the night before—an innocent bystander who took a bullet in the head as he was on a porch clipping someone's hair.

"It just goes on," she said. "The silent suffering."

Chaise lived on the other side of the Chrysler complex. He too was about to graduate from Southeastern High. A good kid who showed neighborhood children how to work electric clippers, his dream was to open a barbershop. The morning after he was shot, Chaise's clippers were mysteriously deposited on his front porch, wiped clean and free of hair. There was no note.

If such a thing could be true, Chaise's neighborhood is worse than Je'Rean's. The house next door to his is rubble smelling of burned pine, pissed on by the spray cans of the East Warren Crips. The house on the other side is in much the same state. So is the house across the street. In this shit, a one-year-old played next door, barefoot.

Chaise's mother, Britta McNeal, thirty-nine, sat on the porch staring blankly into the distance, smoking no-brand cigarettes. She thanked me for coming and showed me her home, which was clean and well kept. Then she introduced me to her fourteen-year-old son, De'Erion, whose remains sat in an urn on the mantel. He was shot in the head and killed last year.

She had already cleared a space on the other end of the mantel for Chaise's urn.

"That's a hell of a pair of bookends," I offered.

"You know? I was thinking that," she said with tears.

The daughter of an autoworker and a home nurse, McNeal grew up in the promise of the black middle class that Detroit once offered. But McNeal messed up–she admits as much. She got pregnant at fifteen. She later went to nursing school but got sidetracked by her own health problems. School wasn't a priority. Besides, there was always a job in America when you needed one.

Until there wasn't. Like so many across the country, she's being evicted with no job and no place to go.

"I want to get out of here, but I can't," she said. "I got no money. I'm stuck. Not all of us are blessed."

She looked at her barefoot grandson playing in the wreckage of the dwelling next door and wondered if he would make it to manhood.

"I keep calling about these falling-down houses, but the city never comes," she said.

McNeal wondered how she was going to pay the $3,000 for her son's funeral. Desperation, she said, feels like someone's reaching down your throat and ripping out your guts.

It would be easy to lay the blame on McNeal for the circumstances in which she raised her sons. But is she responsible for police officers with broken computers in their squad cars, firefighters with holes in their boots, ambulances that arrive late, a city that can't keep its lights on and leaves its vacant buildings to the arsonist's match, a state government that allows corpses to stack up in the morgue, multinational corporations that move away and leave poisoned fields behind, judges who let violent criminals walk the streets, school stewards who steal the children's milk money, elected officials who loot the city, automobile executives who couldn't manage a grocery store, or Wall Street grifters who destroyed the economy and left the nation's children with a burden of debt? Can she be blamed for that?

"I know society looks at a person like me and wants me to go away," she said. "'Go ahead, walk in the Detroit River and disappear.' But I can't. I'm alive. I need help. But when you call for help, it seems like no one's there.

"It feels like there ain't no love no more."

I left McNeal's porch and started my car. The radio was tuned to NPR and *A Prairie Home Companion* came warbling out of my speakers. I stared through the windshield at the little boy in the diaper playing amid the ruins, reached over, and switched it off.

CHANG-RAE LEE

Magical Dinners

FROM *The New Yorker*

SO PICTURE THIS: Thanksgiving 1972. The Harbor House apartments on Davenport Avenue, New Rochelle, New York, red brick, low-rise, shot through with blacks and Puerto Ricans and then a smattering of us immigrants, the rest mostly white people of modest means, everyone deciding New York City is going to hell. Or, at least, that's the excuse. The apartments are cramped, hard-used, but the rent is low. Around the rickety dining room table, the end of which nearly blocks the front door, sit my father, my baby sister, myself, and my uncle, who with my aunt has come earlier this fall to attend graduate school. They're sleeping on the pullout in the living room. In the abutting closet-size kitchen, my aunt is helping my mother, who is fretting over the turkey. Look how doughy-faced the grownups still are, so young and slim, like they shouldn't yet be out in the world. My father and uncle wear the same brow-line-style eyeglasses that have not yet gone out of fashion back in Seoul, the black plastic cap over the metal frames making them look perennially consternated, square. My mother and my aunt, despite aprons stained with grease and kimchi juice, look pretty in their colorful polyester blouses with the sleeves rolled up, and vol-leying back and forth between the women and the men is much excited chatter about relatives back home (we're the sole perma-nent emigrants of either clan), of the economy and politics in the old country and in our new one, none of which I'm paying any mind. My sister and I, ages five and seven, the only ones speaking English, are talking about the bird in the oven—our very first—and already bickering over what parts are best, what parts the other

should favor, our conception of it gleaned exclusively from television commercials and illustrations in magazines. We rarely eat
poultry, because my mother is nauseated by the odor of raw
chicken, but early in the preparations she brightly announces that
this larger bird is different—it smells clean, even buttery—and I
can already imagine how my father will slice into the grainy white
flesh beneath the honeyed skin of the breast, this luscious sphere
of meat that is being readied all around the apartment complex.

We like it here, mainly for the grounds outside. There's a grassy
field for tag and ballgames, and a full play set of swings and slides
and monkey bars and three concrete barrels laid on their sides,
which are big enough to sit in and walk upside down around on
your hands (and they offer some privacy too, if you desperately
need to pee). There's a basketball court and two badly cracked asphalt tennis courts that my parents sometimes use, but have to
weed a bit first. So what if teenagers smoke and drink beer on the
benches at night, or if there's broken glass sprinkled about the
playground. We're careful not to lose our footing, and make sure
to come in well before dark.

And you can see the water from here. I like to sit by the windows when I can't go outside. With the right breeze, at low tide
the mucky, clammy smell of Echo Bay flutters through the metal
blinds. Sometimes, for no reason I can give, I lick the sharp edges
of the blinds, the combination of tin and soot and sludgy pier a
funky pepper on the tongue. I already know that I have a bad habit.
I'll sample the window screens too, the paint-cracked radiators, try
the parquet wood flooring after my mother dusts, its slick surface
faintly lemony and then bitter, like the skins of peanuts. I like the
way my tongue buzzes from the copper electroplating on the bottom of her Revere Ware skillet, how it tickles my teeth the way a
penny can't. My mother scolds me whenever she catches me, tells
me I'm going to get sick, or worse. Why do you have to taste everything? What's the matter with you? I don't yet know to say, It's your
fault.

One of my favorite things is to chew on the corner of our red-
and-white-checked plastic tablecloth backed with cotton flocking
and watch the slowly fading impression of my bites. It has the flavor
of plastic, yes, but with a nutty oiliness, and then bears a sharper
tang of the ammonia cleaner my mother obsessively sprays around

our two-bedroom apartment. She'll pull out the jug of bleach too
if she's seen a cockroach. There are grand armies of cockroaches
here, and they're huge. She keeps the place dish clean, but it's
still plagued by the pests stealing over, she is certain, from the
neighboring units. Twice a year, the super bombs the building and
they'll be scarce for a few weeks, until they show up again in the
cupboard, the leaner, faster ones that have survived. You'll hear a
sharp yelp from my mother, and a slammed cabinet door, and then
nothing but harrowing silence before the metallic stink of bug
spray wafts through the apartment like an old-time song. I know I
shouldn't, but sometimes I'll breathe it in deeply, nearly making
myself choke. For I'm a young splendid bug. I live on toxins and
fumes. My mother, on the other hand, is getting more and more
frustrated, hotly complaining to my father when he gets home:
we've lived here for more than a year, and no matter what she does
she can't bar them or kill them, and she's begun to think the only
solution is to move, or else completely clear the kitchen of food-
stuffs, not prepare meals here at all.

Of course, that's ridiculous. First, it's what she does. She does
everything else too, but her first imperative is to cook for us. It's
how she shapes our days and masters us and shows us her displeas-
ure, her weariness, her love. She'll hail my sister and me from the
narrow kitchen window, calling out our names and adding that
dinner's on — *Bap muh-guh!* — the particular register of her voice
instantly sailing to us through the hot murk and chaos of the playground. It's as if we had special receptors, vestigial ears in our bel-
lies. There's a quickening, a sudden hop in the wrong direction: I
gotta go! My mother is becoming notorious among the kids; they'll
whine, with scorn and a note of envy, Hey, your mom's always calling you! And one big-framed, older girl named Kathy, who has
sparkling jade-colored eyes and a prominent, bulging forehead
that makes her look like a dolphin, viciously bullies me about it,
taunting me, saying that I eat all the time, that I'm going to be a
tub o' lard, that I love my mother too much. I say it's not true,
though I fear it is. Plus, I'm terrified of Kathy, who on other days
will tenderly pat my head and even hug me, telling me I'm cute,
before suddenly clamping my ear, pinching harder and harder until my knees buckle; once she even makes me lob curses up at our
kitchen window, words so heinous that they might as well be rocks.

I remember my mother poking her head out and peering down, her expression tight, confused, most of all fearful of what I might be saying, and immediately I sob. Kathy sweetly tells her that I'm hungry. My mother, who understands little English and is maybe scared of this girl too, softly orders me to come in, then pulls in the casement window.

Once I'm upstairs, she offers me a snack—cookies, *kimbap*, a bowl of hot watery rice, which I eat with tiny squares of ham or leftover *bulgogi*, one spoon at a time. I eat while watching her cook. If she's not cleaning or laundering, she's cooking. Every so often, she'll make a point of telling me she hates it, that she no longer wants to bother but she has to because we must save money. We can't waste money eating out. My father is a newly minted psychiatrist, but his salary at the Bronx VA hospital is barely respectable, and we have no savings, no family in this country, no safety net. We dine out maybe four times a year, three of those for Chinese (there are no Korean restaurants yet), and the rest of the time my mother is at the stove—breakfast, lunch, dinner, as well as making snacks for us midmorning and afternoon, and then late at night for my father when he gets home. The other reality is that my parents don't want to eat non-Korean food; they want to hold on to what they know. What else do they have but the taste of those familiar dishes, which my mother can, for the most part, recreate from ingredients at the nearby A&P. She's grateful for the wide, shiny aisles of the chilled supermarket and its brightly lit inventory of canned goods and breakfast cereals and ice cream, but the cabbage is the wrong kind and the meat is oddly butchered and the fish has been set out on the shaved ice prefilleted, so she can't tell how fresh it is, and she can't make a good broth without the head and bones and skin. But she makes do; there's always garlic, often ginger and scallions, and passable hot peppers. We still have a few cups of the ground red-pepper powder that friends brought over from Seoul, and every once in a while we can get the proper oils and fresh tofu and dried anchovies and sheets of roasted seaweed on a Sunday drive down to Chinatown.

We adore those Chinatown days. I love them especially because it means we skip church and the skeptical regard of the pastor and his wife and the bellowing Hananims and Amens from the congre-

gation that for me are calls to slumber—a break that I see now
my parents welcome too. Somewhere on Bayard or Mott Street,
we'll have a lunch of soup noodles or dim sum and do the shopping with an eye on the time, because the parking lot is expensive
and by the hour, and, despite the parade-level litter and the grimy
bins of dying eels and carp and the lacquer of black crud on the
sidewalks, which she would never otherwise tolerate, my mother
seems calmed by the Asian faces and the hawker carts of fried pot
stickers and gooey rice cakes and the cans of stewed mackerel and
chiles filling the shelves. She'll go unexpectedly slowly through
the crammed aisles of the dry-goods store, lingering over selections that aren't exactly what she's looking for but that nonethe-
less speak to her in a voice I imagine sounds very much like her
own: Take your time, silly girl. Enjoy yourself. You're not going
anywhere. Soon enough, the bags of groceries are teetering like
drowsy siblings between my sister and me in the back seat of our
navy-blue Beetle as we swerve up the FDR Drive. The seats are covered in a light-gray leatherette stippled like the back of a lizard,
which I'm constantly picking at with my fingernail, inevitably running over with my tongue. It tastes of erasers and throw-up. My father is one of those people who drive by toggling on and off the
gas pedal, lurching us forward for brief stretches and then coast-
ing, the rattling of the fifty-three-horsepower engine establishing
the dread prophetic beat, my sister and I know, of our roadside
retching—one of us, and sometimes both, barely stumbling out of
the car in time to splash the parkway asphalt, stucco the nettles.
Now, with the odor of dried squid and spring onions and raw pork
enveloping us, we'd be doomed, but luckily we don't have too far
to go to get back to New Rochelle; my father will let us out before
searching for a parking spot, my sister and I sprinting for the playground while my mother goes upstairs to empty the bags.

On those post-Chinatown evenings, she'll set out a plate of fluke
or snapper sashimi to start (if she finds any fresh enough), which
she serves with *gochu-jang* sauce, then broiled spareribs and scal-
lion fritters and a spicy cod-head stew along with the *banchan* of
vegetables and kimchi, and it's all so perfect-looking, so gorgeous,
that we let out that whimpering, joyous, half-grieving sigh of people long marooned. Yet often enough, apparently, the dishes don't
taste exactly the way they should. My father, the least imperious of

men, might murmur the smallest something about the spicing of a dish, its somewhat unusual flavorings, and my mother will bitterly concur, lamenting the type of fermented bean paste she has to use, the stringy quality of the meat, how these Chinatown radishes have no flavor, no crunch, instantly grinding down her lovely efforts to a wan, forgettable dust. We protest in earnest, but it's no use; she's not seeking compliments or succor. She can get frantic; she's a natural perfectionist and worrier made over, by this life in a strange country, into someone too easily distraught. In Korea, she's a forthright, talented, beautiful woman, but here, at least outside this apartment, she is a woman who appears even slighter than she already is, a woman who smiles quickly but never widely, a foreigner whose English comes out self-throttled, barely voiced, who is listening to herself to the point of a whisper.

Never quite up to her own exalted standards, she is often frustrated, dark-thinking, on edge. Periodically I'll catch her gripped in fury at herself for not quite comprehending, say, the instructions on a box of Rice-A-Roni or Hamburger Helper (seemingly magical dinners that my sister and I whine for, despite not actually liking the stuff), revealed in her wringing the packet like a towel until it's about to burst, then remorsefully opening it and smoothing it out and trying to decipher the back of the box again. I do something similar with toys that I can't get to work properly, or am tiring of, or sometimes—and with an unequaled, almost electric pleasure—the ones I value most. I'll take the claw end of a hammer and pry open the roof of a Hot Wheels car, the enamel paint flaking off from the twisting force and gilding my fingertips. I'll squeeze the clear plastic canopy of the model P-51 Mustang I've carefully assembled until it collapses, the head of the tiny half-pilot inside shearing off. We are mother and son in this way—we share a compulsion we don't admire in the other but never call out either, and right up to the unsparingly frigid night she dies, nineteen years later, and even now, another nineteen on, I'll prickle with that heat in my foolish, foolish hands.

A few years earlier, when we briefly lived in Manhattan—this before I can articulate my feelings for her, before I understand how completely and perfectly I can hurt her—I make her cry because of a fried egg. She cooks an egg for me each morning without fail. I might also have with it fried Spam or cereal or a slice of American cheese, which I'll unwrap myself and fold over into sixteen rough-edged pieces, but always there is a fried egg, sunny-side up, cooked in dark sesame oil that pools on the surface of the bubbled-up white in the pattern of an archipelago; try one sometime, laced with soy and sweet chili sauce along with steamed rice, the whole plate flecked with toasted nori. It'll corrupt you for all time. But one morning I'm finally sick of it, I've had enough. She never makes an exception, because it's for my health—everything is for my health, for the good of my bones, my brain, for my daunting, uncertain future—but rather than eat yet another, I steal into her bedroom with my plate while she's talking on the telephone with Mrs. Suh (at that time her only friend in the country) and drop it onto her best shoes, black patent-leather pumps. And here's the rub: there is no sound a fried egg makes. It lands with exquisite silence. This is the dish I've been longing to prepare.

Do I confess what I've done? Does my face betray the crime? All I remember is how my mother, still holding the phone, and my baby sister, usually squirming in her high chair, both pause and stare at me as I return to the kitchen table. My mother bids Mrs. Suh good-bye and stands over me, eyeing my plate swiped clean save for the glistening oil. Without a word from either of us, I'm dragged forth, her hand gripping my elbow, and we're inexplicably moving. It's as if a homing beacon only she can hear were madly pinging from her bedroom, where I've left the sliding closet door open for all to see my work: the yolk broken and oozing inside the well of one shoe, the rubbery white flopped over the shiny ebony toe. It's a jarring, bizarrely artful mess; boxed in Lucite, it could be titled "Stepping Out, 4," or "Mother's Day Fugue," but of course she can't see it that way because she's hollering, her morning robe falling open because she's shaking so violently, stamping her foot. The end of the robe's belt is bunched in her tensed fist, and I think, She may kill me, actually kill me. Or my father will do the job when he gets home. But I'm hugging her leg now, my face pressed against her hip, and as much as I'm afraid for myself, I'm confused too, and frightened for her, for tears are distorting her eyes, and she's saying, in a voice that I will hear always for its quaver of defiance and forfeit, how difficult everything is, how wrong and difficult.

She's too indulgent of us, especially of me. I love to eat, so it's easy for her, though also at times a burden for us both. Each morning at breakfast, after the egg, she asks me what I want for dinner, and except when my father requests Japanese-style curry rice, which I despise (though I enjoy it now) and show my disgust for by dragging my chair into the kitchen and closing the louvered doors to "get away" from the smell, my choice is what we'll have. As with an emperor, my whims become real. Dinners-from-a-box aside, I have wide-ranging tastes, but increasingly it's American food I want, dishes I encounter while eating at friends' apartments, at summer camp, even in the cafeteria at school: meat loaf (with a boiled egg in the middle), southern fried chicken and mashed potatoes, beef Stroganoff over egg noodles, lasagna. These dishes are much heavier and plainer than ours, but more thrilling to me and my sister and perhaps even to my parents, for it is food without association, unlinked to any past; it's food that fixes us to this moment only, to this place we hardly know.

My mother, having no idea how the dishes should taste, at first struggles to prepare them, going solely by recipes that she copies into a small notebook from a new friend in the building, Mrs. Churchill, an always smiling, blond-haired, broad-shouldered woman who hails from Vermont and has a shelf of classic cookbooks. It's excruciatingly slow going at the A&P as my mother runs down her shopping list—it's as if she were at the library searching for a book in the stacks, trying to find the particular spices and herbs, the right kind of macaroni, the right kind of cheese or cream (heavy or sour or cream or cottage cheese and a perhaps related cheese called ricotta and the deeply puzzling cheese that is Parmesan, which comes in a shaker, and is unrefrigerated), the right canned tomatoes (chopped or crushed or puréed—what, exactly, is "puréed"?), each decision another chance to mar the dish beyond my ignorant recognition. I can be tyrannical, if I wish. I can squash her whole day's work with a grimace, or some blithe utterance: It's fatty. It's too peppery. It doesn't taste the same. You can watch her face ice over. Shatter. Naturally, she can't counter me, and this makes her furious, but soon enough she's simply miserable, her pretty eyes gone lightless and faraway, which is when I relent and tell her it's still good, because of course it is, which I demonstrate by shoving the food in as fast as I can, stuffing my awful mouth.

Her lasagna is our favorite of that suite, though to taste it now I fear it might disappoint me, for the factory sauce (which I demand

she use, this after noticing jars of Ragú at both the Goldfusses' and
the Stanleys') and the rubbery, part-skim mozzarella, the cut-rate
store-brand pasta, the dried herbs. But back then, it's a revelation.
Our usual dinners feature salty fish and ginger, garlic and hot pepper; they are delicious in part because you can surgically pick at
the table, choose the exact flavor you want. But this is a detonation
of a meal: creamy, cheesy, the red sauce contrastingly tangy and a
little sweet, the oozing, volcanic layer cake of the pasta a thrilling,
messy bed. Maybe I first have it at Ronnie Prunesti's house, or Mrs.
Churchill delivers a show model, but all of us are crazy for it once
my mother begins to make it. We choose our recipe (was it on the
box of macaroni?), our tools. I remember how she carefully picked
out a large Pyrex casserole dish at Korvette's for the job, a new
plastic spatula, two checkerboard wooden trivets, so we can place it
in the center of the table, and for a few years it becomes a Friday
evening tradition for us. She makes it in the afternoon after dropping me off in town for my junior bowling league, and when she
and my sister pick me up I hardly care to recount my form or my
scores (I'm quite good for a second-grader, good enough that my
father decides that I should have my own ball, which is, whether
intentionally or erroneously, inscribed "Ray") owing to the wonderful smell on their clothes, clinging to my mother's thick hair —
that baked, garlicky aroma, like a pizzeria's but denser because of
the ground beef and the hot Italian sausages she has fried, the
herbal lilt of fennel seeds.

My father gets home early on Fridays, and while he takes off his
tie and washes up for dinner my sister and I set the table with forks
and knives (but without chopsticks, since I insist that there be no
side of rice and kimchi at this meal, as there is at every other), folding the paper napkins into triangles. My mother brings out a bowl
of iceberg-and-tomato-and-carrot salad, a dish of garlic bread, my
sister waiting for the Good Seasons Italian dressing to separate so
she can start shaking it again. I wonder aloud if my father ought to
retrieve from the top of the kitchen cabinet the clay-colored ceramic bottle of Lancers they got as a present (they rarely drink), if
only because it makes the table look right. They do, although the
wine is old, for they forget that they opened it a month before,
when a classmate came through New York. But no matter. They
don't know that the wine has soured. My mother will lift out fat

squares of the casserole, the fine strings of cheese banding across the table; I scissor them with my fingers and flinch at the tiny-striped burn. We feast. Only my sister can eat just one. Who cares that it's too rich for us to handle, who cares that our family afflic-tion of mild lactose intolerance will surely lead to guffaws and antic hand-fanning during the Friday night repeat of the Million Dollar Movie. Here is the meal we've been working toward, yearning for. Here is the unlikely shape of our life together—this ruddy pie, what we have today and forever.

This is what a boy thinks, a boy with a tongue for a brain, a heart.

Now my mother is nearly done baking the turkey. Bake she must, because there's no Roast setting on the oven. It reads "Roast" in Mrs. Churchill's beautifully handwritten instructions, and the Churchills have gone away for the holiday. There's no one else we can call—at least, no one who would know. It certainly smells good, as if we were going to have a soup of pure fat. Yet my mother desperately peers in at the bird, the tendrils of her hair stuck against her temples, biting her lower lip, as she does whenever she's frustrated or unsure of herself. She has been basting it with margarine and the pan juices, but I can see she's deeply worried, for the bird was still slightly frozen when my father shoved it in, and we've been baking instead of roasting and we have no meat thermometer ("Why didn't I buy one!"), and at some point amid the continuous conversation with my uncle and aunt we've lost ex-act track of the time.

My mother has readied other food, of course, if none of the tra-ditional accompaniments. We'll have the bird and its giblet stuffing à la Churchill (a recipe I still make), but the rest of the table is laid with Korean food, and skewed fancy besides, featuring the sort of dishes reserved for New Year celebrations: *gu jeol pan*, a nine-compartment tray of savory fillings from which delicate little crepes are made; a jellyfish-and-seaweed salad; long-simmered sweet short ribs; fried hot peppers stuffed with beef; and one of my favorites, thin slices of raw giant clam, whose bottom-of-the-sea essence al-most makes me gag, but doesn't quite, and is thus bracing, gal-vanic, a rushing of the waters. Yet because of what's happening in the kitchen, we're not paying much attention; we're distracted by

our celebrity guest, so buxom and tanned. My mother decides it's
time; a piece of plastic has popped up from the breast, though exactly when she's not sure. My father helps her pull the turkey out
and they lift it from the pan, cradling it with butcher string, onto
the platter. We quickly take our places. Do we remove the stuffing
now or serve it directly from the bird? The instructions don't say.
After some discussion, it's decided that it should be left in — the
bird might look too empty, sad. My father wields the new carving
knife he's bought, a long, scary blade with a saw-toothed edge on
one side and smaller serrations on the other. My mother winces.
The knife strobes: the first cut is deep, surprisingly easy.

MADGE McKEITHEN

What Really Happened

FROM *TriQuarterly*

FIND THE NORTH CAROLINA Department of Correction Public Access Information System website. Enter the name of the offender. Write down the seven-digit offender ID number. Click on the box to see the photograph. Or you can do this later.

Write down the name of the correctional institution in which he is incarcerated. Write down the name of the corrections officer who will coordinate your visit. If you are invited.

Ask a friend who is a lawyer to search the record to make sure the offender is not insane. Write down the name and telephone number of the lawyer who handled the offender's appeal and who is now a judge. Call him. If you must leave a message, say *I am considering visiting . . .* and use the offender's name . . . Say *I am a friend of . . .* and use the victim's name. Say you would appreciate his thoughts on what to expect, given his knowledge of the offender's mental state. Be direct (others have called before you with similar questions).

Answer the phone courteously at 8:30 on a summer Saturday evening. Thank him for calling back. Listen to the judge say *You should go.* Listen to him say that once you've been incarcerated twelve years, most visitors, even mothers, stop visiting. Listen to him say *Murderers are not like the shark in* Jaws, *they are not monsters, usually* and *They are more like you and me than we may want to know.*

Thank the judge and walk quickly outside because you know walking in the city helps everything. Walk to the river. Walk along the river for a while. Watch normal people doing normal things. Find balance.

Return home. Take a note card from the desk by the front door and write the request for an invitation to visit. Be direct. Make it three sentences.

Remember that you knew the offender. Remember what he has done. Remember he can invite you or he can refuse. Remember her.

Use *sincerely* to close. Put the note in an envelope and address it. Put a stamp on the envelope and look again at the address. Check the seven numbers after his name. Make sure you have them right. Leave the envelope by the door to be mailed Monday morning.

Tell one person you trust that you are requesting an invitation to visit a murderer you know in prison. Say *Yes, life sentence.* Say *No, no chance of parole.* Listen when your friend asks *Why are you going?* Listen to yourself when you say *Because I loved her.*

Early on Monday walk to the post office two blocks away and drop the card in the inside mail slot.

Wait for a response.

Call the other two who knew her well when you did. Talk together. Mention her freckles, her strawberry blond hair, how good she was in math, how well she danced, how much you laughed together, what a ringleader she was, an instigator, how she was the first among you to have sex but not by much, how you went over every detail she would give up that night at the Pizza Inn all-you-can-eat buffet. Say you have been thinking about her because you are all turning fifty. Do not bother them with your thoughts of visiting prison.

Wait for an invitation.

Find the Christmas cards with family photos she sent each year. Look at the two of them and their three children on the beach, costumed, poised, staged, fun—one year in ski clothes, another in Mickey Mouse ears. Look at her children. Count back—estimate five, eight, twelve that morning. Count forward—estimate nineteen, twenty-one, twenty-five now. Probably older.

Look at the newspaper clipping your mother sent of the first-born's wedding. Look at the old photos of her wedding. Call the other two friends again. Call her mother. Do not leave a message. Remember more high school silliness, a little college silliness, the long blank of the years after. (Note: remembering a blank may leave you quiet.)

Ask yourself why you get to be alive.

Take the long envelope fat with pages out of your mailbox. Read the tiny handwriting pressed hard into the notebook paper on two sides. Twenty pages. Notice the putdowns. Notice the excess verbiage. Imagine that he has little else to do. Notice no kindness.

See the invitation to visit the offender in prison. Notice his words. Put the pages back in the envelope and look at the calendar. Find three dates. Write back. Receive a response. Choose a date. Rent a car. Drive 528 miles to Bayford Correctional Institute. Think of her first car—that red Triumph Spitfire. Remember her energy, the curves of her body, her hands.

Drive all day. Do not call anyone. Be quiet. Listen to music. Be quiet. Drive down the Delmarva Peninsula, the out-of-the-way place that it is, especially at the southern tip. Drive over the Bay Bridge Tunnel. Keep driving. Do not stop.

Arrive in Oriental at the B&B you booked. Let yourself in. Follow the instructions left on the table by the door. Find your attic room. Brush your teeth. Wash your face. Go to bed. Stare at the ceiling.

Hear *You are there for* her . . . *to see, ask, hear . . . because she isn't.*

Sleep. Awake and find the muffin and coffee at the base of the stairs to the attic room. Dress in clothes that cover. Notice the rain on the rental car. Notice that the town is still quiet. Notice that there are more sailboats than cars in this town called Oriental. Follow the MapQuest directions to the prison. Notice it is all gray and wet—the building, parking lot, fence, razor wire.

Look at the official visitor instructions that came in the mail. Take only your car keys, four dollar bills, your lip balm, and your driver's license. Lock the car. Wait with the others outside the kiosk that looks like a Cineplex ticket booth. Look neither worried nor curious. Do not look directly at the other visitors.

Wait for the loud buzzer to sound. Line up. Show ID. State the name and number of the offender. Sign your name. Go through metal detectors. Pass through automatic doors that open and shut with a *Star Trek*–like *whoosh*. Continue inward. Wait for more automatic doors to open and close—two of them. Enter what looks like a cafeteria.

Hear the guard say *The offender must sit facing the clock.* Sit in the chair with its back to the clock.

Look at him when he enters. Show nothing. See how much older he looks. See that he has no teeth. Listen for two hours.

Notice he always says *The tragedy that happened.* Notice he never says *I killed.* Ask *Why could you not just let her go? Why leave the children with neither parent?* Hear *I had come to believe they would be better off with her mom.* Hear *It takes courage to do difficult things.* Hear *Like the men who flew into the World Trade Center towers.* Hear no remorse. Hear no regret.

Buy a soda from the vending machine as the visitor instructions permit. Hand it to him. Sit back down.

Wait for the time to be up. When the time is up, walk to the door. (Note: You may feel oily, dark, in need of a Brillo pad to scour off everything that has come toward you in these hours, and the feeling may be physical and metaphorical.) Drive north through the Great Dismal Swamp. Keep driving. Drive home.

Receive the hundreds of pages of letters he sends over the next six months. Save them for a while. Keep thinking of her. (That part is not hard.) Write from her son's perspective. Write it as fiction. Write from her perspective. Listen.

Ask. *Where are her words?*

Shred his.

Wait several years. Attend a wedding. Be sociable. Hear the charming man next to you talk about his four children, his wife, that his father killed his mother when he was small, his career, his hopes for his children, his love for the grandmother who raised him. Talk to him about family and fun and food and New Orleans. Laugh. Dance with your man.

Hear her now. Hear *Love life.* Hear *Love especially those who have no need for the word "lugubrious."* Hear *That's it.*

Say back *What really happened is your life.*

CARYL PHILLIPS

Rude Am I in My Speech

FROM *Salmagundi*

PERHAPS THE MOST ARRESTING MOMENT in the first act of
Shakespeare's *Othello* occurs when the soldier is asked by the Duke
of Venice to respond to the accusation that he has "beguiled" Bra-
bantio's daughter, Desdemona, away from the protection and
safety of her father's house. The soldier is an outwardly confident
man, full of pride and bombast, and hugely aware of his celebrity
in Venice. He addresses the Duke. "Rude am I in my speech," he
says, then spins a masterfully persuasive narrative full of lyrical elo-
quence which the Duke acknowledges would have ensnared his
own daughter too. The poised, silver-tongued soldier is vindicated
and the play can proceed. What is firmly established in this first act
is that Othello is an outsider both racially and socially. In this thor-
oughly demarcated Venetian world where Michael Cassio is simply
"a Florentine," the "old black ram," although he claims to be de-
scended from "men of royal siege," is regarded as little more than
an "extravagant and wheeling stranger." For the full length of the
first act, what Shakespeare does *not* allow us to see is that for all
Othello's public success there is at the center of his personality a
kernel of self-doubt, a tight knot of anxiety, which is eventually ex-
ploited by his ancient Iago. During this first act the soldier appears
to be in control. He plays games, protesting that he has a clumsy
tongue even though his language betrays no hint of rudeness or
foreign taint. If Othello possesses any self-doubt, or inner discomfort, its origins are not rooted in language. What if he had begun
his mellifluous speech with, "Rude am I in my visage"? Would this
self-assured black migrant to Europe have had the confidence to

stand before the Duke of Venice and play fearlessly with notions of identity and belonging that are rooted in race as opposed to language, or would this be to trespass too close to the source of his well-hidden self-doubt?

Almost ten years ago, I arranged to meet my father at lunchtime in a hotel in Manchester. The night before I had given a reading at a local bookshop, and that afternoon I was planning to move on to Liverpool and give another reading at the university. My father lives maybe an hour away from Manchester, and so this seemed an opportune moment to get together. What made the meeting unusual was the fact that we had not seen or spoken with each other for some years. I came down into the hotel lobby a little early, but there he was, already sprawled out on a sofa and watching the news on the television. He saw me and stood up. I was glad to see him. He had not changed much, and we hugged and I suggested that we go to another hotel around the corner, which had a nicer restaurant. There were very few people in the place and the hostess seated us and gave us our menus. She asked if we would like a drink to start with. My father ordered a Scotch and I asked for a glass of Sauvignon Blanc, and, having informed us of the specials, the hostess left us alone. Five minutes later a waitress arrived with our drinks. As she withdrew we raised our glasses and clinked, and then I sipped and grimaced. My father asked me if there was a problem and I said that the wine was not Sauvignon Blanc. It tasted like Chardonnay. I signaled to the waitress and then I saw a flicker of panic pass across my father's face. He asked me if I couldn't drink it. I said, "Why, it's not what I ordered." The waitress came over and I explained the situation. She shrugged her shoulders and took up my glass. There was no apology, but there was no surliness either as she disappeared from view. My father remained quiet and I could see that he was uncomfortable. For a few moments I made inane conversation; at last the waitress returned with the new glass of wine and I tasted it. Better, I thought, so I nodded and thanked her and she left us alone. However, this incident caused the atmosphere between father and son to become strained.

First-generation migrants to Europe, from wherever they may originate, have to learn quickly how to read the new society in order to successfully navigate their way forward. Sometimes this involves learning when to remain quiet, and somewhat compliant, and not risk causing offense. When West Indians first arrived in England in the 1950s, countless pamphlets were thrust into their hands which explained to them the ways of the English. They were instructed that they must line up at bus stops in an orderly fashion, and not keep working when their fellow laborers were on a tea break, and it was suggested that they should try to join a trade union, and perhaps they should not bring food that smelled "foreign" to work. In common with many immigrants, they were being taught how to tread carefully, the unspoken contract being that in time they would learn the rules and become familiar with how the society worked; so much so that one day they might be considered domesticated. Whether they would ever become fully fledged insiders was not discussed, but for many first-generation migrants this was not something that was necessarily desired. The hope on both sides was for some vestige of tolerance and respect.

There are, of course, two places where new immigrants can find some relief from these anxieties of belonging. First, at home with their families, where the rules are of their own making and no local person can prevent them from being kings and queens in their own castles. Behind closed doors they can cook their own food, listen to whatever music takes their fancy, and curse the locals in whatever tongue or dialect they choose. And then of course there is the world of the pub, or the club, or the café, where immigrants gather together socially and over a drink compare notes with others of their own tribe. The home and the social gathering place constitute zones of psychological relief for immigrants. In such spaces one doesn't have to be called Sam or Son, or take aggressive orders from ignorant people half one's age. In the kingdom of the home, or in the citadel of the club, first-generation migrants are free to be whoever they imagine, or remember, themselves to be, and there is no expectation that they should perform the shape-shifting dance that immigrants often have to execute in order to safely negotiate a passage from sunup to sundown. Of course, the more successful the immigrant, the more difficult it can be to keep in touch with the "club." Upon assuming a white-collar job as a foreman, or an executive role in a company, the rules become more complex, for there are now men and women above you and men and women below you, and with the job comes a salary increase and perhaps a move to a new neighborhood where there are less of you and more of them. To keep contact with fellow migrants one has to now travel further, both physically and psychologically.

During the first, Venetian act of Shakespeare's play, before the action moves off to Cyprus, it is clear to us that Othello, this "extravagant and wheeling stranger," is a man who is a long way from home. In Venice he is an exotic celebrity, and as such the Duke is inclined to overlook the social and cultural transgression of not only an interracial marriage but a secret one, therefore allowing Othello to indulge in behavior that would almost certainly be frowned upon if attempted by a noncelebrity. This being the case, this extravagant stranger appears to be untroubled by the fact that he has recourse to neither home nor club as places to which he might retreat and recuperate from the daily fatigue of living a performative life, and he appears content to veer dramatically between rhetorical swagger and self-deprecating bluster like a kite snapping in the wind. Apparently he feels that his success is such that there is no need for him to be aware of the unwritten Venetian rule book which tells him that he must line up in an orderly fashion for a gondola, and don't even think about cooking chickpeas or couscous, and whatever you do don't mess with the local ladies, especially the titled ones. Our celebrity migrant considers himself above and beyond such restrictive nonsense. By the end of Act One the newly married man truly believes that he has crossed over into full acceptance, but the truth is, without family or peer group, and without societal knowledge born of vigilance and judicious interaction, he is incapable of making sound decisions about something as basic as knowing who to trust. It soon becomes lamentably evident that, far from being in control of the situation and participating as an insider, our black first-generation migrant to Europe is about as unmoored as any man can be.

My father is no Othello. He may have polished up a few words and phrases here and there, and done a little studying of the dictionary, but to this day he remains admirably rude in speech. But then again he has never been a vital or essential cog in British life and occupied the role of supermigrant. What West Indian immigrant has? In fact, what immigrant has? As a first-generation migrant he has always been aware of the home and the club as zones of sanity in which he can be himself. Like most second-generation children, I have at times been puzzled and frustrated by his dependence upon one form or another of the "club," and irritated by the taciturn manner in which he often exercised his authority in the home; not that he was always wrong. When I was fifteen or sixteen, I remember one Saturday night standing upstairs in front of the mirror and preparing myself to go out to the church discotheque. Eventually I ventured downstairs wearing tight blue nylon bellbottoms, black platform shoes, a pink shirt with a huge collar that was trimmed in brown piping, and a black-and-white-checked jacket. My father was sitting at the kitchen table and he looked up at me over the top of his newspaper. He shook his head and said, "Somebody tell you that shit matches?" The second generation was stepping out into England with a confidence and brashness that, in retrospect, could have used a little more of his cold water being poured upon it. It was his house and he was trying to tell me something about how to look and comport myself out there on the streets, like the time a year or two later when I passed my driving test and he told me that I must be very careful if I was out driving at night with a white girl in the passenger seat. He warned me that I should be prepared to have the police stop and harass me for no other reason than the fact that I was with a white girl. Again he was passing on knowledge which was meant both to help prepare me for life in England and to reaffirm who he was when in his own private sphere. I listened, and I assumed that my father knew what he was talking about, for at the time he had a white wife.

As a reader and a writer, I am interested in loneliness and isolation, and I have found myself returning time and time again to consider those who have suddenly realized themselves to be marooned. Richard Wright's Bigger Thomas in that huge Chicago mansion, scared out of his mind and not knowing whether to stay put or flee; Ibsen's Oswald, recently returned to Norway with his body eaten away by disease and his mind racked with pain at the bleakness of his own country; James Baldwin's David, alone in a house in the South of France at precisely the time his lover, Giovanni, is about to be guillotined in Paris; Shusaku Endo's medical intern, Suguro, whose conscience begins to torment him as he remembers the past and finds himself increasingly detached from daily reality. However, I know of no character in literature more profoundly alone and isolated than Shakespeare's pioneer migrant

Othello, who, once he passes beyond the imaginary security of his life in the great city of water, suddenly finds himself adrift with no son or daughter to measure his situation against, no peer group to bond with at the end of the day, no Venetian home to return to, and loving a local woman whom he eventually decides he cannot trust. No wonder he loses his mind.

Immigrants will continue to enter Europe, and initially they will be unsure of how to be an Italian, or how to be a Dane, or Irish or Greek. It takes many years for a first-generation migrant, of any race, to become socially confident, and perhaps, in the end, it is only those closest to them, the second generation, who can fully understand the price they pay as they grapple with self-doubt and attempt to hitch their fortune (and talent) to a new country. I am beginning to feel that witnessing and recording the predicament of the first generation is a responsibility, because by the time we reach the commendably brash third generation, a parental comment about one's dress, or how to be circumspect in the street, is likely to be met with a bemused and slightly disdainful "What are you on about?" As the grandchildren enter fully and boldly into the country with not only the temerity of an Othello but, crucially, armed with the social knowledge and understanding that the Venetian resident didn't have, or seem to desire, the kernel of self-doubt which speaks to either social standing or race is, in their lives, beginning to disappear. Nervous hesitation will once again be visited upon the next wave of first-generation migrants, wherever they might hail from, and to the list of potential sources of anxiety to be negotiated we might add religious belief. Rude am I in my speech. Rude am I in my visage. Rude am I in my faith. When I left my father in Manchester that lunchtime, and took the train to Liverpool, I began to think about first-generation diffidence, and again I reflected upon the supreme loneliness of the migrant to Venice, who also had a white wife, but it never occurred to him that the police were going to pull him over, until, of course, it was too late.

BRIDGET POTTER

Lucky Girl

FROM *Guernica*

IN 1962, I WAS NINETEEN, working in my first job, living in my first apartment, having sex with my first real boyfriend. Michael was a tall, thick-haired Italian from the Bronx. For birth control, I was using fluffy pink foam from an aerosol can. I had heard about it from dark-banged, bespectacled Emily Perl in the television production office where I had my first job. I was the floater, filling in when a secretary went to lunch or the switchboard operator needed to go to the bathroom. Emily was a researcher and married. She used the foam as backup to her diaphragm. At the time it was illegal for a gynecologist to prescribe a diaphragm for a single woman, and I didn't have the nerve to lie. As for condoms, what little I knew of them was that they were disgusting, unreliable, and boys didn't like to use them anyway.

Emily Perl knew a single girl who had been buying the pink foam illicitly from a pharmacy on Madison Avenue and using it—no diaphragm—without a problem. It was a spermicide. When the white-coated pharmacist handed me the plain white box of contraband from beneath the counter I tried to ignore his knowing leer. Sperm killer sounded safe and safe is what I wanted to be.

I used the pink foam.

My period was late.

Historian Rickie Solinger in her book *Wake Up Little Susie* describes what it was like to have an unwanted pregnancy in 1962. The woman might be "futilely appealing to a hospital abortion committee; being diagnosed as neurotic, even psychotic by a mental health professional; expelled from school (by law until 1972); unemployed; in a Salvation Army or some other maternity home; poor, alone, ashamed, threatened by the law." There was also an acute social stigma attached to an unwed mother with an illegitimate child; maternity homes were frequently frightening and far away. All counseled adoption. The only alternatives were a shotgun wedding or an illegal abortion.

According to a 1958 Kinsey study, illegal abortion was the option chosen by 80 percent of single women with unwanted pregnancies. Statistics on illegal abortion are notoriously unreliable, but the Guttmacher Institute, a respected international organization dedicated to sexual and reproductive health, estimates that during the pre–*Roe v. Wade* years there were up to one million illegal abortions performed in the United States each year. Illegal and often unsafe. In 1965, they count almost two hundred known deaths from illegal abortions, but the actual number was, they estimate, much higher, since the majority went unreported.

Michael and I checked around for remedies. First we had a lot of energetic sex, even though we were hardly in the mood. That didn't work. One night I sat in an extremely hot bath in my walk-up on Waverly Place while Michael fed me a whole quart of gin, jelly jar glass by jelly jar glass. In between my gulps, he refreshed the bath with boiling water from a saucepan on the crusty old gas stove. I got beet-red and nauseous. We waited. I threw up. Nothing more. Another night I ran up and down the apartment building's six flights of stairs, Michael waiting at the top to urge me to go back down and do it again.

On a Friday evening, I drank an overdose of castor oil. By midnight I had horrible cramps of the wrong kind in the wrong place.

When my period was a month late I gave up hoping for a false alarm and went to visit Emily Perl's gynecologist. His ground-floor office in a brownstone on a side street on the Upper East Side was genteel but faded. So was he, a short, stern old man with glasses perched on the top of his head and dandruff flakes on his gray suit jacket. As I explained my problem, he shook his head from side to side in obvious disapproval of the loose behavior that was the cause of my visit. He instructed me to pee in a jar. The test results, he said, would take two weeks.

At that time pregnancy testing involved injecting a lab rabbit with human urine and watching for its effects. I waited to hear if the rabbit died. I learned much later that all lab rabbits used for pregnancy tests died, autopsied to see the results. It was code.

My rabbit died.

Michael was Roman Catholic and at twenty-two was willing to get married but unenthusiastic. We could, he supposed, live with his parents in the Bronx. I didn't know what I wanted to do. My upper-class English parents would have been appalled and, I was sure, unsupportive. Confused, ashamed, scared, and sad, I decided to try to get an abortion.

Try was the operative word. I asked the gynecologist for advice. He told me that the law prohibited him from helping me in any way, but he offered to check me later for infection. The idea of infection alarmed me but I thought his gesture was nice.

I'd heard that after twelve weeks the procedure became extremely dangerous. So I had four weeks left to borrow money, find a way to do it, and get it done.

Emily Perl knew someone who knew someone who knew someone who had been taken care of by a woman in an apartment on West Eighty-sixth Street. When Michael and I arrived, she put the chain on the inside of the door and peeped through the crack. She let me in but demanded that Michael wait in the lobby. The room was dark, overheated, and smelled of boiled cabbage. I glimpsed a big Victorian wood-framed red velvet couch and a round oak pedestal table through the dinge. In her fifties, the woman had an Eastern European accent, suspiciously black hair, and smeary scarlet lipstick. She was curt.

She would "pack" my uterus and send me home, where I must rest. For a day or two. When I started to bleed I must return, and she would take care of it. What would she put inside me? I asked clumsily. "Stoff," she replied. Where would she "take care" of it? I asked. She pointed to a door. "In ze udder room." I must "svear" not go to a doctor or a hospital. I understood the chilling threat. "It's nowting," she said. "If you wanna now is fine. Five hunnerd dollars. Cash."

My rent was $60 a month. I earned $60 a week, $47 after taxes. I could barely make it Friday to Friday. I thanked her and fled. There had to be a cheaper, safer way.

There was. Within a couple of days Emily Perl, born researcher, came up with the Angel of Ashland, Pennsylvania. Dr. Robert Spencer was a legend, a general practitioner inspired by compassion to perform, it is said, somewhere between 40,000 and 100,000 illegal abortions over his sporadic career. His price was $50. He worked in a sterile environment with an anesthetist and used an orthodox medical procedure called dilation and curettage. What did that mean? I asked Emily. Opening and scraping, she told me. I was sorry I had asked. His clinic had been closed down by the law, but she gave me a contact number at a motel somewhere in Pennsylvania. I should say I wanted an appointment, saying simply that I needed a D & C. It was affordable, sane, and safe.

I called. The woman who answered told me Dr. Spencer was unreachable, he would be unreachable for about five months. I pressed. I might even have cried. The woman in the motel somewhere in Pennsylvania finally told me that he was in jail.

Emily's last suggestion was based on a rumor. There might be a place in the Santurce district of San Juan, Puerto Rico, called the Women's Hospital that would give an abortion. It might cost $250. She knew nothing more. I was becoming frantic. Michael was unable to do much more than hold my hand. I had two weeks left. I was on my own.

Sneaking into an empty office at work and locking the door, I picked up the phone. The overseas operator found the number and placed the call. The connection was crackly, and the man who answered neither confirmed nor denied that they would help. I asked if I would need more than $250. That might be okay, he said vaguely. I should come down if I wanted to know more. Not on a weekend, he warned.

I would go. I would need money for the airfare, money for a place to stay for a couple of nights, and money for the abortion. It would add up, I speculated, to about $500.

Michael offered to ask his father, a shoemaker with a repair store on Canal Street, but he couldn't tell him what he needed the money for, and he wasn't sure if his father would have it to lend. I had never asked my parents for money, and they had never offered it. If I did now, they would assume, rightly, that their prediction that I would get into some kind of dreadful trouble had come true. I couldn't face them.

Emily Perl's husband was a book editor. They lived in an apartment with real draperies. They gave dinner parties at which they served wine in long-stemmed glasses. Maybe she had an extra $500. Borrow it from the office, she suggested. Bosses like their employees to feel obligated. They'll get it back by deducting it from your paycheck.

So I sucked in my breath and asked the young partner in the television production company. He didn't ask what it was for. I had been obvious, sniffling and red-eyed around the office. "I'll talk to the accountant," he said. The accountant gave me a check the next day.

It wasn't such a rare occurrence, I learned later.

I had money to fly to Puerto Rico, stay a couple of nights in a motel, and have the procedure taken care of by a doctor in a hospital. I bought a ticket on Pan Am for a Sunday evening flight there and a Tuesday night flight back. The airfare was $100. I picked a place to stay a short distance from the hospital, the White Castle Hotel. There was a White Castle on the corner of Seventh Avenue and Eleventh Street, a block from my apartment, which served a quarter-inch-thin gray burger, pellucid squares of chopped onion on top, on a saccharine sweet bun that dissolved in your mouth without a chew.

I climbed down the stairs from the Pam Am flight at San Juan airport, and as I stepped onto the tarmac, my white patent-leather kitten-heeled shoes sank in, ruined. I had a change of clothes, a nightgown, a toothbrush and toothpaste, a copy of *Henderson the Rain King*, $350 in American Express traveler's checks, and $150 in cash.

I checked into the White Castle Hotel after dark and gave the clerk $100 in traveler's checks. The rest were for the procedure. The cash was for taxis and food. The room smelled of disinfectant and stale cigarettes, but it was air-conditioned. Lucky. I hadn't thought to ask. It was one hundred and three degrees that dark night in San Juan.

In the morning, the clerk gave me directions. I didn't want him to know my destination, but I couldn't risk spending money on a taxi. The hospital, I gleaned from the map, was a long walk away.

It looked like a friendly suburban institution, built of clean white brick with a sweeping U-shaped driveway. As I walked up the steps under the white-columned portico to the entrance, I allowed myself to believe for the first time that this would work.

The lobby was quiet. Behind a desk stood an official-looking young man in a white coat. I approached tentatively, standing in front of him, praying that he spoke English. He looked up and asked, "Jes?" I had practiced this speech a million times. On the plane. As I tried to sleep. When I woke that morning. On the walk over. Out loud, I said that I had been told on the telephone from New York that I could get a D & C. I want to make an appointment. For today. Please. He nodded and slid me a form to fill out. This was going to work.

He asked me my age.

Nineteen.

He shook his head.

"Oh, no no no. Too young. Only after twenty-one."

I begged, pleaded, told him I had borrowed money to get there, that I didn't have any more, that I was desperate. He told me to leave.

As I walked toward the door, the rain began to fall, splashing back up a foot or two, a few people on the road outside caught in the downpour, running to escape but instantly drenched. I stepped outside, but it was useless. Already dripping, I ducked back in and asked meekly if I might wait until the storm passed. I sat on a brown couch, the backs of my thighs sticking to the plastic surface.

I would be returning pregnant. I wept silently, hoping that anyone who saw me would mistake the tears sliding down my face for rain from the deluge outside. My paperback copy of *Henderson the Rain King* was sodden. Outside, it rained on. I would go back to the White Castle, call Michael, tell him the news, get a plane back to New York that day. I would be able to save a few dollars. But I would have to keep this baby.

I sat and waited. And waited. As I started to pull myself together to leave, a tiny brown man in the green uniform of an orderly approached me, skittish, surreptitious. He held a crumpled piece of lined paper in his hand torn from a notebook. "Go dere," he said in a stage whisper. He offered me the scrap, then disappeared.

Written in pencil was a name and an address. My dress was wet, my tarmacked shoes stuck to the ground as I walked. I had proud long hair then that I ironed straight. It frizzed in the humidity. I handed a cabdriver the paper. He spoke no English, but I could tell that he thought I was mistaken, that I didn't want to go there. That it was far. Yes, yes. I nodded emphatically at the paper, taking it back from him and pointing with my finger at the address. Finally I understood his words: *twenty dollars.* I handed him money and off we went, out of San Juan, on dirt roads for what seemed like hours, to a small village built around a grassy square. The square was still, empty save for a few mangy-looking dogs, a couple of chickens, and two old men sitting on a bench playing a board game. He dropped me in front of an open building, which appeared to be someone's house.

A small man glanced at me from inside, and pointed to the whitewashed stairs that rose along the wall. At the top stood a second man, dressed in white pants and an undershirt. His massive shoulders and arms were those of a wrestler. He must be a bodyguard, I thought. But he immediately started talking about the money in fluent, barely accented English. He could take care of me, but traveler's checks were no good to him. I didn't have enough money for the cab fare to the hotel and back again on top of the $250 that he was demanding. Are you alone, he asked? Yes, I said. We agreed on $200. He would wait. I returned in the twilight with the cash.

A wooden table, no anesthesia, a scraping sound, and a newspaper-lined metal bucket. I moaned. Be quiet, he demanded. Or did I want him to stop? No, no. Go on. Please. Go on.

When it was over he warned me not to fly for two days, gave me two sanitary pads, and called a taxi. By now it was night. The roads seemed ruttier in the dark, every bump jarring my sore body. It was still Monday. I had to change my flight to Wednesday. At the hotel I slept on and off, not knowing day from night. Tuesday, in the dark, I went out to the little bodega across the street and bought some cheese and peanut butter snacks in little rectangular cellophane packages. Peanut butter sticks to the roof of my mouth, so I grabbed a bottle of Coca-Cola. That didn't seem healthy, so I added an orange. I had nothing to cut it with in the hotel room, and the peel didn't want to come off, so I bit off the top, sucked the juice out of it, and threw it empty but whole into the garbage.

Michael met me on Wednesday night at Idlewild. We rode the

bus in to the Port Authority. I was tired and craving red meat. We took the IRT downtown to our favorite place for a cheap-enough steak dinner. It was owned by Mickey Ruskin, who became famous later as the proprietor of Max's Kansas City. I had a filet steak, a baked potato, a salad with blue cheese dressing, all for $9.99. The vodka was extra. So was the carafe of house red. Michael paid for dinner, and I felt full and satisfied and safe. The name of the place was the Ninth Circle, the lowest region of Dante's Hell, below which lies only Lethe, the river of forgetfulness.

In the morning I called Emily's gynecologist. He saw me the same day. He examined me and wrote a prescription for penicillin just to be sure. He told me to call if the bleeding got worse. It didn't. I was one of the lucky ones. According to the Guttmacher Institute, in 1962—the year I made my trip to Puerto Rico—nearly sixteen hundred women were admitted to just one New York City hospital for incomplete abortions.

In the *New York Times* in June 2008, Waldo Fielding, a retired gynecologist, described his experience with incomplete abortion complications.

"The familiar symbol of illegal abortion is the infamous 'coat hanger'—which may be the symbol, but is in no way a myth. In my years in New York, several women arrived with a hanger still in place. Whoever put it in—perhaps the patient herself—found it trapped in the cervix and could not remove it . . . Almost any implement you can imagine had been and was used to start an abortion—darning needles, crochet hooks, cut-glass salt shakers, soda bottles, sometimes intact, sometimes with the top broken off."

Three years after my trip to San Juan, illegal abortion officially accounted for 17 percent of all deaths attributed to pregnancy and childbirth in the U.S. It is speculated that the actual number was likely much higher.

LIA PURPURA

There Are Things Awry Here

FROM *Orion*

I FOUND A PERIMETER, THANK GOD, and I'm walking. I'm making an hour of it, finding a way to get my breathing going hard. These four big lots with big-box stores must compass a mile. Measuring helps. I am here (quick check: yes, panting and sweaty) but it feels like nowhere, is so without character that the character I am hardly registers at all. So I'll get to work, in the way I know how:

Here is a farmer entering the black field. He's a proper farmer, bowlegged and leathery, with a serviceable rope looped over his arm. But the farmer comes out of a logoed truck and the rope links up to a ChemLawn can and off he goes to tend the weeds asserting through the asphalt. He pisses I don't know where during his long day in the sun. His hat's a tattered red GO BAMA cap. His tin lunch pail is a bag from Popeyes, just down the road (I mean *highway*).

Here is a rancher coming over a rise, backlit and stiff, sure hands on the reins, eye for the dips that would wreck a fetlock. He's nearly cantering over the brown grass, cropped short to begin with, but hey, he's on contract, it's the fifteenth of the month, so he comes to harrow the grass at the edge of the lot. The rancher rides masterfully and the mower goes fast; he turns sharply, leans into the bit, and the beast resists not at all.

Here are the animals branded and waiting, they're tired, they stopped where the grass was fresh and a pond provided. It's dusk coming on, a slight chill picking up that turns them toward home, but they don't raise their heads, catch a scent of dog, of roundup coming. The herd's mixed. "MsBob" is all in with "Luvbun" and "GoTide." "Bubbaboy," "Nully," and "Sphinx" are there too. The stock are purebred Camaros, Explorers, Elantras, Legends. Docile and ragged; worn, overfed.

More is wrong.

The flags are frozen. They're fifty feet high but don't move in wind and they carry no sentiment, like "these we hoist high over our small town/farm/ranch to keep alive spirit, memory, fervor . . ." The flags have names: *Ryan's, Outback, Hooters* (best saloon in town, I'd say, judging by all the horses tied up out front). *IHOP. Waffle House. Walmart* on a far — I'd like to say *hill* but that's out of the question, the hill's been dozed, subdued into *rise.*

Here is a field between parking lots — real grass and dirt with bottles tossed in, amber longnecks, flat clears of hard stuff. The word *artifact* comes, but it's bumped out by *garbage,* the depths are all wrong, and in a matter of weeks it will all be turned over. Not a field's breaking. Not loamy and clod-filled. More Tyvek and tar. By which things are wrapped, laid in, erected. How easily the new names for "seasons" come forth: *undeveloped, developing, development, developed.* Skirting the site, I lose options like *fallow,* that yearlong rest wherein land regains strength. I'm losing the language for thoughts about gleaning. *Crop* goes to *cropping* as in Photoshop fixing. (And *Photoshopping* — wow, *that* gets confusing.)

Here is a farm woman, her shawl held against wind. It's late February in Tuscaloosa and the tornadoes that hit farther south last week are still lending their kick. She leans into the gust as she crosses, with bags, the black earth (that black below tar), the damp earth (I say *earth* out of habit, I see), but it's very well marked, white lines intersect, and the acre or so she's covered (I'm holding on here, with *acre* as measure) is *field* distance, but it's not a field anymore. She's juggling bags and pinning her nametag, she works at the Cobb, the town's multiplex, and she's late for her shift. On my next turn around the series of lots (where, remember, I'm walking, trying to get my own body into the scene), she'll be behind glass, with money and tickets. Smoothing her hair. Gulping her Big Gulp. Settling. (*Settler. Settlement.* Sigh.)

A bit farther on, here is a mailbox with its red flag flipped up, in front of the Marriott, my closest neighbor (I'm a Hilton Tuscaloosa guest for a week). It's a wooden mailbox on a wooden post, which means "rustic" — and truly, it *is* weatherworn. Around each fire hydrant — the hotels here in parking-lot land are each fitted with two stumpy blue ones—grows a thicket of bushes. To hide the hydrant. Though in any small town, hydrants are red and freestanding on actual street corners. This greenery means to convey "tended garden." Which makes the hydrant a reverse sort of flower, one that emits water. Which I guess fits the whole upended scene.

Here are four tall trees in a tangly grove—former trees because now they're dead, though a grove, I know, accommodates all forms of growth and decomposition, all cycles and stages. Long, bare branches and rough, broken ones alternate all the way down. It's the kind of ex-tree that might draw an owl (that's what I'm conjuring, a native barred owl), it's got to be full of grubs just beginning to stir, and it offers a safe, clear view of the land. In the air is the scent of burning *something*. Highway and rubber. Diesel and speed. In fact, it's all over—a smell, if I'd known it as a kid, I'd hardly notice, or only on days when the wind kicked up. Poor farm wife in her booth, her hair tangled and blown. Gusts helping my rancher into his stable, right up the ramp and the tailgate slams shut. And my farmer—he's holding his rope low and firm while it leaks a bright poison as yellow and brief as a corn snake, sunning, then startled, then disappearing back into the ground.

Here in the lot is some corrugated cardboard I thought was an animal's vertebrae (sign of hope, life in burrows!). Here the Brink's truck is outside the Cobb, and the driver is armed, as he's been since transfers of loot began. Here, with a thought to my love up north, I pluck a dandelion (it escaped the farmer), the gesture complete as it's always been, small, flowery symbol of tender missing. I passed a shard of—it looked like pottery (domestic life/human scale!)—but close up was a shorn chunk of thick plastic.

And before the Committee on Irrevocable Mistakes chose this to do to the land—plant tar, seed commerce— *here* was what?

What was here, that a body moved through it?

Back in my room I can't shake the sensation (despite my dandelion in a plastic cup, curtains wide open, basket of apples to naturalize things). A strangeness, an insistence is hovering. The strangeness makes me say aloud to myself, *Something* had *to be here, something* had been.

Something made me make stand-ins, cutouts, cartoons. It made me possessive, led me to say "my rancher, my farmer, my good farmer's wife"—*mine,* because I had to make them. From scratch. Out of *something.* Had to make them *look like.* A past. "The past." I conjured clichés (they come fashioned with roots). I had to make something, because the land couldn't do it. The land gave nothing. Gave nothing up. There was no plan, no narrative here, or tether-back-to. Just boxes to eat in. Big boxes for shopping. One boxy theater with nine movies plexed in. The parking lots gaped. Snipped, sprayed, and divided. Unpeopled. Tidied for no one.

Real land is never sad in its vastness, lost in its solitude. Left alone, cycles dress and undress it, chill-and-warm so it peaks, hardens, slides, swells. Real land hosts—voles, foxes, cicadas. Fires, moss, thunder. Rolls or gets steep. Sinks, sops, and sprouts. But this land didn't read. It babbled the way useless things babble—fuzzy bees with felt smiles, bejeweled and baubley occasional plaques, ConGRADulation mugs/frames/figurines. Capped, crusted, contained, so laden with stuff—how can it breathe?

Here, surely, went people with thoughts, in the past—and not as I conjured them, fleet, makeshifty odes, dumb stock-assumptions, citified cartoons, with force of wind and vast stretch of blacktop shaping my story of them very poorly. (Points, maybe, for hale traits I assigned: reticence, dignity, industriousness, skill!) My folks were as flat as those cowboy silhouettes slouched up against mailboxes, but the drive to olden them, tie them back to the earth, give them good pastoral work was real.

Let me start over, since this is America, land of beginnings. I'll try again, since after one night's stay, *here* doesn't clarify at all. Let me start very simply with my simple problem:

Here, it's February 2008, and I can't figure out how to get my body to land in a land where the present's not speaking. Where stories won't take, and walking is sliding. I found a cadence to quiet the chatter, a word useful for focus and pacing out steps— *refuse,* which I used as both re-FUSE and REF-use, resistance-meets-garbage, iambic/trochaic, singsongy, buoyant—but alas, it ordered not much. So today I go searching in earnest. To the library first (always, always), then around the corner to Special Collections where I blurt my question to the expert on duty: *At the site of the Cobb—that whole south side of town* ("mess of emptiness," I'm conveying with pauses) — *by the Big K and Hooters* ("that awful nowhere" suggested by sighs), *before all that, what was* there? *Ah,* she says, disappearing in the back, then returning with a stack of yellowing magazines. *Here, try these.*

I find a clear table, spread the magazines out, and turn the dry pages.

Once it was February 1942 here. It was British Cadet Class 42E at the Alabama Institute of Aeronautics, a wartime flying school operating in cooperation with the U.S. Army Air Corps. Here First Captain Wheeler wrote in *Fins and Flippers,* the cadets' magazine, a note of gratitude to the American trainers "for interpreting their training system in a manner intelligible to we British Cadets."

Here, in their monthly, the cadets and their officers noted the welcomed small acts of American civility and laughed over their own displacement (moors! Tuscaloosa!), all in the literary conventions of the time—yearbooky, vignettish, clean-cut, and well-mannered.

And just for a moment, the ugliness recedes (note of gratitude for the cadets, as they hover around, high in the blue, learning dials and gauges and jostling each other; note of—I can't help it —pleasure, as I read to myself and their lovely accents kick in). The pour of blacktop, the gray icing of curb, I'm being assured now, *isn't* the earth. That's its burned crust. That's its sackcloth for unholy times, before the rapture comes and restores, assumes the earth back to woods, fields, shores where I might ramble and stroll —little myth I can't help invoking, which more commonly goes, in my head, wordlessly: *It'll get better, it'll be righted, cleaned, and made pure, it will, how bad could it be, see how perfectly blue the sky is!* (That's stock-Lia talking, brightly, brightly because the ugliness hurts, the wincing is constant; that's the me rucksacked up and ready for hiking, neverminding the dark and gathering clouds, grabbing a poncho, and let's go everyone!)

Here, near the Cobb, is the land where Mac wrote, in *Fins and Flippers,* a little piece called "Our London":

> I remember the sun setting over the last rugged corner of Britain in a blaze of crimson magnificence, that we saw when the ship sailed in August. I remember seeing the lights of Toronto start to blink from a small island on Lake Ontario. But best of all—I remember London.
>
> Though I am many thousands of miles away, I see her constantly, not as she stands now, bruised and battered, but as she was when I spent my adolescent initiation within her walls; and I am sorry that I was not able

to appreciate her then as I do now. For in those days, Regent Street just signified to me the road that led from Piccadilly Circus to Oxford Street. Charing Cross was just a station that served my purpose in going south. The same applied to Fleet Street, Cheapside and Soho, and a host of other fine places . . .

Here, my students and I are reading Virginia Woolf, who worked in Mac's London, right through the war, this very same war, on her own piece, "A Sketch of the Past." Almost every entry begins with a mere nod to the war outside her window. Instead, it's her past, her lost houses, land, family—whole eras gone, irreplaceably gone— that demand recounting:

> As we sat down to lunch two days ago . . . John came in, looked white about the gills, his pale eyes paler than usual, and said the French have stopped fighting. Today the dictators dictate their terms to France. Meanwhile, on the very hot morning, with a blue bottle buzzing and a toothless organ grinding and the men calling strawberries in the Square, I sit in my room at 37 Mecklenburgh Square and turn to my father.
> . . . Yesterday . . . five German raiders passed so close over Monks House that they brushed the tree at the gate. But being alive today, and having a waste hour on my hands . . . I will go on with this story . . .

Here, it's London for us, when we gather, my students and I, three hours each night to talk about books, language, art—forms of flight, forms of landing. With my cadets, it's getting less strange. All this sitting and reading together helps.

Here, Ryan, one of my hosts, brought me an umbrella since I came unprepared for sudden storms. Here, Group Captain Leonard Thorne notes, as I do, the Tuscaloosa residents' "wonderful hospitality and friendship."

Nights, here, I am much impressed by my Hilton stack-up of pillows. (I can easily be made to feel rich by an abundance of bedclothes, plumping them while watching bad late-night TV, letting the excess fall to the floor.) Seems I would have played nicely with RAF Hazlehurst, who "still thinks a pillow is a weapon and not a headrest." We'd have blurred the room with soft flying weapons. "Born and bred in Derbyshire. Educated at Winchester. 'Dick' to his buddies . . ." He's the bareheaded one, no leather helmet-and-goggle set, or dress cap all the others wear, in their *Fins and Flippers* photo.

And here is E. G. Gordon, transferred from the Royal Artillery Anti-Aircraft, born in London, educated at Kingsbury School, Middlesex, whose chief sport is boxing, who "claims to be the shortest man in the RAF and so lives in constant dread of six-foot blind dates." Here, layered over the land, are his jitters, which, from his photo, it seems he makes light of: his flight cap is precipitously tilted, one side of his mouth hiked, mischievous, laughing, his tie expertly knotted, his meticulous uniform sharp pressed and not especially diminutive-looking. Whatever he left behind of himself, whatever I sensed on my walk, subatomic, molecularly present— that which I now know to call E. G.—was right *here*. Was so young. In the photo, he's no more than twenty. If he's alive now, he's older than my father.

Here, I walk into class thinking, *Really I have nothing to say to these people, the proper study of writing is reading, is well-managed awe, desire to make a thing, stamina for finishing, adoration of language,* and so on about reverie, solitude, etc. Here, sitting down, I'm going over my secret: *I don't want to be inspiring, I just want to write, and they too should want that—let's all agree to go home and work hard.* I walk in, I see people with books, stacks of books I've asked them to read. Besides Woolf, there's James Agee (let's take that out, class), who lived with and wrote of the poorest white sharecroppers of Alabama (nice convergence—Alabama!) and whose force of nature, *Let Us Now Praise Famous Men,* was published in 1941, as he might add, *Year of Our Lord,* to dignify the event. *Event:* I choose my word carefully, friends, for, as Agee writes, "This is a *book* only by necessity . . . let's turn to page xi . . ." Now I'm cooking. I, in my flight suit (black sweater and jeans), look into the faces of my cadets. Everyone's eager. We walk to the runway. We find the ignition.

Here, I am escorted to the Dreamland for barbecue, and with Brian, my student, eat my first banana pudding. Here, A. T. Grime, flight lieutenant, wrote, "Anxious experiments are being carried out by the devoted Mr. Davies, our Dietician, with the object of providing an acceptable Yorkshire Pudding a la Tuscaloosa, to satisfy the palates of our gourmets. This I think is typical," he continued, "of the efforts made by all at this school . . . to make your pilgrimage a memorable experience." The banana pudding is so sweet, so custardy, full of bananas and cakey white fluff, so heavy and childish, if I'd grown up with it, I'd miss it too, when abroad.

Here, in 2008, the assistant in charge of visitors is a "Fifi." (That's

Ryan.) Here, in 1942, the novices en route to becoming pilots first class were "Dodos." Fifis and Dodos. What a menagerie this land raised up.

Here, the novices have their own games: flag football with elaborate e-mail invitations. "As you can see, we at the UAEDFL—University of Alabama English Department Football League—are incredibly dedicated to our sport; we always give 110% and we play hurt . . . come play this Saturday at 11 and feel the RUSH." Here the cadets' training program offered "archery, horseshoes, swimming, tennis, tumbling, softball, volleyball, boxing, relays, calisthenics and for recreation golf, checkers (Chinese and regular), chess, cards, music, reading, singing and movies." Posted at 10:59 one night: "After incessant whining on the listserv and the occasional snide (yet sheepish!) remarks in the graduate student lounge, the English Department comes up with an unbelievable plan to raise money by playing flag-football . . . Can this ragtag band of writers, researchers, instructors and critiquers settle their views on Derrida before it's too late?" And stanza one of an eleven-stanza poem called "Cadence, Exercise," by cadet J. S. Peck, goes:

> Throughout the U.S. Armies wide
> Stand formations side by side
> Their contempt they'll never hide
> for Calisthenics!

Here's Flight Lieutenant Garthwaite, RAF administrative officer, in his monthly bulletin "Over to London": "To those at home we send our sincerest hopes for the future. Although not on the field of battle ourselves, we do but gird ourselves for the great and final overthrow of Naziism. Let us hope and trust the coming year will see this war through . . . and . . . not a little by the fruits of our learning over here."

Yes, here they learned their recitations: maximum speeds and service ceilings; flight ranges, fuel capacities, and armaments carried by the Arvo Lancasters, Armstrong Whitleys, and Bristol Beaufighters they'd be flying over the skies at home, soon, soon.

I knew in this vacancy *something* asserted. Something strange—that is, real—and insistent was here. The land didn't mean to be torn and tar-covered, wasn't meant to sprout stock farmers, farm women, and ranchers. The land asked to be considered, and seriously. The land wanted to speak—past the bunkers of rolled insulation, past the earth-eating backhoes and yellow concoction my farmer (okay, *working stiff,* bare hands in the poison, then wiping his nose) force-fed the grass. Here, the land must have been green by the runways. Some of the big trees still here must have seen it. Yes, it must've been lush once, before hotels started turf wars along Marriott/Hilton lines, and thick vines choked the trees, and the tractors came and the hot blacktop poured, so the SKUs of Big K —hundreds of thousands—might take root and flourish.

I was returned—but not to an Eden, for there were airstrips and the screams of takeoffs, supply roads were laid down for fuel and equipment, the contrails of jets streaked the air, burned, scented, inscribed the quiet so the feel of the whole experience—the desire to serve, the fear of serving—would return whenever humidity, fuel, barbecue combined rightly for the novices.

I was returned, but more in this way: someone dreamed of getting the word, high over Berlin, to top-speed it east toward the Polish border, the Führer, *he's there!,* it's the hamlet of Gierloz, fix your sights, son, load, steady, and—. Someone considered the glory, the fame, posing for photos with requisite wounds. Family pride, shining future. The world's gratitude. Because the *boys* must have thought it, because *I* had the thought, it must have been lingering. The thoughts must have held on, hovering, jittery, wanting some rest. Such thoughts were preserved, but nowhere on the land. Nothing *cadet* was marked here, not poems or pudding, jaunty caps, homesickness. Instead, here were lots, grids, boxes, all manner of automata—doors that opened without human touch allowing the body to float right on in and get down to the business of buying.

Here's where the splintered, close barracks were raised—and then razed, plowed under into a new kind of cloverleaf: blacktopped, clovery only from air.

When the land would not speak and my characters failed, when the land was muffled and my characters stock, this piece was born.

Here is my seed. Here is my search, trail, map of convergences.

Here is the thing I made in place of—*what,* exactly?

What did I find myself wanting? Something simple and telling —say a shop revealing the "character of the people upon whom the town depended for its existence." Even better (and this from

Thomas Hardy's England), "a class of objects displayed in a shop window . . . scythes, reap-hooks, sheep-shears, bell-hooks, spades, mattocks and hoes at the ironmongers; beehives, butter firkins, churns, milking stools and pails, hay rakes, field flagons and seed lips at the cooper's, cart ropes and plough harnesses at the saddler's; carts, wheelbarrows, and mill gear at the wheelwrights and machinist's; horse embrocations at the chemist's; at the glover's and leathercutter's, hedging gloves, thatcher's kneecaps, ploughman's leggings, villager's patterns and clogs . . ." Oh, boots to lace up against scalding and scraping! Commerce boiled, reconstituted — oh, made rhythmic with breath, heavy with being — even objects transparent as the jewel-colored jars of preserves in the pantries of farmhouses I've known — apricot suns, the flushed hot-dawn tomatoes, deep dusk-purple plums put up, sealed, stored away, would shine with this presence.

I wanted a footpath, a field edge — a *sidewalk*. People at ease with neighbors and chatting. A simple plaque at the site of — whatever: *Here the cadets of 42E sat to eat their first grits*. Scrap of wing or propeller on the Hilton's faux mantel. *Fins and Flippers* next to every Gideon's Bible.

What did I find? Some Februaries that matched — one then and one now; some novices each with their good fights and good words, their gratitudes, civilities, and homey soft puddings.

I wanted to know what happened here, on land like this.

Now I know.

People learn to fly through it. And then they go home.

RACHEL RIEDERER

Patient

FROM *The Missouri Review*

1

THE BUS WILL HAVE TO MOVE. I'm under its rear tires on the passenger side, and with the crowd, the driver can't see me in the mirror. "Can you please tell him to move?" I say to someone leaning over me. It is easy to be calm because I cannot really have been run over by a bus.

I look for my friend Simone. She is short and curvaceous, with warm brown Caribbean skin and long black hair. We have been out together, dancing in a sweaty blue-neon nightclub with pulsing music and dancers with seductive silhouettes gyrating on pillars. Earlier, she had helped me pick out the pink-and-red shoes that are now squished under the tires. She would make the driver move the bus, but I can't see her.

In an emergency, you cannot just say, "Somebody call 911," because everyone will assume that someone else will do it, and no one will call. This is called "the Problem of Collective Action." I pull my cell phone and driver's license out of my jacket pocket and hand them to a stranger and tell the stranger to call an ambulance.

It's about two in the morning, a weekend in late November; there can't be a bus on my leg. I am a junior in college, and tomorrow I am going to a big tailgate where I will drink beer and hot chocolate with peppermint schnapps, laugh with my friends in the cold. A few minutes ago I was standing on a corner in downtown Boston, in a crowd of about two hundred students waiting to be taken back to campus. The tall charter bus, with gleaming white sides and purple lettering, its tinted windows well above eye level if you are beside it, came around the corner. We were standing on the street, and it pulled up fast, right by the crowd. And then those of us standing furthest out in the street were up against it—the hot, smooth flank of the bus on one side, the pressing crowd on the other. Someone beside me fell, and then I fell. While I was still lying on the cold asphalt, the bus moved forward a little, and its tires rolled onto my leg. It stopped there, breathing its exhaust and the smell of hot rubber on me. Do all buses have four tires in one cluster like this, two across and two deep? Two of the tires are sitting on my left leg, and my right leg is wedged into the little crevice between the pairs.

But this isn't a real event; it is a saying: "I feel like I got hit by a bus." You say this when you have gone for a long run without stretching and wake up the next morning with soreness in long-forgotten muscles. It does not happen in real life, certainly not to me.

The bus moves forward, off my left leg, over my right leg, and then off me altogether. The weight must have been deadening my nerves; the sensation that was uncomfortable a moment ago has exploded, the pain in my leg taking up all the room in my brain. Someone picks me up and moves me to the sidewalk. I feel small. The cold cement feels good. There's an ambulance, and now Simone is here. She will go to the hospital with me, but she has to ride in the front. I lie in the cargo hold and beg the EMTs for drugs. They cannot give me any and ask what hospital. I shouldn't have to make this decision; I don't even know the names of any Boston hospitals, and what good are EMTs who are powerless to choose a hospital or relieve pain?

At the hospital, everything is moving; my stretcher is being thrust into wide, swinging doors. White coats and bright-colored scrubs flash against the bright white walls. There is forceful talking and the beeping of machinery. People surround me. They put an IV in my arm, and a beady-eyed nurse says that she put morphine into the IV bag, but she is a liar and a sadist, I can tell from her pinched face, which cannot even approximate a look of compassion. I know from the feeling in my left leg that there is not a single drop of morphine in the ridiculous plastic bag.

My left leg is purple and scarlet and mustard yellow. It would be grotesquely beautiful, but the tire mark and gravel embedded in the flesh ruin this effect. The sadistic nurse touches my ankle and says it is broken. They will do an x-ray to confirm and send me home in an air cast, with crutches. She is wrong. If broken ankles felt like this, people would not have them so often.

I demand anesthesia. I cannot leave the hospital. I have to be unconscious. Now. She laughs. I try begging. "Please," I say, and my eyes tear for the first time. I repeat myself, screaming, so she will know I am not kidding. She is sorry, she claims, but she has given me the maximum dosage. That's not my fucking problem, and I tell her so.

She wants to cut the shoe off my left foot; I cannot let her. I love these shoes! They are Mary Janes, but they are soft and have soles like sneakers, and they are pink with red checkers. My swollen ham foot is bursting out of the left shoe, but I can still unhook the small silver buckle. I sit up, and while I am unstrapping the cute, salvageable, only slightly torn shoe from the ruined foot, another nurse, clearly Beady Eyes's nemesis, comes in. "Here, I thought we should have given you this in the first place." She plunges a needle into one of the connector sockets on the IV tube. The throbbing leg goes numb. The panic subsides. I love her. I have to know what she gave me.

"How do you spell it?" I ask, and as the room blurs and quiets, I hear: "D-I-L-A-U-D-I-D."

Semiconscious and calm, I am full of solutions. Emergency rooms need to be bright and well-lit, but someone should have remembered that all the sick and injured people are lying on their backs, scared and disoriented, and staring into rows of fluorescent lights doesn't help. I will mention it to someone.

It has only been a few minutes since the angel nurse gave me the medicine. Now a tall, handsome black doctor is standing at my feet, looking at my leg in a way that worries me. He is touching parts of my enormous Technicolor calf and ankle—my leg is now a column, the same size below the knee as above—and asking can I feel it. Sometimes I can. He touches my toes and asks if I can move them. I wiggle them. At least, I order them to wiggle. They refuse. The nurse and doctor exchange words about nerve damage and crush syndrome. I try again, try asking the toes to wiggle. Try cajoling, sweet-talking them. I revise: they don't even have to wiggle, just bend a little. They are unmoved.

My toes would have bent. My feet are pretty and obedient. They are slender with high arches. Yes, they are callused on the bottom, but they are nothing like this fat red blob that has had all the foot shape squashed out of it. "We are going to operate right away," the doctor tells me. "We are going to do everything we can to save your leg."

I have seen enough medical dramas to know that when doctors try to save a limb, it gets amputated. When I go to hospitals, I get stitches or an air cast, not an amputation. If my leg is amputated, I will never fall in love and get married. I will either be a bitter, one-legged old maid or else I will have to troll around on the Internet and join some sort of online group for fetishists of lopsidedness and half limbs. Maybe I will get a discount on pedicures — but no, actually, how could I even bring myself to paint the toenails on my remaining foot? Does a cyclops wear mascara?

This can't be real. Maybe I never went to the steamy, pulsing blue club outside which buses mangle legs and thrust people into metallic-smelling fluorescent hospitals. I have read about lucid dreaming; if you want to be lucid in a dream, there are a few techniques. Try to flip on and off a light-switch — it will not work. Or try to read text or numbers — you will not be able to. Your dream self has only to remember that if you cannot read and use light switches, you are dreaming. With practice, good lucid dreamers can control their dreams. I have done this only once. I dreamed I was in the ocean, about to drown in a huge oncoming tsunami. I panicked but then realized that I am never in the middle of tropical oceans in real life, so this could not possibly be a tsunami situation and I must be dreaming. I calmly flew into the air and hovered while the wave rolled past beneath me.

2

Please remove any jewelry before surgery. I hand the nurse a fistful of tongue ring, nose ring, and earrings. The handsome doctor is an "orthopedic traumatologist," and he introduces me to a plastic surgeon who will help in the surgery. I gesture to my nose and say, "Oh, no, I'm not here for this. It's actually my leg that's the problem." He doesn't get it and begins explaining that plastic surgeons do more than cosmetic surgery; they work on all kinds of soft tissue. I already knew that, but I don't bother explaining because they have given me a little something to calm me down, and I sink into sleep.

I wake up in a dim beige room with soft light peeking in from the window where the blinds are drawn. My leg hurts. A lot. My leg hurts—it must still be there if it hurts this much, and I should be excited that it is still attached to me, but the ripping pain makes that impossible. My mom has come all the way from Kansas City, so it must be at least the next day. Mom, with her strong pianist's fingers and her brown eyes and brown hair, straight and fine like mine, only shorter—a familiar fixture in this strange room. She is stroking my hair and saying soothing things to me, which is nice, but medicine would be better, and I ask her to get the nurse. The ICU nurse, Joey, is a tall, muscular man in his forties with a trim, dark beard and mustache. I tell him my leg hurts, and he starts to talk about morphine and maximum dosages. This time I do not swear; I say simply that morphine does not work on me and I need something called "Dilaudid: D-I-L-A-U-D-I-D." He smiles and disappears into the bright white hallway, closing the door behind him and reinstating the dimness.

There is a faded baby-blue blanket over my legs, and tubes run from beside the bed up under the blanket. "Will they have to—" I cannot finish the question, but my mom knows what I mean— she must be wondering too—and she says that the doctors do not think they will have to amputate my leg. They have cut some slits into the tissue and left them open to relieve the pressure.

When Joey returns, he plunges a needle into the IV socket, and a familiar warmth rolls gently into my brain, flushing out panic and muffling the pain. Joey says I have strong legs, and we talk about kickboxing, which I take at my gym and which he teaches at the Y. He has a high voice for a man so muscular and dark, and when he speaks, it is slow and friendly, with lots of inflection, not like the rushed, flat-affect speech of the ER nurses. He says I will kickbox again someday because I am strong; he can tell. "Yeah," I say, trying to mimic his cheerful tone, but as I say it I start to cry.

A few days have passed. I have been moved from the ICU to the "Med/Surg" floor, where my off-white wallpapered room has a large window that looks out at pale late-autumn sky and the gray of other hospital buildings. I still have the light blue blanket. Two plastics residents come and debride my leg every day. The muscle of my shin was torn off the bone. It has no blood supply, but the doctors decided not to remove it—they hope that if it sits there long enough, blood vessels will grow in and reattach the muscle to the rest of my body. Meanwhile, it dies a little every day, the muscle that used to move my foot up and down. In the first surgery, the doctors cut four long slits into my leg and left them open—now there is no skin on the front of my shin. It is wrapped in gauze and then a layer of plastic wrap to keep it sterile. When the doctors change the gauze, which they do daily, it tears off small chunks of dead tissue. This is supposed to stimulate cell regrowth, but it doesn't feel regenerative. The first few times they did it they put me under general anesthesia, but they can't do that anymore.

General anesthesia shuts down your digestive tract. The nurses told me this to explain why I need laxatives and suppositories. Using a bedpan is embarrassing, but when it is difficult, it's worse. And so it is good to have less anesthesia. I try to remember this when the two residents come and change the dressing while I squeeze my mom's hand.

3

My mom has moved into the hotel down the street from the hospital, and she is in my room almost all the time. She's an excellent patient advocate, making sure the doctors check on me frequently and demanding that the nurses up my pain meds whenever their maximum dosages are not enough. We talk about getting extra Valium for debridings, how to wash my hair, how to insert suppositories—not walking.

She has gone down the hall to talk to a nurse, or maybe to call my dad, when a new nurse comes in. He is my age, tall and slender and tan, with dark eyes, heavy eyebrows, and thick brown hair. I am feeling alert and more normal than I have in days, and we chat about ordinary things. He is in the nursing program at Northeastern; he knows someone I know, and I ask if he likes his program, and he asks me what I study. For a few minutes, while smiling and talking and feeling a little awkward and shy, I am like myself. Then he says he is going to give me a sponge bath, and I am again a crippled patient talking to one of her many health-care providers. I stink. I have been sweating into the once-crisp white sheets, and they are soft and damp. One of the medications makes my sweat smell tangy and chemical, and my hair is greasy, but though I badly need a bath, I am mortified at the prospect of this glossy-haired young man soaping and rinsing me limb by limb, and I ask him if we can do it later.

He leaves the room, and I can feel that the bed is wet and hot where I am sitting. I am not incontinent—but then again, until four days ago I was not a person whose legs got crushed by buses or had to worry about sponge baths. I reach between my thighs, and my hand comes back bloody. I am not supposed to have my period, but obviously my body is no longer trustworthy, and all the organs are working together to perpetrate the perfect betrayal. I cannot get out of bed, and if I press the nurse call button the dark-haired young nurse will come back in here, and I cannot—will not—talk to him about my period. Despite my best efforts, I am crying again, and the only thing I can think to do is yell "Mom!" repeatedly, like some terrible child at the grocery store.

The nurse comes back in and wants to know what's wrong and how he can help, and all I can do is sob and tell him to get my mom. I am regressing. But it's not even regression; I didn't tell my mom when I got my first period in the sixth grade. Now I am twenty years old, blubbering like some insane, menstruating baby. My mom helps clean me up and gets a female nurse to change my bedding and give me a sponge bath. The young male nurse, she assures me, will not be assigned to me again.

4

It is Thanksgiving, and I have been in the hospital for six days. My father and brother have come for the holiday, and my friend and roommate, Johanna, is here too. She is from Ireland and doesn't go home for the holiday. She always hugs me as soon as she comes in, and I love to smell the cigarette smoke in her curly blond hair and feel the cold that clings to her jacket; it is as close as I come to going outside. We all make fun of the hospital cafeteria's greasy and chewy attempt at Thanksgiving dinner, but we don't care. When I was about four years old, my parents made a tape of me talking about the first Thanksgiving, and they play it every year for anyone who will listen. On it, I talk in a baby voice about how the Indians made best friends with the Pilgrims and shout a singsong imitation of Miles Standish inviting Chief Massasoit over for hot dogs. My parents imitate the whole monologue for Johanna. Normally I would blush and protest this performance, but tonight I don't care. I laugh along with the rest of them.

After dinner, my family goes back to the hotel. Johanna stays. Tall and thin, she can just barely curl her long legs and torso into a cozy ball on the chair next to my bed. She comes here a lot, though I am usually too foggy to be good company. Sometimes after I fall asleep she sits in the chair and presses the button that releases the pain meds into my IV every ten minutes or so, and I stay numb and asleep that much longer.

After my family goes home, Johanna sits in the chair next to the bed, and we watch a movie on the little TV mounted on the wall. It is a romantic comedy, and it looks cheesy but good, I say. Johanna laughs — because, she tells me, we have watched the movie several times together already, and every time I wake up from my opiate sleep and see it on, I say as if I have never seen it before that it looks pretty good. The movie channel at the hospital plays the romantic comedy and two children's movies on a never-ending loop. Johanna reminds me that we have watched all three.

Tonight she reads me a funny story about an American tourist in Ireland, in her thick accent with its soft vowels and lilting inflection. Usually she takes a cab back to our dorm, where she sleeps in the room adjacent to my empty one. Tonight she hunkers down in the chair next to my bed, and when I wake up in the middle of the night for my next round of drugs, she is still there, wrapped in her long blue-gray sweater, sleeping.

5

I have been in the hospital for more than two weeks, and I haven't seen my leg yet. The pale blue blanket stays on even when the nurse bathes the rest of my body, even when they move me into the chair next to the bed to change the linens. Usually I lie back and look at the ceiling during dressing changes, but I am getting curious, and today I am going to watch.

I promise myself to be stoic. I will not cry or bite my hand. Worse things have happened to better people, I sometimes repeat to myself. My dad used to say this in a fake hillbilly accent, the same voice in which he said, "Well, it sure beats a poke in the eye with a sharp stick," when things went wrong. Political prisoners, rape victims, starving orphans, homeless addicts—these people have it hard. You are a privileged college student whose leg hurts.

So, no crying. The nurse uses blunt-edged, crooked scissors to cut away the plastic wrap and the top layers of bandages. The gauze underneath is caked with blood, which I was expecting, but also with something surprisingly dark yellow, the iodine that they've swabbed onto the wound as an antiseptic. She wets the bandages, and as she peels away the final strips, with little bits of flesh stuck into the white gauze netting, she always asks me in between strips if I need a break. I don't take one because if she just keeps going, it will be over faster. My leg from my hip to the knee looks normal, just a bit shrunken, since the muscles have atrophied. My knee is swollen, and two inches below the knee my leg becomes a steak. The skin is gone from most of the front and side, and there is just a mess of red tissue about three inches across that extends nearly the length of my shin. Below the meaty exposed parts is what used to be an ankle, where my leg used to narrow, where you could see my Achilles tendon in the back and the little circular bones protruding on either side. Where my ankle should be, there is a thick yellow-and-purple cylinder connecting the wound area to the clubfoot, which is wider than it used to be. It's completely black on the top and bottom, but the sides are still fleshy. I am told that the black crust is dead soft tissue that probably will fall off and let out the new pink skin that is—maybe—growing underneath it. A few weeks ago the sight of this would have made me queasy, but I am sick of feeling weepy and nauseated with my brokenness. Today it makes me mad.

If you are in the hospital, people will say ridiculous things to try to cheer you up. "Sometimes pain is its own form of prayer," they say if you have told them you are not interested in praying. "God has a plan for everyone," they say with kind smiles. You will lie in your hospital bed and think that if there is a god—a possibility that seems more and more remote every time someone puts a glycerin suppository, blood thinner, or seizure medication into what used to be the beautiful machine of your body—he or she probably does not have enough free time to make individualized plans for everyone. People may scold you for your doubt—gently, because you are in poor health—and remind you that God works in mysterious ways. You will be tempted to shout at them that if God planned for you to get run over by a bus, then he is at best a poor plan-maker or, more likely, a sadist.

Simone, who studies religion, is assuring me that "everything happens for a reason." I want to scream at her that people have two working legs for a reason and that her statement is a copout that weak people turn to when they realize they have zero control over their lives.

But it is impolite to shriek at people who have taken the time to visit you and who only want to help, so I murmur something non-committal.

6

The doctors do not talk about amputation anymore. They talk about physical therapy options, explain the various braces and orthotic devices that could make up for the fact that I cannot flex my foot out of its constant semipointed position. Every day Mom reads me the cards that come in the mail: sweet messages, votes of confidence. Many say they are proud of me for being strong, or being brave. These make me laugh. How would I be strong or brave? There is nothing for me to do here except take the medicine I am given, follow the doctors' instructions, and try to wiggle my foot. You have to make choices to be brave, and I don't have many. I can choose to tell dumb jokes to visitors, and I can choose to cry when I'm alone instead of in front of people.

There is comfort, though, in mottoes, and eventually I find my own, a trite and simple mantra but one inarguably true: *All things must pass.* My parents have the George Harrison album with this title. On the cover, the long-haired hippie lounges in soft lighting on soft grass in front of a stand of pine trees. When people talk to me about divine plans and mysterious ways, I know they are wrong, but I also know this: one day I will not be in this hospital bed anymore. One day I will wake up somewhere else, and on some day after that I will wake up and my first thought will be something other than dying muscles and opiates.

Sometimes the motto is not effective: when my leg hurts a lot, like now, or when being bedridden frustrates or humiliates me more than usual, I mentally scream at my leg. *Fucking bastard asshole leg of betrayal! Et tu,* motherfucking *leg?* If it had been amputated I could have gone home. I wouldn't have to have heparin injected into my stomach twice a day to keep the blood from clotting in the open wound or take Neurontin to dull the stabbing pain in my feet that is supposed to be promising because that is what it feels like when nerves grow back or take laxatives to counteract the effects of the narcotics that have shut down my intestines and made my mind so hazy that I cannot read the books that well-intentioned friends have heaped into my room.

But I can only go so far down this mental pathway before my anger suddenly gives way to empathy for the leg. It was a good leg; it had a strong calf muscle and flexible joints, and it was a slow runner but good at yoga and did not deserve to be crushed by a bus and have its insides put outside to be picked at delicately by scalpels and torn off clumsily by gauze. I was the one who took it downtown to the club, after all. I know this is irrational, but if the bus and the leg don't have to play by the rules, then neither do I.

Simone comes to visit often, and she sits in the straight-backed chair to the right of the bed, and out the window behind her there is snow falling. Sometimes she wants to talk about the night of the accident; it was a trauma for her too, after all. She rode in the ambulance and called my parents in the middle of the night, and waited in the hospital hallways alone until other people arrived. That night I had chosen between two pairs of shoes. I wanted to wear some stiff red patent-leather monsters with thick four-inch heels. They are ridiculous, and they hurt my feet, but they are sexy in a kitschy way, and sometimes only they will do. Simone talked me into wearing the soft, flat, checkered ones. They would be better for dancing, she said while we were sitting in my room planning the night, holding up different outfits and drinking cheap red wine from a box. She was right: the pink-and-red shoes were perfect for dancing.

But if I had worn the crazy heels, my feet would have hurt, and I would have gotten cranky early in the night. I would have insisted we go home a half-hour earlier, and we would have taken a different bus, one without a maniac driver. If I had been really lucky and gotten a blister, I might even have insisted we take a cab, and we could have avoided buses altogether, and I wouldn't be here now. I would be in the snowy city outside the window, walking around on

two functional legs, wearing a heavy, long coat and smoking a cigarette, drinking coffee from a wax-lined paper cup instead of lying
here in a thin hospital gown and sipping water from the dull peach
plastic cup that's always on my bed tray. Simone, with her sensible
shoe suggestions — this is all her fault.

7

I am watching the two plastics residents slice away the dead bits
around the edge of my leg. The part of the muscle that could po-
tentially be viable shrinks every day, with every chunk that is pulled
off clinging to a bandage and every sliver they carefully cut away.
It's crazy to watch them and not care that they are doing this. They
gave me a different drug, something called Versed, a way to avoid
general anesthesia and the heavy doses of narcotics they have been
giving me. It doesn't make you unconscious; it doesn't even make
you not feel pain — it just makes the pain not matter. Here I am,
watching them slice, feeling them slice, and I just don't care. I am
sitting up, watching, and asking them how they got interested in
medicine. I can hear that my yammering questions sound drunk
and slurry, which isn't fair because I am not drunk; I am thinking
perfectly clearly, except that I am watching them cut strips of shin
sashimi out of my body. I am telling them how interesting this drug
is, and they are saying please lie back down. But I'm determined to
talk to them about how when I was in high school I really wanted
to go into pharmaceutical research and invent the perfect recre-
ational drug, something really cool and interesting but with no effect on memory or emotion. It seems like they are ignoring me,
but maybe they just need to concentrate. Is this stuff addictive? I
want to know. They slice in silence, no longer amused. They talk
about "adjusting," and the anesthesiologist who has been creeping
around behind me fiddles with something, and I'm really tired
now, so I guess I will lie back down. And sleep.

8

It is almost Christmas. My friend Jack is coming to visit today. He
is back from Kenya; there he spent the semester studying wildlife
management and visiting Masai villages where the houses are made

of cow dung. He called yesterday to tell me he was back. He has not had e-mail or phone access while he was away, but his girlfriend sent him a letter telling him I was in the hospital. He said it was the scariest letter he had ever gotten, which made me feel important. Before he left for Africa I had a persistent crush on him. We read the same books and liked the same music, and I was good at making him laugh; I wonder if I still am. He has never returned my crush, but knowing he will be at the hospital makes me nervous in a prehospital way, when succeeding or failing at dating and flirtation were central and the stakes high. My mom is washing my hair in a basin, going back and forth to the bathroom and refilling the water cup for each rinse. She massages my scalp with her fingers, giving me good scalp-massage shivers. She brought me a blow dryer, and today I'll brush and blow-dry my hair by myself, and my hair will be straight and shiny for the first time in a month.

Jack is here before I am done, and I yell to him to wait in the hallway until I look presentable. But I am suddenly conscious of my medical-chemical pungency and yellow complexion and remember that my face is glassy-eyed and always either puffy or shrunken. Suddenly my plan to claw my way back to normalcy with a hair dryer seems ridiculous, and I haven't seen my friend in months, so I call to him to just come in. He looks the same, his light brown hair a little shaggier than usual, his face still narrow and eyes still bright blue. He talks to me the same way he always has, quickly, excitedly, unaccustomed to me being a slow-witted, tired patient. He tells me stories about soccer games and sunsets and creatures and gives me a carved wooden statue of a thinking man sitting up, leaning forward with his elbows on his knees and his head resting in his hands. I have been inside my small off-white room for weeks, and I love the statue for coming from somewhere so sunny and hot and far away.

9

For several days I have had a mysterious machine attached to my leg. It sits on a side table by the foot of the bed, whirring. It is about the size of a car battery, and a tangle of tubes snakes from the machine under the blanket. They must be attached to my body because the clear plastic tubes have red and yellow fluids in them, being sucked in and pushed out. It is a wound VAC, the plastic surgeon is telling me, and it is supposed to help the tissue regrow.

The wound VAC is plugged into the wall, but tonight the nurse shows my mom how to switch it to battery power so I can leave my room. They pick me up and set me in the wheelchair, which has a special attachment so I can keep my left leg horizontal while my mom pushes me around. My hip, knee, and foot have to stay on the same plane; if my leg is lowered, too much blood rushes in and it feels like being pricked with thousands of needles. We go down the hallway to the elevator bank. It looks like a hotel, with the muted gray carpeting and pale floral and landscape art in faux-classy gold frames on the walls. Mom asks if I want to go outside. I look out the window—fat, lazy snowflakes fall in the streetlight. Yes. I don't have a coat at the hospital—I was wearing a lightweight dusty blue jacket when I was admitted last month—but Mom bundles me in blankets, and we get in the elevator and go. The wheelchair bumps and shakes the wound VAC in my lap when we wheel across the little gap into the elevator.

Outside, the freezing air stings the inside of my nose as Mom wheels me across the asphalt and onto the sidewalk, and we look up at the hospital together. It is like we are in a stark urban snow globe. This part of Boston is all hospitals, side by side. A dark blue bus pulls into the patient drop-off circle several feet away. The brakes on the chair are not faulty, the sidewalk is not slippery, and the bus driver sees us, but this logic does not stop my breathing from quickening. It is late, and there are no other cars. We stay for a few more minutes, shivering pleasantly in silence before heading back inside.

10

I can hear friends' voices in the hallway. Christmas is a few days away. They have brought lights, and they spend several minutes stringing up the multicolored strands. They tell me about school and the winter formal. By now I have stood up, leaned on crutches, and screamed at the needle sensation when I lower my leg. The muscle might reattach. I might regain some control of my foot. I tell them these things and joke about having thrown myself under the bus to avoid exams.

It is late when they leave. I sit up in bed, unable to sleep, staring at the Christmas lights. The room looks warm and cheerful with the fluorescent overhead lights off and the yellow, blue, green, and magenta glowing in a square around me. My mom has been talking to the doctors about getting me transferred to a hospital in Kansas City soon. They will take me there in a special medical helicopter so I can travel with all my drugs and machines. At the new hospital, they will graft skin onto the exposed bone and tissue of my leg, and I will have scars instead of wounds.

I think about some far-off future day when something will happen to me—I will meet someone, do something, go somewhere—that could only happen because the texture and timing of my life were changed by having my leg crushed by a bus and living for a season in a hospital bed. This is not the same as "Everything happens for a reason," but it will do. In the multicolored quiet, I can imagine a time when this will be over.

Peroneus longus tendon transfer: surgical procedure in which the tendon that moves the foot side to side is cut from its anchor on the lateral side of the foot and reattached to the top of the foot, restoring some of the patient's dorsiflexion. After a few months of physical therapy, the patient will likely be able to walk on her own.

PATRICIA SMITH

Pearl, Upward

FROM *Crab Orchard Review*

CHICAGO. SAY IT. Push out the three sighs, don't let such a
huge wish languish. Her world, so big she didn't know its edges,
suddenly not enough. She's heard the dreams out loud, the tales
of where money flows, and after you arrive it takes *what, a minute?*
to forget that Alabama ever held sugar for you.

She wants to find a factory where she can work boredom into
her fingers. She's never heard a siren razor the dark. She wants
Lucky Strikes, a dose of high life every Friday, hard lessons from a
jukebox. Wants to wave goodbye to her mama and a God not particular to ugly. Just the word *city* shimmies her. All she needs is a
bus ticket, a brown riveted case to hold her dresses, and a waxed
bag crammed with smashed slices of white bread and doughy fried
chicken splashed with Tabasco. This place, Chicago, is too far to
run. But she knows with the whole of her heart that it is what she's
been running toward.

Apple cheeks, glorious gap-tooth fills the window of the Greyhound. For the occasion, she has hot-combed her hair into shivering strings and donned a homemade skirt that wrestles with her
curves. This deception is what the city asks. I dream her sleeping at
angles, her head full and hurting with future, until the bus arrives
in the city. Then she stumbles forth with all she owns, wanting to
be stunned by some sudden thunder. Tries not to see the brown
folks—the whipcloth shoe shiners, the bag carriers—staring at
her, searching for some sign, craving a smell of where she came
from.

How does a city look when you've never seen it before? Grimace and whisper hover everywhere. It is months before she realizes that no one knows her name. No one says Annie Pearl and means it.

She crafts a life that is dimmer than she'd hoped, in a tenement flat with walls pressing in hard and fat roaches, sluggish with Raid, dropping into her food, writhing on the mattress of her Murphy bed. In daytime, she works in a straight line with other women, her hands moving without her. *Repeat. Repeat.* When her evenings are breezy and free and there is change in her purse, she looks for music that whines, men in sharkskin suits, a little something to scorch her throat. Drawn to the jukebox, she punches one letter, one number, hears her story sung over and over in indigo gravel. And she cries when she hears what has happened to homemade guitars. They've forgotten how much they need the southern moon.

At night when she tries to sleep, Alabama fills her head with a cruel grace, its colors brighter, and its memory impossibly wide. She remembers the drumbeat she once was.

My mother, Annie Pearl Smith, never talks with me of Annie Pearl Connor, the girl she was before she boarded that Greyhound, before she rolled into the city. The South, she insists, was the land of clipped dreaming, ain't got nones and never gon' haves. Alabama only existed to be left behind. It's as if a whole new person was born on that bus, her first full breath straining through exhaust, her first word *Chicago*.

But from her sisters I heard stories of what a raging tomboy she was, how it seemed like she was always running.

Whenever I dream her young, I see red dust on her ankles and feet. Those feet were flat and ashy, steady stomping, the corn on her baby toe raw and peeled back. No shoes could hold them. Those feet were always naked, touched by everything, stones asked her to limp and she didn't. Low branches whipped, sliced her skin, and they urged her to cry and she wouldn't. Blood dripped and etched rivers in rust.

She was a blazing girl, screech raucous and careening, rhymes and games and dares in her throat. Her laugh was a shattering on the air. Playing like she had to play to live, she shoved at what slowed her, steamrolled whatever wouldn't move. Alabama's no fool. It didn't get in her way.

What was down south then, then where she romped and ran? Slant sag porches, pea shuck, twangy box guitars begging under blue moons. Combs spitting sparks, pull horses making back roads tremble, swear-scowling elders with rheumy glares fixed on check-erboards. Cursed futures crammed into cotton pouches with bits of bitterroot and a smoldering song. Tragic men buckling under the weight of the Lord's work, the grim rigidity of His word. The horrid parts of meat stewed sweet and possible. And still, whispers about the disappeared, whole souls lost in the passage.

There was nothing before or beyond just being a southern girl, when there was wind to rip with your body and space to claim. Her braids always undid themselves. She panted staccato, gulped steam, and stopped sometimes to rest her feet in meandering water. But why stop when she was the best reason she knew to whip up the air?

And yes, she also owned that slower face. She could be the porch-swinging girl, good to her mama and fixed on Jesus, precious in white collar ironed stiff and bleached to the point of blue. She could make herself stand patient in that Saturday morning kitchen assembly line, long enough to scrape the scream from chitlins and pass the collards three times under the faucet to rinse away the grit. She could set the places at the table and straight sit through endless meals she doesn't have time to taste.

She wore that face as Saturday night's whole weight was polished and spit-shined for Sunday morning. Twisting in the pew and gri-macing when her mother's hand pushed down hard on her thigh in warning. *Girl, how many times I got to tell you God don't like ugly?* To her, righteousness was a mystery that rode the edge of an or-gan wail. She'd seen the Holy Ghost seep into the old women, watched as their backs cracked, eyes bulged, careful dresses rose up. She wondered how God's hot hand felt in their heads, how they danced in ways so clearly beyond them. Decided there would be time enough for this strange salvation. First she had to be young.

All the time her toes tapped, feet flattened out inside her shoes. The sun called her name and made her heart howl. She was a drumbeat, sometimes slow and thoughtful on deep thick skins, most times asking something, steady asking, needing to know, needing to know *now,* taking flight from that rhythm inside her. Twisting on rusty hinge, the porch door whined for one second 'bout where she was. But that girl was gone.

I dream her brave, unleashed, naughty the way free folks are. Playing and frolicking her fill, flailing tough with cousins and sisters, but running wide, running on purpose, running toward something. She couldn't name this chaos, but she believed it knew her, owned her in a way religion should.

At night, the brooding sky pushed down on her tired head, made her stay in place. She sweated outside the sheets. Kicked. Headed somewhere past this.

Anybody know how a Delta girl dreams? How the specter of a city rises up in her head and demands its space and time? How borders and boxes are suddenly magic, tenements harbor pulse, and the all there is must be a man with a felt fedora dipped lazily over one eye? She was turning into a woman, tree trunk legs, exclamation just over her heart. Alabama had to strain to hold on.

Oh, her hips were always there, but suddenly they were a startling fluid and boys lined the dust road and she slowed her run to rock them. Soon she was walking in circles. Then she was barely moving at all. Stones asked her to limp and she did. She was scrubbing her feet in river water and searching for shoes.

Chicago.

Chicago.

The one word sounded like a secret shared. And, poised in that moment before she discovered the truth, Annie Pearl Connor was catch-in-the-breath beautiful. She was sweet in that space between knowing and not knowing.

Months later, her face pressed against a tenement window, she is a note so incredibly blue only the city could sing it.

She has to believe that love will complete her.

And so she finds him, a man who seems to be what Chicago lied and said it was. He smolders, gold tooth flashing. He promises no permanence. She walks into the circle of his arms and stands very still there. There must be more than this, she believes, and knows she must fill her body with me, that she must claim her place in the north with a child touting her blood. Hot at the thought of creation, she is driven by that American dream of birthing a colorless colored child with no memories whatsoever of the Delta.

It is a difficult delivery, with no knife slipped below the bed to cut the pain. In a room of beeping machines and sterilized silver, she can't get loose. Her legs are bound. Her hands are being held down. She screams, not from pain but from knowing. My mother has just given worry to the world.

There will be no running from this.

This child is a chaos she must name.

ZADIE SMITH

Generation Why?

FROM *The New York Review of Books*

HOW LONG IS a generation these days? I must be in Mark Zuckerberg's generation—there are only nine years between us—but somehow it doesn't feel that way. This despite the fact that I can say (like everyone else on Harvard's campus in the fall of 2003) that "I was there" at Facebook's inception, and remember Facemash and the fuss it caused; also that tiny, exquisite movie star trailed by fan-boys through the snow wherever she went, and the awful snow itself, turning your toes gray, destroying your spirit, bringing a bloodless end to a squirrel on my block: frozen, inanimate, perfect—like the Blaschka glass flowers. Doubtless years from now I will misremember my closeness to Zuckerberg, in the same spirit that everyone in '60s Liverpool met John Lennon.

At the time, though, I felt distant from Zuckerberg and all the kids at Harvard. I still feel distant from them now, ever more so, as I increasingly opt out (by choice, by default) of the things they have embraced. We have different ideas about things. Specifically we have different ideas about what a person is, or should be. I often worry that my idea of personhood is nostalgic, irrational, inaccurate. Perhaps Generation Facebook have built their virtual mansions in good faith, in order to house the People 2.0 they genuinely are, and if I feel uncomfortable within them it is because I am stuck at Person 1.0. Then again, the more time I spend with the tail end of Generation Facebook (in the shape of my students), the more convinced I become that some of the software currently shaping their generation is unworthy of them. They are more interesting than it is. They deserve better.

*

In *The Social Network* Generation Facebook gets a movie almost worthy of them, and this fact, being so unexpected, makes the film feel more delightful than it probably, objectively, is. From the opening scene it's clear that this is a movie about 2.0 people made by 1.0 people (Aaron Sorkin and David Fincher, forty-nine and forty-eight respectively). It's a *talkie,* for goodness' sake, with as many words per minute as *His Girl Friday.* A boy, Mark, and his girl, Erica, sit at a little table in a Harvard bar, zinging each other, in that relentless Sorkin style made famous by *The West Wing* (though at no point does either party say "Walk with me"—for this we should be grateful).

But something is not right with this young man: his eye contact is patchy; he doesn't seem to understand common turns of phrase or ambiguities of language; he is literal to the point of offense, pedantic to the point of aggression. ("Final clubs," says Mark, correcting Erica, as they discuss those exclusive Harvard entities, "not finals clubs.") He doesn't understand what's happening as she tries to break up with him. ("Wait, wait, this is real?") Nor does he understand *why.* He doesn't get that what he may consider a statement of fact might yet have, for this other person, some personal, painful import:

> ERICA: I have to go study.
> MARK: You don't have to study.
> ERICA: How do you know I don't have to study?!
> MARK: Because you go to BU!

Simply put, he is a computer nerd, a social "autistic": a type as recognizable to Fincher's audience as the cynical newshound was to Howard Hawks's. To create this Zuckerberg, Sorkin barely need brush his pen against the page. We came to the cinema expecting to meet this guy, and it's a pleasure to watch Sorkin color in what we had already confidently sketched in our minds. For sometimes the culture surmises an individual personality, collectively. Or thinks it does. Don't we all know why nerds do what they do? To get money, which leads to popularity, which leads to girls. Sorkin, confident of his foundation myth, spins an exhilarating tale of double rejection—spurned by Erica and the Porcellian, the finaliest of the final clubs, Zuckerberg begins his spite-fueled rise to the top. Cue a lot of betrayal. A lot of scenes of lawyers' offices and miserable, character-damning depositions. ("Your best friend is suing you!") Sorkin has swapped the military types of *A Few Good Men* for a different kind of all-male community in a different uniform: Gap hoodies, North Face sweats.

At my screening, blocks from NYU, the audience thrilled with intimate identification. But if the hipsters and nerds are hoping for Fincher's usual pyrotechnics they will be disappointed: in a lawyer's office there's not a lot for Fincher to *do*. He has to content himself with excellent and rapid cutting between Harvard and the later court cases, and after that, the discreet pleasures of another, less-remarked-upon Fincher skill: great casting. It'll be a long time before a cinema geek comes along to push Jesse Eisenberg, the actor who plays Zuckerberg, off the top of our nerd typologies. The passive-aggressive, flat-line voice. The shifty boredom when anyone other than himself is speaking. The barely suppressed smirk. Eisenberg even chooses the correct nerd walk: not the sideways corridor shuffle (the *Don't Hit Me!*), but the puffed chest vertical march (the *I'm not 5′ 8″, I'm 5′ 9″!*).

With rucksack, naturally. An extended four-minute shot has him doing exactly this all the way through the Harvard campus, before he lands finally where he belongs, the only place he's truly comfortable, in front of his laptop, with his blog:

> Erica Albright's a bitch. You think that's because her family changed their name from Albrecht or do you think it's because all BU girls are bitches?

Oh, yeah. We know this guy. Overprogrammed, furious, lonely. Around him Fincher arranges a convincing bunch of 1.0 humans, by turns betrayed and humiliated by him, and as the movie progresses they line up to sue him. If it's a three-act movie it's because Zuckerberg screws over more people than a two-act movie can comfortably hold: the Winklevoss twins and Divya Navendra (from whom Zuckerberg allegedly stole the Facebook concept), and then his best friend, Eduardo Saverin (the CFO he edged out of the company), and finally Sean Parker, the boy king of Napster, the music-sharing program, although he, to be fair, pretty much screws himself. It's in Eduardo—in the actor Andrew Garfield's animate, beautiful face—that all these betrayals seem to converge, and become personal, painful. The arbitration scenes—that should be dull, being so terribly static—get their power from the eerie oppo-

sition between Eisenberg's unmoving countenance (his eyebrows
hardly ever move; the real Zuckerberg's eyebrows *never* move) and
Garfield's imploring disbelief, almost the way Spencer Tracy got all
worked up opposite Frederic March's rigidity in another courtroom epic, *Inherit the Wind*.

Still, Fincher allows himself one sequence of (literal) showboat-
ing. Halfway through the film, he inserts a ravishing but quite unnecessary scene of the pretty Winklevoss twins (for a story of nerds,
all the men are surprisingly comely) at the Henley Regatta. These
two blond titans row like champs. (One actor, Armie Hammer, has
been digitally doubled. I'm so utterly 1.0 that I spent an hour of
the movie trying to detect any difference between the twins.) Their
arms move suspiciously fast, faster than real human arms, their
muscles seem outlined by a fine pen, the water splashes up in individual droplets as if painted by Caravaggio, and the music! Trent
Reznor, of Nine Inch Nails, commits exquisite brutality upon Ed-
vard Grieg's already pretty brutal "In the Hall of the Mountain
King." All synths and white noise. It's music video stuff—the art
form in which my not-quite generation truly excels—and it dem-
onstrates the knack for hyperreality that made Fincher's *Fight Club*
so compelling while rendering the real world, for so many of his
fans, always something of a disappointment. Anyway, the twins lose
the regatta too, by a nose, which allows Fincher to justify the scene
by thematic reiteration: sometimes very close is simply not close
enough. Or as Mark pleasantly puts it across a conference table, "If
you guys were the inventors of Facebook you'd have invented Facebook."

All that's left for Zuckerberg is to meet the devil at the cross-
roads: naturally he's an Internet music entrepreneur. It's a Generation Facebook instinct to expect (hope?) that a pop star will fall
on his face in the cinema, but Justin Timberlake, as Sean Parker,
neatly steps over that expectation: whether or not you think he's a
shmuck, he sure plays a great shmuck. Manicured eyebrows, sweaty
forehead, and that coked-up, wafer-thin self-confidence, always
threatening to collapse into paranoia. Timberlake shimmies into
view in the third act to offer the audience, and Zuckerberg, the
very same thing, essentially, that he's been offering us for the past
decade in his videos: a vision of the good life.

This vision is also wafer-thin, and Fincher satirizes it mercilessly.

Again, we know its basic outline: a velvet rope, a cocktail waitress who treats you like a king, the best of everything on tap, a special booth of your own, fussy tiny expensive food ("Could you bring out some things? The lacquered pork with that ginger confit? I don't know, tuna tartar, some lobster claws, the foie gras, and the shrimp dumplings, that'll get us started"), appletinis, a Victoria's Secret model date, wild house parties, fancy cars, slick suits, cocaine, and a "sky's the limit" objective: "A million dollars isn't cool. You know what's cool? . . . A *billion* dollars." Over cocktails in a glamorous nightclub, Parker dazzles Zuckerberg with tales of the life that awaits him on the other side of a billion. Fincher keeps the thumping Euro house music turned up to exactly the level it would be in real life: the actors have to practically scream to be heard above it. Like many a nerd before him, Zuckerberg is too hyped on the idea that he's in heaven to notice he's in hell.

Generation Facebook's obsession with this type of "celebrity lifestyle" is more than familiar. It's pitiful, it pains us, and we recognize it. But would Zuckerberg recognize it, the real Zuckerberg? Are these really *his* motivations, *his* obsessions? No—and the movie knows it. Several times the script tries to square the real Zuckerberg's apparent indifference to money with the plot arc of *The Social Network*—and never quite succeeds. In a scene in which Mark argues with a lawyer, Sorkin attempts a sleight of hand, swapping an interest in money for an interest in power:

> Ma'am, I know you've done your homework and so you know that money isn't a big part of my life, but at the moment I could buy Harvard University, take the Phoenix Club, and turn it into my ping-pong room.

But that doesn't explain why the teenage Zuckerberg gave away his free app for an MP3 player (similar to the very popular Pandora, as it recognized your taste in music) rather than selling it to Microsoft. What power was he hoping to accrue to himself in high school, at seventeen? Girls, was it? Except the girl motivation is patently phony—with a brief interruption, Zuckerberg has been dating the same Chinese American, now a medical student, since 2003, a fact the movie omits entirely. At the end of the film, when all the suing has come to an end ("Pay them. In the scheme of things it's a parking ticket"), we're offered a Zuckerberg slumped before his laptop, still obsessed with the long-lost Erica, sending a "friend request" to her on Facebook and then refreshing the page, over and over, in expectation of her reply . . . Fincher's contemporary window-dressing is so convincing that it wasn't until this very last scene that I realized the obvious progenitor of this wildly enjoyable, wildly inaccurate biopic. Hollywood still believes that behind every mogul there's an idée fixe: Rosebud—meet Erica.

If it's not for money and it's not for girls, what is it for? With Zuckerberg we have a real American mystery. Maybe it's not mysterious and he's just playing the long game, holding out: not a billion dollars but a hundred billion dollars. Or is it possible *he just loves programming?* No doubt the filmmakers considered this option, but you can see their dilemma: how to convey the pleasure of programming—if such a pleasure exists—in a way that is both cinematic and comprehensible? Movies are notoriously bad at showing the pleasures and rigors of art-making, even when the medium is familiar.

Programming is a whole new kind of problem. Fincher makes a brave stab at showing the intensity of programming in action ("He's wired in," people say to other people to stop them disturbing a third person who sits before a laptop wearing noise-reducing earphones), and there's a "vodka-shots-and-programming" party in Zuckerberg's dorm room that gives us some clue of the pleasures. But even if we spent half the film looking at those busy screens (and we do get glimpses), most of us would be none the wiser. Watching this movie, even though you know Sorkin wants your disapproval, you can't help feel a little swell of pride in this 2.0 generation. They've spent a decade being berated for not making the right sorts of paintings or novels or music or politics. Turns out the brightest 2.0 kids have been doing something else extraordinary. They've been making a world.

World makers, social network makers, ask one question first: How can I do it? Zuckerberg solved that one in about three weeks. The other question, the ethical question, he came to later: Why? Why Facebook? Why this format? Why do it like that? Why not do it another way? The striking thing about the real Zuckerberg, in video and in print, is the relative banality of his ideas concerning the "why" of Facebook. He uses the word *connect* as believers use the word *Jesus,* as if it were sacred in and of itself: "So the idea is really that, um, the site helps everyone connect with people and share information with the people they want to stay connected with . . ." Connection is the goal. The quality of that connection, the quality of the information that passes through it, the quality of the relationship that connection permits—none of this is important. That a lot of social networking software explicitly encourages people to make weak, superficial connections with each other (as Malcolm Gladwell has recently argued),[1] and that this might not be an entirely positive thing, seems never to have occurred to him.

He is, to say the least, dispassionate about the philosophical questions concerning privacy—and sociality itself—raised by his ingenious program. Watching him interviewed, I found myself waiting for the verbal wit, the controlled and articulate sarcasm of that famous Zuckerberg kid—then remembered that was only Sorkin. The real Zuckerberg is much more like his website, on each page of which, once upon a time (2004), he emblazoned the legend *A Mark Zuckerberg Production.* Controlled but dull, bright and clean but uniformly plain, non-ideological, affectless.

In Zuckerberg's *New Yorker* profile it is revealed that his own Facebook page lists, among his interests, minimalism, revolutions, and "eliminating desire."[2] We also learn of his affection for the culture and writings of ancient Greece. Perhaps this is the disjunct between real Zuckerberg and fake Zuckerberg: the movie places him in the Roman world of betrayal and excess, but the real Zuckerberg may belong in the Greek, perhaps with the Stoics ("eliminating desire"?). There's a clue in the two Zuckerbergs' relative physiognomies: real Zuckerberg (especially in profile) is Greek sculpture, noble, featureless, a little like the Doryphorus (only facially, mind —his torso is definitely not seven times his head). Fake Mark looks Roman, with all the precise facial detail filled in. Zuckerberg, with his steady relationship and his rented house and his refusal to get angry on television even when people are being very rude to him (he sweats instead), has something of the teenage Stoic about him. And of course if you've eliminated desire you've got nothing to hide, right?

It's *that* kind of kid we're dealing with, the kind who would never screw a groupie in a bar toilet—as happens in the movie—or leave his doctor girlfriend for a Victoria's Secret model. It's this type of kid who would think that giving people *less* privacy was a good idea. What's striking about Zuckerberg's vision of an open Internet is the very blandness it requires to function, as Facebook members discovered when the site changed their privacy settings, allowing more things to become more public, with the (unintended?) consequence that your Aunt Dora could suddenly find out you joined the group Queer Nation last Tuesday. Gay kids became un-gay, partiers took down their party photos, political firebrands put out their fires. In real life we can be all these people on our own terms, in our own way, with whom we choose. For a revealing moment Facebook forgot that. Or else got bored of waiting for us to change in the ways it's betting we will. On the question of privacy, Zuckerberg informed the world, "That social norm is just something that has evolved over time." On this occasion, the world protested, loudly, and so Facebook has responded with "Groups," a site revamp that will allow people to divide their friends into "cliques," some who see more of our profile and some who see less.

How "Groups" will work alongside "Facebook Connect" remains to be seen. Facebook Connect is the "next iteration of Facebook Platform," in which users are "allowed" to "'connect' their Facebook identity, friends and privacy to any site." In this new, open Internet, we will take our real identities with us as we travel through the Internet. This concept seems to have some immediate Stoical advantages: no more faceless bile, no more inflammatory trolling: if your name and social network track you around the virtual world beyond Facebook, you'll have to restrain yourself and so will everyone else. On the other hand, you'll also take your likes and dislikes with you, your tastes, your preferences, all connected to your name, through which people will try to sell you things.

Maybe it will be like an intensified version of the Internet I already live in, where ads for dental services stalk me from pillar to post and I am continually urged to buy my own books. Or maybe the whole Internet will simply become like Facebook: falsely jolly, fake friendly, self-promoting, slickly disingenuous. For all these reasons I quit Facebook about two months after I'd joined it. As with all seriously addictive things, giving up proved to be immeasurably harder than starting. I kept changing my mind: Facebook remains the greatest distraction from work I've ever had, and I loved it for that. I think a lot of people love it for that. Some work-avoidance techniques are onerous in themselves and don't make time move especially quickly: smoking, eating, calling people up on the phone. With Facebook hours, afternoons, entire days went by without my noticing.

When I finally decided to put a stop to it, once and for all, I was left with the question bothering everybody: Are you ever truly removed, once and for all? In an interview on *The Today Show,* Matt Lauer asked Zuckerberg the same question, but because Matt Lauer doesn't listen to people when they talk, he accepted the following answer and moved on to the next question: "Yeah, so what'll happen is that none of that information will be shared with anyone going forward."

You want to be optimistic about your own generation. You want to keep pace with them and not to fear what you don't understand. To put it another way, if you feel discomfort at the world they're making, you want to have a good reason for it. Master programmer and virtual reality pioneer Jaron Lanier (b. 1960) is not of my generation, but he knows and understands us well, and has written a short and frightening book, *You Are Not a Gadget,* which chimes with my own discomfort, while coming from a position of real knowledge and insight, both practical and philosophical. Lanier is interested in the ways in which people "reduce themselves" in order to make a computer's description of them appear more accurate. "Information systems," he writes, "need to have information in order to run, but information *underrepresents reality*" (my italics). In Lanier's view, there is no perfect computer analogue for what we call a "person." In life, we all profess to know this, but when we get online it becomes easy to forget. In Facebook, as it is with other online social networks, life is turned into a database, and this is a degradation, Lanier argues, which is

> based on [a] philosophical mistake . . . the belief that computers can presently represent human thought or human relationships. These are things computers cannot currently do.

We know the consequences of this instinctively; we feel them. We know that having two thousand Facebook friends is not what it looks like. We know that we are using the software to behave in a certain superficial way toward others. We know what we are doing "in" the software. But do we know, are we alert to, what the soft-

ware is doing to us? Is it possible that what is communicated between people online "eventually becomes their truth"? What Lanier, a software expert, reveals to me, a software idiot, is what must
be obvious (to software experts): software is not neutral. Different
software embeds different philosophies, and these philosophies, as
they become ubiquitous, become invisible.

Lanier asks us to consider, for example, the humble file, or
rather, to consider a world without "files." (The first iteration of
the Macintosh, which never shipped, didn't have files.) I confess
this thought experiment stumped me about as much as if I'd been
asked to consider persisting in a world without "time." And then
consider further that these designs, so often taken up in a slap-
dash, last-minute fashion, become "locked in," and, because they
are software, used by millions, too often become impossible to
adapt, or change. MIDI, an inflexible, early-1980s digital music
protocol for connecting different musical components, such as a
keyboard and a computer, takes no account of, say, the fluid line of
a soprano's coloratura; it is still the basis of most of the tinny music
we hear every day—in our phones, in the charts, in elevators—
simply because it became, in software terms, too big to fail, too big
to change.

Lanier wants us to be attentive to the software to which we are
"locked in." Is it really fulfilling our needs? Or are we reducing the
needs we feel in order to convince ourselves that the software isn't
limited? As Lanier argues:

> Different media designs stimulate different potentials in human nature.
> We shouldn't seek to make the pack mentality as efficient as possible.
> We should instead seek to inspire the phenomenon of individual intel-
> ligence.

But the pack mentality is precisely what Open Graph, a Facebook innovation of 2008, is designed to encourage. Open Graph
allows you to see everything your friends are reading, watching,
eating, so that you might read and watch and eat as they do. In
his *New Yorker* profile, Zuckerberg made his personal "philosophy"
clear:

> Most of the information that we care about is things that are in our
> heads, right? And that's not out there to be indexed, right? . . . It's like

hard-wired into us in a deeper way: you really want to know what's going on with the people around you.

Is that really the best we can do online? In the film, Sean Parker, during one of his coke-fueled "Sean-athon monologues," delivers what is intended as a generation-defining line: "We lived on farms, then we lived in cities, and now we're gonna live on the Internet." To this idea Lanier, one of the Internet's original visionaries, can have no profound objection. But his skeptical interrogation of the "nerd reductionism" of Web 2.0 prompts us to ask a question: What kind of life?[3] Surely not this one, where 500 million connected people all decide to watch the reality TV show *Bride Wars* because their friends are? "You have to be somebody," Lanier writes, "before you can share yourself." But to Zuckerberg, sharing your choices with everybody (and doing what they do) *is* being somebody.

Personally I don't think final clubs were ever the point; I don't think exclusivity was ever the point; nor even money. E Pluribus Unum — that's the point. Here's my guess: he wants to be like everybody else. He wants to be liked. Those 1.0 people who couldn't understand Zuckerberg's apparently ham-fisted PR move of giving the school system of Newark $100 million on the very day the movie came out — they just don't get it. For our self-conscious generation (and in this, I and Zuckerberg, and everyone raised on TV in the eighties and nineties, share a single soul), *not being liked* is as bad as it gets. Intolerable to be thought of badly for a minute, even for a moment. He didn't need to just get out "in front" of the story. He had to get right on top of it and try to stop it breathing. Two weeks later, he went to a screening. Why? Because everybody liked the movie.

When a human being becomes a set of data on a website like Facebook, he or she is reduced. Everything shrinks. Individual character. Friendships. Language. Sensibility. In a way it's a transcendent experience: we lose our bodies, our messy feelings, our desires, our fears. It reminds me that those of us who turn in disgust from what we consider an overinflated liberal-bourgeois sense of self should be careful what we wish for: our denuded networked selves don't look more free, they just look more owned.

With Facebook, Zuckerberg seems to be trying to create something like a Noosphere, an Internet with one mind, a uniform environment in which it genuinely doesn't matter who you are, as long as you make "choices" (which means, finally, purchases). If the aim is to be liked by more and more people, whatever is unusual about a person gets flattened out. One nation under a format. To ourselves, we are special people, documented in wonderful photos, and it also happens that we sometimes buy things. This latter fact is an incidental matter, to us. However, the advertising money that will rain down on Facebook—if and when Zuckerberg succeeds in encouraging 500 million people to take their Facebook identities onto the Internet at large—this money thinks of us the other way around. To the advertisers, we are our capacity to buy, attached to a few personal, irrelevant photos.

Is it possible that we have begun to think of ourselves that way? It seemed significant to me that on the way to the movie theater, while doing a small mental calculation (how old I was when at Harvard; how old I am now), I had a Person 1.0 panic attack. Soon I will be forty, then fifty, then soon after dead; I broke out in a Zuckerberg sweat, my heart went crazy, I had to stop and lean against a trash can. Can you have that feeling, on Facebook? I've noticed —and been ashamed of noticing—that when a teenager is murdered, at least in Britain, her Facebook wall will often fill with messages that seem to not quite comprehend the gravity of what has occurred. You know the type of thing: *Sorry babes! Missin' you!!! Hopin' u iz with the Angles. I remember the jokes we used to have LOL! PEACE XXXXX*

When I read something like that, I have a little argument with myself: "It's only poor education. They feel the same way as anyone would, they just don't have the language to express it." But another part of me has a darker, more frightening thought. Do they genuinely believe, because the girl's wall is still up, that she is still, in some sense, alive? What's the difference, after all, if all your contact was virtual?[4]

Software may reduce humans, but there are degrees. Fiction reduces humans too, but bad fiction does it more than good fiction, and we have the option to read good fiction. Jaron Lanier's point is that Web 2.0 "lock-in" happens soon; is happening; has to some degree already happened. And what has been "locked in"? It feels important to remind ourselves, at this point, that Facebook, our new beloved interface with reality, was designed by a Harvard sophomore with a Harvard sophomore's preoccupations. What is your relationship status? (Choose one. There can be only one answer. People need to know.) Do you have a "life"? (Prove it. Post pictures.) Do you like the right sort of things? (Make a list. Things to like will include movies, music, books, and television, but not architecture, ideas, or plants.)

But here I fear I am becoming nostalgic. I am dreaming of a Web that caters to a kind of person who no longer exists. A private person, a person who is a mystery, to the world and—which is more important—to herself. Person as mystery: this idea of personhood is certainly changing, perhaps has already changed. Because I find I agree with Zuckerberg: selves evolve.

Of course, Zuckerberg insists selves simply do this by themselves and the technology he and others have created has no influence upon the process. That is for techies and philosophers to debate (ideally techie-philosophers, like Jaron Lanier). Whichever direction the change is coming from, though, it's absolutely clear to me that the students I teach now are not like the student I once was or even the students I taught seven short years ago at Harvard. Right now I am teaching my students a book called *The Bathroom* by the Belgian experimentalist Jean-Philippe Toussaint—at least I used to *think* he was an experimentalist. It's a book about a man who decides to pass most of his time in his bathroom, yet to my students this novel feels perfectly realistic; an accurate portrait of their own denuded selfhood, or, to put it neutrally, a close analogue of the undeniable boredom of urban twenty-first-century existence.

In the most famous scene, the unnamed protagonist, in one of the few moments of "action," throws a dart into his girlfriend's forehead. Later, in the hospital, they reunite with a kiss and no explanation. "It's just between them," said one student, and looked happy. To a reader of my generation, Toussaint's characters seemed, at first glance, to have no interiority—in fact theirs is not an absence but a refusal, and an ethical one. *What's inside of me is none of your business.* To my students, *The Bathroom* is a true romance.

Toussaint was writing in 1985, in France. In France philosophy seems to come before technology; here in the Anglo-American world we race ahead with technology and hope the ideas will look after themselves. Finally, it's the *idea* of Facebook that disappoints. If it were a genuinely interesting interface, built for these genuinely different 2.0 kids to live in, well, that would be something. It's not that. It's the wild west of the Internet tamed to fit the suburban fantasies of a suburban soul. Lanier:

> These designs came together very recently, and there's a haphazard, accidental quality to them. Resist the easy grooves they guide you into. If you love a medium made of software, there's a danger that you will become entrapped in someone else's recent careless thoughts. Struggle against that!

Shouldn't we struggle against Facebook? Everything in it is reduced to the size of its founder. Blue, because it turns out Zuckerberg is red-green colorblind. "Blue is the richest color for me—I can see all of blue." Poking, because that's what shy boys do to girls they are scared to talk to. Preoccupied with personal trivia, because Mark Zuckerberg thinks the exchange of personal trivia is what "friendship" *is*. A Mark Zuckerberg Production indeed! We were going to live online. It was going to be extraordinary. Yet what kind of living is this? Step back from your Facebook wall for a moment: Doesn't it suddenly look a little ridiculous? *Your* life in *this* format?

The last defense of every Facebook addict is *But it helps me keep in contact with people who are far away!* Well, e-mail and Skype do that too, and they have the added advantage of not forcing you to interface with the mind of Mark Zuckerberg—but, well, you know. We all know. If we *really* wanted to write to these faraway people, or see them, we would. What we actually want to do is the bare minimum, just like any nineteen-year-old college boy who'd rather be doing something else, or nothing.

At my screening, when a character in the film mentioned the early blog platform LiveJournal (still popular in Russia), the audience laughed. I can't imagine life without files, but I can just about imagine a time when Facebook will seem as comically obsolete as LiveJournal. In this sense, *The Social Network* is not a cruel portrait of any particular real-world person called "Mark Zuckerberg." It's a cruel portrait of us: 500 million sentient people entrapped in the recent careless thoughts of a Harvard sophomore.

Notes

1. See "Small Change: Why the Revolution Will Not Be Tweeted," *The New Yorker*, October 4, 2010.

2. See Jose Antonio Vargas, "The Face of Facebook: Mark Zuckerberg Opens Up," *The New Yorker*, September 20, 2010.

3. Lanier: "Individual web pages as they first appeared in the early 1990s had the flavor of personhood. MySpace preserved some of that flavor, though a process of regularized formatting had begun. Facebook went further, organizing people into multiple-choice identities, while Wikipedia seeks to erase point of view entirely."

4. Perhaps the reason why there has not been more resistance to social networking among older people is because 1.0 people do not use Web 2.0 software in the way 2.0 people do. An analogous situation can be found in the way the two generations use cell phones. For me, text messaging is simply a new medium for an old form of communication: I write to my friends in heavily punctuated, fully expressive, standard English sentences — and they write back to me in the same way. Text-speak is unknown between us. Our relationship with the English language predates our relationships with our phones.

Not so for the 2.0 kids. When it comes to Facebook, the same principle applies. For most users over thirty-five, Facebook represents only their e-mail accounts turned outward to face the world. A simple tool, not an avatar. We are not embedded in this software in the same way. 1.0 people still instinctively believe, as Lanier has it, that "what makes something fully real is that it is impossible to represent it to completion." But what if 2.0 people feel their socially networked selves genuinely represent them to completion?

SUSAN STRAIGHT

Travels with My Ex

FROM *The Believer*

SOUTHERN CALIFORNIA IN MID-JULY. My ex-husband and I
were headed to Huntington Beach because that's where The Baller,
a shooting guard who'd been playing basketball since she was
seven, wanted to celebrate her eighteenth birthday.

(We have three daughters—herewith known as The Scholar,
The Baller, and The Baby.)

"I hate Huntington," I said. "My least favorite beach."

"I didn't want to go either," my ex-husband said. We were driving
behind my van, the dark green Mercury Villager I. Today my van
was packed with teenagers. Behind the wheel was The Scholar.
Next to her, The Baller. In the backseat, The Baby, along with Neka,
one of our daughter's high school teammates. And in the middle
was Bink, another former teammate, and The Baller's boyfriend.
We call him our Laurie. My house, full of my little women (though
they are all taller than I am), has for years seen various successions
of boys who have tried to be the equivalent of Louisa May Alcott's
Laurie. This one seems close. Our Laurie is willing to sit on the
couch with all three girls and any attendant girls and watch *She's
the Man* or *Fired Up!* He cooks for himself. A lefty quarterback, he
throws the tennis ball accurately and untiringly for the dog. His
favorite phrase, uttered with deadpan sympathy: "That's unfortunate."

"Look at this traffic," I said. "This is why I hate going through
Orange County."

The I-91 freeway. Four lanes *each way,* often the most congested
in the nation.

My ex-husband and I have known each other since the eighth

grade, when he was a basketball player and I was an ex-cheerleader. (My mother had run me over, accidentally, with her own 1966 Ford station wagon, effectively ending my career two weeks after it began.)

I looked at his foot on the gas pedal. He hardly ever wears sandals. Regulation boots at his correctional officer job. Size fourteen. When we were in high school, and he was an All-County power forward, one of his nicknames was Feets. Mine was It-Z-Bits. He's six-four and goes 305 pounds. I'm five-four. 105.

We have been divorced now for twelve years. But we still see or speak to each other almost every day. Where we live, in the easily jeered-at Inland Empire, we know countless ex-couples like us. Whether it's because we can't afford to move away after we divorce or we're just too lazy to dislike each other efficiently and permanently, it seems to work.

The Scholar would be a junior at Oberlin, and this summer received a research fellowship at Cal Tech. The Baller would start USC in weeks, with nearly a full scholarship. The Baby had just won a DAR (Daughters of the American Revolution) award for her history scholarship at her middle school.

But that's why I was broke. Two kids in college. A California economy in shambles. My upcoming pay cut: 10 percent. Feets: 14 percent pay cut from the county juvenile institution.

He works graveyard. That meant he'd slept for two hours, after spending the night watching two teenage boys charged with a gruesome murder.

By 2 P.M. we'd gone about thirty miles in traffic that was now, unbelievably, stop-and-go. We talked about how many police cars we'd seen that summer, how everyone we knew was getting tickets, how The Scholar and The Baller had both gotten their first citations this year under dubious circumstances. "Revenue," Feets kept saying. "The state is broke. They have to make money, and it has to be on us."

A California Highway Patrol car drove past us on the right, then pulled alongside the green van. The cruiser slowed, at the rear of my van's bumper, and then pulled back up to the side and hit the flashing lights.

"What the hell?" I said.

"He's pulling her over," my ex-husband said, resigned. "Of course he is. Car full of black kids in the OC."

The patrolman was shouting at The Scholar through the loud-speaker.

My ex-husband said, "I'm going, too. He's not gonna pull any shit. I'm not having it."

My husband has a history with cops. He's the six-four Black Guy, the one that fits the description, the one who was seen carrying the shotgun earlier, the one the gas station attendant saw and acciden-tally stepped on the silent alarm, the one who "attacked" a cam-paign worker in Pittsburgh, the one who carjacked Susan Smith, the one you make up, but in reality the one who gets out of his car to help a woman change a tire and she nearly falls into a ditch, she runs away so fast.

"He better not mess with her," my ex-husband said.

"It's D——," I said. That's our Laurie's name. "He's gonna make D—— get out of the car."

Our Laurie is the six-five Black Guy, the one with elaborate braids under his NY Yankees cap, the one wearing size thirteen shoes and a South Carolina T-shirt because he'd just gotten a schol-arship offer from the Gamecocks, the one who'd returned only the day before from the high school All-American basketball camp in Philadelphia, the one with brown skin almost exactly the same shade as my ex-husband's, the one we tease our daughter about because she always said the last thing she ever wanted to do was replicate my life.

"Where you from?" one officer yelled at us, and another held the barrel of his shotgun against Feets's skull, pushing it farther and farther until the opening seemed to be inside his ear, under his huge Afro. It was August 1979. Westwood, California.

Where you from? Where's your license? Where's your car? Is it stolen? Why are you here? Why aren't you in Riverside?

We'd driven eighty miles from Riverside, the land of uncool, of orange trees and dairy farms and a tiny downtown. I was ready to begin my sophomore year at USC. Feets played basketball for Monterey Peninsula College, and our friend Penguin was a line-backer for a junior college in Riverside County. After the beach, they wanted to cruise the streets of Westwood, the paradise we'd seen only in movies.

Feets wore tight khaki pants, a black tank undershirt, and a cream-colored cowboy hat on his big natural. Then two police cruisers sped onto the sidewalk where we walked, blocking our path. Four officers shoved us against the brick wall.

I remember how it smelled.

He was their target, I realized quickly. Power forward. His shoulder blades were wide, dark wings; he was spread-eagled against the wall.

He fit the description.

A black man with a shotgun and a cowboy hat was seen threatening people at UCLA, one of them shouted.

The cop who'd taken me aside looked at my license. *Why'd you come all the way from Riverside to L.A.? Where's your car? Whose car is it? Does your mother know you're with two niggers?*

Penguin was talking back to the cops, refusing to give them his license, and I thought they were going to shoot Feets. Through his ear.

They said a few more things to him, things I couldn't hear. They lowered the shotgun. He lowered his arms. They told us to find our car and leave L.A. "Go back to Riverside!" They said they'd follow us, and that if they saw us walking again, they would shoot on sight.

The patrol car shadowed us as we walked. My boyfriend walked slowly, slightly ahead of me. I knew he was afraid of the bullet that might still come, if he moved wrong. We went back to where we belonged.

What did the highway patrolman want? The Scholar had been going thirty-two miles an hour, between stops. She had always signaled.

"The right taillight's going out again," my ex-husband said.

"My seat belt is still broken," I said.

My ex-husband fishtailed in the dirt of the shoulder, trying to pull ahead of the van and the cruiser. The patrolman was yelling louder, his voice echoing off our door. "Ignore the white truck," he shouted.

"Pull behind him!" I shouted.

"No, then he'll get scared," my ex-husband was shouting.

I knew what he thought: if the officer got scared, he might shoot us.

The Scholar stopped, and the cruiser stopped, and my ex-husband accelerated and went around one more time, a terrible

dance which wasn't funny but it kind of was when the highway patrolman leaped out of his vehicle then, agitated, staring at us, holding both arms wide in the air, saying, *What the hell?*

He had reddish blond hair, big shoulders, sunglasses.

He looked straight at me, and frowned. And that was good.

Oddly, this summer I read *Travels with Charley:* John Steinbeck, riding in his truck, named Rocinante, with a camper shell on the
back, with his large French poodle, named Charley, who is "bleu"
when clean, which means black. When they hit New Orleans, a
man leans in and says, "Man, oh man, I thought you had a nigger
in there. Man, oh man, it's a dog. I see that big old black face and I
think it's a big old nigger."

Once Feets and I were camping across the country in a different
truck—a blue Toyota with a camper shell—and we spent an un-
easy hot night in McClellanville, South Carolina. At dawn, he got
up and took a walk beside the Intracoastal Waterway. While we
slept, the campground had filled with hunters. I lay in the camper,
and from the open window near my head, I heard a father say to
his young son, "See that big nigger? That's a big nigger, right there.
When you get older, I'm gonna buy you a big nigger just like that."

I never told Feets exactly what the man had said. I just said there
were scary people here and we should pack up and leave. We did.

If there's anything scarier than Fits the Description, it's Routine
Traffic Stop.

The names or faces we've learned over the years. A brother in
Signal Hill. Rodney King. The Baller's basketball coach's brothers,
both of them. My younger brother's best friend. Shot nineteen
times in his white truck as he maneuvered on the center divider of
the freeway, having refused to pull over. He might have been high.
Either hung up on the cement or trying to back up. No weapon. A
toolbox. He'd just delivered a load of cut orangewood to my driveway.

"I ain't getting out," Feets said. He had his hands on top of the
steering wheel.

"I know! I'm going," I said. I needed to get my wallet.

"He better not mess with her," he was saying.

"I'm going!" I said. We both knew it was my job. I bent down to
get my pink leather tooled wallet. My job is to be the short blond

mom. At school, at basketball games, at parent-teacher conferences, in the principal's office when a boy has called The Baby
a nigger and the male vice principal sees my ex-husband—BIG
DOGS shirt, black sunglasses, folded arms the size of an NFL line-
backer's, and a scowl—and looks as if he'll faint.

My job is to smile and figure out what's going on.

By the time I got out of the car, the patrolman was looking at me,
and The Scholar was pointing at me.

The traffic roared past on the freeway, twenty feet away from the
silent weigh station. I took my sunglasses off and felt my mouth
tighten. Who had smiled like this? (A foolish smile that angered
someone. Custard inside a dress. What?)

"Why did you stop? What are you doing?" the cop said loudly at
me.

"That's my mom and dad," The Scholar said, aggrieved. She
wasn't scared. She was pissed. Her default setting.

"We're on our way to the beach for a *birthday party!*" I said, cheery
and momlike. "Her dad and I didn't want to get separated, 'cause
in this traffic we might never see each other again!"

The little women hate when I do this. They imitate me viciously
afterward. They hate that I have to do it, and that I am good at it.

"What's the problem?" I asked. "Is it that darn seat belt?"

(Who smiled like this?)

The officer squinted at me, then at the van.

"One of the male passengers wasn't wearing his seat belt." But
then he said drily, "He's wearing it now."

He asked for license and registration and insurance, and I made
jokes about how deep in the glove compartment the registration
might be, and I pulled the insurance card from my wallet, and the
registration was outdated and he glared at me but went back to his
patrol car.

The Scholar started a low invective about California's urgent
need for revenue, and I leaned into the window to say to our Laurie, "You weren't wearing your seat belt? You always wear your seat
belt!"

He said, "It wasn't me. It was Bink."

Bink is darker than he is, nineteen, wearing her hair tucked into
a black cap, wearing a huge black T-shirt. She rolled her eyes, furious.

"He's coming back," someone said. The officer approached the other side of the van. "I need the male passenger to open the door. Open the door," he said.

Bink opened the door slowly.

He asked Bink for her license. He didn't let on that he'd thought she was a guy. He didn't ask her or our Laurie to get out of the car. I stopped having visions of people lying on their faces in the dirt. He wrote the ticket, our Laurie looked straight ahead, at The Scholar's hair, and The Baller looked straight ahead, out the windshield, and I knew Feets was watching in the rearview without moving. I stood awkwardly near the driver's-side window until it was done.

It wasn't until that night that I felt my mouth slide over my teeth again and I remembered. A foolish, dazzling smile. Custard.

Toni Morrison's novel *Sula*. The mother and daughter are on a train traveling from Ohio to Louisiana, and when the white conductor berates them for being out of the Colored car, the mother smiles at him, a placating, unnecessary show of teeth, and the black passengers hate her, and her daughter is ashamed of the custard-colored skin, and her weakness.

About twenty miles earlier, outside Corona, I'd been telling my ex-husband what I'd heard three days ago. I'd given one of our many nephews a ride home after football practice, with The Scholar. We'd spent a long time in the driveway of my father-in-law's father's house, talking to two of his brothers, three cousins, and a family friend. There is always a crowd in the driveway, because the house is not air-conditioned, and the beer is in a cooler, and there are folding chairs, card tables, and stereo speakers hung on the wrought iron supports for the carport. It's the nerve center of communication for the entire neighborhood.

We talked about the newspaper article about the police review of the 2006 shooting of our coach's brother. The commission had found no fault, though the brother was pulled over three times in thirty minutes, the first time because "he had a weird look" and the second time because after the patrol car continued to follow him, he ran a stop sign and made a U-turn. The official report said he had struggled when the officers attempted to put him in the back of the car for questioning. Witnesses said he was trembling, his hands shaking, and that the officers said they were arresting him.

His brother had been shot by deputies when he was very young. One officer said the man's brother reached for his Taser; the other officer shot him. The witnesses, who spoke mostly Spanish, said the man's brother did not reach for the Taser.

Mr. T, a friend, said he'd been pulled over this year in the mostly white neighborhood where he'd lived for a decade. The officers said he fit the description of a robbery suspect. He gave them his ID. The suspect was described as six feet, 185 pounds, and in his thirties. Mr. T is five-eight, rotund, and in his sixties. He was told to get out of the car and lie on his stomach on the sidewalk. He refused repeatedly, and was kept there for over an hour while the officers berated him and asked him questions.

One brother-in-law was stopped while riding his bicycle to work at 5 A.M. He is a custodian at the community college. He was told drug dealers often use bicycles now. He was given a ticket for not having reflective gear.

The father of a basketball teammate was made to lie handcuffed in his own driveway for an hour by city police, who'd been called because his neighbors didn't recognize him when he sat on his block wall. He was wearing sweatpants, working in the garden. He is an LAPD officer.

Every single friend and relative in the driveway had a story.

The Baller got her first citation earlier that year, in January. The highway patrolman followed her for five miles on the highway and had her pull over into the parking lot of a strip club. Our Laurie was in the passenger seat. He was questioned at length, about his identification, his address. The patrolman didn't believe that he was seventeen. When our daughter called me, she was crying. She said she was afraid of what I would say.

She was right. I was furious, but not about the ticket. "When you get pulled over, you put D—— in danger," I shouted at her. "You're risking his life. Don't drive even four miles over the speed limit! He could have been shot and killed!"

Only some mothers say that to their children.

It took two more hours to get to Huntington Beach and find a parking space.

The six-four Black Guy and the six-five Black Guy arranged themselves on chairs. They were surrounded by us and six more girls on the blankets now, friends of The Baller's, eating chicken and watermelon and cupcakes.

Feets didn't go in the water, as he usually did when the girls call him the whale and, even now, try to jump on his back. He read and dozed. He had slept two hours.

Our Laurie went in the water. He was alone for a long time, the farthest out in the powerful waves of that day, and because he was so tall the water reached only his chest.

Feets had a huge natural. We used to stand in the mirror together, back in 1979, and with his ancient, tiny black blow dryer I did my hair like Farrah Fawcett and then he blew out his Afro.

His hair is short now, with a lot of gray, under his ballcap.

Our Laurie always has braids, under his ballcap. It's the braids that make people nervous. The hat. The long shorts. The intricate tiny braids that his mother makes every week, that cross his skull in complicated patterns and just touch his shoulders.

The Baby said, "Why does everyone make fun of watermelon and fried chicken anyway? Why did people always talk about Barack and watermelon?"

The Scholar said, "Oh, my God, could you be any more annoying? Learn your history, okay?"

"Why don't you ever eat watermelon, Daddy?" she asked him.

"'Cause it's nasty," he said. "Just like green peas. They made me eat it when I was a kid, and I ain't a kid now."

He was slumped in his chair, half asleep. His feet were covered with sand.

When I was pregnant with The Scholar, everyone in the driveway teased us. "You got size-five feet and he got them size-fourteen boats. What the hell is that baby gonna look like?"

Who said it? Him, or one of his brothers? Or did I dream it? "What if it's a short baby with his feet? It'll be like one of those plastic clowns—you can punch it and punch it and it'll pop right back up, on them cardboard feet."

That night, he called at eleven fifteen. He was on shift. "They make it back okay?" he said, quietly, anxiously, in the echoing vacuum of the cement walls.

We had left the beach in his truck after only two hours. He had to sleep before work.

"They came back about forty minutes after we did," I told him.
"For real?"

"I guess they got cold," I said.

Maybe they had been nervous. We didn't talk about it. "You working security?" I said. "You gonna fall asleep?"

He said he had court calendar, making the schedule for juvenile offenders who would be escorted in in the morning. He has to shackle and prepare them. He'd already told everyone at work about the seat belt. A lot of coworkers had gotten tickets this summer. "Revenue," he said again. Then he said, "I just wanted to know they made it back," and hung up.

I stood in the kitchen doorway. Our Laurie was on the couch, with the little women heckling him while he took out his braids, which were full of sand. They had never seen his shoulder-length curls before, and they kept trying to take pictures with the cell phone.

CHRISTY VANNOY

A Personal Essay by a Personal Essay

FROM *McSweeney's*

I AM A PERSONAL ESSAY and I was born with a port wine stain and beaten by my mother. A brief affair with a second cousin produced my first and only developmentally disabled child. Years of painful infertility would lead me straight into menopause and the hysterectomy I almost didn't survive.

I recently enrolled in a clinic led by the Article's Director and Editor for a national women's magazine. Technically, we were there to workshop and polish ourselves into submission. Secretly, though, we each hoped to out-devastate the other and nail ourselves a free-lance contract.

I wasn't there to learn. I've been published as many times as I've been brutally sodomized, but I need to stay at the top of my game. Everyone thinks they have a story these days, and as soon as they let women in the Middle East start talking, you'll have to hold an editor hostage to get a response. Mark my words.

There were ten of us in the room. The Essay Without Arms worried me at first, but she had great bone structure and a wedding ring dangled from a chain on her neck, so I doubted her life has been all that hard.

Two male essays wandered in late. They were Homosexual Essays, a dime a dozen, and publishers aren't buying their battle with low self-esteem anymore. Even if their parents had kicked them out, I'd put money on a kind relative taking them in. It wasn't as if they'd landed in state care, like I had, and been delivered straight into the wandering hands of recently paroled foster parents. Being gay is about as tragic as a stray cuticle, and I wasn't born a Jehovah's Witness yesterday.

I presented my essay first, and tried not to look smug as I returned to my seat. The Article's Director let out a satisfied sigh and said, "I see someone's done this before." Yes, someone had. I've developed something of a reputation in the industry for taking meticulous notes on my suffering. It was a lesson learned the hard way after my year in sex slavery was rendered useless from the effects of crank on my long-term memory.

The third essay that read absolutely killed. She'd endured a series of miscarriages and narcoleptic seizures living in a work camp during her youth in communist China. Initially I was worried, but then I thought, whatever, good for her. There are twelve months in the year, and if Refugee Camp walked away with January, the April swimwear issue would be the perfect platform for my struggles with exercise bulimia. I don't mean to sound overly confident, but much of the unmitigated misfortune that has been my day-to-day life has taught me the importance of believing in myself.

Next up were two Divorce Essays, which came and went, forgettable at best. The Editor's critique suggested as much. Alopecia followed. She had promise, but was still clearly struggling for a hook. Every essay who's been through chemo or tried lesbianism ends up bald. Bald isn't the story. Alopecia was heading in the right direction, loving herself, but she was getting there all wrong. I think she needed to focus on not having eyelashes or pubic hair. Now that's interesting. *That's* an essay.

The last kid was unpublished and new on the circuit. It was hard to figure out what we were up against with this one. He walked up to the podium unassisted, bearing no visible signs of physical or mental retardation. Maybe it was something systemic, or worse still, the latest wave of competition to hit the market: a slow-to-diagnose mental illness. I tried to relax. It was hard to build story arcs off problems cured by pills. Problems caused by pills, on the other hand, sold on query alone. Shit. Maybe he was an addict.

His essay was weird. I think he was about a Tuesday. Not the Tuesday of an amputation, just a regular any old Tuesday. He persisted on beginning sentences without the personal pronoun *I* and comparing one thing to another instead of just out-and-out saying what happened. I was trying to track his word count but lost myself momentarily as he described the veins in a cashier's hands. It reminded me of my grandmother, her rough physical topography a testament to a life of hard work. We all leaned in during one of his especially long pauses, only to realize he wasn't pausing, he was done.

The Refugee Essay applauded loudly, but quite honestly, I think her tepid grip on English and admitted narcolepsy barred her from being a qualified judge. The Gay Essays joined in too, but they'll clap for anything with a penis and a Michelangelo jawline.

My ovations, on the other hand, are earned, and this essay never once told me how he felt about himself. Although, I have to admit, if I'd been him during that section where his father didn't even open the gift, I'd have been devastated by the rejection. Not of the thing itself, but of what it represented. Like it wasn't a gift so much as it was longing in the shape of a box, wrapped up in a bow.

Look, it wasn't like this essay didn't have potential. I think everyone in that room agreed he had a certain something. But talent takes time. Inoperable tumors just don't sprout up overnight, and psychotic breaks are nothing if not slow to boil.

The Article's Director didn't bother to give him any feedback. One of the Divorce Essays tried to pipe in about the unsatisfying ending, but the Editor silenced her with the stop sign of her raised palm. Wordlessly, she stared at this essay with a sorrow that reminded me of the last look the man I believed to be my father gave me before heading to Vietnam, only later to return a person wholly different from the one who left. "You deserve something better than this," the Editor said, "yet for rules I follow, but did not create, I can't help you."

I thought about this essay a lot over the next few days, like he was beside me, equal parts familiar and strange. But the thing about life is that you simply cannot settle for melancholy, even when it's true. You are not a tragedy, you are a personal essay. You must rise above and you must do it in the last paragraph with basic grammar and easily recognized words.

Anyway, come November I will be buying every copy of *Marie Claire* I can get my one good hand on! You'll find me on page 124. If you haven't looked death straight in the eye or been sued by a sister wife, you won't see yourself in my story. But you will find solace in knowing your own problems are petty and banal. I have ascended victorious from the ashes of immeasurable self-doubt and pain. And I have not simply survived, I have flourished.

JERALD WALKER

Unprepared

FROM *Harvard Review*

WE DROVE CAUTIOUSLY through the downpour, making the kind of small talk one would expect of strangers, when my companion slid a jacket from his lap, exposing his penis. It rose up high through his zipper, like a single meerkat surveying the land for trouble. To be sure, there was trouble to be had because, despite being a skinny seventeen-year-old, I never left home without my razor.

But what I'd really needed that morning was an umbrella. Rain had begun falling in sheets a few minutes earlier as I'd sprinted to catch the Seventy-ninth Street bus, which pulled away just before I reached it. My frustration had not had a chance to sink in when an Oldsmobile stopped in front of me. The driver offered me a ride. I was immediately put on guard, since random acts of kindness were rare for the South Side of Chicago. In the instant before I opened the passenger door, I decided that a robbery would put me back only six dollars, making it worth the risk. But if he had designs on my leather Converse All Stars, as had a previous robber, I might have to offer some resistance, depending on whether or not he drew a gun.

The other robber had not. He'd merely dragged me into an alley and begun punching my face while explaining, *"This is a stickup, motherfucker!"* Next he searched my pockets, finding and taking my only dollar and a bus transfer. He cursed and hit me once more. Then he jabbed a finger at my shoes. "Give me those!" he commanded. "Give me your coat too!" He didn't seem to mind that it was winter and the ground was covered in snow. After he fled with my belongings, I went back to where he had accosted me to wait for the bus that would complete the final leg of my trip to basketball practice, due to start in twenty minutes at 7 A.M. When the bus arrived, I explained to the driver what had happened. He waived the fare, gave me a tissue to wipe my bloodied nose, and a few miles later deposited me between stops, right at the fieldhouse door. This had happened five years earlier, when I was only a child of twelve. And unarmed.

"So, do you play sports?" this driver was asking me. He wore a large Afro and lush sideburns that reached to his chin, typical of the current style. I figured him to be around fifty.

"Little bit," I said.

"What do you play?"

"Hoops."

"Oh, yeah?"

I nodded. "Yeah."

"What position?"

"Point guard."

"Going to shoot some now?"

I shook my head. "Work."

"What do you do?"

"I'm a lab assistant at the medical center."

"What does a lab assistant do?"

"Clean piss and shit from test tubes."

"Does that pay well?"

I looked at him. "Well enough."

We stopped at a red light. The wipers slapped at the rain, filling the silence. The penis continued its watch. I looked around myself, amazed at how dark it was for midmorning, and at how many people, like me, had been caught unprepared. They darted about beneath newspapers or stood huddled in doorways, while I sat relatively dry, convinced that both my six dollars and my All Stars were safe. It was my body this man wanted, and that, I believed, was safe too. When the subject of sex was broached—verbally, that is—I would simply state that men weren't my thing. I relaxed in my seat and waited for his proposition, hoping it wouldn't come before we'd traveled the remaining ten blocks to the elevated train station, where he'd agreed to take me.

Meanwhile, fifteen hundred miles away in Atlanta, another black male may also have believed his body was safe, just prior to being slain and dumped in the Chattahoochee River.

His name was Nathaniel Cater. His murder was unusual only in the fact that he was twenty-seven, much older than the other victims, and in the fact that there had been other victims. Twenty by that point, all of them between the ages of nine and fourteen, and all of them black males. The first murder had occurred two years prior, in 1979—a fourteen-year-old boy found in the woods, a gunshot to his head. Nearby was the boy's friend, who had been asphyxiated. A few months later, a ten-year-old boy was found dead in a dumpster. And then a strangled nine-year-old; a stabbed fourteen-year-old; a strangled thirteen-year-old; murder after murder until the capriciousness of Negroes could no longer be sustained as a viable cause. There was clearly a holocaust in the making, a systemic denial of future black generations, a conclusion that flowed logically from the vicious legacy of the Deep South. This was the work of the Ku Klux Klan, people believed, and I believed it too. The South, as promised, was rising again.

Each night, on the evening news, I watched efforts to keep it down. New York's Guardian Angels, the Reverend Jesse Jackson, and grieving parents gave press conferences. There were images of helicopters flying over homes and of bloodhounds sniffing through parks. Psychics traveled through time and returned with tips and warnings. Confidential hotlines collected the names of would-be killers. Rewards were posted. Sammy Davis Jr. and Frank Sinatra gave a benefit concert. Green ribbons were worn. And through it all, the murders continued to mount, until June 21, 1981—just a month after I'd accepted the ride with the stranger—when the police arrested a twenty-three-year-old man named Wayne Williams.

Being male, single, introverted, and a loner, Williams fit the general profile of a serial killer, except for the all-important fact that he was black. And so rather than a collective sigh of relief in the black community, there was broad outrage, for we all understood that we were *not* serial killers. The arrest of Williams was a smoke screen, it was decided, another cover-up by white supremacists of their sordid deeds. Sure, we had some rotten apples among us, your garden variety of thugs, burglars, prostitutes, gangbangers, and dope dealers. We even had middle-aged men in cars who'd solicit sex from teenaged boys, but the torturing and execution of people for sport or at the behest of inner voices, that *pathological shit,* was the strict domain of white folks. It wasn't in our DNA.

That's why we'd not produced an Ed Gein, for instance, the man whose barbarity inspired the movies *Psycho* and *Silence of the Lambs.* When his ten-year killing spree ended, it was discovered that he lived, literally, in a house of horrors, with the flesh of his victims serving as furniture upholstery, jewelry, and clothing. His mother's heart was simmering on the stove. John Wayne Gacy was another; he killed twenty-four boys and men, cutting their throats while in the act of raping them. And how about Herman Mugett, the doctor who was said to have murdered over two hundred women by asphyxiating them in a secret chamber in his office? Then there was Albert Fish, who may have mutilated and killed up to one hundred boys; Ted Bundy, the necrophiliac who applied makeup to his victims and slept with them until they decomposed; David "Son of Sam" Berkowitz, who killed women by order of howling dogs. The list also includes Richard Angelo, Jeffrey Dalmer, Gary Ridgeway, Andrew Cunanan, but no one knew of them yet, because it was still only the spring of 1981, a month before Wayne Williams's arrest and a year before his conviction of the Atlanta Child Murders. All during the trial he maintained his innocence, and I, convinced not of a lack of evidence—there was plenty—but only of our genetic superiority, was among the many blacks who believed him.

As we approach the thirtieth anniversary of these crimes, Williams has yet to own his guilt. I use this occasion to own mine. My belief that blacks could be only so bad was equivalent to the view, promulgated since slavery, that we could be only so good; to hold one of these views necessitates the holding of the other. And both views, albeit used for different purposes, place false restrictions on our humanity. At the time of Williams's conviction, I was incapable of reaching this conclusion. The seed of it was planted, however, only three weeks later, when a thirty-three-year-old black man from Michigan, "Coral" Eugene Watts, confessed to killing forty women and girls. His preferred modi operandi were death by drowning, strangling, and stabbing, and his preferred race was white. This was in part why he was so difficult to capture, since a defining trait of serial killers is that they rarely kill outside of their own ethnic group, and this was the same trait that, ironically, made the case stronger against Williams. But just as many blacks came to Williams's defense, the impulse was to defend Watts as well, for here might be a vigilante of sorts, an intensely angry brother out to exact the ultimate revenge on his oppressor. That argument couldn't hold water, though; all it took was for Watts to explain that he'd dreamed of killing women since he was twelve, describe at length his conversations with demons, and express his need to drown some of his victims in order to keep their evil spirits from floating free. This was no vigilante. This was just a man — as vile and deranged as any white counterpart who had preceded him or who would follow. And he, like Wayne Williams, and like Gein, Bundy, Mugett, and the others, belonged to us all.

As did my driver. As did I. And so the scenario in which we found ourselves that rainy morning was susceptible to the full range of human behavior, not merely the one I had envisioned and, luckily, the one that played out. A block from my destination, he removed a twenty-dollar bill from his shirt pocket and positioned it on the seat between us. Just before that we'd spoken of the Bulls, the White Sox, the storm, and then, as the train station came into view, he circled the conversation back to my job at the medical center. "I wouldn't care for that," he said. "Do you like it?"

"It's just a job," I said. "Pays the bills."

It was the wrong thing to say, or maybe it was the right thing, because my reference to money brought the issue to the fore. It was then that he'd produced the twenty-dollar bill. "Would you like to make a little extra?" he asked, winking at me. "Have a little fun in the process?"

I stated the response I'd mentally rehearsed since he'd exposed himself: "Sorry, brother, but men just aren't my thing."

"I can give you forty," he said quickly, as if he'd been mentally rehearsing too. I told him no again. He swore. But I didn't panic. I didn't reach for my razor. I repeated my position and thanked him for the ride. We drove the rest of the way in silence. Just before he stopped the car, he pulled his jacket back onto his lap, picked up the money, and in this manner — without theft, without violence, without murder, without the slightest decrease in my stupidity — the trip came to an end.

The Washing

FROM *The Washington Post Magazine*

I HADN'T PLANNED to wash the corpse.

But sometimes you just get caught up in the moment.

Through a series of slight miscalculations, I am the first of the deceased woman's relatives to arrive at the March Funeral Home in west Baltimore on this Monday morning. The body of the woman whom everyone in the family refers to simply as Dadee, which means "grandmother" in Urdu, is scheduled to arrive at 10 A.M., after being released from Howard County General Hospital in Columbia. I get to the funeral home at 10 A.M. and make somber chit-chat with the five women from the local mosque who have volunteered to help with funeral preparations, which includes washing the deceased's body.

According to Islamic practices, family members of the same gender as the deceased are expected to bathe and shroud the body for burial. But because it's such a detailed ritual and because so many second-generation American Muslim families have yet to bury a loved one here, mosques have volunteers to assist grieving families. These women have come from the Islamic Society of Baltimore, where Dadee's funeral prayer service will be held this afternoon.

When the body arrives at 11:30 A.M., I am still the only family member here, and the body-washers naturally usher me in to join them for the ritual cleansing. It feels too late to tell them that technically I'm not a relative. When I first met the women an hour ago and spoke to them in my halting Urdu, it seemed unnecessary to explain that I was only about to become Dadee's relative. That she was the visiting grandmother of the woman engaged to marry my younger brother. That she had flown in from South Africa just ten days earlier to attend the upcoming wedding. That the only time I'd ever seen Dadee was last night at the hospital, a few hours after she died of sudden cardiac arrest, and then I hadn't even seen her face. When I had arrived at the hospital after getting the call from my brother, a white sheet was already drawn up over Dadee's face and tucked around her slight, eight-decade-old frame.

But the body-washers are understandably in a bit of a hurry. They've been kept waiting. And these genuinely kind women, five middle-aged homemakers, have their own responsibilities to get back to. I call my brother's fiancée to tell her the women want to start the hour-long washing, and she gives the go-ahead because she and her parents are still at the hospital. I tell the washers they can start, and they look at me expectantly. "Let's go," they say in Urdu. "Uh, okay," I reply. It's not that I don't want to wash the body. It's actually something I've wanted to experience for a while. Earlier in the year, I told the funeral coordinator at my mosque to keep me in mind if the need ever arose when I'm available. A few years ago, I attended a daylong workshop on how to perform the ritual. It's just, I didn't think today was going to be the day. I didn't think this was going to be my first body. I had come here, on this fall day in 2008, only to offer emotional support to my future sister-in-law and her mother.

I mutely follow the women through a heavy door marked "Staff Only," then down a flight of concrete stairs into the recesses of the funeral home. I'm starting to feel as though I'm trapped in one of those old *I Love Lucy* episodes, where Lucille Ball finds herself stomping grapes or smuggling cheese and has no idea how to stop this runaway train. We reach a large open room, where I see some gurneys and a simple coffin—upholstered in blue fabric with a white interior. Another doorway leads into a smaller private room that has been set up for ritual washings such as these, one of the volunteers tells me. From the doorway, I see Dadee's form in her hospital-issue white body bag, zipped all the way up. She is lying on a metal gurney, which, with its slightly raised edges, looks like a giant jellyroll pan. It has a quarter-sized hole at the bottom, near Dadee's feet, and the silver tray is tilted slightly so the water we will use drains into a utility sink.

I am not afraid of dead bodies. I have seen one up close three times in my thirty-six years: in high school at the funeral of a friend's father; as a police reporter when I took a tour of the local morgue; and more recently when a friend's ill baby died. But this is the first time I will touch a corpse, and *that* I am a little nervous about. But I'm also grateful for the opportunity. In Islam, it is a tremendous honor to give a body its final cleansing. The reward is immense — the erasure of forty major sins from your lifetime's record. Few people I know have ever washed a body. Because my parents and their peers moved here from Pakistan as young adults, most of them missed the natural opportunity to wash their own parents' or grandparents' bodies when they passed away overseas. And because few of my Muslim peers have lost their parents, we are two generations that don't know what to do when the time comes.

I feel blessed not to be experiencing my first washing with one of my own loved ones, when I would be numb from loss. I would have had little time to prepare myself because Muslims are buried immediately after death — the same day when possible. There is no embalming, no makeup, no Sunday finery for the deceased. There is no wake, no long speech, no cherrywood coffin with brass handles. There is simply the ritual washing, the shrouding in plain white cloth, a funeral prayer that lasts five minutes, and then the burial — preferably the body straight into the dirt, but, when required by law, placed in a basic coffin.

Body-washers put on sterile scrubs to protect us from whatever illness may have stricken the deceased. First I tie on a large paper apron. Then come rubber gloves. I see one of the women pull on a second pair of gloves over the first, and I follow. Next are puffy paper sleeves that attach from elbow to wrist and are tucked into the gloves. Then big paper booties. And finally a face mask with a large transparent plastic eye shield. By the end, I look like a cross between an overzealous nail technician and a Transformer.

I watch the women unzip Dadee from her body bag. As it opens, I see her face for the first time. Muslims believe that at the moment of death, when a soul that's headed to heaven emerges from its body, it slips out as easily as a drop of water spilling from a jug. But a soul that's headed to less heavenly places emerges with great difficulty, like a thorny branch being ripped through a pile of wet wool. I'm relieved that Dadee's face is peaceful, the way you hope somebody's grandmother's face would appear.

I stand by Dadee's feet, on her right side, and watch the women gently lift and rock Dadee to free her from the body bag. She's still dressed in her blue-and-white hospital gown. One of the women slowly lifts the gown, while another drapes Dadee with one of the same long aprons that we are all wearing. Not for one moment are any private areas of the body exposed. In the ritual Islamic bathing, the body is to be given the utmost respect. Not only is it to stay covered at all times, but the washers are to remain forever silent about anything negative or unusual they may witness—for example, if there is an unexpected scar, or deformity, or tattoo. In this, a human's most vulnerable of moments, she is guaranteed protection by her family and community.

It is time to begin the washing. A thin rubber hose is attached to the faucet in the utility sink, and one of the women turns on the water, adjusting it until it is comfortably warm, as prescribed by Islamic tradition. Because I'm the only "relative" in the room, I'm expected to perform the lion's share of the washing, but the women see that I have no idea what I'm doing, so they resume control, leaving me in charge of the feet. The first time I touch Dadee's feet, I am surprised. I expect the corpse to be cold, but it feels warm. Then again, she left this shell less than a day earlier. Perhaps these things take time.

A Muslim's body is generally washed three times from head to toe with soap and clean water. The right side is washed first, then the left. During the final washing, a softly fragranced oil is rubbed onto the body. The body has to be repeatedly tilted from one side to the other, and it is harder than I expected to maneuver the dead weight of a human form. Dadee's feet keep getting in the way of the hole at the bottom of the table, and every few minutes, the water pools up there and I have to lift her leg.

Fifteen minutes into the washing, my brother's fiancée and her mother knock at the door. The granddaughter is too distraught to join in and watches tearfully from the doorway. But Dadee's daughter-in-law dons the gear and steps into her family role. She is understandably traumatized, having been the one to find Dadee collapsed at their home in Columbia last night and having performed CPR to try to revive her. This is her first time washing a body too. I can't tell if she wants me to stay and keep washing, or leave, because we've met just a handful of times in the three months since my brother proposed to her daughter. But she doesn't say anything, so I stay.

*

Washing a body in this way, it's impossible not to flash forward to
your own ending. I have lain on a table like this before, draped
strategically with white cloth, comforting hands laid on me. But
that was just for a massage at the Red Door Spa. When I imagine
my own washing, I see myself being handled by loved ones: my two
oldest friends, Farin and Sajeela; my brothers' wives; my mother
and mother-in-law. I've also asked two women at my mosque whom
I adore to participate. Maybe I'll live long enough to have a
daughter-in-law in the room with me. Should I be so lucky, even a
granddaughter. The more I see, the more I appreciate the way a
Muslim's body is handled after death. There is so much gentleness,
so much privacy. The body isn't left unattended in the short span
between death and burial. It unnerves me when, walking through
the funeral home's hallway, I look into a room and see a dead man
lying on a gurney, unattended. I wonder how long he has been
there, how he has been handled, who has had access to him.
Whether the water that ran over his body was warmed.

The body-washers pass the rubber hose back and forth to each
other and to me and my soon-to-be relative, who strokes her
mother-in-law's hair and washes it. At the end, we dry Dadee with
clean white towels and slide several towels underneath her, with
their edges hanging over the sides of the gurney. We then roll her
gurney into the adjacent room where the coffin awaits for her
transport to the mosque. We station her gurney next to a second
one, where one of the women has already laid out Dadee's funeral
shroud, called a kafan, made of five white cloths of different sizes.
We use the towels underneath Dadee as handles to lift her to the
second gurney. Pieces of the white fabric are folded around
Dadee's body and secured with ropelike strands of the same cloth.
One of the volunteers, Rabia Marfani, assembles these fabric kits
at home, using cotton/polyester bed sheets that she buys at Walmart.

When the cloth that wraps the hair back is tied on Dadee, she
seems strangely transported. She looks so small and fragile, like a
little girl with a bonnet tied around her hair. Finally, a large cloth is
folded around the entire body, completely enclosing her. It's tied
shut with the ropelike strands, and the body looks almost like a
wrapped gift. Together we lift Dadee into the coffin. One of the
women shows me and Dadee's daughter-in-law how to open the
fabric around Dadee's face, should any of her family members

ask to see her one last time at the Janazah prayer service at the mosque.

Afterward, I hug each of the body-washers and thank them deeply for their help. Although Dadee is not exactly my relative, I feel as though these women have done me a huge personal favor, expecting nothing in return. When I ask Marfani why she has participated in this custom more than thirty times in her fifty years, she replies: "It's our obligation. And there is so much reward from God . . . One day I will also be lying there, and somebody will do this for me." She started as a teenager in Pakistan, assisting when her grandmother and aunt passed away. She encourages younger women to volunteer or just watch, because this knowledge needs to be passed on.

We all then raise our hands and pray, asking God to forgive Dadee's sins, to give her the best in the next life. I inwardly alternate between speaking to God and speaking to Dadee. I ask God to welcome her; I wish Dadee good luck on this ultimate pilgrimage. Islam teaches us that after the soul is removed from the body, it briefly faces God to learn its fate, then is returned to the body while on its way to the grave. There it awaits its full reckoning on the Day of Judgment. Though Dadee is no longer of this world, she can continue to earn blessings based on what she has left behind— through righteous offspring who pray for her forgiveness, through knowledge that she has spread to others, or through charitable work whose effects outlast her.

I pray for Dadee, and I also apologize to her for a mistake she doesn't know I nearly made. In today's mail, after the funeral, Dadee's family will receive my hand-addressed invitation to her for a wedding reception hosted by my parents. Earlier this week, I had argued with my brother over the unnecessary expense of mailing separate invitations to multiple family members at the same address. I had considered just sending a joint one. In the end, how grateful I am that I did it his way. Of course you deserve your own invitation, Dadee, after flying across the world to witness your granddaughter's wedding.

I ask God one last time to have mercy on her soul. As I pick up my purse and turn to leave the room, I address my final words to both of them: "Innaa lillaahi wa-innaa ilaihi raje'oon." To God we belong, and to God we return.

Contributors' Notes

Notable Essays of 2010

Contributors' Notes

HILTON ALS is a staff writer at *The New Yorker.* He also writes for the *New York Review of Books.*

MISCHA BERLINSKI is the author of *Fieldwork: A Novel.*

KATY BUTLER, a 2004 finalist for a National Magazine Award, has written for *The New Yorker,* the *New York Times, Mother Jones, Salon, Tricycle,* and other magazines. She was born in South Africa and raised in England, and came to the United States with her family at the age of eight. "Everything Is Holy," her essay about nature worship, Buddhism, and ecology, was selected for *Best Buddhist Writing 2006.* In 2009 she won a literary award from the Elizabeth George Foundation, administered by Hedgebrook, a colony for women writers where she was a resident. "What Broke My Father's Heart" was named a "notable narrative" by the Nieman Foundation for Journalism at Harvard, won a first-place award from the Association of Health Care Journalists, and was named one of the 100 Best Magazine Articles of All Time. Butler has taught narrative nonfiction at Nieman Foundation conferences and memoir writing at Esalen Institute. Her current book project is *Knocking on Heaven's Door: A Journey Through Old Age and New Medicine* to be published in 2013. She lives in the San Francisco Bay Area.

STEVEN CHURCH is the author of *The Day After the Day After: My Atomic Angst, Theoretical Killings: Essays and Accidents,* and *The Guinness Book of Me: A Memoir of Record* (winner of the 2006 Colorado Book Award). His stories and essays have been published in *Agni, Fourth Genre, Brevity, The Pinch, Wag's Revue, Colorado Review, North American Review, Waccamaw, The Pedestrian,* and many other places. He teaches in the MFA Program in

Creative Writing at Fresno State and is a founding editor of the literary magazine *The Normal School*.

PAUL CRENSHAW's stories and essays have appeared in *The Best American Essays 2005, Shenandoah, North American Review, Southern Humanities Review, Hayden's Ferry Review,* and *South Dakota Review,* among others. He teaches writing and literature at Elon University. "After the Ice" is one of a collection of essays set mainly in the writer's hometown in Arkansas.

TOI DERRICOTTE, a professor of English at the University of Pittsburgh, has published four books of poems, *The Empress of the Death House, Natural Birth, Captivity,* and *Tender,* winner of the 1998 Paterson Poetry Prize, as well as a memoir, *The Black Notebooks,* a *New York Times* Notable Book of the Year. She is the recipient of a Guggenheim Fellowship, two fellowships in poetry from the National Endowment for the Arts, and two Pushcart Prizes. She is the cofounder of Cave Canem, the workshop/retreat for African American poets. Her most recent book of poetry, *The Undertaker's Daughter,* will be out in October.

MEENAKSHI GIGI DURHAM's short stories, essays, and scholarly articles have appeared in a variety of publications, including *The Chronicle of Higher Education* and *Ellery Queen's Mystery Magazine.* She is the author of *The Lolita Effect* and coeditor of *Media and Cultural Studies: Key Works.* She is an associate professor of journalism at the University of Iowa, where she has taught since 2000. She is currently at work on an academic book, a variety of essays and short stories, and a novel.

BERNADETTE ESPOSITO learned to investigate air disasters at the NTSB Training Center in Ashburn, Virginia. Her essays have been winners of or finalists for a Pushcart Prize, the University of New Orleans Writing Contest, the Plonsker Prize, and a Santa Fe Writers Project Literary Award. She is finishing a collection of essays on plane crashes and teaching math in Laramie, Wyoming.

CHRISTOPHER HITCHENS is a contributing editor to *Vanity Fair* and a visiting professor of liberal studies at the New School. He is the author of numerous books, including works on Thomas Jefferson, Thomas Paine, George Orwell, Mother Teresa, Henry Kissinger, and Bill and Hillary Clinton, as well as his international bestseller and National Book Award nominee, *God Is Not Great.* His most recent book is a memoir, *Hitch-22.*

PICO IYER is the author of two novels and seven works of nonfiction, including *Video Night in Kathmandu, The Lady and the Monk, The Global Soul,* and, most recently, *The Open Road.* An essayist for *Time* magazine since 1986, he also writes frequently for the *New York Review of Books, Harper's*

Magazine, the *New York Times,* and many others. His next book, an extended essay on fathers, Graham Greene, and hauntedness, *The Man Within My Head,* comes out in the spring of 2012.

VICTOR LAVALLE is the author of a collection of stories, *Slapboxing with Jesus,* and two novels, *The Ecstatic* and *Big Machine,* for which he won the Shirley Jackson Award, the American Book Award, and the Ernest J. Gaines Award for Literary Excellence. He is a 2010 Guggenheim Award winner and an assistant professor at Columbia University's School of the Arts. About "Long Distance" he says: "This essay actually came about when I was asked to write about my life *after* having lost a great deal of weight. And yet, when I sat down to work, all I could do was return to that time when I was much heavier and deeply unhappy. Why? I sure didn't miss those days. And yet, I felt I couldn't write about my present without touching on that past. But, of course, I never reach the true *present* in the essay. Maybe I still don't know how to talk about a life with greater happiness. Or I'm still trying to break free from the romance of misery. That has destroyed better writers than me."

CHARLIE LEDUFF was awarded the 2001 Pulitzer Prize for National Reporting for his contributions to a *New York Times* series, "How Race Is Lived in America." The author of two books, *Work and Other Sins: Life in New York City and Thereabouts* and *US Guys: The True and Twisted Mind of the American Man,* he has written and hosted shows for the Discovery Channel and the BBC. His upcoming memoir is titled *Detroit: An American Autopsy.*

CHANG-RAE LEE is the author of four novels: *Native Speaker, A Gesture Life, Aloft,* and most recently, *The Surrendered,* which was a finalist for the Pulitzer Prize. He teaches at Princeton University.

MADGE McKEITHEN has written essays that have been published in literary journals, anthologies, newspapers, and online. Her first book, *Blue Peninsula: Essential Words for a Life of Loss and Change,* was published in 2006. Born and raised in North Carolina, she moved to New York City in 2003 and began teaching in the Writing Program at the New School, work she will continue online while teaching in person in Tashkent, Uzbekistan.

CARYL PHILLIPS is the author of nine novels (*The Final Passage, A State of Independence, Higher Ground, Cambridge, Crossing the River, The Nature of Blood, A Distant Shore, Dancing in the Dark,* and *In the Falling Snow*), four books of nonfiction (*The European Tribe, The Atlantic Sound, A New World Order,* and *Foreigners*), and four stage plays (*Strange Fruit, Where There Is Darkness, The Shelter,* and *Rough Crossings*). Besides several screenplays, he has written many dramas and documentaries for radio and television. A Fellow of the Royal Society of Literature, he currently is a professor of English at Yale University. His most recent book is a collection of essays, *Colour Me English*.

BRIDGET POTTER was born in Brompton-on-Swale, Yorkshire, and came to the United States as a teenager in 1958. She spent the first forty years of her career in television, beginning as a secretary, then as a producer and an executive, including fifteen years as senior vice president of original programming at HBO. In 2007 she earned a BA in cultural anthropology from Columbia University. This year she will complete an MFA in nonfiction, also from Columbia, where she has been an instructor in the University Writing Program. She is currently working on her first book, a memoir/social history of the 1960s, from which her essay "Lucky Girl" is adapted. She has two grown daughters and lives in Manhattan and Wassaic, New York.

LIA PURPURA's recent books include *On Looking*, a finalist for the National Book Critics Circle Award in nonfiction, and *King Baby* (poems), winner of the Beatrice Hawley Award. Her awards include NEA and Fulbright Fellowships, three Pushcart Prizes, the Associated Writing Programs Award in Nonfiction, and the Ohio State University Press Award in Poetry, among others. Recent poems and essays appear in *Agni, Field, The Georgia Review, Orion, The New Republic,* and *The New Yorker,* and her new collection of essays, *Rough Likeness,* will be out in January 2012. She is writer in residence at Loyola University in Baltimore, Maryland, and teaches in the Rainier Writing Workshop MFA Program.

RACHEL RIEDERER has written for *The Nation, Science,* and *The Rumpus,* among other publications. She holds a BA from Harvard and an MFA from Columbia, where she taught academic writing. She is currently at work on a book of travel narrative and environmental reportage about Lake Victoria.

PATRICIA SMITH is the author of five books of poetry, including *Blood Dazzler,* chronicling the tragedy of Hurricane Katrina, which was a finalist for the 2008 National Book Award, and *Teahouse of the Almighty,* a National Poetry Series selection. Her work has appeared in *Poetry, The Paris Review, TriQuarterly,* and *The Best American Poetry 2011*. She is a Pushcart Prize winner and a four-time individual champion of the National Poetry Slam, the most successful poet in the competition's history. Currently she is a professor at the City University of New York/College of Staten Island and is on the faculty of both Cave Canem and the Stonecoast MFA program at the University of Southern Maine.

ZADIE SMITH is the author of three novels, *White Teeth* (2000), *The Autograph Man* (2002), and *On Beauty* (2005), which won the 2006 Orange Prize for Fiction. She is also the author of *Changing My Mind: Occasional Essays* (2009) and the editor of a story collection, *The Book of Other People* (2007).

SUSAN STRAIGHT has published seven novels, including *Highwire Moon,* which was a finalist for the National Book Award, and the companion novels *A Million Nightingales* and *Take One Candle Light a Room,* which follow a family from slavery in Louisiana to contemporary life in California. Her new novel, *Between Heaven and Here,* is forthcoming. She has written essays for the *New York Times,* the *Los Angeles Times, The Believer, The Oxford American, Harper's Magazine, Salon,* and other publications.

CHRISTY VANNOY writes an ongoing column of stories for McSweeneys. net and is currently working on her first book. She lives in New York City.

JERALD WALKER is the author of *Street Shadows: A Memoir of Race, Rebellion, and Redemption,* recipient of the 2011 PEN New England/L. L. Winship Award for Nonfiction and named a Best Memoir of the Year by *Kirkus Reviews.* His essays have appeared in numerous periodicals and anthologies, including *Creative Nonfiction, The Harvard Review, Mother Jones, The Missouri Review, The Iowa Review, The Best African American Essays,* and twice before in *The Best American Essays.* Walker is an associate professor of creative writing at Emerson College. "Unprepared" is from a collection of essays in progress.

RESHMA MEMON YAQUB wouldn't even be fit to write a grocery list were it not for her guardian editors: Michelle Gaps, Leslie Morgan Steiner, Lynda Robinson, Betty Wong, Bonnie Miller Rubin, Stephen Franklin, Carol Kleiman, Diane Debrovner, Laszlo Domjan, John Dowd, Sydney Trent, Sally Lee, Fred Hiatt, John Koten, Dan Ferrara, Tom Nawrocki. Writers she adores to the point of having pretend conversations in her head with them: Christiane Northrup, Brian Doyle, Lisa Kogan, Anne Lamott, Justin Halpern, Iris Krasnow, Michael Pollan, Louise Hay. Her stories owe many glorious plot twists to Zain, eleven, and Zach, seven. Ditto their dad (Amer) and grandparents (Ali, Razia, Muhammad, Nasreen). Costars: Sophie, Sana, Yousef, and Maryam. Miss Yaqub lives in Bethesda, Maryland. Her next project is an investigation into the whereabouts of two missing people: Mr. Right and Ms. Memoir Literary Agent. Sightings may be reported to her via Facebook.

Notable Essays of 2010

Selected by Robert Atwan

Notable Special Issues of 2010

James F. Hoge, Jr., November/
December.

Hedgehog Review, Does Religious
Pluralism Require Secularism?, ed.
Jennifer L. Geddes, Fall.

In Character, The Humility Issue, ed.
Charlotte Hays, Winter.

Kenyon Review, Work by North
American Indigenous Authors,
guest ed. Simon Ortiz, Winter.

Michigan Quarterly Review, Growing
Up Motown, ed. Angela D. Dillard,
Fall.

New Letters, Families, ed. Robert
Stewart, vol. 76, no. 2.

New Literary History, What Is an Avant-
Garde?, eds. Jonathan P. Eburne
and Rita Felski, vol. 41, no. 4.

New Quarterly, To List Is Human,
guest ed. Diane Schoemperlen, no.
114.

Pen America, Correspondences: A
Forum, ed. M. Mark, no. 12.

Portland, Water as Soul, ed. Brian
Doyle, Spring.

Prism International, 50th Anniversary
Retrospective, eds. Rachel

Knudsen and Elizabeth Ross,
Winter.

Seneca Review, The Lyric Body, guest
eds. Stephen Kuusisto and Ralph
James Savarese, Spring.

Shenandoah, A Tribute to Flannery
O'Connor, ed. R. T. Smith,
Spring/Fall.

Southern Review, Baseball, ed. Jeanne
M. Leiby, Spring.

Southwest Review, Style as
Performance/Performance as
Style, eds. Willard Spiegelman and
Rhonda Garelick, vol. 95, nos. 1
& 2.

Ten Spurs, The Best of the Best:
Literary Nonfiction of the
Mayborn Conference, ed. George
Getschow, no. 4.

Tikkun, God and the 21st Century,
ed. Michael Lerner, March/April.

Western Humanities Review, Hybrid/
Collaborative Work, eds. Craig
Dworkin, Paisley Rekdal, and
Lance Olsen, Summer.